Dangerous

This is a work of fiction. Names, characters, places, and incidents are products of the author's imagination or are used fictitiously and are not to be construed as real. Any resemblance to actual events, organisations, or persons, living or dead, is entirely coincidental.

Copyright © 2025 by Lottie Moore.

All rights reserved. No part of this book may be reproduced, distributed, or transmitted in any form without written permission from the author, except for the use of brief quotations in a book review.

This book is written in British English, but is set in America with American characters meaning phrases and some spellings may differ.

In this story, certain minor aspects of NFL football may have been changed for the sake of the plot and narrative. These changes are fictional and not reflective of actual game rules and logistics. But I have tried to stay as true to it as I can.

This book contains mature themes such as sexual content and references to addiction, PTSD and suicide.

It is intended for an 18+ audience.

Cover design by Georgia at Pixel and Quill Studio.

Contents

Dedication	1
1. 1: Mae	3
2. 2: Nathan	12
3. 3: Mae	23
4. 4: Nathan	31
5. 5: Mae	40
6. 6: Nathan	49
7. 7: Mae	60
8. 8: Nathan	74
9. 9: Mae	83
10. 10: Nathan	100
11. 11: Mae	110
12. 12: Nathan	124

13.	13: Nathan	134
14.	14: Mae	144
15.	15: Mae	157
16.	16: Nathan	169
17.	17: Mae	180
18.	18: Nathan	195
19.	19: Mae	209
20.	20: Nathan	220
21.	21: Mae	226
22.	22: Nathan	240
23.	23: Mae	261
24.	24: Mae	270
25.	25: Nathan	280
26.	26: Mae	289
27.	27: Nathan	305
28.	28: Mae	316
29.	29: Nathan	326
30.	30: Mae	337
31.	31: Nathan	350

32.	32: Mae	366
33.	33: Nathan	372
34.	34: Nathan	382
35.	35: Mae	396
36.	Epilogue: Nathan	407
37.	What's To Come	414
38.	About The Author	415

Dedication

For those of you who need a dirty-talking football player in your life.
I got you.

1: Mae

Losing your job is tough.

Losing the job you've always dreamed of is even harder.

My manager—or rather, ex-manager—sits behind her desk with a pinched face. I knew something was up the moment she asked me to step into her office.

The dreaded office. The office where no conversation is ever good. Most employees leave crying or red-faced.

I want to flip the table and tell her she can't do this, but the harsh reality is that she can. I've only been at the veterinary practice for four months, and I'm still on probation.

"Budget cuts," she'd told me before asking me to hand my *in-training* badge back over. I'd wanted to jam the pin into her thumb as revenge, but I decided against it. Cindy can be petty, and the last thing I need is her telling every other veterinary practice in the country not to hire me.

The scent of cheap antiseptic lingers in the air, and dog and cat anatomy posters hang wonkily from the walls, the eyes of the cartoon animals feeling like an audience as they judge me. I glower back at them, a chill running down my spine.

It's freezing in here. But I suppose heating the place costs money—money the company just doesn't have.

"You're a good worker, Mae. You really are, but we simply cannot afford to have this many trainees anymore."

"You're the only vet practice in the state that offers this kind of training program," I tell her as if she doesn't already know. "School is too expensive."

Joining a vet practice that was part of the Veterinary Training Academy—which means we get to learn on the job while being paid a lower salary—seemed like the only route I could take.

"We appreciate the work you've put in." Cindy shrugs her shoulders, clearly at a loss. "Your contract ends today. I'm sorry."

I stand, allowing my chair to scrape against the tiled flooring. "Did you not consider this before taking on so many of us?"

It's a rhetorical question. I don't want her response. Her words mean little to me. There's no point in trying to soften the blow when I moved from Montana to Colorado for this opportunity, and I can barely afford my rent as it is. My lease is almost up, and after next month, I'm going to need to either enter another year-long contract with my greedy landlord or find somewhere else to live.

But the cost of moving is steep.

I leave the practice for the final time with hunched shoulders and begin the drive home. My gaze lands on myself in the rearview mirror, and I huff at the sight of my half-lidded, heavy eyes.

Four months wasted.

It feels like a massive kick in the teeth.

"And it's another win for the Missarali Storks! Montana will be proud!" the radio presenter blasts, making me jump. My stupid car is jacked, and the radio turns on whenever it wants. Getting it fixed is low on my priority list, though. "They're doing well this season, but I'm not sure they can keep it together with everything going on—"

I groan as I switch it off with twitchy fingers. I've never been a sports fan, and I'm certainly not interested in hearing about how the Missarali Storks are doing in the season.

It brings my mother to mind—the coach for their cheerleaders.

She told me moving away was a mistake. That I wouldn't be able to handle it.

Twenty-five is a perfectly normal age to chase your dreams, but she insisted I was too young and wouldn't survive in such a cut-throat industry.

It only confirmed that she would never change. She cares about one person and one person only: herself.

"So, does that mean you're coming home?" My best friend, Flo, asks on the other end of the Bluetooth line as I weave in and out of traffic, desperate to get home and throw myself onto the couch so I can eat my feelings. A tub of cinnamon ice cream is screaming my name right now.

I can spend tomorrow searching for new veterinary practices to apply to, but for now, I want to wallow and imagine myself throwing darts at a life-size photo of Cindy's big head.

"I don't know. That's a big decision."

Not one I want to think about right now.

"So was moving out of state to pursue your dream, but you did that. If Colorado doesn't have what you need, find somewhere that does. I'm sure other states are in need of a young, hot veterinary nurse."

I hum. "Even if it's miles away from you?"

I hear my best friend pause from her end. I know she's desperate for me to return to Montana, but she'd never say it. She knows how long I've wanted this.

"Whatever makes you happy, Mae. I'd offer for you to stay with me, but if my landlord found out, he'd have me evicted, and the last thing I want is to end up living on the streets with the rats."

"Why not? You'd blend right in." My lips tug into a smile.

"Haha, very funny."

"I'm going to see if I can get by. I'll start looking for other veterinary practices that offer the same training program. Some positions may have opened up."

I'm not holding out much hope, though. Not a lot of veterinary practices offer the program.

"You could always just marry a rich man, you know?"

"Well, when you find one that's actually hot, well-mannered and not a raging asshole, let me know. Colorado's seriously lacking in that department."

Flo laughs and says, "I'll keep an eye out for you," before ending the call as I pull up outside my apartment.

I glare at the brick's peeling paint and chipped windows. The balconies show severe neglect, with overgrown weeds and rusted outside furniture. My old roommate used to smoke out there, and instead of throwing her cigarette buts away, she'd litter the floor with them, leaving it stinking of smoke.

We hadn't settled for the worst place in town, but this apartment complex isn't far off. It was within budget, though, and I'd told myself that the second I had enough money, I'd move to a nicer location—away from her. But then she disappeared and left me struggling to pay her half of the rent.

I knew I should have made her sign some kind of contract. The lease is solely under my name, but our landlord, Greg, doesn't care who stays here as long as he gets his rent money on time.

She always gave me strange vibes, but I was under pressure to find somewhere to live at such short notice, and having someone to split the monthly rent with sounded like a good idea at the time.

That was before she began chipping off parts of random people's headstones and bringing them home to perform seances. It scared me half to death to hear her screaming in the middle of the night, surrounded by candles, claiming that a ghost had appeared and tried to possess her body.

Safe to say, I'm not going to miss her.

I breathe in the chilly November air before entering my apartment.

Dropping my bags by the front door, I shrug off my white veterinarian coat that I have no use for anymore, laying it over the back of my small, green couch. It's second-hand and lumpy, with a gaping hole in the back, but it was free, and that was all that mattered at the time when I had nothing to spare.

Chump, my tortoise, glances up at me from his pen, his slow movements making me smile. His little legs stick out from underneath his thick shell, moving in the most awkward and ungraceful way. He's not cute. Not in the same way a puppy or kitten is, but he's mine, and I appreciate his sagging skin and beady eyes regardless.

He feels no need for social interaction, so he doesn't mind me being gone most of the time. But it's nice to have someone to come home to. I tell him my problems, and although I know he doesn't understand me, it's nice to have someone—or something—there to listen.

He's expensive to house. His food and bedding don't come cheap. But I'd never consider giving him up. He's part of a memory I don't want to forget—my last tie to my father.

Settling down on the couch, I allow my head to flop back, my eyes fixated on the ceiling above. The silence feels too loud. It's giving me time to think. There's a sudden absence of purpose that rushes through me, knowing I won't be waking up at the crack of dawn tomorrow to tend to dogs with respiratory problems and cats with parasites.

I'll be starting from scratch, but I'm not a quitter. There's no point sitting here feeling sorry for myself when it won't change anything.

I'm dragged from my thoughts by a knock at my door, and I roll my eyes and prepare to plaster on a smile for my neighbour, who probably needs toilet paper again, but I'm surprised when Greg is standing on the other side.

He gives me little time to compose myself.

"Mae, your rent. It's late."

I furrow my brows, eyes tracing over his receding hairline and lopsided eyes before realising how rude it is to stare. It's hard not to when he looks like a gerbil, though. "Late? No, it's not."

He looks at me as if I'm pulling his leg. "Yes, it is. Haven't you seen any of my emails? Your payment for last month didn't go through."

"Are you sure?" I immediately grab my phone and sift through the countless emails I haven't had time to open.

A cold wave rushes over me, a knot forming in my stomach as Greg says, "Do I look as if I'm not sure? I have the paperwork."

I exhale heavily. This day just keeps getting better and better. I'm almost waiting for some cringy TV host to jump out from my closet and yell, "Ha! You just got pranked!" but as the seconds tick by, I realise that's not going to happen.

"I'm really sorry, Greg. I thought I had enough in my account. I'll get you the money as soon as possible."

His shoulders drop, releasing the stiff tension he's holding as disappointment floods his eyes. "This is the second time your rent has been late. I'm sorry, Mae, but if I don't get the money by the end of the day, then I'm afraid I'm going to have to ask you to leave."

He doesn't wait for my response; instead, he saunters down the steps without another word for dramatic effect. His too-tight suit constricts his body, making his movements wooden.

After closing it, I allow my head to drop down to rest against my apartment door. My tongue skates across the front of my teeth as I laugh in disbelief despite the fact that nothing about this situation is remotely funny.

I'm drowning, and there are no buoyancy aids available, leaving me stranded out at sea, barely afloat.

Clenching my spare hand into a fist by my side as I strangle my phone with the other, I gulp in dread, knowing what I need to do.

There's no way I can get this money to Greg in time, and even if I could, I know I can't afford to stay here in the long run. Not without my veterinary nursing job.

Fuck.

My chest constricts as I flick through my contacts, hovering over my mom's name, unsure whether to tap or pull away. I'm not ready for what she'll have to say, but I know I'm going to have to bite the bullet.

She picks up after a few rings, and after an awkward and mostly one-sided conversation, it looks like I'm heading back to Montana to visit Mommy Dearest.

2: Nathan

Cone drills will be the death of me.

Sweat trickles down my forehead as I clutch the football to my side, the fake green grass of the stadium blurry as I jog. The rhythm of my heart pounds in my ears, and my quads ache with every step.

"You're not running for the bus outside the mall, gentleman!" booms my coach, bracing his hands on his capped head, his lips turning down in a frown. "We're over two months into the regular season, and you'll be lucky to pull your uniforms over your heads without having asthma attacks during your next game!"

I press my lips together. As the team captain, it's part of my job to motivate these guys, but we're slacking, and we have a reputation to uphold. The Missarali Storks made it to the final four teams in the NFL Playoffs last year, and although it was disappointing not to make it all the way, we intend to win the Super Bowl this time.

I can't see that happening with the way we're training though.

We've been winning, but the games have all been close. I don't like sitting so near the cliff's edge, wondering when you're due to tip so far that you plummet to the cold, hard ground. Uncertainty isn't a nice feeling.

I'm not in the mood today. I hate hounding people, and no matter how hard Coach Darrell pushes these guys, some of them seem to struggle. We're good, but not so good that we can rely on it to take us to the Super Bowl. Hard work can get us there, and that's what I've been trying to remind them.

This job takes the best out of us. It strips us down, beats us senseless and leaves us bare.

Not only is it physically exhausting, but mentally, too. If you don't win, you lose. Nobody celebrates second place. It's the first loser—something my father loves to remind me of.

The media watch our every move. Every single thing we do is under a microscope. But it comes with the job. It's something we have to put up with if we want to be successful football players.

"Hit the showers, guys!" I order them once Coach blows the whistle, hiking my thumb over my shoulder towards the locker rooms. The stadium is deathly silent as my team files off the grass and down the tunnel. I can tell they're disappointed in the way practice went today.

Darrell tuts, flicking his cap off, letting it drop to the ground. "Nathan, please, give them some words of wisdom."

"What do you want me to say, Darrell?" I question, close enough with him to be on a first-name basis.

"You're one of the oldest here. You have the most experience. Say something. Anything. They're burned out, and we haven't even made it to the Playoffs yet."

I clap him on the shoulder as I pass him. "I'll try, but you can't force passion. If we push them too far, they'll break."

My father spent my entire life pushing me to live and breathe football back in Bozeman, and look where it got us—blood relatives who view each other as mere acquaintances.

Strangers, even. We just so happen to share the same DNA.

As I follow the rest of my team towards the locker rooms, cheerleader Coach Renee—she removed the accent a couple of years ago because she claimed it made her quirkier—struts past me, narrowing her eyes into slits.

She's always hated me, but after last season, she's been on my back. Like an annoying fly that won't stop buzzing around my head and reminding me how much of an inconvenience I am to her.

I don't give her the reaction she wants, though. Instead, I stroll right past her and enter the locker room without a second glance.

If there's one thing I've learned from Renee Bexley, it's that provoking her only fuels the fire-breathing dragon.

I'm surprised I have any hair left after the amount of times we've butted heads.

I remain quiet as I shower and get dressed, and when I'm done, Bennett barges his shoulder into mine in a friendly manner. "Head up, Slater. You'd think it was a loss against the Memphis Tycoons during the Playoffs all over again with the face you're making."

"It will be if we don't get our shit together."

Bennett Quinn is a joker, but if anything, he's a talented quarterback. Probably one of the best players on the team, but he needs more media training. He's made more than a few mistakes at press interviews, which doesn't reflect well on the team. I know he's trying though, so I can't bring myself to have my back up about it. Mainly because he's one of my best friends.

"I sent you some more interviews to study. Watch them," I tell him.

It pisses me off that it's my job to media train my team. Other teams hire people for that kind of shit, but our manager, Peter, doesn't want to spend any more money than he feels is necessary.

I swear *Dollar* could be his middle name.

Or perhaps *Money-Hungry Pig* would be a better fit.

Bennet dips his chin, holding his hand up to his forehead to mimic a salute. "On it, Chief."

I roll my eyes and say a quick goodbye to the rest of the guys, heading towards Emmanuel's store on the outskirts of Missarali, near the airport. I haven't seen him for a couple of weeks, and we're due a catch-up.

I run my hands through my dark hair and down my stubbly face before putting my cap on, only now realising how exhausted I am. Sleep and I haven't been the best of friends lately. My team is stressing me the fuck out, and a lot of the responsibility to get them back on track falls upon my shoulders, according to the media and the man I'm unfortunate enough to call my biological father.

Be a leader. You're not being enough of a man. This is your team, and you're letting them down. Get them up to scratch because you're going to embarrass yourself if you don't.

My father's words ring loud and clear in my head. He doesn't check up on me too often, but when he does, it's because the season has started, and he feels the need to criticise me on something he's seen about the Missarali Storks in the news or a game he watched where we didn't play our best.

You'd think he was an ex-NFL player by how he judges me, but it was just a dream he didn't have the skills to accomplish. He wasn't good enough, and so he pushed his desire onto me. I was practically playing football the day I came out of the womb.

My weekends weren't spent playing in the park or getting ice cream. No, I was being brought to tears while my father yelled at me about my catching or throwing techniques. And what did I receive for crying? Drills. More and more until my tiny body couldn't stand any longer.

I never allow myself to wallow, though. There's nothing I can do but just get on with it.

The wine store bell rings loudly as I push the door open, and Emmanuel's beaming face catches my attention.

"Nathan, it's good to see you!"

I shake his hand. "You too, Emmanuel. I wanted to come sooner, but I've been pretty busy."

"I see that." He steps aside, gesturing to the wall behind his cash register, a cut out of me from a magazine stuck up with a thumbtack. I'm smiling—a very forced smile—holding the ball above my head after scoring the winning touchdown at our last game.

Emmanuel's grin is so proud that it causes my heart to thump erratically inside my chest. In a way, he's been somewhat of a father figure, and God knows I need one with the one I've been cursed with.

Instead, all I got from my birth father was a *good job. Now, on to the next game* text.

The bell rings behind me, signalling someone has walked in, but I pay them no mind as Emmanuel holds up a finger to me and rushes around me to help them.

I gaze at the rows of alcohol lined up on the metal shelving. The dim light above flickers, the coolers humming, taking me back to the day I first barged in here as a young kid with my head held high and my chin jutted out in fraudulent confidence.

I was so determined, yet so frightened.

I straighten the red cap on top of my head and wander through the aisles, picking up a few bottles of expensive-looking champagne and reading their backs as I wait for Emmanuel to finish up with his customer.

"I'm looking for something nice for a family member. I'm visiting."

That voice. It's like nectar—smooth and sweet. The hairs on the back of my neck spike up.

I've never been overly interested in women. I haven't had the time. Sex is fun, but it's been a while since I've been able to relax enough to enjoy a night with someone. My father loves to remind me that dating a woman won't win me the NFL, and he's right.

All it'll gain me is more heat from the media. Questions. And I hate being questioned.

I slowly move towards the part of the store where Emmanuel and his customer are, the soft pop music playing through the speaker above clouding my footsteps.

Then, the customer laughs.

She fucking laughs, and my brows knit together, my jaw ticking. It's the sweetest sound I've ever heard. Melodic. Like a symphony. Every muscle in my body tenses as I round the corner, and I swallow harshly as I spot the most beautiful woman I've ever seen.

Tanned, smooth skin.

Hair the colour of honey, wavy and flowing over her bare shoulders.

A smattering of freckles dotted over her button nose.

A body with curves in all the right places, her hips hugged by a pair of skin-tight jeans that flare out at the bottom, accentuating her toned ass.

Her smile—bright and straight.

However, the grin isn't quite reaching her almond-shaped eyes. It's a smile that someone puts on to hide their anticipation. Their nerves. Their dread. Like a mask. It's something I used to do every day until I gave up and finally allowed myself to accept how I truly feel.

Trapped.

The young woman gazes at me, shifting as she attempts to focus on whatever Emmanuel is saying about his wine selection. However, her eyes continue to flicker to my form, as if silently asking me why the hell I'm standing here, listening.

But there's something else swirling inside of those irises. Curiosity, perhaps. Her gaze glides up and down my body, and judging by the slight flush to her cheeks, it's clear she's intrigued by what she sees.

The feeling is mutual.

Her fluffy eyebrows scrunch as she takes a large, sleek bottle from Emmanuel's hands, hers delicate and small in comparison. "I can't afford this one. Maybe something a little less... nice." She drags her bottom plump lip into her mouth and clears her throat. Embarrassment doesn't quite reach her face, but I can practically see her mind whirling—worried she's entered a store with extortionate pricing.

I know I should walk away. Leave them to it. But it's like my feet are stuck to the tiled flooring. I can't help but stay put—just allow myself to enjoy the presence of the beautiful woman for a minute longer before she disappears, and I never see her again.

"Ah, yes, of course." Emmanuel places the bottle back onto the shelf before clicking his fingers and mumbling to himself. He disappears around the corner, appearing to be looking for a specific wine he has in mind.

The woman watches me with interest before rolling her glossed lips together. She reaches for a bottle, spins it around and reads it.

Why the fuck are her lips so tempting to me?

I need to pull my head out of the gutter.

"That one's not good," I say, and she raises her eyebrows at me, taken aback by my comment. I nod my head toward the wine bottle she's holding. "Or so I've heard."

I'm never usually the type of person to talk to strangers, but for some stupid reason, in the comfort of Emmanuel's store, the words tumble out of my mouth with fluidity.

She laughs again, and the sound goes straight through me. "Good to know." Her chin dips in a simple nod. "I like that men are breaking the stereotypes and drinking wine now. It gets them in touch with their… softer side." A humorous smile reaches her pink lips as she places the bottle back on the shelf. She shrugs. "Or, so I've heard."

I press my tongue to the roof of my mouth at her joke, a small chuckle desperate to come out, but I don't grant it permission. Instead, I settle for a curve of my lip.

But I lower my eyes as her bag droops from her shoulder, and as she attempts to sling it back over, it clips a bottle on the shelf.

It tumbles to the ground and smashes into a thousand pieces, the sound causing her to jump. A small yelp escapes the young woman's mouth, and I can see the cogs turning in her head as she glances down with parted lips and an irritated face.

"Fuck me," she mutters as she shakes her head from side to side.

The wine she's knocked off the shelf is expensive, and judging by her paling face and hopeless eyes, she can't afford it.

She bends down to, what I assume is, pick up the broken pieces, and I scowl.

"You'll cut yourself," I tell her, taking a few steps forward, the tips of my shoes stopping just before the puddle of fancy red wine.

The smell is strong and acidic, causing me to grimace, my nose stinging.

Emmanuel rounds the corner with saucers for eyes. His mouth downturns into a frown as he glances at the liquid seeping into the cracks in the flooring.

He's a good person, and he doesn't deserve to lose out on money, especially because his shop isn't exactly a booming business.

The woman turns to him with pursed lips. "Shit, I'm sorry, I—"

"Here's the money for the wine, Emmanuel," I say, reaching into my pocket, pulling out some cash, and handing it to him.

I'm doing this for him. The sad look on his face is causing my stomach to twist in a harrowing way. It has nothing to do with *her*.

I nod once, my eyes shifting to her for the last time. It's hard to drag them away, but after a few seconds of studying her, I do, turning my attention back to Emmanuel. "I didn't mean to drop it. I apologise."

And with that, I turn on my heel and walk out of the store, unable to stay inside another second.

One: because the stench of the wine is sending me into a spiral.

And two: because I can't bear to be around that woman any longer; otherwise, I'll want to know her name. Where she's from. What she does. And I refuse to get attached to another woman just for them to let me down again.

The prospect of that is far too dangerous.

3: Mae

One condition. There was one condition to me returning home. I had to join my mom's fucking cheerleading squad. And I, being as desperate as I'd been, had agreed.

I'm seriously debating whether I've made the right choice, though. Granted, I'm only going to be a fallback, but I'm still required to attend every practice and learn every routine.

Apparently, the fallback had a family emergency and had to leave the state. I'm hoping there are no more issues with anyone, which means I can hang out on the sidelines instead of performing in front of everyone.

The thought of that makes me want to be sick.

My mom has been coaching the Missarali Storks cheerleaders for the past five years. I was an enthusiastic dancer when I was younger, but I gave it up when I reached the age of fourteen, and that didn't bode well with her.

Our relationship has always been rocky. We've never seen eye-to-eye—with her being a very materialistic and uptight person—but over the past few years, her dislike for me has grown.

Cam, my brother, is her favourite. He's a physiotherapist for the Storks—a job he managed to get because of her. In her opinion, he's making the most of his life, heading down the right path. He has his ducks in a row.

I have ducks. They're just in an unorganised huddle right now.

Safe to say, she didn't appreciate the wine as a gift. I'd scratched off the price tag—since the cost is very much a deciding factor on whether she likes a present or not—but her face had told me immediately that I'd made the wrong call.

"Red wine gives me headaches," she'd said before setting it down and reviewing the house rules.

My mind was somewhere else, though.

I'd vaguely recognised the man from the wine store, but I couldn't pinpoint who he was. His olive-coloured eyes had caused my heart to skip a beat, the noise around me having faded to a distant hum for a few seconds. I couldn't quite focus on what the worker had been telling me about his extensive wine selection.

The clothing of the mystery man had fitted him well. A little *too* well. He was muscular, but not in an overdone way. Lean. Athletic. And all I could do was imagine myself running my hands down his—what I assume would be—chiselled abs.

But then reality set in and wine was suddenly all over the floor.

It seems the Gods above refuse to give me a day when nothing goes wrong.

All I want is a day, and then they can go back to wreaking havoc.

The mystery man had paid for my wine. It was a kind gesture that had caused me to click my teeth shut with surprise, but when he owned up to my mistake and walked out without another word, my tummy did that strange *flip-flop* thing where it feels like it's taken up gymnastics.

I also hate to admit that my eyes had been glued to his ass as he made his escape.

The walls of my mother's house are painted a dull beige, the furniture bright white and uninspiring. She prefers simplicity and it shows in her taste of decor.

"Practice starts tomorrow," she tells me as I fold a pair of black workout shorts and stuff them in the dresser. I didn't bring much—just a large suitcase and Chump—which cost me an arm and a leg to transport.

Greg obviously wouldn't let me keep my furniture in the apartment back in Colorado, so my mom paid for it to be moved into storage as part of our deal.

"It's going to take me a little while to get my fitness level back up," I warn her, mentally berating myself for not keeping up with my running regime. It was hard with the little time I had. That, and curling up on the couch with a creamy hot chocolate, was always a whole lot more tempting than pulling on a pair of tight-as-fuck leggings and running until my lungs gave out.

"Well, you better find your feet quickly. I don't want to introduce you as my daughter and then have you bring the team down. That wouldn't look good on me."

I give her a blank look. When I was younger, I used to speak back to her. I wasn't afraid of challenging her behaviour, but I've learned that doing so only spurs her on. She feeds off it, loving a challenge.

"I'm speaking to everyone after practice tomorrow. There's something very important happening this season." My mother's tone is bitter.

She looks bothered, but I don't ask her what's wrong. I know better than to do that because she always finds a way to spin the problem around and make it my fault.

"Met any hot football players yet?" Flo asks me through the phone, and I laugh as I wait outside the Missarali City stadium, where the cheerleaders and football players train.

"No, it's my first day, Flo." My smile flattens as I see my mom pull up, parking her gleaming Porsche right beside my thousand-year-old rental one. I'd scraped the bottom of the barrel to get it yesterday, but it seemed I was doing the garage a favour by taking it off their hands for the time being. Nobody wanted it, and their faces were a picture when I'd stopped by last night and enquired about it. "Flo, I need to go, but we'll meet soon, okay? I miss you."

"I miss you more."

My clammy hands slide my phone back into my bag.

I've never struggled when meeting new people. I'm not shy, but there's something about walking into a tight-knit girl group that causes my stomach to twist in the most uncomfortable way. Being a newbie is never fun, and I feel like I'm about to plunge headfirst into shark-infested waters.

Taking a deep inhale, I step through the doors. I'm sure my mom doesn't want to walk in with me.

The stadium is stunning, surpassing all expectations.

Bright grass is laid out, with white spray paint marking it. Rows of seats climb so high they look like a gigantic wave about to storm over me. Enormous jumbotrons hang in every corner, most likely bigger than my old apartment's living room.

Chatter fills the air, female voices, all excited and eager, and once they spot me, their delicate eyebrows raise, glossy lips parting.

Fuck, they're obviously all gorgeous.

"Girls," my mom starts from behind me, "because of Gwen's sudden family emergency, I've found us a new member of the team. This is my daughter, Mae. You'll make her feel welcome, I'm sure."

A tall brunette rushes over to me, wrapping my hand in hers in a bone-crushing handshake. She even smells amazing. "Hey, I'm Sophia—the team Captain."

"Mae," I introduce myself.

"She's only here temporarily, so there's not much of a need for pleasantries," my mother says with a heavy sigh. "We're eating into crucial practice time. Let's get started."

I'm walking on eggshells here. I can feel my mother's disapproval hanging in the air, worried I'll taint the perfect cheerleaders she's moulded.

I don't push it though—I can mingle later—so I drop my bag down and join the girls, trying my hardest to wear as genuine of a a smile as I can. However, it's hard when everyone's looking at me like I'm fresh meat.

Is staring at the newbie until she's unbelievably uncomfortable some kind of initiation process or something?

Safe to say, I'm not nearly as fit as I thought I was. I knew it was going to be a struggle, but fuck me. After an hour of practice, my heart feels like it's about to burst out of my chest. I almost fell to my knees with gratitude when my mom announced we'd finished for the evening.

I grip my water bottle with sweaty palms, chugging down as much of it as possible.

"You get used to it," comes a confident voice from beside me, and I put a stop to the tsunami of water streaming into my mouth to take a look at the tall blonde. "I remember my first class. I couldn't walk the next day."

I chuckle. "Great. I'm looking forward to that."

"Ice and stretching are going to be your best friends." She smiles—bright and welcoming, her face gleeful. "I'm Poppy."

"Mae."

"So, what's it like being the cheerleading coach's daughter?"

I shrug. I don't want to insult my mother, especially because all the women here probably like and look up to her. You'd have to be an idiot not to realise how much she enjoys working with these girls.

Her eyes were gleaming the entire time they were dancing, and then, they'd flicker over to me, and she'd roll them, reprimanding me for not kicking high enough or for having a bent elbow.

Her standards have always been high. Sky-high. It's one of the reasons I gave up dance. I hated how much of a perfectionist she was. No performance was ever right.

"It's a new experience, for sure. I'm not that much of a football fiend."

Poppy nods, eyes rolling. "Oh, trust me, I know. My brother's—"

"Alright, girls," my mother calls, waving everyone over, "I have something I need to talk to you about, but we're going to need to wait until the football fools get here."

"Fools?" I whisper, sensing the animosity in the air.

"She hates them," Poppy says as we join the crowd of women sitting on the scratchy grass. "This is so weird. We don't usually have meetings with the guys."

Everybody quietly babbles beside us as we sit with our knees hugged to our chests, my sweaty blue sports bra and shorts uncomfortable against the hot flush of my skin.

My mother picks at her nails, a tell-tale sign she's agitated. She flicks her golden hair over her shoulder with dismissal as a capped man—who I assume is the coach of the football players—strolls through the tunnel leading to the field. He's followed by a group of athletic men.

I take in their varying heights and builds, some tall and lean while others are stocky and powerful, all of their eyebrows furrowed as they glance down at us, clearly just as confused as we are.

But my eyes bulge out of my head as they land on the man who's been at the forefront of my thoughts since the incident at the wine store yesterday.

4: Nathan

Fuck... *her*. Really? I grind my teeth together.

Her tanned and toned arms tighten around her legs, and her pink lips part slightly as our eyes meet.

She looked beautiful under the lights in the wine store, but here, all sweaty and aghast... shit. I don't want to look at her, but my eyes keep finding their way back.

She's a problem I don't need.

I have enough on my plate.

I plaster a scowl onto my face, snapping my eyes away and standing on the side of my clustered teammates—as far away from her as I can get.

I try my best to ignore her presence, but I can't help myself. Her barely-covered skin has a glowy sheen to it. Her wavy hair is pulled back into a tight ponytail, with loose pieces on either side of her slender face. It's flushed, but I can't tell if that's because she's been training or because she's recognised me from yesterday.

I was an idiot for paying for the wine, but I truly believed I'd never see her again. And now here she is, part of the Missarali Storks Cheerleading Squad.

I pray she doesn't put me on a pedestal, expecting me to converse with her in passing. Ask how she is at games. Take an interest in her life.

That's not me. I'm not interested in her in the slightest.

I was doing it for Emmanuel.

We're here for a meeting, but Darrell gave little away about why. We don't socialise with the cheerleaders that often, and for good reason after what happened last season.

Renee clicks her tongue, pulling out her phone, scanning the screen. "Right, are we ready?" She turns to Darrell, who gestures for her to proceed.

"Do you know what this is about?" my teammate, Samuel, asks, his arms crossed, face unimpressed. No doubt he's supposed to be on a date right now. I swear the guy has worked himself through the entire female population of Missarali.

"No idea."

"Let's be frank," Renee's tone is icy, "the media and fans aren't happy with you guys." She's addressing my team. "After what happened last season, they think that—"

"Hold on," Darrell interjects. "I was told this applies to both the football players and cheerleaders. That's why this is a group meeting, Renee."

She glares, her jaw so tight it looks like it's going to break. "As I was saying, it's not looking good for the Missarali Storks, and Peter has come up with a plan to debunk the stories about how the players, and cheerleaders if you will"—she rolls her eyes—"aren't taking this seriously." Her gaze lands on me, head tilting.

A chuckle escapes me. "I don't know why you're looking at me like that, Renee," I say loudly. "I'm not a puppeteer for my teammate's dicks. They're all grown men with free will, and the same applies to your cheerleaders. All those relationships last season were consensual."

A few small gasps from the more uptight cheerleaders capture my attention, but when my eyes flicker to *her* again, she appears to be holding back a snicker.

It causes me to pinch my eyebrows together. None of the cheerleaders would ever dare laugh at Renee.

Last season, one of my players knocked up one of the cheerleaders, and another couple was photographed making out in a subway station. I'm still not sure why Renee blames me, but according to her, I'm the most influential member of the group, and I didn't step in. So, apparently, it's my fault.

I'm thirty-three, and a lot of these players are barely pushing twenty-two. I've learned that you can't try to control youngsters in that kind of way. The more you push, the more they reel back.

That, and I'm not in charge of who they decide to have sexual relations with. I don't control them, and I don't want to. As long as it doesn't affect the way they play, I don't care who they fuck.

Renee looks like she's about to combust, and Darrell shoots me a warning look, but I wave his concern away. She's always treating me like I'm scum on the bottom of her shoe, and occasionally, I like to show her that her opinion means absolutely nothing to me. If she wants to test me, then I'll test her right back.

A small smile graces my lips as Renee diverts her eyes.

"Onto Peter's plan. He wants to create a positive look for the Montana Storks, including having the football players and cheerleaders seen publicly together, doing charity work. *Not* getting handsy."

I roll my eyes.

Right, like that's going to work. The fans and media are going to think what they want. There's no point manipulating their beliefs.

Darrell speaks now. "You're all going to be paired up with a member of the other team and then put into groups of four. Your job as partners is to keep the other in check. Make sure they don't step out of line and do or say anything at these charity events that could hinder the team."

I mentally scoff. I'm not about to babysit a cheerleader. I have much more valuable things to do with my time.

"We want you all to complete this charity work to the best of your abilities. Show Montana that you care. Not only about football, but the community. Right now, you've been painted out as people who prioritise money and sex."

The media's perception of my team is fucking stupid. It couldn't be further from the truth. I know fame, money, and sex are not the reason they're here.

We're misrepresented—looked at as people who care about our salaries and scandals more than anything else. Some of the players are serial daters, but they're open about it. The women they see know they don't want to settle down. It's just sex, and both parties are aware of that.

"Might I remind you all of the no-fraternisation rule that's come into play this season," Renee booms. "Anyone seen having anything other than a professional relationship with a member of the other team will immediately be cut. Those are not only my rules, but Peter's too."

She shoots a blazing look over at Darrell, and eventually, he shakes his head and says, "And mine, too."

The last people I want to hang around with are the cheerleaders. I don't have anything against them personally, but they're a link to Renee, and I don't need them feeding back to her and causing even more trouble for us. She has a way of spinning everything we do into something negative.

I can practically feel the tension streaming through my veins.

It seems Bennett can sense it too, as he glances at me with raised eyebrows. A look that says *dude, chill out. You seriously need to get laid.*

But fucking women doesn't score touchdowns—another famous line from my father, Kevin Slater, or as I like to call him in my head, the leech.

Football is all he cares about. So, in turn, it's all I care about.

It's all I *can* care about.

I hate how he's programmed me to be this way, but your childhood shapes you, and mine was the rectangular shape of a football field.

My eyes flicker to… *her* again, and my chest tightens. It was bad enough when she was wearing a cami top and jeans at the wine store, but now she's in front of me in sweaty gym wear, and it takes all the strength I have to peel my eyes away.

"Do we get a say in who our partners are?" Sophia asks, raising her hand.

"Absolutely not," snaps Renee. "In fact, Darrell and I came together to pair you up with people we believe you'll be least compatible with."

Samuel scoffs beside me. "Like an anti-matchmaking service?"

I can see Darrell fighting a smile, and I know he finds this almost as ridiculous as we all do. But Peter's the boss, and what he says goes. "If you want to call it that, yes."

I run a hand down my face. We need the extra time to train, and instead, Peter is adamant about mopping up our image.

You know what'll really clean up our image? Winning.

A baby's cry whips me from my thoughts, and I turn my head to see Evan storming through the tunnel, holding onto his two-year-old son, Leo, with one arm. Droplets of tears dribble down Leo's chubby cheeks, and Evan presses a soft kiss to the side of his head before glaring out at the rest of us.

His growly behaviour causes me to chuckle.

"Evan West, how many times have I told you, no children at meetings? And you're late," Darrell groans, pinching the bridge of his hooked nose as Evan approaches us.

"When Leo's nannies learn to be on time, then so will I."

"Are they actually late, or did you fire another one?" I laugh.

"Fuck off, Slater," he huffs, but it's all friendly.

Bennett gasps, leaning forward to place his hands over Leo's tiny ears, causing the small child to stop crying and giggle. "That's no way to talk in front of a kid."

"Oh, come on, Quinn. He's heard worse."

I feel sorry for Evan. Leo's mother wants nothing to do with either of them. Not only did she pack up and leave once Leo was born, but she hasn't called since. She's living it up, now engaged to some famous hockey player, and I doubt she's been truthful about birthing a child to her fiance. Not even the media know who Leo's mother is.

Renee clicks her fingers at us—trying to gain our attention—as if we're dogs. "This is what I'm talking about—fools... all of you. Listen out for your names and your partner. We want you to choose somewhere to volunteer with your group. We have some charity events lined up that we'll all be attending, too. But we can talk about those during another meeting."

I'm hoping I'll be paired with someone like Sophia or Madison. I don't know much about them, but I've spoken to them in passing a few times. They seem like easy girls to work with, and that's what I need—an easy ride.

Anyone but *her*.

Because she looks like a fucking rollercoaster.

And I hate rollercoasters.

I keep my arms crossed as I listen.

"Madison and Evan, Kelly and Samuel, and Clara and Jason and Rebecca and Michael…"

My throat feels tight. I don't know *her* name, but judging by how she hasn't reacted, it hasn't been called out yet. I arch my eyebrows daringly at Renee as she glances at me, her mouth downturned before continuing to read the names and groups.

Her eyes are deadly. Challenging.

"Lastly, Bennett and Poppy," she pauses, "and Nathan and my daughter, Mae."

My lungs constrict, and I glance down at *her* as she follows Renee's gaze, her hazel eyes widening as they quickly rake over my body before focusing back on my taut face.

Fuck me.

I bite down on the inside of my cheek.

Because not only am I partnered up with this girl who causes my self-control to shed with every look she gives me, but she's Renee Bexley's fucking daughter.

5: Mae

"A no-fraternisation contract? Really?" The ballpoint pen hangs limply from my fingers as I glance up at my mother from the armchair in her office.

"Do you think rules don't apply to you, Mae? You get treated the same as everybody else." Her lips are pressed together as she slims her eyes, daring me to challenge her.

She's hoping I will. It means she can assert her dominance.

I clamp my teeth down on my bottom lip, stopping myself from making a snarky comment. I can be a bigger person.

I skim over the written words on the sheet of paper quickly before signing it.

Him.

I'm paired up with him.

Nathan Slater.

Not being big into sports, I didn't truly recognise him at the wine store, but my heart almost fell out of my butt when he walked through that tunnel.

The captain of the Missarali Storks. The heartthrob that every horny sports fan longs to have just one wild night with. The so-called untouchable and forbidden man—always wearing that intimidating scowl that sends people running.

He's around six feet three and all muscle. He's sculpted. Toned. His body matches his personality. Hard and impenetrable. Or so I've heard from the media.

He didn't seem like that at the wine store though.

"Mae? Are you even listening to me?"

I stare at my mother with wide eyes. "Sorry. What?"

"Nathan Slater. He's a piece of work. He has no control over his teammates, so do what you need to do regarding the charities and stay away from him."

"If you hate him so much, why did I get paired with him?"

"Because I know he won't risk ruining his career to mess around with my daughter." My mother glances down at me like I'm some whore who's going to beg him to fuck me. Like she's done this just to piss him off.

I fight the urge to spit bitter words at her, but I don't need to be reminded of how I'm staying in her house for free for the tenth time today.

"The last thing I need is you being impregnated by one of them."

I scoff. "Mom, seriously. The last person I'm going to fuck is a football player."

"Have I made myself clear?"

I stand from my seat. "Like the contract threatening me with legal action wasn't enough?" My tone is grim, but my mother's never paid any mind to my unhappiness. She doesn't care about how her words affect me.

I exit her office and head toward the stadium field where the meeting was being held before my mother called me into her office. We'd been told to discuss where we want our first charity appearance to be within our groups before heading home.

I catch a glimpse of bright blonde hair, and Poppy waves me over. Nathan is standing beside her with his arms crossed over his chest, his workout clothes tight around his athletic body. Under the dim lights in the wine shop, I couldn't properly see all his features, but beneath the bright stadium rays, I take notice of more than I should.

More than what's appropriate.

His lips are plump, surrounded by a smattering of stubble. He has a square jaw and high cheekbones, with thick eyebrows framing his face, hovering over his narrowed eyes. His dark hair is tousled and slightly damp—fresh from a shower after what I assume was a gruelling training session on the practice field outside.

"Mae, this is Bennett," Poppy introduces me, gesturing to the beaming man beside her. He's your standard good-looking football player. Tall. Muscular. Great hair and teeth.

He holds his hand out to me and shakes mine with a smile.

"And this is Nathan, he's—"

"We've met." The words roll off my tongue before I can stop them, and Nathan widens his eyes at me, his jaw flexing. He looks displeased—almost like he's irritated I disclosed the information.

Poppy cocks her head. "You have?"

"I mean, kind of. I was buying wine."

"Wine?" Poppy appears as if she wants to pry, but she takes one look at Nathan's rigid posture and clicks her tongue, deciding to change the subject.

Seems he's not so keen to talk about that.

"Well, how about we hit a bar to discuss our plan to change the world?" Bennett suggests, the corner of his lip curling up into a smile.

"Did you not hear a word Renee and Darrell said? I think the last thing they want us to do is go out drinking together," Nathan grumbles.

"It's a drink, Nathan, not a foursome. They're not here, anyway." Bennett gestures around us. Other groups have dispersed.

"They didn't specifically say we had to discuss it here." Poppy smiles, shrugging innocently. "Mae?"

All heads turn to me, and the way Nathan looks at me like he wants me to decline their offer frustrates me. If there's one thing my friends say is my best quality, it's doing the exact opposite of what other people want me to do. Especially when they scowl at me the way Nathan currently is.

I hold my head high. "I wouldn't mind checking out the city."

Something flickers behind Nathan's eyes and his jaw ticks.

I continue to smile, daring him to object.

But he doesn't.

Poppy and I quickly hit the showers, and the boys wait for us outside the stadium. Bennett gives me brief directions to a bar called The Salty Dog, and although I'm concerned my car will fall apart on the journey there, I make it to the parking lot without a hitch.

The bar is a small, rustic-looking place with high beams and a wooden interior. The windows are small and foggy, letting in little light and giving it a sleepy feel. The dim lights overhead illuminate the worn, polished bar top smattered with droplets of beer, making it slightly sticky, and there's a line of peeling leather stools tucked neatly under it.

A small *Help Wanted* sign sits in the window, but it's old, tattered, and looks like it's been there for a while.

"Hey, guys. What'll ya have?" asks the bartender as she rinses her hands under the faucet behind the bar. She looks fed up already, and it's only seven-fifteen.

"Hey, Amber." Bennett smiles. "I'll take whatever beer you recommend. We're mid-season, so something light."

She nods, turning to Poppy and me. "You guys?"

We both order berry ciders.

Amber turns to begin prepping the drinks, causing me to blink since she didn't ask Nathan what he wanted. But after a few minutes, she places a tall glass in front of him, making me tilt my head in curiosity. "Here's your water, Nathan."

"Thanks." He grips the glass with his thick fingers and moves to a table in the far corner, sitting with a huff.

He moves with corded muscles, uptight and highly strung, and my eyes skate over his toned back, berating myself for looking at him in such a way. It pisses me off that he's blessed with the face of an angel but has the personality of The Hulk.

It smells like old people in here, and not the rose-scented perfume kind of old, but the musty old book kind of smell. It's not unpleasant, but it isn't inviting either. It makes my nose wrinkle before the bartender passes me my drink.

Bennett laughs. "Good luck with him as a partner, Mae." He tilts his drink toward me, head nodding towards Mr Grumpy Pants in the corner. "You're going to need it."

I run a hand down my face, sipping my cider. "Thanks. I think I'm in for an interesting season."

Poppy's mouth turns flat at the conversation, but she doesn't say anything as we sit at the table Nathan's claimed.

"Does anyone have any charities in mind?" Bennett asks, and Nathan's eyes shift to me. I can see him analysing me with no shame. He's trying to sus me out. But there's a way that his gaze collides with my own that makes my stomach tense.

"I don't want to do anything dull," Poppy says, swirling her finger around the rim of her cider bottle. "Something fun."

Bennett clicks his fingers as if he's devised a brilliant idea. "I could ask my uncle if we could—"

"No," Nathan interrupts. "Working at your uncle's ranch doesn't count as charity work."

"Ranch?" I ask.

Poppy laughs. "Bennett, here, is a real country boy at heart. Runs a ranch with his uncle that he lives on during the off-season."

I'm intrigued. Considering my mother limits the amount of time her cheerleaders spend in the football player's company, Poppy sure does know enough about them.

My eyebrows hike up, and I peek under the table to take a look at Bennett's tennis shoes, humming with a small smile. "Cowboy boots at the dry cleaners?"

Nathan chokes on his water, and Bennett booms with laughter, his palm hitting the wooden table. "Can't wear them around these guys," he says with a grin. "They'd tarnish them."

"You should see his uncle. He comes to Bennett's games wearing his cowboy hat. I've never seen him without it, but, strangely, it's kind of hot."

"Please keep those kind of thoughts to yourself. I don't want to imagine you fucking my sixty-year-old uncle." He grimaces at Poppy before tipping his beer in my direction, quickly recovering. "So, Mae. You've joined the team mid-season. There's got to be a story behind that?"

"So nosy," Nathan mutters. His perfectly carved face is glowering again, and I resist the urge to ask him if he came out of his mother with a face that disgruntled... and hot.

"My mom needed someone. I used to dance, so I have experience, and yeah, here I am." I shrug. It's not an overly interesting story. Especially because I'm unwilling to explain how I lost my dream job.

I'd asked my mother not to disclose that information, and I was thankful when she actually agreed—most likely because she doesn't want people to think of her daughter as a failure. But it works for me, so I don't mind. "I'm only here for the rest of this season, though. Then, I'll be moving to start a veterinarian nurse training program."

Nathan's head tips, his face deadpan, shoulders broad and barely fitting between the wall and Bennett's. "Where'll you be moving? Somewhere far away?"

Annoyance sparks inside me, and I open my mouth to make a bitter remark about him needing to change his name from Nathan Slater to Nathan Sourpuss, but Poppy speaks first.

"Animals!"

Nathan looks confused as he turns to the excited blonde. "Yes, that's what a veterinarian does?"

"No, animals are fun. Let's work at an animal shelter. We can walk the dogs, cuddle the cats, feed the... hamsters? Do they have hamsters there?" Pride swarms her. "The community will love that."

Bennett nods. "Not a bad idea."

I smile, trying to fight the excitement that rushes to my face, but volunteering at an animal shelter is right up my alley. "I'm happy with that. It sounds fun."

Bennett cocks an eyebrow at his teammate, and Nathan swallows, taking another sip of his water, swiping the excess off his bottom lip with his tongue.

Why does he have to do that when I'm supposed to find him the most unappealing man alive?

"I don't care," he responds.

Bennett sniggers, holding his drink up to cheers us, sending me a wink. "To good luck this season. Some of us are going to need it more than others."

I sigh. And looking at how Nathan glares at his football friend like he wants to knock the beer glass right out of his hand, Bennett's right.

6: Nathan

I tap my foot on the dirt path outside the Missarali City Animal Shelter, the sound of dogs barking and heavy metal doors being opened and closed coming from behind me. The air is bitter today, and I glare down at the goosebumps on my skin, checking the time on my watch for what feels like the tenth time this minute.

I'm a punctual person—another trait I picked up from my father.

At least this one is useful though.

Darrell seemed intrigued when we informed him of the place we'd decided to volunteer at. There's something comical about Montana's big, beefy heartthrobs—the media's words, not mine—having photos taken cuddling tiny, fluffy kittens.

I won't be surprised if the animals scamper off with their tails between their legs.

Bennett's laughter catches my attention, and I turn to him, Poppy and Mae with a scowl as they stroll across the parking lot. "You're late."

Poppy lets out a whistle. "What size steel rod have you got up your ass today?" She giggles as she moves past me into the animal shelter with Bennett, leaving Mae staring after her with stunned eyes, shock evident on her face from the comment.

She's wearing a pair of leggings and a sweatshirt, and I can't help but let my gaze travel lower than necessary. Her rounded hips are accentuated, and I clear my throat and gesture for her to enter the shelter in front of me.

Definitely not because I want to get a look at her ass.

Because I don't.

The smell of cleaning products wafts up my nose as we step into the reception. It causes it to crinkle up, overly sensitive to the alcohol in them.

A million and one thoughts race through my mind whenever the smell is present, but I've learned to ignore them. Push them away. Project the intense sensation into another notion instead—something more positive. Something that will actually benefit me, because dwelling on my past certainly doesn't.

We get ourselves checked in and are made to wear name badges that indicate we're volunteers. Photos of us are taken, and I plaster on a smile. Darrell and Renee need to approve of these, and if we don't look happy to be here, they won't make the cut and won't be released to the press.

A sense of guilt spikes inside me. We're only here to clean up our image. It screams entitlement, and I disapprove of using these charities this way. But either way, they're getting help, so I suppose it's a win-win situation.

Mae appears giddy, entirely in her element here, much more at ease than a few days ago at the bar. It was impossible to miss the way her eyes lit up with excitement when Poppy brought up volunteering here. I hadn't expected such a bright reaction from her, like the clouds had cleared and the sun had come out.

"We've got some dogs that need some attention, and the cat area needs cleaning," the lady behind the desk tells us, a wide grin on her face.

"I'm allergic to cats," I state, and Mae turns to me with a frown.

"Why didn't you say that when we discussed the idea of volunteering here the other day?" Her hands are on her hips as she subtly scolds me.

Why does a sick part of me not mind it?

"Because I don't care where we volunteer."

I'm not afraid to admit that I don't let people in. I keep chit-chat to a minimum—except with the people I trust. Because caring can be hazardous.

As a child, I cared way too much, and it came back to bite me in the butt when trying to accomplish what I was supposed to. Or what was expected of me. I learned the hard way. Caring only dwindles your chances of being happy, because when everything in your life goes to shit, you end up disappointed that it didn't work out.

Bennett studies me, shaking his head and muttering something about not wanting to clean up cat shit, but he keeps the complaint quiet enough so that the lady helping us—Sheila, I believe her name is— doesn't hear.

"I love cats," Poppy speaks up, raising her eyebrows at me— silently warning me to be nice—before beckoning Bennett with a nod of her head and heading down the corridor.

I huff. I'm not one for surface-level conversation, and the last person I want to have that with is Coach Renee's daughter.

I have my back up when it comes to Mae. I'd be the same with any of the cheerleaders, but there's something about her being the daughter of the woman who despises me and wants me off the team that makes it ten times worse.

Maybe it also has something to do with the fact that she's drop-dead gorgeous, too. I can already tell she has a mouth on her, and I know she's going to drive me up the fucking wall.

I just have to get through this season, though. These charity appearances won't last forever, and then I won't have to see her again. She'll be leaving, and our paths won't cross again.

We're led down the barren corridor, where the sound of dogs crying for attention gets louder. Rows of kennels line the wall, with worn-out toys and blankets scattered over the floor. The walls are painted a cheerful yellow, but it does little to mask the underlying sadness lingering in the eyes of the dogs, all gawking up at us with a mixture of hope, fear and anticipation.

Mae kneels in front of one of the kennels and coos at the excitable brown dog, eyes expanding. He rises on his hind legs, licking her fingers through the wire, letting out enthusiastic yips.

"Hi, gorgeous boy."

"Came in as a stray with a nasty wound on his leg the other day, that one. The vet here got him stitched up, but be careful of it," Sheila informs us, the middle-aged woman nodding down at the young dog. "He's yet to be named. A bit of a handful, but I'm sure you'll cope." She grins down at Mae, who's still fussing over the pup.

I can't tell what breed he is. He looks like a strange mix, and I know this gives him less of a chance of being chosen for adoption. People come here hoping to find the perfect dog, and looks are a huge factor.

This dog is cute. There's no doubt about that, but he's... unique.

"You look like you have a little bit of beagle in you, don't you, bud?" Mae questions the dog as if he's about to talk back.

Sheila raises her eyebrows. "You think? We couldn't put our finger on it."

"I think so. I can already tell he's a major sniff-head."

Sheila cackles before leaving us to it, letting us know she'll be at reception.

I almost want to beg her to come back because I don't want to be left alone with Mae when I have no idea what I'm supposed to talk to her about.

But I resist the urge.

The way Mae crouches down—it makes her sweatshirt rise, and a tiny sliver of midriff shows. I hone in on the smooth skin, jaw popping as I try to yank my gaze away but fail.

I feel like a fucking creep.

We spend the next hour opening up each pen with a green sticker on—indicating the dog is friendly—and giving them the attention they're desperate for.

I can't imagine being locked away all day, every day, hoping someone will walk past and notice you. Help you.

I resonate with them in a way. Even as a kid, I was pushed to exhaustion. I'd openly vocalise at football practice how tired of playing competitively I was, hoping for a coach or parent to hear and tell my dad to lay off me, but nobody ever noticed. Or if they did, they decided not to say anything. I was stuck. Trapped in my father's web he'd so perfectly spun for me.

I lean down to pet the dog Mae's holding onto, and she laughs, gazing up at me with those big hazel eyes that glisten far too much for their own good.

"He's not going to bite. He just wants to say hello."

The big pitbull-looking dog whines, his butt wiggling as his tail swishes from side to side, hitting the side of his plastic bed. It makes a loud thumping sound.

I move into a crouching position, unsure of what to do as the dog crawls over my lap, shoving its snout into the crook of my neck with affection.

It's wet and slobbery, and I grimace, angling myself so he no longer has access to my clavicle.

Mae stifles a laugh. "I think he likes you. Or he can smell your sweat."

I grimace mentally. Mae is teasing. I know I don't smell. I'm freshly showered.

She takes notice of my rigid posture. "You're not scared of dogs, are you?"

A few days ago, Mae and I barely spoke, and when we did, our words were short and snappy. But it seems that being in the presence of animals has snatched away any negativity from her, putting her in a good mood.

"No. I just don't want them in every one of my crevices." I move my hand upwards to pet the dog's head, his skull round and bulbous under my fingertips.

Mae hums before turning to the dog that trots back over to her and lands in her lap, telling him, "I've always wanted a dog, but I have to settle for a tortoise for the moment. I don't have the time for a menace like you."

I arch my eyebrows, clicking my tongue as I blink. "A tortoise?"

"Yeah, Chump." Her eyes snap to mine.

"Chump?"

Who the hell named it that? They deserve to be incarcerated.

Mae doesn't strike me as the type of girl to have a reptile as a pet, but it dawns on me that I don't actually know her at all.

And it'll make things so much easier if we keep it that way.

We settle into silence, nothing but the sound of dogs yipping and the ceiling fan whirring filling the room.

I usually feel so at ease with silence, but for whatever reason, I'm not.

Now that I've been in Mae's presence for a length of time, I begin to take note of every detail of her face. Each tiny freckle. The small dimple beside her lip. The white scar at the tail of her eyebrow, running into her hairline. I try my best not to look for too long, but I can't help but wonder how she got it. It looks like the injury had been deep.

A childhood accident, perhaps? Kids are always falling out of trees or tumbling off trampolines.

"Have you ever had any animals?" she suddenly asks me, and I release a deep breath, running my tongue along the front of my teeth.

"No."

There's a tense pause before she huffs, narrowing her eyes and shaking her head. "Are you always this grumpy?"

The question catches me off guard, and I cock my head at her, pursing my lips.

"I'm not grumpy," I respond, but she tilts her head and raises her eyebrows at me. "I'm sorry if spending time with the daughter of the woman who has it out for me doesn't benefit me." My tone is calm—monotone, even. I rarely ever lose my temper—unless it's out on the field.

My comment causes her molars to clamp down, and a scowl takes over her usually harmonious features before she curses. "Look, I don't know what's gone on between the two of you, but I'm trying to make the best out of a shitty situation here. I don't particularly like football, so I'm not jumping for joy either. But we're partners, and you can either get over it or sulk for the rest of the season. Either is fine by me."

There's a howl from the kennel next to us, and Mae huffs, piercing hazel eyes boring into mine before she steps out of the small kennel to tend to the other lonesome pup.

I don't know how to react. I understand she's frustrated with me, and I understand I haven't exactly been welcoming, but this woman is stirring thoughts within me that I don't need. Or want.

I run a hand down my face.

God, this would be so much easier if she was a bitch to me.

My phone vibrates in my pocket, and I yank it out, huffing as my father's name flashes on the screen. I debate declining his call, but he'll only persist and make whatever he has to say to me an even bigger deal than necessary if he knows I'm ignoring him. Moving on autopilot, I push the emergency exit door open and step out into the cool breeze.

"What?" I say through gritted teeth.

I hear his agitated chuckle on the other end of the line. "Hello to you too, son."

"You've never been one for pleasantries."

I imagine him smiling—the type of smile that could curdle cream. The cocky bastard. "Are you ready for the game on Thursday?"

Football. Always football. We haven't spoken about anything else for years.

"Yes," I bite out.

"Are you going to win?"

"Do I look like a fortune teller?"

Some could mistake Kevin Slater's questioning for passion, but it's so much more than that. He's always used pressure to get to me. Even at the age of thirty-three, he still treats me like I'm an easily mouldable child—using the same techniques to make me feel like a failure.

It's a shame he taints the sport I had the potential to enjoy.

I try to talk to him as little as possible, but he loves to play the role of the doting father for the tabloids, attending my games when he can and wrapping his arms around me in a spine-crushing hug when we win, posing for the cameras.

Journalists would have a field day if they found out I hate him, and he hates me just as much. I don't want to give them anything more to talk about, so I allow my father to fake his devotion to me. It's just easier.

"Clear your head, Nathan," he spits. "You can't let this slip through your fingers. You don't want to disappoint everyone all over again, do you?"

I clench my jaw.

"Make your mother proud."

With that, I hang up the phone, crushing the metal between my fingertips, wanting nothing more than to see it crack just like my inner child does whenever he brings up the woman who deserved better.

The woman I wish I could have saved.

7: Mae

My muscles ache. It feels like a thousand tiny needles are pricking into my skin whenever I take a step. Training has been challenging, but I'm slowly getting used to it. My cardiovascular skills have always been pretty favourable, and even though I'm not at the top of my game, I'm gaining it back quickly.

It just sucks that it hurts so damn much.

My mother approved of our animal shelter photos. However, she did specify that Bennett's hand was a little too low on Poppy's waist.

With all honesty, it looked perfectly friendly to me, but Poppy received some choice words from my mother and I have a feeling that she's going to stand with a bargepole-sized space between the two of them the next time we take a photo.

I see Nathan in passing during training. His glances always last a little longer than necessary before his face settles back into a glower, and he ignores my presence. Sometimes, when we leave practice, he's out on the second field running extra laps. Sweat trickles down his bare chest, tanned skin stretching over thick, corded muscles.

I find myself slowing my walking pace down or fumbling around with my bag just so I can spend a few extra seconds with my eyes on him.

He's just so fucking hot.

And I hate it.

After our conversation on the first day at the animal shelter, he completely shut off. He didn't speak. And neither did I. There was tension lingering in the air, and he kept drifting off, seeming to be distracted by his own thoughts.

I told him he can sulk all he wants, but if he's going to do that, then I'm going to make it just as uncomfortable for him as it is for me.

Because Mae Bexley doesn't roll over for anyone.

I've been subjecting him to annoying questions at the animal shelter all day today, using it as a distraction from glancing at his veiny forearms when I know he's not looking.

While cleaning the dog leashes, I asked, "So what do you do besides just throw a ball?"

While re-stocking the kibble in the pantry, I asked, "So what does your helmet actually do besides make you look silly?"

And while playing rope with the beagle-looking dog, I asked, "How old is too old for someone to play, if you catch my drift?"

I received minimal answers every time, but never silence. Nathan didn't blank me. He responded, even if I was bothering the fuck out of him.

My insinuation about his age made him freeze, though, and I swear I saw the corner of his lip flick up the tiniest bit before he flattened them again.

It was all I needed to see to spur me on.

"So what do you do once you've caught the ball again?" I ask as we exit the animal shelter, putting on my best dumb girl voice, tilting my head to the side and blinking a few times.

He gazes down at me with that same old taut jaw, eyes flickering to Poppy and Bennett, who are already getting into their cars.

I've been questioning him about football all day, forcing him to talk to me, and it's funny watching him frustrated as I pretend to still not understand.

"I told you, I run."

My gaze flickers down his body. "With those legs?"

Nathan deadpans me.

If looks could kill.

"Wait, so how do you score a goal?" It takes all my strength not to burst out laughing once I see him press the heels of his palm into his eye sockets and curse. "What?" I question with fake innocence. "I'm a cheerleader now. I need to know these things."

"A cheerleader who doesn't like football." He shakes his head, removing his hands from his face, mouth downturned.

"A cheerleader whose uniform still doesn't fit her." They didn't have time to tailor me an outfit, so I had to wear a spare set a size too small at last night's game.

Nathan shrugs. "Hadn't noticed."

A scoff falls from my throat. "Alright, Mr *I'm going to stare at you from across the field.*"

Irritation flickers in his eyes. "I don't stare at you. Why would I stare?"

"Whatever helps you sleep at night, quarterback." I arch an eyebrow at him and turn to lean against my car. Once I'm not facing him, I smile to myself. But I'm exhausted. Keeping up this chirpy act is tiring.

He can be a grouch if he wants to, but I'm curious how long he can keep it up.

Two can play at this game.

"You know I'm a wide receiver and not a quarterback, right?"

"That does ring a bell, actually." I play with my cuticles. "Why don't you tell me about that whole two-point convention thingy again?"

"*Conversion*," he corrects me. "It's called a two-point conversion. Do you seriously not know a thing about football? You're on a cheerleading team. You're supposed to know this stuff."

Now I've got him talking. That's probably the most he's said to me in one go all day.

I lift my shoulders in a shrug. "Am I? I think all I'm supposed to do is stand on the sidelines and look pretty."

"Cheerleaders are more than looking pretty," is his casual response, surprising me.

I hum, nodding. I can't tell if Nathan's being serious or pulling my leg, but his face is blank as his eyes dart from each feature of my face.

He's standing there, bathed in the golden light. The rays highlight every angle of him, his sharp and defined face looking like Gods sculpted it.

His shirt clings to him in the heat, but he isn't sweaty. In fact, he smells like citrus—lemony and fresh. I'm not even sure if he's wearing cologne or if it's just his natural manly scent fixing with the smell of his laundry detergent.

My suspicion is the latter.

"Why is there a no-fraternisation rule?" I blurt out, and Nathan's eyes go comically wide for a second before he composes himself. "Has it always been that way? Signing a contract seems a little excessive."

"Do you always talk this much?" His words could be mistaken for judgment, but looking at Nathan's face, he's genuinely wondering—face, perhaps a little pissed off.

"When I'm curious, yeah."

He averts his eyes. "The rule was only put into practice this season. Before then, no one had ever really spoken about it. But hushed relationships got in the way. So," he gestures his hands outward, "hence the contract." His brows tighten. "Look, I'm sure you've got stuff to do, and so do I. I can't spend all day explaining things to you."

I hum, unaffected, taking note of the dropping sun. I need to get home before it gets dark. My rental car's headlights don't work much better than a dying firefly.

Before I go, I shoot Nathan a small smile, telling him, "I was just messing with you all day, by the way. I did my research. I know a lot about football," and I hear his exhale of frustration as I spin on my heel in the direction of my car.

Something is heavy on Nathan's mind tonight. It's obvious with the way he plays during the game.

His limbs look heavy—like some invisible force is weighing him down. His face is sharper than usual, and I pick up on how he scans the bustling crowd, his eyebrows pinching and nostrils flaring. As if he's searching for someone.

He doesn't move with the fluidity I expect him to. His movements are jerky and calculated, and his opponents can predict his next move before he puts it into play, meaning they take control of the ball for most of the first two quarters.

I can't make out what the crowd are saying, but it's clear they're not happy. I have to give the team props because they completely ignore them, blocking them and their complaints out.

I stand on the sidelines, shimmying my pom-poms. The red and white cheerleading outfit that's too small causes my breasts to spill out more than I think is acceptable. I thank whoever is looking over me that all I have to do is stand by and hype up the crowd without needing to perform any of the routines tonight.

I'm not sure I'd survive the mortification of having my tits fall out on live television.

Although I'm sure it would make me pretty popular.

Nathan and I meet eyes from across the grass, and his gaze drops to my breasts for a split second before he blinks, shakes his head and averts them, zoning back into the game.

I can feel my skin beginning to flush.

He catches the ball and shoves his way past a few players from the opposing team who try to take him down. I swear I can hear their bones snapping and bodies twanging.

The Missarali Storks are winning, but I know these sorts of games can change at the drop of a hat. All it takes is for someone to be in the wrong place at the wrong time, and it gives the opponent an opportunity to slip through.

And that's precisely what happens.

Bennett now has control of the ball, but he's forced to the ground. There's nobody there to pass it to, causing the crowd to throw their hands up in irritation.

I watch with a rigid posture, forgetting I'm supposed to be easing the crowd. The phoney smile drops from my face as I crane my neck to get a better look at Nathan, who's dragging himself from the floor after having been tackled.

Bennett shakes his head in frustration as his captain helps him to his feet. The jumbotrons above show them having a conversation. It isn't heated, but I can tell they're having some choice words with each other, and after a few seconds, Nathan clips the back of Bennett's helmet in a friendly manner.

The rest of the game doesn't go as smoothly as they'd like. The Missarali Storks win, but only by three points, which is too close for everyone's liking.

A win is a win in my book, though.

When Poppy and I enter the cheerleading locker room, we can hear Coach Darrell talking with the team in their own locker room through the wall.

"That was a close one, boys. We nearly lost it out there, but thankfully, you pulled through. I'm proud."

Poppy has her ear to the wall, finger to her lip, telling me and the other girls to be quiet.

There's another voice. I don't recognise it, but they sound older. Grumpier. "Watching you out there made me nervous, so I can't even begin to imagine how the fans felt. Nathan, where was the teamwork?"

I knit my eyebrows together.

The team won. What's the need to pick on them? Nathan was playing to the best of his ability out there. They all were.

"I don't know why you're directing that question at me," is Nathan's response, his tone icy. Each word drips with a confident disdain that should repel me, but instead, I find myself drawn to the danger.

"Well, you're the captain, aren't you?" A scoff. "Are you even taking this seriously?"

The man speaks with such condescension.

Nathan is in his thirties. He's not a child, and it's perplexing that he's being spoken to as if he is.

"And what are *you* to this team?" he responds, making the rest of the team mutter under their breaths. "Just a nosy man using his family connections to force his way into the team's locker room. You're not supposed to be in here, so I suggest you leave."

There's silence and a muffled response, but the sound of heavy footsteps indicates someone's walked away, and judging by how I can still hear their coach and Nathan speaking, it's neither of them.

"Sounds to me like they're going to drive those boys to insanity one of these days," I say, rolling my eyes and pushing myself off the door. After peeling the too-small outfit off my sore body, I grab my bag and change into my sweats.

I'm meeting Flo tonight. I haven't seen my best friend for months, and I'm beyond excited—almost as excited as I am to get away from my mother for the night.

She's been berating me for my choice of meals, telling me that if I don't lay off the carbs, I'm going to gain weight, and she can't have an overweight cheerleader on the team. It's funny coming from someone who believes that a sliver of seasoned lettuce and two rice crackers with a thin layer of jelly on them is a sufficient meal.

One night, it was enough to make me scoff my dinner of vegetable lasagne down right in front of her, a proud smile on my face as she glared at me with disgust before mumbling something about having an animal as a daughter.

I wonder if she's going through some intense menopause or something.

I wave a quick goodbye to the girls before exiting the locker room and entering the corridor, keeping an eye out for anyone who I think would fit the voice I'd heard speaking to Nathan and his team.

I'm nosy.

I can't help it.

"Hey, Mae-Mae!"

I turn at the nickname, a laugh bubbling up my throat as my brother, Cam rounds the corner. He opens his arms wide, pulling me to his chest.

He's been away on vacation with some friends and only got back this morning for tonight's game.

"Cam, how have you been? I've missed you."

He nods, his ashy brown hair falling in front of his face, his matching hazel eyes boring into my own. "I'm good. Listen, I'm sorry that the veterinarian program didn't work out for you, but I know you'll get another shot at it. How can they say no to this face?" He boops my nose teasingly, and I shove his hand away with a mixture of a groan and a snicker.

I assumed my mother would tell Cameron about what had happened to me. It's embarrassing having to admit you lost your dream job and had to move back in with your mother, but my brother has always been supportive, and I know he would never make me feel small for something I have no control over.

His eyes scan my bag, my medication pouch filled with epi-pens sticking out. He uses his pointer finger to push it back in so it doesn't fall out. "Still got those allergies, huh?"

"I don't think an allergy to nuts is something you just grow out of, Cam."

He shrugs. "I think I just feel sorry for you because you could never have any of Grandma's peanut brittle. Honestly, it was life-changing."

My eyes roll as I swat at his arm. "She'd pluck her nose hairs while making the mixture. Somehow, I don't think I was missing out on much." I shoot him a toothy grin. "How are you finding working here?"

"It won't be for forever. It's just to get my foot in the door, and then I'll apply for other teams to help physio. Can't stay in Missarali my entire life."

Cam's four years older than me and has always been drawn to the sports world. He never had the desire to play but instead wanted to be on the sidelines, helping the team behind the scenes.

Becoming a physiotherapist seemed like the perfect fit for him. And God knows my mother couldn't be more thrilled with his career choice. She's so proud of him, and honestly, there's a small part of me that wishes I knew what that felt like.

But then I remember that I don't need her approval. I don't care what she thinks of me.

"How's Mom treating you?"

I bring my fingers to my lips, picking at them—something I've always done when unhappy. Cam detects my uncertainty immediately, sighing. "It's—"

"Mae, come on, what's going on?"

Our mother is a sensitive topic for us. We're both aware she's not my biggest fan, but it's not something we've spoken about openly—besides the one time we both got drunk while out with friends and I cried to him about being made to feel like a failure. He tried to help by speaking to her about it, but she did nothing but call me an attention seeker, and it made the situation a million times worse.

He wants to stick up for me, but doing so only hardens things. It's why he keeps her at arm's length now.

"She's being her usual self. It's fine. I'm here for a season, and then I'll be moving. I can handle it."

"Do you want to come and stay with me?" Cameron's lips curl upwards at the question. He knows what the answer is going to be.

I deadpan him. "No, thank you. Last time I stayed, I didn't get a wink of sleep because all I could hear was one of your roommates fucking through the paper-thin wall. Their moans are forever etched into my brain." I fake a shiver. "I'm scarred for life."

My brother booms with laughter. "I won't lie to you and say it's got much better."

I glance down at my phone as it pings, quickly reading over Flo's text. "I need to go, but let's get dinner next week?"

"Sure. I need to go and give these pussies their massages, anyway. Nathan's hamstring keeps seizing up."

My mouth suddenly goes dry.

Images of Nathan's thick thighs oiled up flash into my mind without warning, and I clear my throat, nodding, trying to keep my face neutral.

I'm sure it's the same thought every horny viewer tonight had as Nathan shucked his helmet off and doused his face in a stream of water to cool down, droplets trickling down his stubbled face and dripping onto his neck, sweat sticking to his football gear.

I've never wanted to be a droplet of water before.

But there's a first time for everything.

"Mae?" Cam barks at me loudly, jolting me from my *very* vivid thoughts. "You haven't eaten anything with nuts in, have you? Your face has gone all red."

My hands fly to my cheeks, prodding at the flaming skin. "No. What? No."

My brother eyes me up suspiciously before nodding slowly. "Right, well. I'll see you next week. Text me."

"Yup, bye." I have to stop myself from speed-walking out, disbelief flooding through my system at almost being caught fantasising over Nathan Slater.

I don't know why my mind went there. He's a cranky asshole who hates me. And I hate him.

I can't deny he's hot. I can't deny that his voice makes the hair on the back of my neck spike up.

But he's... him.

And I'm me.

And allowing my head to go there—even for a split second—is far too dangerous.

8: Nathan

My father has some nerve. I'm unsure exactly how he manages to get past security and sneak into our locker room after every game. But I imagine all he has to do is show the security a few photographs of him and me together, and they let him through, thinking he's a proud father who just wants to congratulate his son.

But he'd stormed in here as if he were a coach. Not only did he speak to me like shit, but my team, and that's a line he knows not to cross. I'm protective of them. They don't deserve to be subjected to his deprecation.

Cam, our physio, calls me into his office, and I lie down on the small cot he's set up. It's far too small for my six-foot-three frame, and I shift uncomfortably, the scratchy paper on top of it gyrating against my skin.

"You've got to invest in a bigger bed, Cam. I beg you," I say, allowing my head to flop back onto the plump pillow.

He chuckles, oiling his hands up and manoeuvring my leg upright, my knee pointing to the ceiling. He gets to work, and I hiss in pain, gritting my teeth.

Cam's a decent guy who joined the team last season after finishing school. However, he's Renee's son, and although he claims he isn't overly involved in her life, I'm still wary of him. But he has a job to do, and so do I.

"Well, maybe you guys should just stop growing," he responds as he digs into my skin with the pad of his thumbs, my hamstring screaming, tense and tight.

"Ease up, man."

He stops and gestures for me to flip over. With every press and knead, the tension my body so desperately wants to hold onto begins to dissipate, the pain transforming into nothing more than a dull throb.

Massages are known for being relaxing, but sports massages are far from pleasurable. It's almost as if Cam gets satisfaction from causing us pain.

Is that what they taught him in school? To be a psychopath?

"How's the volunteering going? I saw the photos."

"Fine. We're going back to the animal shelter tomorrow."

"You don't strike me as an animal kind of guy."

I don't respond, opting for a low grunt instead. As a child, I was desperate for a bunny. I still remember the day my parents got into a raging argument because my mother came home with one as a surprise for me.

My father wasn't best pleased, and he threatened to boil it for dinner. I spent that evening crying into my mother's shoulder while hugging Tiggles—a name nine-year-old me had come up with—but when I woke up the following day, Tiggles was gone.

My father had made my mother return him. He claimed I didn't have time for pets. That they were a waste of time and it was only going to die and leave me heartbroken, distracting me from practice.

"How's Mae settling in?"

Cam's question catches me off guard. I clear my throat, feeling the frustration begin to rebuild in my body as I think of Mae's delighted face when we stepped into the animal shelter and how I'd rained on her parade by being a grouchy asshole.

Does a part of me feel bad? Yes. But can I let it distract me? No.

Something is fascinating about her, though. Not only because she's beautiful but because of how she carries herself. The apparent bone-deep love she has for animals. The fake smile she plasters on even though there's sadness lingering deep within those almond-shaped eyes. That smart mouth of hers, snarky comments slipping out before she can bite her tongue.

I can't help but find the strange combination somewhat intriguing.

And I don't fucking know why.

Mae is Renee's daughter and Cam's sister.

Our ships may be crossing right now, but they have different destinations. She's here for a short time before leaving to start her veterinarian training.

And I'll still be here. Doing all I know how to do.

"Nathan? You're not going to nut, are you?"

"Shut up," I grumble, running a hand down my face, sighing when Cam raises his eyebrows at me, pressing me to answer his first question about his sister. "Yeah, Mae seems good," is all I can bring myself to say.

He hums. "My mom giving you a hard time about keeping your hands off her?" He's kidding. He knows I don't mess with the cheerleaders, but the question still irks me.

Without permission, my head conjures up a scene of Mae and I together. In bed. No clothes. Sweat coating our bodies as our lips lock, and her body trembles beneath mine.

Fuck, she'd sound good moaning my name.

"I wouldn't risk my entire career for a one-night stand."

"So you're saying that if your career wasn't on the line, you might consider it?" Cam wears a cheesy grin, but I can see a glint of something else behind his eyes. It looks like protectiveness, and I completely understand where he's coming from.

The idea of anybody here touching my own sister makes me feel sick. She's a consenting adult, sure, but we both know I'll always see her as my baby sister. It's just the way it is.

I bite the inside of my cheek. "No."

Mae and will never go there. I don't want it to go there. She pisses me off.

"Good. Okay." Cam steps back from me and claps his hands together. "You're all done. Come back if the muscle is giving you trouble between now and the next game."

"You know it will."

It's the effect of consistently pushing my body to its limit, but I don't know any other way of life. When I'm not training, a member of another team is, which means they could better their skills beyond mine. I'm not as young as I once was, and some new, fresh twenty-one-year-old could be just around the corner, ready to take my spot.

I reach forwards to push the door open, but as I lay my hand on the metal knob, Cam stops me with a low clear of his throat.

"Nathan, I don't want to be *that* guy, but I'm being serious about not going there with Mae. I don't think you would, but I just have to put it out there. She's had a tough childhood and doesn't need any more drama in her life. Not from our mom. Not from the media. And not from a football player."

I offer him a stiff nod as a reply, exiting his office. I'm not a man of many words, but I'm sure Cam can tell I've taken his concern seriously.

Still, much to my dissatisfaction, I can't help but wonder what Mae experienced in her childhood to make Cam so protective of her.

Usually, I wouldn't give a fuck, and that's what's irritating the hell out of me.

DANGEROUS

Football hurts.

So does being tackled to the ground and having the cracked part of your helmet near your mouth bend and stick into your chin.

It's halftime, and even though the medics rush over to tend to me, I wave them away. I need time to breathe.

My father is watching me from his seat, eyes sharp. Even though we're winning, I know he's not impressed with the injury I've just sustained.

It made you look weak he'll tell me later.

I exit the playing field and head to the men's locker room, where I clean myself up. It's a minor injury, but the skin on the face is thin, with more blood vessels close to the surface, meaning it doesn't stop oozing.

My teammates won't be too worried about me. I often disappear during halftime to give myself a pep talk—and to avoid my father's less-than-sympathetic one.

As I exit the locker room, I almost walk into a petite figure, and I gaze down to see Mae standing in front of me, her tits fucking distracting as they sit perfectly on her chest.

I get they didn't have time to make her a custom outfit, but could they not have stuck her in something a little less enticing? I shouldn't find the coach's daughter this good to look at.

"What are you doing?" I question as I narrow my eyes at her.

She tilts her head at me like it's obvious. "Going to the bathroom. Is that okay?" She crosses her arms over her chest.

I tilt my head to the sky.

Fuck me.

I don't need to see that.

Most people don't speak to me. They avoid me, and I can't blame them. I'm not the warmest guy to be around when on-season. I don't have the patience for small talk and I'm not known for sugar-coating things. People keep their distance besides those who know me well, and honestly, that suits me just fine.

But then there's Mae.

She doesn't recoil when I shoot her a sharp comment or an infamous glare. If anything, she fires right back with that smart mouth of hers. I'd want most people to back off, but a part of me enjoys the back talk with her.

It's like she knows how to handle me.

I find it endearing.

But I remind myself I need to keep my distance.

"That's fine with me, princess."

Her eyebrows hike up at the nickname.

It's what I've been calling her in my head since I found out she was Renee's daughter.

"Princess? Why the hell am I a princess?" She looks taken aback and places her hands on her hips before jutting them out.

"You're related to the queen." I roll my eyes. "That makes you the princess."

She doesn't look impressed, bordering on offended. I just know she's going to come back with something, and I tilt my head to the side, waiting. Why the hell do I enjoy teasing her so much?

After a few seconds, a cocky smile finds its way to Mae's face. "Right. Well, Nate—oh, can I call you Nate?"

My eyes flare. "No."

"Good. You took quite a hit there, Nate." She laughs. "Sure you're not suffering from a concussion or something?"

I fucking hate that nickname, and she knows it. She's clearly done her research. A part of me is flattered.

Still hate the nickname, though.

"Football is a contact sport. I'm used to it."

She nods to my chin, eyes rounding just the tiniest bit. "It's still bleeding."

I wipe it with my sleeve.

"Well, that's a sure way to get an infection."

"Nothing a little dirt can do to me, princess."

Mae's jaw flexes as I step back. "Don't call me that."

I move past her, shaking my head, a tiny chuckle slipping out from between my lips. "That's a hard pass."

I can feel the steam radiating from her, hitting my back. Not a fan of football puns.

Noted.

9: Mae

"Well, aren't these cute?" teases Flo as she turns her phone in her hand, showing me the screen.

I roll my eyes at the photo of Poppy, Bennett, Nathan, and me at the animal shelter. Nathan's arm is around my shoulder in a friendly manner, his teeth blinding white as he smiles at the camera. His presence commanded the room without even trying, and it seems to happen wherever he goes. People look no matter what he does, and that pressure must be crushing.

Flo skips to the next photograph on a sports social media account that Peter sent the photos to. It shows Poppy cradling a snow-white cat to her chest, her head tilted back with laughter as Bennett crouches down behind her, his face contorted with displeasure as he scrapes a crusty pile of cat shit off the tiled flooring.

Poppy and I have been exchanging messages, and she's been sending me videos of our routines to help me when she notices me struggling a little during practice. I find her easy to speak to, possibly a little overbearing, but I like it.

She's a ball of energy, and it's contagious. I can't help but feel in a good mood when around her.

Flo swipes again, revealing a photo of Nathan and I. The adorable beagle mix dog with the stitched-up leg—or Mr No Name as we now call him—is on my lap, his tongue lolling out as he licks my exposed collarbone. Nathan is beside me, his head slightly tilted, the smallest of smiles gracing his lips.

It was for the camera, though. As soon as the volunteer handed back the phone and disappeared, he went straight back to his favourite place—Grumpy Town.

"You should frame this one," Flo says, arching her eyebrows at me, and I turn away from her and shake my head. I don't want to think about anything other than the turkey-club sandwich she made for me.

"I don't want Nathan Slater on my wall," I tell her, my mouth full.

"Very ladylike." She pauses. "And why not? He's gorgeous. I wouldn't mind seeing that every day."

"He's an ass. He looks at me like he wants me to drop dead."

Okay, maybe that's *slightly* dramatic.

He's grinding my gears, though. We're both stuck in the same position. We don't want to be doing this—although I don't mind volunteering at the animal shelter—so the best we can do is try and make it work for the time being.

He's making it damn difficult, though.

Especially because he walks around with that body of his, which makes me literally drool.

"You should fuck him."

I almost choke, attempting to wash my sandwich down with Flo's hefty glass of wine. She doesn't have a filter, and although I've come to expect it, she sometimes takes me off guard. "Flo, that is *not* happening."

Her eyes narrow, and she flips her ashy hair behind her shoulder. "Not with that attitude."

"There's a no-fraternisation contract I've signed, and did you also miss the part where I said he looks at me like he wants me to drop dead?"

Flo sips her wine, but I can see her smiling against the glass.

"Can we please just change the subject?"

My best friend shoots me a look that says *We'll talk about this another time* before agreeing. "How's the vet program search going?"

I shrug. "I haven't found any openings."

"You'll get there. Keep your head up." Flo pats the top of my head. "Looking down too much will give you a permanent double chin."

"You're so weird." I burst out into laughter.

She smirks at me. "But you wouldn't have me any other way."

"Hmm, honestly, I'd prefer you a little easier on the eye."

She slaps my arm. She knows I'm kidding. Flo's absolutely gorgeous with her long, ashy brown hair, ocean-blue eyes and tall and slender figure.

"Fuck you and your lame ass for not having sex with a hot football player when you have the chance."

"Trust me, Flo. There's no chance there. Not that I'd want to even if there were."

She drags her bottom lip into her mouth, stifling a laugh. "Sure, I'll be a good friend and pretend I believe you, Mae."

We've got two days left volunteering at the animal shelter, and to say I'm disappointed is an understatement. I've loved spending my spare time here.

The camera flashes as we pose for another photo, and Nathan immediately steps away from me, almost as if touching me has burned him.

"Okay, we're a little short today," explains Sheila, her grey hair tied back into a neat bun. "Our vets are both busy on a course, and two more staff members are off sick, so you'll see less of us wandering around. So far, though, you've all been amazing, and it's an honour to have you."

My heart blossoms with admiration. Sheila comes here almost every day. Sure, she gets paid, but the government doesn't give her much. To her, that doesn't matter, though.

I can see the want in her eyes. The need to be here doing this. It's the same thing I imagine sparks in me when thinking about working in an environment similar to this.

The same thing I imagined I'd see in Nathan's eyes when out on the field, but he often looks dead behind them. Like he needs a fucking break.

I see the pain behind Bennett's fake smile as Sheila suggests he and Poppy attend to the cats again, having no doubt he really executed all of the cleaning while Poppy spent the entire time cuddling the kittens.

He doesn't sell her out, though.

"We're happy to work with the dogs again," I say.

The tension flows from Nathan beside me, his gaze lingering on me briefly as we walk down the corridor towards the dog kennels. Mr No name wiggles his butt from side to side, and he leaps into my lap after I open the door.

I glance up at Nathan, who is standing on the other side of the kennel, arms crossed, leaning back against the wall. He offers the dog a treat from his pocket before stepping back again.

"So... how are people responding to the photos?" I question, trying to fill the silence.

But also because I'm genuinely curious.

I've decided I'm not going to subject him to questioning today.

"The media seem to be happy with them."

I'm not going to be part of the team forever, so it doesn't affect me much. But that doesn't mean I'm not glad the media seem to be laying off the Missarali Storks. I don't like the idea of anyone being subjected to unnecessary scrutiny. I know how it feels.

"What are they saying?"

Nathan shrugs. "I don't follow social media, but Bennett says they're pleased with what we're doing."

"Well, I'm glad they no longer see you guys as dreaded soul-crushers." A chuckle escapes me at the media's dramatics. "I don't get why they care that you guys mess around with women, anyway. You have money, looks and fame. Sleeping around is inevitable. There's no issue with it."

People have always been sensitive when it comes to sex.

A knot forms in my stomach as Nathan's eyebrows knit together, his lips pressing into a thin line as his eyes slim. "I don't mess around with women."

I internally groan. I hadn't meant it as an insult.

"I didn't mean it like that."

"Not everything the media say about us is accurate, you know?"

I didn't mean to offend him by stating he sleeps around. Nathan's talented, rich, and gorgeous, and I have no doubt he has women snapping at his heels.

But then again, he always has his head so deep in the game. Perhaps he really does stay away from women.

"Nathan, I—" I stop talking as soon as I notice the blood on my hands, and Nathan's eyes go wide as he takes a step forward, concern clear on his face.

Mr No Name is still ecstatic at our arrival, and he shows no sign of being in pain, but when I glance down at his leg and see the blood dribbling from it, I curse. "His stitches have come loose."

I swear I see relief spread across Nathan's features once he realises it's not me that's bleeding, but I shove those thoughts away.

He quickly steps away to inform one of the workers about the dog's condition, and after noticing their concern about being short-staffed when they come to check on the dog, I suggest we take him to the vet to save them the trouble.

Mr No Name has no objections to clambering into my old, rusty rental car—I'd offered to drive so as not to get blood on Nathan's expensive Audi's seats—and he waits patiently in the car's footwell as we make our way to the vet.

The drive is silent, and although awkward, I'm thankful for it.

I sit with my body hunched over as we wait for the vet to stitch Mr No Name up. The surgery is quiet, with only a lady holding a pet chinchilla on her lap—the rodent giving us the stink eye and definitely freaking Nathan out, judging by his perplexed eyebrows.

The silence is stretched thick and heavy, surrounding us like fog. My gaze flickers to the side of Nathan's face for a second, and his jaw flexes, keeping his eyes straight ahead, boring into the back of the ripped, leather waiting room chair in front of him.

The air feels charged, filled with nervous energy.

I don't understand how he's sitting here and not choking. Instead, he's as still as a statue.

I'm picking my lip nervously, and I realise I can taste blood. I pull my fingers away from my mouth, sucking on my bleeding bottom lip.

"I'm sorry," I say after a heavy sigh, and Nathan turns to me. "I didn't mean to offend you. I thought I was being... supportive, but it came out wrong."

The lack of response I receive is suffocating, and I gaze into Nathan's olive-green eyes, guilt hitting me hard in the chest. The last thing I want to do is make this more difficult for both of us.

He swallows. His Adam's apple bobs up and down, and my eyes trail down the thick muscle of his neck. He looks defeated as he leans forward and rests his linked hands on his knees. "Don't worry about it. I was being touchy."

"I just want you to know I didn't mean it in the way you think I did. I don't think you're a man-slut or anything like that."

The corner of his lip twitches at the word *man-slut*, but he holds it down. "Mae, just don't worry about it. Okay?"

My chest fills with oxygen at the way he says my name. It rolls off his tongue so easily. So seductively.

I have to remind myself that we're aiming to be civil here. And these aren't the sorts of things you think about when trying to be civil with someone.

I offer him a curt nod. "Okay."

Nathan's eyes drop to my lips, and my stomach twists, my heart thumping inside my chest at how he's looking at me.

A few seconds later, he's still staring at my mouth.

Fuck me.

But a wave of reality drenches me when he says, "Your lip is bleeding."

"What?"

"Your lip. It's bleeding."

"Oh."

I rise from my seat and grab a tissue from the front desk, pausing there as I gently dab at my lip, needing the moment to myself. I can't believe I thought—even for a brief second—he was looking at me in any other way than friendly.

Am I really *that* horny?

God, I need to get laid.

LOTTIE MOORE

I haven't celebrated Thanksgiving properly in years. Sure, Flo invites me over to her place on the city outskirts if Cam's busy, and she'll do an awful job carving a turkey. But it's not the same as celebrating with your own family.

Although, Flo is as close to family as I can get—besides my brother.

Sometimes, her mom will join, too, and she'll spend the entire meal talking about why she thinks aliens will come down to Earth one day and take over. It's her favourite topic once she's had a few glasses of wine.

But it always cheers me up.

However, this Thanksgiving, I'm spending it at Coach Darrell's house. Poppy wouldn't let me bail.

The room is bustling—full of football players and cheerleaders—and Sophia hands me a glass of wine as she smiles at my perplexed expression. "Peter's idea. Wants to get some nice photos of the team being thankful and all."

Is everything Peter does just for show?

I've only just stepped into the room, and I already feel the sudden urge to down my drink to feel more comfortable. Comfortable family settings have always been strange for me. I've never really experienced it.

Hazel—Darrell's wife—rushes up to me, engulfing me in a warm hug. "It's so lovely to meet you, Mae. I hope you're keeping the guys on their toes."

My gaze flits to Nathan, whose jaw is set as he leans back on a stool. His dark jeans wrap around his thick thighs—not too tight, but not too loose—and his T-shirt clings to his muscles in the most natural way. I can tell he's just thrown the outfit on. He doesn't need to try to look good because he does anyway.

His hair's a little messy, looking like his fingers have run through the dark strands a few times. I wonder how soft it is. What it would feel like to tug on while—

Hazel clears her throat in front of me, releasing a giggle. "Has the drink got to you already, dear? You're staring into space."

"Oh, yeah." I offer her a smile, and we tap our glasses together.

"Hazel, honey, do we have any more wine?" Darrell asks from the stove, his sleeves rolled up as he stirs the contents of a pot with a spoon.

"Oh, yes, in the back shed. Let me just—"

She looks flustered, glancing down at the canapes she was in the middle of preparing before she came to introduce herself to me.

I place a hand on her wrist. "Let me get the wine, Hazel. You have enough to do."

Her eyes twinkle with gratitude. "Thank you, Mae. The shed's just at the end of the backyard. If you could grab a few bottles, that would be really helpful."

I dip my chin to my chest in a nod, placing my glass of wine on the counter. "Of course."

Hazel snaps her fingers, head peering over to look at the nearest football player.

Nathan.

"Go with her," she instructs. "We're near the mountains. Rattlesnakes sometimes like to pay a visit."

His lips flatten as his eyes meet mine, but he doesn't argue as he stands from the stool he's sitting on. His fresh, lemony scent hits me, and I try to keep my face neutral before turning and exiting through the back door.

Our footsteps crunch lightly on the gravel path, and the scent of damp earth and smoke from nearby bonfires mixes with the crisp winter air. I can feel him behind me, moving with a confident stride like he always does, and I peer down the backyard, which is scattered with lights. They're not bright enough that I'm able to see, though.

I quickly lose my footing—thanks to Poppy's suggestion I wear my wedged heels—and my ankle twists, sending me stumbling. My heart races for all the wrong reasons, and I close my eyes as the ground rushes up to meet me.

But it doesn't quite get there.

"Are you okay?" Nathan's concerned voice cuts through the air. But it's not his words I'm focused on. It's the thick, corded arm wrapped around my waist.

I'm suddenly acutely aware of how warm he is—my back against his stone-like chest—and as I fight the urge to lean into his touch, I step away from him, brushing my clammy hands on my pant legs.

"Yeah, thanks," is all I can muster before I turn my back on him and continue walking down the yard.

I swear I hear him sigh, but I'm not so sure.

Do I talk to him? I don't know what I'm supposed to say, especially after that.

"Do you like turkey?" is what I settle on.

"What?"

"It's Thanksgiving. Turkey. You know... the bird that gobbles, do you like it?" I run a hand through my hair. This is so fucking stupid.

"Yes, I like Turkey," is his confused response, but it's paired with a humorous exhale.

I don't want to turn around to see his face right now. I just know he's looking at the back of my head like I'm crazy.

Because I feel crazy.

We reach the small shed. It was only a good few yards away, but it might as well have been miles away with how constricting that walk felt.

Pushing the door open, I flick on the light, but it does little to illuminate the space around us. My eyes squint as I try to take in my surroundings. There's an old motorcycle in here collecting dust, and I side-step it, afraid that if I get too close, a cockroach will launch itself onto me. Toolboxes cover the floor—more than anyone would need—with hammers and spanners poking out of each one, meaning the lids can't close.

It's creepy, to say the least.

"Are we just going to stand here, or are we going to get the wine?" Nathan asks me, and his husky voice kickstarts my limbs, encouraging me to take another step forward.

I reach down once my eyes begin to adjust, meaning I can see the small cluster of bottles in the corner. But as I bend, Nathan takes a quick breath.

"What?"

"Mae, don't freak out, but there's a giant spider on your back."

My spine goes rigid, and I shoot back up into a standing position. "No, there's not!" My heart stutters in my chest. Small spiders I can deal with, but hearing there's a 'giant' one on me turns my blood to ice.

I know it can't hurt me, and I do love all animals, but that doesn't mean I want them on my back.

"Please tell me you're joking." My hands are frozen at my sides.

He shakes his head slowly, his eyebrows pulled taut. His eyes flicker to my lower back, where I assume the spider is sitting.

"When you say big...?"

He doesn't respond, and that tells me all I need to know. I have the equivalent of Shelob on my back.

I take note of the sly smile on his face, and I clench my fists. "It's not funny, Nathan! Don't laugh!"

He wipes his hand across his mouth as if to cleanse the laugh from it.

"Nathan, please get it off." I'm making an effort not to shout, but my patience is wearing thin. I'm on the verge of tearing my shirt off right in front of him just to rid myself of this itchy skin feeling. Tears prick my eyes. The uncertainty of not knowing what the spider looks like makes it so much worse. I'd feel more at ease if I could see it, but since I can't, my imagination is spiralling with thoughts of what it might look like.

Is it poisonous?

Black and hairy?

Is it a jumping one? Some can jump.

"Okay, okay, turn around. Calm down for me, princess." I almost jolt at the nickname, but I can't find it within myself to demand he cut it out right now.

I can tell he's on the verge of laughing again, but he stifles it as he twirls his index finger, releasing a quiet whistle once he catches sight of the creature again.

If it looks that big in the dark, how big would it look in the light? I don't even want to think about it. Clamping my eyes shut, I brace my hands against the shed wall, shuffling closer to Nathan and bending so he has easy access.

This is a suggestive position, but I don't give a fuck right now.

He doesn't say anything, and I clear my throat. "Nathan?"

"Hold still." He sounds like he's breathing heavily through his nose.

"Holding," I respond with gritted teeth.

Nathan's hands are on my back after a few seconds, fingers delicate. The sensation is oddly calming, soothing my racing heart, but I don't let my mind go there.

He's getting a creepy crawly off my back. There's nothing sexy about this at all.

On instinct, I lean back again, trying to get this spider as close to Nathan as possible so he can quickly swipe at it.

He gulps from behind me.

"Please..." I take a deep breath. "Have you got it?"

No reply.

Only silence.

"Nathan," I say firmly.

Then, his fingers are gone from my spine, and I'm straightening myself and turning around to see him cupping his hands together.

"I assume you don't want to see it?" he says, already turning around, body standing tall.

"No, thank you. Please just take it outside, but don't kill it."

"I'm not that heartless," he tells me as he turns left towards the bushes beside the shed.

DANGEROUS

I don't like spiders. Don't want them on me. So why the hell am I hoping for another one to crawl onto my back so I can bend over for Nathan again?

10: Nathan

The flash of a camera makes me cringe, so I pull the brim of my cap further down to help cover my face, shielding myself from the array of desperate reporters in front of us who are keen to get a money-worthy shot.

We're at a press conference to discuss our thoughts on our upcoming game, but nobody really wants to talk about that. All these frenzied reporters want is the gossip in our personal lives.

Who we're dating. What cars we drive. Celebrities we've partied with. Family issues we have.

It's what makes them the big bucks.

I hate these things, but Peter says they're compulsory. He wants to keep the team relevant. That way, he can make as much money as possible. It doesn't matter to him that we get eaten alive every single time.

"Evan, is the rumour that Ella Baxter is the mother of your child true?" a reporter asks, and I glower, opening my mouth to defend my friend. But Evan gets there before me.

"Does anyone here actually want to talk about football? Why does my son concern you?" He looks fed up. People are always making ridiculous assumptions about who Leo's mother is, and Evan has made it abundantly clear that he will never reveal her identity.

He doesn't want the drama. Or the lawsuit she threatened him with if he were to sell her out.

"Is that a yes?" the reporter presses, and Evan glares at him—eyes so piercing you'd think the reporter would shrivel up and make a run for it, but he stays put, a slight smirk on his lips. He knows if Evan doesn't actively deny it, then he can sell a story on the pop singer, Ella Baxter, being the possible mother of Leo.

Coach Darrell shoots Evan a look from down the conference table, silently telling him to deny it if he wants to avoid another story.

He pinches the bridge of his nose, his dark hair falling in front of his eyes. "No, Ella Baxter is not Leo's mother. I've never even met the woman, so I don't know where you're getting that from. But unless anyone actually has a question about football—which is what we're here to talk about—I won't be wasting my time."

The tidal wave of news reporters erupts into low hums, scribbling down in their notebooks and flashing their cameras.

The heat of the overhead lamps sizzle my skin, and I squint my eyes as they pulse, wishing I'd brought my glasses with me.

I hate wearing them, though.

Whenever I do, news reporters focus on me, latching onto the fact that women love it. Their photos sell for more.

I dislike being the reason these assholes make money. They have zero respect for us.

"I think what Evan is trying to say here is that we all have a passion for football," Bennet begins, clearly having taken notes on the media training I'd assigned him, "and we're excited about our next game. We want everyone else to look forward to it just as much as we are, so why don't we discuss that instead?"

Darrell pats him on the back, agreeing, offering him a proud smile.

The response is clearly practised and polished, but it doesn't matter if it makes the team look professional.

A reporter cackles. His stick-thin body looks like it's about to crumble under the camera's weight hanging from his neck. He takes the microphone being held out to him, clutching at it with his lanky fingers. "Unfortunately, boys, stories about football don't sell, and we have a living to make."

I stop myself from criticising the man. I get it. I do. They have families to feed, but exploiting us is not an ethical way to earn a living.

"Nathan." I mentally roll my eyes as he points at me. "What do you have to say to the people who view your team as a bunch of thirsty players, only interested in satisfying themselves with the cheerleaders as if they're toys? Don't you think they deserve more respect than that?"

I huff. I'm tired of this question. It's the same every time, but they just word it differently, trying to catch me out and get me to say something less than favourable about our cheerleaders—to paint me as a sexist pig.

Nobody on my current team has touched one of the cheerleaders. The people who did last season were let go by Peter for creating too much drama, and Renee did the same with the women.

"I believe we've been over this, but I'll reiterate it for you. The relationships and interactions you saw between players in my team and our cheerleaders last season were consensual. I can assure you we treat women with the utmost respect, and if I discover anyone on my team to be doing any less than that, then I'm not afraid to call them out on the behaviour." I grind my teeth together. "We're here to play football, though. That is our main focus."

More humming. More scribbling. More flashing of cameras.

It bores me.

My mind wanders back to that moment with Mae in Darrell's shed. Even though a monstrous, furry spider was on her back, I wasn't focused on that. I was looking at the curve of her lumbar. The way her palms lay flat against the shed wall as she bent over for me. How her legs parted, shaking slightly. It had made me immediately go hard, so thank fuck it was dark in there.

I can't get a fucking boner over Mae Bexley.

Another question aimed at Bennett through the microphone brings me back to reality.

The reporters leave me alone after my professional answer, realising they can't get anything juicy out of me today. They look at me with their stupid faces, though—as if they're begging me to open up and tell them about what's happening in my personal life.

What personal life? I don't have time for anything else.

Mae's comment about me messing with women at the animal shelter bothered me. I was grouchy with her, and maybe I shouldn't have been, but hearing that she felt that way intensified the irritation flourishing in my chest.

She and that mouth of hers get on my nerves.

Have I slept with women? Of course. But do I see myself as someone who toys around with their emotions and drops them once they've given me what I want?

Absolutely not.

That's something I would never do.

I have more respect for them than that.

I usually don't care much about what people think of me. I ignore it because I know it's not the truth. Sure, it's frustrating at times, but it doesn't keep me up at night.

But knowing Mae thinks the same... it doesn't sit right with me. I don't want her to see me that way. I want her to know I'm more than the headlines.

The conference is over quickly. Darrell cuts it short after a reporter asks one of my teammates why he looks like he's gained a bit of weight, and I order the sleazy reporter to be banned from all future conferences.

The fucking nerve.

Evan leans up against the wall in the corridor, clamping his eyes shut and cursing under his breath.

"You okay?" I ask him, my mouth downturned. It was a shit show in there, and he received the brunt force of the hit.

He opens his eyes, looking drained—like all the life has been sucked out of him. "Yeah."

"Evan, have you been getting any sleep?"

"Honestly... no. Leo caught a cold a few days ago, and I've been up every couple of hours trying to settle him."

"What about his nanny?"

Evan scoffs. "*What* nanny?"

His response causes me to tilt my head, a groan escaping. I press the heels of my palms into my eye sockets, rubbing in frustration. "Look, I know you're protective of Leo, but we're in the middle of a season. You can't go firing every nanny after one shift."

"None of them give a shit about my kid, Nathan. They take the job because of who I am, and I'm fucking tired of having people use Leo as an excuse to wiggle their way into my life."

"I can see that." I nod to the bags hanging beneath his dead eyes. "You can't play the way you are, though."

Evan opens his mouth to speak, but I hold my hand up to stop him.

"I'm doing this because I care about you, West. You're not playing Monday. You're resting."

His eyes expand to saucers. "What? You can't do that."

"I can. I'll make the suggestion to Coach. You're burning out, Evan, and there's no way you can continue the rest of the season this way. I'll babysit Leo tonight."

My friend grunts, shaking his head, but deep down, I know he's relieved. I've given him an out, which he so desperately needs. He's a great father. He always puts his kid first, but he's neglecting himself. He can't take care of Leo the way he wants to if he carries on this way. And he knows that, which is why he doesn't object.

"I'll drop him off at six."

"Make sure to bring more than one pack of diapers. Last time, he shit through them in an hour."

Leo glares at me with pale grey eyes—just like his father. He's sitting in his high chair, having thrown his entire plate of spaghetti and meatballs I'd prepared onto the floor.

"Well, this is a first for me," I tell the salty kid. "No one's ever turned their nose up at my cooking."

Leo blows out a snot bubble, and I immediately wipe it away.

Bracing myself against the green plastic of his high chair, I gaze into his eyes challengingly. "Okay, Leo. What's it gonna take for you to eat something?"

All I receive as a response is a loud "Yuck."

"Your daddy said you love this," I say, bending down and scraping the food off the floor before dropping it in the trash.

Leo's still getting over his cold. He's no longer running a fever, but Evan supplied me with medication just in case. I'm glad my friend is getting some well-needed rest, but I can't help but feel out of my depth here. I love Leo. He's a great kid, but because he's comfortable with me, he tests me.

Swiping him from his high chair and placing him on the floor, I begin to mop, huffing to myself as I watch the small kid take hold of his favourite dinosaur toy and throw it to the other end of the kitchen. The plastic reptile hits my rack of spices, causing a jar of chives to plummet to the floor. Luckily, it doesn't smash.

I curse—low enough so that Leo can't hear—and turn to see he's run into the living room and is now scaling the couch as if it's Mount Everest, spaghetti sauce smeared around his mouth, staining the leather.

He's acting up because he doesn't feel well. He's usually a good kid, and this kind of behaviour isn't typical for him.

"Hey, buddy." I crouch down in front of him. "How about we get you to bed? Are you sleepy?"

Leo shakes his head. "Not tired."

"Of course you aren't," I groan, tilting my head back to stare at the ceiling.

Pulling my phone from my pocket, I sigh with relief. It's been over an hour since I last received a text from Evan. He always worries when I take care of his son, and while I understand why, he needs to learn to trust people.

I laugh at the irony of my own thoughts.

The last thing I can tell anyone to do is trust someone.

Suddenly, Leo bursts into a sob, snot running from his nose, his cheeks flushed. He reaches out for me, and I scoop him up in my arms and rub circles on his back, gently shushing him.

It only makes him cry harder, though, mumbling about missing his daddy.

Calling Evan isn't an option right now, though. He looked like a zombie at the press conference. I was surprised he didn't collapse onto the table.

"Hey, hey, it's okay." I keep my voice quiet. "You'll see your daddy tomorrow. Do you want some warm milk? That always makes me feel better."

I'm lying. Who the fuck likes drinking an entire glass of milk? But I'll say anything to calm Leo down.

He shakes his head, his words muffled as he sobs into my chest. I can't make heads or tails of what he's saying.

We need to try and find Leo a nanny who he connects with. That way, Evan will feel more comfortable, but he has his guard up. When you first meet him, he's a stone-cold wall, and no doubt, it scares everyone who tries to work for him off.

Darrell has even taken one for the team before and got his wife, Hazel, to babysit Leo during a few games, but he expressed that it was a one-time thing and Evan shouldn't get used to it.

After thirty minutes of continuous crying from Leo—the tiny human showing no sign of stopping anytime soon—I pull out my phone and call the one person I know who can advise me in this situation.

They pick up on the first ring.

"Poppy, I need your help."

11: Mae

I have a newfound dislike for the media. I'd watched the Missarali Storks press conference on TV and was dumbfounded to discover that these reporters weren't there to get the juice on football after all.

They treated the guys like caged animals, attempting to back them into corners. They showed no respect, and I breathed a sigh of relief once Darrell cut the conference short. Evan looked particularly pissed off, and rightfully so.

The mother of his son is nobody's business but his own.

Nathan was calm and collected—like usual. He showed little emotion besides the odd flicker of frustration whenever a reporter asked an out-of-pocket question. Although I tried to watch everyone, my eyes gravitated to him, even when he wasn't talking.

He looked good in a cap.

Okay, maybe *good* is an understatement.

My mom is on the phone when she walks into the kitchen where I'm eating. A part of me wants to shy away from her—cover my food so she can't see—but then I remind myself that I don't give a fuck.

"Alright, Cam, put it in the diary, and I'll book it." My mom is smiling. It's not something I see often, but then again, she doesn't have much reason to smile around someone she dislikes. She cuts off the call, her eyes dropping to my plate before she sighs and pours herself a cup of coffee.

She sits opposite me. The tension is thick in the air, and I meet her eyes, raising my eyebrows. The only reason she'd willingly be sitting here with me is because she has something to talk to me about.

"Are you okay?"

"I'm more than okay." She flicks her perfectly blown-out hair behind her shoulder. "Cam's taking me out for dinner for a catch-up, so I'm going to need to leave practice a little early on Saturday. Can I trust you to hold the fort down?"

I resist snorting. It sounded to me like she'd been the one to ask Cam to dinner, but I resist voicing that opinion.

"Sophia's the captain. Isn't she in charge?"

My mom rolls her eyes. "Obviously, but the football players will be there at the same time, so I need you to let me know if there are any strange interactions between anyone."

"Why does it sound like you're just waiting for someone to mess up? I don't want to be your spy." I'm trying to make friends, and snitching on people is not the way to do it—not that there's anything to snitch about. As far as I've seen, everyone's been professional.

Even if I had bent down in front of Nathan in a shed with my ass hovering over his dick.

Concern flourishes on my mother's face, the creases her makeup has settled into deepening. "Is there a reason for that, Mae? Is something going on with you and any of the—"

"I'm going to stop you right there." I hold up my palm. "I don't want to hear what you're about to ask."

"You were a little angel when you were younger, Mae. What happened? I don't know if you have hormonal issues or some deep-rooted trauma because of your father, but he's not—"

"Don't bring up Dad," I bite out, standing from my chair, blanching. "Our relationship issues have nothing to do with him."

My mother stares at me, cocking her head before finally saying, "Have you considered therapy?"

That's enough to drive me out of the kitchen, memories of my father surfacing.

His smile.

His laugh.

His compassion.

I miss him.

And I need to get the heck out of here.

Flo's travelling for work, but Poppy's always asking me to grab coffee or lunch with her. I call her, and she picks up after a few seconds.

"Mae?"

"Hi, Poppy. I know this is really random, but is there any chance you're free tonight? I'm going over one of our routines, but I'm just not getting it."

Lie.

I know the routines like the back of my hand now, but I don't want to have to explain to her that my mom is impossible to be around. It doesn't feel like an appropriate thing to say.

"I was waiting for you to want to hang out." She laughs. "Sure, come over. I'll text you my address."

I feel a little cowardly running away from my mom, but she's the one person I can never get through to, and leaving the house and giving myself a little time to cool off is the best thing I can do so I don't fall into the trap of arguing with her.

I quickly reach Poppy's apartment. It's in a nice area, with large oak trees crowding over it, sheltering it from the precipitation falling from the sky.

The entrance is framed by lush greenery, carefully manicured plants lining the gravel pathway. I admire the large windows stretching from floor to ceiling, giving me a good view of the sleek and sophisticated interior.

I'm sure I look flustered and riled up, but I can't bring myself to care. Poppy's seen me looking worse.

I buzz number three, and the loud hum from the heavy glass door indicates I've been granted access. I realise I should have brought something as a thank-you for letting me visit, and I make a mental note to offer to pay for her lunch sometime—I'll briefly be getting a part-time job here so I have some disposable income.

The stairs are steep and glossed, and I can see the faint outline of my footprints on each one behind me, the rain making the mud outside claggy.

Rattling my fist against Poppy's door, I nervously shift my weight from foot to foot. I'd forgotten to change into training attire to back up my lie that I want to practice a routine, and it's going to look awfully strange showing up in a pair of denim shorts.

But hopefully, she'll look past that.

The door is pulled open, and I open my mouth to greet Poppy, but my eyes land on a very confused Nathan instead. A very confused—shirtless—Nathan.

Oh my God.

I feel the colour drain from my face, and my stomach spins, along with my head.

"I—I'm here to see…" Without thinking, my gaze drops to Nathan's toned, tanned chest, and after hearing him clear his throat, I snap my eyes back up. His eyebrows are hiked up, asking me what I'm doing here.

I could ask him the same question.

"Nathan! Let Mae in!" Poppy calls from another room.

"You knew she was coming?" he asks her, but I can tell he's trying to keep his voice hushed. I'm not sure why.

He steps aside, his fingers clutching the door tightly, and I'm surprised it doesn't crack the wood.

It feels like sweat is dripping down the back of my neck, and I instinctively graze my fingers against it to check. Once I realise it's only slightly damp, I breathe a sigh of relief.

I move past Nathan into the apartment, my bare shoulder brushing against his chest, goosebumps dancing across my skin from the contact. It's clear he notices, too, because he takes a sudden step back, bringing his hand to rub at the spot, the veins in his hand pronounced.

Poppy rounds the corner, dressed in a pair of pyjamas, her blonde hair pulled up into a messy bun.

"Sorry, I had a couple of unexpected visitors, but we can still go over the routine." She laughs, gesturing to Nathan.

I arch an eyebrow. "A couple?"

"Yeah, Leo's here. Evan's son."

"Oh," I mutter, confusion wrapping around me and strangling me like a python. I crane my neck to look at Nathan, trying very hard to ignore how good he looks. His hair is wet, and it appears he just got out of the shower, water droplets dripping down his neck and catching the light from the bright lamp beside him.

I've seen him shirtless from a distance... but close up, he looks other-worldly.

My abdomen tightens.

"Look at her face!" Poppy suddenly bursts out into a fit of laughter, causing me to cross my arms over my chest defensively.

"My face is fine."

"Unless you consider being the shade of a tomato as fine." Nathan lifts his eyebrows—the rest of his face sullen—and I shoot a scowl at him.

"I thought you knew," Poppy tells me, tilting her head and tapping her chin with her finger.

"If you two are fucking, please just don't tell me. I can't defend you if you admit it." I dig my teeth into my bottom lip, hearing Nathan scoff from behind me.

"Mae, Nathan's my brother."

Shock hits me hard in the chest, and relief spreads through my veins. My reaction causes Poppy to giggle before gesturing for me to follow her into the living room.

It exudes a warm and inviting ambience, with a muted couch in the middle and an array of colourful throw pillows covering it, adding a splash of colour.

She settles down on the couch, places her feet on the wooden coffee table in front of her, and turns down the volume of the TV.

Nathan grimaces from the doorway to the living room. "Why is Mae here, Poppy? Leo's sleeping in the next room."

"Hello? Right here," I grumble.

"Why don't you go and put on a shirt and stop making *my* guest uncomfortable before you start asking *me* questions in *my* apartment?" Poppy remarks, gaining a glare from her brother before he trudges down the corridor, only to return a moment later with a navy T-shirt covering his chest.

I'm disappointed.

I was enjoying the show.

"Much better."

My eyes flicker between the pair. They're so different. Nathan's tanned with green eyes. He has dark features. Poppy has fair skin. Her hair is a dirty blonde colour, and her eyes are icy blue. She's sunny and bright, whereas Nathan is dark and sombre.

"Same dad, different moms," Poppy clarifies after spotting me analysing them both, and I nod, blinking to clear my head. "Not that I would even consider our dad family."

"We don't need to talk about Dad."

She rolls her eye at her brother, turning to me. "Nathan's just grumpy because he and our father hate each other, but they have to pretend they're the best father-son-duo in the NFL. In fact," she nods at him, "when are you not grumpy?"

Exactly what I said.

"I'll perk up once I can retire," Nathan mutters, though I can't tell if he's serious or not. I was under the impression that football was his whole life, so hearing that he's actually looking forward to retiring catches me off guard.

"Well, I suppose you're not getting any younger," I say, and Poppy erupts in fits of laughter, choking on the water she just took a sip of.

"I get enough old man jokes from my team. I don't need them from you, too." I can tell he's trying to put on a crabby tone, but it's not quite reaching the baseline of his voice, and he watches me before sighing, running his hand down his face. His broad shoulders lean against the doorframe, body swaying slightly.

"Nathan, go to sleep. If Leo wakes up, I'll handle it." Poppy's eyes soften.

"I told Evan I'd look after him. I only needed your help getting him settled. It's not your responsibility, Pops."

His nickname for her loosens my chest up.

She waves away his concern. "I doubt he'll even wake up. The white noise should keep him knocked out."

But Nathan doesn't listen. Instead, he shuffles over to the cream-coloured armchair beside me and sits down. His fingers are inches away from mine. "I'll wait and head to bed when I'm sure he's sound asleep."

"So stubborn," Poppy murmurs, flicking the volume to the TV up a little and pulling a blanket over herself. "Did you really want to run through a routine, Mae?" She shoots me a perplexed look. "You seemed to have them all down in practice the other day. In fact, Sophia congratulated you for being so on point."

I shrug. I've never been a great liar. My emotions are easily readable on my face, so I don't usually bother being dishonest about my thoughts and feelings. "I know, I just—"

"Wanted to get away from your mom?"

I look at her, feeling like a deer in the headlights. "What makes you say that?"

The last thing I want to do is turn the cheerleaders against my mother. She's built up a relationship with them, and I don't want to be the one to shatter it. I'm coming into her space, and it seems wrong to shed light on how she treats me when it doesn't concern or affect anyone else. It's not like I'm staying anyway, and I don't want to create any more issues between us.

I'd rather just forget about her.

"The way she looks at you," Nathan suddenly says, and I whip my head in his direction. "It's the same way she looks at me. Well, very similar." His eyes are still glued to the television, but he's looking through it. Not at it.

My mother tries to stay out of my way during practice. She doesn't speak to me much, but when she does, she uses a tone that could cut ice. I'm always the first person she'll point out during a bad run of a routine.

I'm out of line. My limbs are floppy. I'm off-beat. It's always me.

Most of the time, I've performed the routine perfectly. She just loves to try to destroy my confidence.

I wasn't aware that the cheerleaders had noticed—let alone the football players. Let alone Nathan.

"What's her problem?" Poppy tucks her knees to her chest. "You're her daughter, and it's clear that—"

"You can't just expect people to unpack their family drama with you, Poppy," Nathan grumbles, but a sliver of interest is lingering in his eyes.

"I'm studying psychology. This is excellent research."

"She's not a project." His tone is frosty, and my stomach twists at how he defends me.

Poppy's not trying to intrude. She's just an open book, and she probably doesn't understand why others aren't the same. In a way, it's kind of refreshing. I've been surrounded by people who brush things under the carpet growing up, and it's a habit I've picked up—an unhealthy one.

"It's fine," I say to them both, shrugging. "There's not much to tell when it comes to my mom, though. She wanted her daughter to be a carbon copy of her, but I'm not, so she despises me. I got on with my dad much better than her, and she didn't like that because she's a control freak." I mentally wince at the final few words. It's not something I should be saying openly to one of her cheerleaders, but I now consider Poppy a friend.

"Yeah, I gathered that. She's a good cheerleading coach. I can't fault her for that, but honestly, she doesn't seem like the greatest mother. I've asked her about her family in the past, and she's always shown no interest in talking about you."

"Jesus Christ. You've got to be kidding me," Nathan mumbles as he pinches the bridge of his nose at Poppy's wording.

Her comment stings, but it's not something I wasn't expecting. I know my mother doesn't brag about me.

I don't go around singing her praises for being mother of the year, either.

Poppy pauses, biting down on the inside of her cheek. "Sorry. I think I analyse people a little too much. It comes with the degree. I didn't mean to make you uncomfortable or anything."

I shake my head. "Don't worry. It's actually kind of nice to have someone ask me about it. Nobody ever does, so I don't mind. Don't apologise, Poppy. I trust you not to run and tell my mom. I know you mean well."

That makes her grin. "So what about your dad?"

My breath hitches as my father is dragged into the conversation. A rush of emotion hits me, and I feel myself begin to shut down as I clear my throat, the words jammed.

Not much gets to me. I have a pretty strong backbone, but when it comes to my father—it's a very different story.

I was a daddy's girl. We got on like a house on fire. I still remember the times we'd laugh at stupid cat videos until our sides hurt. The times he'd help me build a fort in the living room and we'd camp there all night with Chump beside us. The times we'd visit the stables near our house and beg the owners to let us ride their horses for an hour, promising to brush them down and muck them out as repayment.

But all those times are just distant memories now—memories I latch onto because I don't want to forget them. I refuse to forget them. I refuse to give up on him.

He's out there somewhere.

Nathan quickly notices my dissociation, and he glares at his little sister, his jaw ticking before he stands up to grab the TV remote, raising the volume to drown out her voice. "Poppy, I'm trying to watch TV. Can you quieten down? This is a good show."

He hasn't been paying attention to it at all, though. I know that because I've been paying attention to him.

I swallow, my lungs expanding as I breathe in oxygen, allowing the happy memories to drift to the back of my mind.

Nobody speaks, and I try my best to focus on the crappy scripted TV show playing on the television before us.

"Nathan, I thought you were tired. Leo's settled now. You can go to bed."

At his sister's voice, he shakes his head, gesturing to the TV. "No, I like this show."

It makes me cock my head because I seriously can't imagine Nathan Slater enjoying a cheesy reality show marketed towards young females.

In fact, I *know* he's definitely not enjoying it because his eyebrows pinch together, and his mouth purses when someone on screen starts an argument with another over a drunken kiss.

I shift myself to be more comfortable on the couch, and I swear I see him raise his eyebrows at me—as if he's asking if I'm going to be okay—but I convince myself it was just my imagination as Leo's shrill cry rockets through the apartment.

12: Nathan

I wake to my phone blaring on the bedside table in Poppy's spare room. "Hello?" I groggily say into it after seeing Evan's name flashing up on screen.

"I've been texting you for the past two hours." His tone is cold. Grumpy fuck.

"And I've been asleep for the past two hours."

Evan clearly doesn't appreciate my comment. He steers the conversation towards his son, who I'm certain is still sound asleep in the room next to me. I'm hyper-aware of his presence, but it's not just him I can feel in the apartment.

Mae stayed over last night. I heard her and Poppy giggling in her room a little past midnight. I even left my door ajar just so I could hear Mae's laugh a little clearer, which is something I'm not proud of.

"Leo's still sleeping off his cold. Poppy was great with him," I tell Evan while brushing my teeth and throwing on a pair of sweatpants.

"Well, maybe if cheerleading doesn't work out for her, being Leo's nanny is on the cards." Evan's tone is semi-playful.

"Did you just make a joke?"

"Shut up. Get my kid ready." He pauses. "But, in all seriousness, Nathan, thank you. It means a lot."

"Hmm. I accept payments in either cash or bank transfer," I kid before hanging up the phone and entering the kitchen, desperate for a cup of coffee.

I struggle to function without the stuff.

As I step through the curved archway into the sleek kitchen, my gaze is immediately drawn to a barely covered Mae, and I'm unable to look away. It's clear she's just woken up—the puffiness of her lips, the frizziness of her hair, and the haze in her eyes all give it away. She's leaning against the granite countertop, a large glass of water in hand, and her fingers grip it a little tighter as she spots me.

"Morning," she says, voice light and airy.

My eyes skate down her body before I snap them back to her face. She's dressed in a pair of tartan pyjama shorts and a cropped T-shirt, her nipples hard against the fabric.

Fuck my life.

What is this woman trying to do to me?

"Hi," I gruff out, turning and boiling the coffee pot.

The last thing I need to see is Mae in skimpy sleepwear, fresh from the bed sheets. My mind is wandering into enemy territory. And it feels fucking good... which isn't ideal.

Because I wish it weren't Poppy's bed sheets she'd just slipped out of.

"Leo slept well," she says, keeping her voice hushed, face a little drained from last night.

It had been the first time I'd seen her so vulnerable. Granted, my sister had pried far too much. It wasn't fair, and I'm definitely going to be having a word with her about pushing people too far.

I dip my chin at Mae's comment as I turn towards her and pray that I don't have a hard-on from thinking about waking her up with my lips on hers.

My hands on her waist.

Head between her legs.

"Yeah, Poppy's great with kids."

"I can tell. She's great with everybody."

My sister's never had many friends growing up. Her brash personality often scares people off when she first meets them.

I'd noticed how her old friends would roll their eyes and look at each other with expressions that said *Why are we friends with this girl?*

It cut me deep to see her repeatedly dropped by people who didn't understand her. Who didn't value or accept her.

But Mae seems different.

She speaks to my sister compassionately and values what she has to say. She doesn't make her feel bad for her views; she accepts her, quirks and all.

"I want to thank you for how you are with Poppy."

Mae's eyebrows arch. "What do you mean?"

"You accept her. You treat her like she's an actual person."

"Of course. Why wouldn't I?"

It confuses me how vastly different Mae is from her mother. In the beginning, I'd assumed she would be a little princess. A brat. Just like her flesh and blood. But she's slowly proving me wrong.

The coffee pot behind me reaches its boiling point. But neither of us moves, and of course, she's standing right in front of the cupboard where Poppy's mugs are. I stretch my jaw as I take a few strides in Mae's direction.

She looks up at me, pink lips popping open, and I'm concerned she's going to drop the frosted glass of water she's desperately clutching onto.

Her tits look incredible from this view, and I do my best to be a gentleman and avert my gaze. Even though I don't want to. Even though all I want to do is drop my head and press my lips to the space where her neck meets her shoulder.

The tension is thick, our shared glance creating a buzz in the air that causes my eyebrows to collapse in on one another as I tower over her.

We're so close.

Too close.

I lift my arm, my palm flat against the cupboard above her head, fingers slowly gripping onto the small knob.

Her sweet strawberry scent lingers in the air around us, her glossy hair gliding across her tanned shoulders as she asks, "What are you doing?"

Her pupils are dilated, and she takes a heavy breath.

My nostrils flare.

I want to tell her how fucking beautiful she looks. How tempting she looks. But there are so many reasons why that can't happen.

She's twenty-five, in the prime of her life. She doesn't belong in a place like Missarali. She's too good for it. Too good for me.

My fingers pull the cupboard open—my elbow just skimming the side of her head—and I grip a mug and step back. "I needed a mug," I tell her, my throat thick.

Mae blinks, her lips creating an *'O'* shape as she quickly steps aside, giving me space.

She hadn't picked up on my *very* subtle hint to move out of my way. And by subtle, I mean practically non-existent. I'm perfectly aware I could have made her do so with a quick, "Excuse me."

But perhaps there was a part of me that didn't want to—just to give me an excuse to get closer to her for even just a second.

"Sam, come on!" I yell across the field as he's tackled to the ground, but he manages to pass the ball at the last second, giving Evan the opportunity to score a passing touchdown.

The crowd goes wild—flailing limbs and mouths so wide they could catch flies. The stands are packed. People have painted their faces red and white—our team's colours. Banners and flags flutter in the air as the clock counts down to zero, indicating The Missarali Storks have won the game by a longshot.

Thank fuck. We needed this big of a win.

We're crawling our way back up. It's not exactly where I want us to be confidence-wise, but this is a huge step up for us. We're showing everyone that we're serious about this. We want to win. Football is our priority.

Bennett engulfs me in a bear hug, yanking out his mouthguard and whacking me on the back of the helmet as a friendly *congratulations*.

I don't bother scanning the crowd for my father. He's not here today, and I know for a fact it's the reason I've played well. I haven't been put off by his scrutiny.

Once in the locker room, freshly showered and wearing dark jeans and a sweatshirt, Darrell enters, beckoning me with his finger.

"What's up?"

"Riley's asking for you." There's a big grin on my coach's face.

Although we were playing against the Pittsburgh Pilots today, they're a team we're pretty friendly with.

Riley, their captain, is an asswipe, though. We have a cordial relationship with one another, but he's too cocky for his own good, and he enjoys talking up our fake rivalry to the cameras, claiming it makes the game more entertaining for everyone involved. I, however, dislike the drama he enjoys creating.

As I exit the locker room, Riley's sly, smiling form comes into eyeline.

"Slater," he says, clapping his hand on my back. "You guys put up a good fight out there. Seems we weren't lucky enough today."

"I don't think luck has much to do with it, Donovan."

He booms with laughter. "Thanks, Nathan. You always know how to perk me up." He pauses. "Listen, a few of the guys and I are heading out for a drink, so why don't you and your teammates join us?"

Riley must sense my reluctance because he pushes my shoulder playfully. "Oh, come on. What do you actually do with your free time? You're never seen out. Ever."

I nod. "And I'd like to keep it that way."

"Riley, what the hell are you doing on our side of the stadium?" Bennett's loud voice thunders from behind me, a broad smile on his face as he wraps his arm around Riley's shoulder.

"Just trying to convince your captain here to come out for a drink with us."

Bennett eyes me up, chuckling. "I'm down for that. As long as we promise there'll be no football talk."

I huff. Bennett can be impulsive sometimes, and I know he tends to say things he shouldn't when he feels comfortable, so in reality, he needs someone there to keep him in check. "Ask Sam if he'll go with you guys. I'd rather go home and do anything else."

More footsteps grab my attention.

"And where do you think *you're* going?" Poppy's sharp voice is hard to ignore.

I tilt my head up to the sky, momentarily closing my eyes. "Peace and quiet. All I want is some peace and quiet."

My sister is studying Bennett, her head tilted, a playful smirk curling the corner of her lip.

His eyes round as if he's been caught red-handed, and he chuckles, hiking his thumb over his shoulder. "We're heading out for a drink."

"And what kind of trouble are you going to get yourself in?"

"You got a babysitter, Quinn?" Riley laughs.

"Something like that," he mutters under his breath as he shoots my sister a look.

My sister hums. "If you're going out, so am I." She points towards her chest. "Remember what our coaches said. I'm on Bennett watch."

He narrows his eyes into slits, but it's far from a glower. "God, woman. Fine, come if you want."

Mae exits the locker room behind us, bag slung over her shoulder, surveying everyone with surprise. "What's going on? Am I missing out on any gossip?"

"Mae's coming too." Poppy links her arm with her friend, almost causing the both of them to topple over with the force.

"Going where?" Mae inquires, her pink hoodie falling from one of her shoulders, the soft fabric skimming down her smooth skin.

I can't help but notice the way Riley's beady blue eyes skate over her bare skin before he barks something about not being opposed to having some cheerleaders join, and I bite down on my tongue in distaste.

"Looks like we're all in," Riley cheers, tousling his light brunette hair, and I can tell he's trying to ensure it looks good for the girls, who aren't even paying attention to him.

He studies Mae as if she's some prize to be won. As if he's decided she's his next conquest.

My restraint is slipping.

Fast.

The last I heard, Riley was dating some millionaire's daughter. They were seen together just last week, holding hands and cosying up while they shopped at some stupidly expensive designer clothing store.

What a fucking pig.

And he gets away with it because he's well-liked by the tabloids. He always gives them the gossip they so desperately yearn for.

Everyone begins to walk down the corridor leading to the VIP section of the stadium parking lot. I watch with a taut jaw, and a sigh leaves my lips when Mae turns to me and raises one dark eyebrow.

"You coming... Nate?" She smirks.

I highly doubt she could come up with some cheesy nickname to playfully tease Riley with. What would she even call him? Ri? Rile?

I mentally scoff. None of them are charming.

We stare at each other for a good five seconds as I chew on the inside of my cheek, her hazel eyes holding me captive, which is a first for me.

They say eyes are the window to the soul, which rings true for her. I swear I can almost *feel* what Mae is thinking with just one look.

I sling my bag higher on my shoulder, forcing my feet to move. "Yeah, I'm coming."

I like to keep a close eye on my sister, so I need to make sure Riley doesn't try anything with her.

But I also feel this strange sense of overprotectiveness toward Mae, and it's definitely not the sisterly kind.

13: Nathan

We opt for The Salty Dog—a quiet bar. The last place we need to be is somewhere where we'll get recognised and stormed for autographs and photographs.

The stereo in the corner plays some cringe-worthy pop song, unrecognisable to my ears, and the small groups of patrons here natter amongst themselves, appearing too old to care about sports and who we are.

The faint smell of tobacco wafts up my nose, and I wonder if somebody's smoking in here or if the scent is so embedded into the furniture that the place continuously smells this way.

I take a sip of my water, eyeing up Riley as he sits at the table with my sister and Mae. His stupidly perfect teeth are on full display as he laughs, voice boisterous and egotistical.

I've always thought Riley Donovan deserves a good throat punch to bring him down a few pegs, but I've never felt so passionate about it until now.

Bennett pulls his cap further down as a group of younger people enter the bar, angling himself so they can't see his face. "Your dad didn't come to the game today."

"He was working."

"I don't see why you don't just tell him to stay the hell away from you."

"Tried that," I respond, tilting my glass towards him. "Didn't go down too well. Besides, he'll take to the media if I try that again, and God only knows what kinds of stories he'll sell on me to try and ruin my name if I try that again."

Bennett's face falls. He sighs, shaking his head slightly. "Shit. Is it really worth putting up with him, though? I mean, no offence, but your dad's an ass."

I shrug, shifting my eyes over to Riley and the others. I pretend to be absorbed in the atmosphere. The chattering of people. The feel of the uncomfortable barstool beneath me. The smell of old wood and dust.

But the way Riley speaks with fluidity and charm and how Mae laughs at whatever he's just said is where my attention really lies.

I hope she's laughing *at* him.

I can sense my eyes tightening, a spark of disapproval flickering inside my chest. Mae doesn't need a guy like Riley. He's non-committal. He loves the chase, but once he's captured his prey, he loses interest and moves on to the next shiny toy.

He hides it well from the media, but football community members talk.

"Man, are you okay? You look like you're ready to throw hands." A chuckle seeps from Bennett. He follows my eyeline and mutters a quiet, "Oh, I see."

"What?" I mutter, snapping my eyes away and jostling my glass, the ice hitting the sides, creating an aggravating *clink* noise.

"Might want to be a little more subtle about that." My best friend is grinning from ear to ear. I swear, I've never seen the guy in a bad mood. Even when we lose a game, he's oddly positive.

"Subtle about what? I'm just looking at them."

He chuckles, winking at me over the brim of his tall glass of soda. "Them? Or *her?*"

My eyes round. The fact that Bennett is even bringing that up is ridiculous. There is no possibility that Mae and I will ever be anything more than professional.

"Shut up, Quinn."

"Denial is a river in Egypt," is his response.

"What the hell are you talking about?"

"Nothing. Nothing at all, my friend." He's laughing, and I see Mae's head turn to take a quick look at us at the sound of Bennett's loud bellow.

She's fresh-faced, having had a shower after cheering. She doesn't do much on the sidelines, but I can't lie and say that her in that red and white uniform—they finally managed to get one tailored to her—doesn't steal my attention away when I should be focusing on the game.

She's a distraction.

A big fucking distraction.

Poppy is engaged in a conversation with one of Riley's teammates. It looks friendly enough, and I know that the guy has a wife and a kid on the way. He's trustworthy, so I'm not that worried.

But Riley is smiling slyly at Mae—as if she's a meal—and she's nodding in agreement.

My gut twists inside of me when he leans forward, almost entering her personal bubble. His large, tattooed hands hover just a brush away from hers, and although Mae doesn't look uncomfortable, she doesn't appear to be encouraging his behaviour either.

She's still, but her face is still friendly.

Does she like tattoos? Is that what she's into? I don't have any. Never felt the need for them.

I huff.

A promising future is on the cards for Mae, so the last person she needs to be mixed up with is Riley Donovan. She doesn't want to be famous. She wants a quiet life where she can tend to animals in peace.

"Oh, shit! You're Nathan Slater and Bennett Quinn!" A man in his late twenties stands beside us, lips stretched out in a smile. "Congratulations on the win, guys. I just watched the game on TV."

I dip my head in appreciation. "Thanks, man. Keep it quiet for us, though, yeah? We're just here for a celebratory drink."

"Oh, of course. Do you both mind signing my—" the fan glances around, snatching up something from the bar counter, "—used napkin?"

Bennett chuckles, pulling a pen from his bag and scribbling on the dirty napkin, making a face when the pen rips through the paper. I quickly do the same as the fan and Bennett engage in friendly conversation, and I refocus on Mae and Riley again.

Dislike blossoms inside my chest as he inches forward a little more, his fingers making contact with hers, eyes lustful.

Oh, absolutely fucking not.

I push my barstool back and march towards their booth.

Their heads twizzle towards me, eyes confused, but Riley's are also laced with agitation.

"You good, Slater?" His teeth click together.

I gesture for Mae to scoot up, and she does immediately, giving me room to squeeze in. "I'm fine, Donovan. Thought I'd join you guys for a bit."

I'm not too sure, but I think I see Mae's shoulders droop in relaxation at my arrival.

"I was just telling your cheerleader here how good her team looked in their cheer uniform. She included."

My fingers twitch, the rings around them suddenly feeling impossibly tight, constricting the blood flow. I press my tongue to the roof of my mouth, eyes honed in on Riley's.

I'm not a petty guy. I'm above all that. But Riley's smug face is testing my patience.

I snap.

"How's that girlfriend of yours, Donovan? You two looked pretty cosy in the tabloids last week."

Mae's jaw ticks, and her form immediately stiffens as she straightens. I force my laugh down because, damn, I've just unleashed a raging bull in her.

Riley knows what I'm doing. I can practically feel the steam radiating off him. There's something funny about how he squirms, trying to muster up a snarky comeback but failing miserably. Instead, he settles for, "Yeah, she's fine. Why?"

I've got the upper hand here. I've just rained on his flirtatious parade, and he can't fucking stand it.

Perhaps I'm enjoying it a little bit too much, but I refuse to let someone use Mae as if she's some kind of plaything. She doesn't deserve it.

"Tonight's win wasn't enough for you, huh?" Riley questions me, simmering rage lingering behind his irises.

"Hold on, so let me get this straight," Mae speaks up, holding her hands up and waving them to get Riley's attention. "You have a girlfriend?" She hums. "Well, she must be *very* proud to have you." Her tone is sarcastic as she crosses her arms over her chest and glares at Riley, and I drag my bottom lip into my mouth to prevent myself from breaking.

"Yeah, she is actually."

"I can't see why," Mae remarks, "because all I see here is a greedy, disloyal asswipe with his head so far up his own ass he's wearing it as a hat. Do you flirt with anything with a pulse?"

"Okayyy," Poppy chimes in, slowly gripping the glass of soda that sits in front of Mae, "I'm just gonna take this away before it ends up on his head."

Mae's comment is enough to have me laughing, especially because Riley stands up and announces he's leaving and doesn't want to waste another second in our presence. His teammates don't follow him, though, and his ego seems to burst even more.

That was fucking gold.

"Well, he was a fucking narcissist," Mae says, letting her head flop back onto the top of the leather booth so she can stare up at the ceiling. She releases a laugh of disbelief.

"Most athletes are."

I want to ask her if she found Riley attractive. If she was fooled by his phoney charm for even a second. But I keep the lid on my jar of vulnerability.

"Hmm, true. I'll remember to stay away from athletes from now on." The comment makes my muscles tighten. "I'll probably end up married to some businessman or something. Someone who comes home every evening in his suit and tie and blabs on about stocks and boring investments, expecting dinner to be on the table at seven PM sharp." She groans, rolling her eyes. "I can't fucking wait."

My mouth is downturned, distaste sour on my tongue. "Don't date a businessman, princess. That sounds dull."

Poppy and the others are distracted by their own conversation, so I use the nickname confidently, finding it funny how Mae's eyes flicker every time.

"Most men are dull."

A niggling feeling grows in my chest. All I want to do is lay her down on this table and prove her very fucking wrong. Because if she thinks all men around here are dull, I'll show her just how dull I can be.

I fiddle with my cap, giving myself something to do with my hands.

Mae will find a man she'll marry someday.

And they won't be an asshole NFL star like Riley.

I grind my teeth, unhappy with the direction my thoughts are heading.

Thinking of Mae married to some bland man who'll probably expect her to cook, clean, and look after the kids while he spends every second of his spare time working bothers me—a lot.

He'll probably give her shit sex, too.

My sister clears her throat beside us, saving me from my mind. "I'm exhausted. Are you guys ready to go?"

I nod, exiting the booth, and Mae does the same. Poppy beckons Bennett over towards the exit with a tilt of her head, and Mae hangs back with me as I grab my duffel bag.

"Thanks for having my back with Riley," she says with a small laugh. "I can't stand men who cheat. It makes zero sense to me, and the last thing I want is to be plastered all over the news as the *other* woman."

That's the last thing I want too.

I keep my face neutral, eyes dipping down to her breasts, cupped by her white, lacey cami top, for a brief second before I flick them back up. "No problem."

Silence descends between us, and I ask her, "Do you like tattoos?"

"Tattoos?"

I nod. "Yeah, on men." God, I sound like a self-doubting little teenager. "Riley has a bunch."

Mae tilts her head, humming. "Tattoos are fine. To be honest, I was too busy looking at his shit haircut."

I roll my lips together, eyes closing for a second as I scoff.

The things that come out of this woman's mouth.

However, I only allow my mask to slip for a second. I blank my face and stare ahead, focusing on the wall with old bottle caps glued to it to create some kind of strangely unique art piece.

"Oh, he gave me this." She holds up a small piece of paper with a mobile number written on it, "but I won't be needing it." Dropping it into her half-drunk glass of soda, she watches it disintegrate with a small smile.

DANGEROUS

He gave her his number?
I run my tongue along the front of my teeth.
Yeah… Riley Donovan and his shit haircut can suck it.

14: Mae

"Still hate shellfish?" Cam asks me, peeking over his menu to wiggle his eyebrows.

I deadpan him. "With a passion."

"Yep, I was right. Moving to Colorado didn't magically give you taste."

Ignoring him, I sip my ice-cold water and order a chicken curry. "So," I ask, shooting him a wry smile, "how's the love life going?"

"Why are you asking me that?"

Cam's been single for a while. He swore off relationships altogether after discovering his girlfriend of four years was cheating on him. I know it hurt him—more than he let on.

Charlotte and I were friendly, but I knew she walked all over my brother, and because he was in love, he allowed it to happen. There was nothing I could say or do to change his mind. It wasn't until afterwards he admitted to me just how toxic their situation had been.

She was training to be a professional dancer, though, and my mother obviously loved her. Hearing about their breakup had sent her into a moody spiral, and she wanted nothing more than for them to rekindle things.

It isn't going to happen, though. Cam has made that very clear.

I shrug. "Just wondering if you've met anybody. You know I want you to be happy."

"Mae-Mae, I *am* happy. I don't need a woman for that."

"You mean you don't need to be in a *relationship* with a woman for that," I correct him. I'm well aware he sleeps around now, but after what Cam's been through, he deserves to have a little fun—Charlotte was while he was ring shopping for the woman he thought he was going to spend the rest of his life with.

"You want to talk about the women I *fuck*?" Cam chuckles, and I fake a gag, waving my hands to stop him from talking.

"No, thank you. I'm good."

"Don't ask, then." He sips his bubbling beer. "How's Nathan?"

Lately, it seems all people want to do is ask me about Nathan Slater. Frankly, I don't know how he is because he's almost impossible to read. Just when I think he's dropping those heavy, rock-hard walls of his, he says something that makes it clear they're very much still up—impenetrable and unyielding.

He wears his icy exterior like armour, his defences pushing anyone within a two-metre radius back.

And then he has the nerve to call me princess.

And act jealous when Riley Donovan is flirting with me. He looked fucking hot doing it, though.

I knew I was never going to call Riley. He isn't my type, but when Nathan stormed over to embarrass him in front of all of us, I wanted to fall out of the booth with laughter.

Because there's one thing I hate, and it's cocky, egotistical men.

"Still looks at the world like he wants to punch every person in sight, but other than that, I think he's fine."

"I mean, he has a reason to look at the world like he does. Have you met his father?" Cam laughs.

I shake my head. "Thankfully, no, but I haven't heard great things."

My brother shuffles his chair forward, pressing his elbows into the table. "He barges into the team's locker room almost every game and speaks to the guys as if he's their coach."

"Why doesn't Nathan just tell him to fuck off?"

Cam raises his shoulders and drops them in a shrug. "I don't ask. But that's something you and Nathan have in common if that'll make this whole partner thing a little easier."

A laugh of disbelief bubbles up my throat. "Okay, I'm not going to bond with Nathan over our mutual dislike for our parents."

Cam's fishing. He's leaning in closer, the casual remark he's just made laced with intent. He's well aware of the bait he just cast—wanting me to bite and tell him that

Nathan and I are actually getting on better than I thought we would.

It's a strange situation.

I no longer feel like Nathan wants to stick forks into his eyes when he's around me, but there's still a strange, charged energy in the air when we're around each other.

I feel uncertain.

Uncertain because I definitely check him out like a friend shouldn't.

Uncertain because I want to learn more about his father and his struggles. Not because I'm being nosy, but because I actually want to understand him.

Uncertain because whenever I see him shirtless, I imagine myself running my hands down his chiselled abs with his lips latched onto my neck.

My body begins to pulse, and my mouth goes dry. I need to change the subject, but Cam beats me to it.

"It was Dad's birthday the other day." He says it as if I'd forgotten.

I wonder what he did to celebrate. Stay in and order himself takeout? Hit the club and party with a bunch of strangers? Or maybe he spent it with his new family... the new family I sometimes convince myself he's found.

"Cam... are you happy without dad?"

My brother immediately tenses up. His Adam's apple bobs up and down as he swallows, but I can practically see the frog stuck in his throat, refusing to move.

Our father leaving isn't a topic we tip-toe around like our mother, but it's not something we speak about often either. There's no need—not when neither of us knows where he is or how he's doing. We mention him casually, but I haven't flat-out asked Cam how he's coping with it for years.

"I think there'll always be a part of me that could be happier with him around."

I scowl. "You say that like we're never going to see him again."

Cam sighs, nervously fiddling with his flannel shirt. "Mae-Mae, he was sick. It wasn't safe for us. I think we need to accept that sometimes, you can't help everybody."

My nose stings, and I rub at it in discomfort. "He's helping himself. That's why he left. He has to come back at some point."

I'm not an idiot, though. I know I'm living in denial, but it hurts less.

My phone interrupts our moment by ringing in my lap, seeming to snap Cam out of his gloomy trance. He clears his throat, gesturing for me to answer it.

I groan at my mom's name.

She never calls me, so it must be important.

"Hello?"

I immediately pick up on the thick and bitter aura she emits from her end. "Sophia isn't going to make it to the next game because of her honeymoon, so you're on." She releases a grumpy huff. "Don't mess this up for me, Mae."

I clutch the phone in my clammy hand.

For some reason, I'm perfectly calm and collected when performing CPR on a dying dog or watching a very risky surgery that could cause a cat to bleed out in seconds. But the thought of getting out and dancing in front of millions of people for a stupid football game frightens the fuck out of me.

Especially because my mom's making me feel like the weight of the world is on my shoulders.

"Have you ever walked a dog before?" I ask Nathan with a frown as he clutches the dog leash in hand—as if it's utterly foreign to him—by the door of the animal shelter, the mud-covered fabric staining his palms. I imagine having something other than a football in his hands is strange.

He deadpans me. "I don't live under a rock."

"You play football. It's practically the same thing."

He releases some strange mix of a chuckle and a huff, and I snap my head to him, thinking he was choking for a second. It looks as if he doesn't quite know how to react to my playful comment.

One could mistake it for flirting, but that's not what I'm trying to do here.

Okay... maybe a little.

But I enjoy seeing the cogs turning in his head when I do. It always looks like he's trying to conjure up some appropriate response, sifting through many that are a little risky before settling on a more safe-for-work one.

Boring.

We're taking Mr No Name for a walk today now that his leg is pretty much healed. It's obvious he's been on walks before, as he lifted his paws for us to put on his harness, and that only makes me feel even sadder for him.

He was once someone's baby—someone's beloved pet—and they abandoned him. Yet, he's so forgiving. He looks at humans as if they stand on a pedestal before him. As if they're superior to him.

If only he knew.

The grass of the field behind the shelter sways gently in the breeze, the mucky green strands crisping up under the warm glow. Wildflowers dot the landscape, their floral fragrance mingling with the earthy scent of the soil beneath our feet. Large trees surround us, too, their leaves vibrant, birds balancing on their branches and chirping as Mr No Name runs beneath them.

It warms my heart. This place is a refuge for the dog, away from the confinement of the cold kennel he currently calls home. He looks so happy, and it immediately brings a smile to my face.

He deserves a home. And a name.

Nathan's stomach growls beside me, and I whip my head to him. "You didn't eat before we came out?"

"I was running laps. Didn't have time." There's a brief pause before Nathan asks, "What's your favourite food?"

I arch my eyebrows. It makes my lips curl upwards because I know he's trying to make casual conversation, and this is his version of it. I appreciate the effort.

It's actually kind of cute.

"My friend, Flo, makes these incredible turkey-club sandwiches. I don't know what she does to them because she refuses to tell me, but I could eat them every day."

"Maybe she wipes her armpits with the bread."

My eyes widen, and I snicker, covering my lips.

Nathan's comment sounded like it was supposed to be a joke, but he said it so casually that it made it funnier.

"Do you know what? Even if she does do that, it tastes damn good, so I wouldn't even mind."

Nathan rolls his eyes above me, his mouth turning down disgustingly.

"What's yours?"

"My what?"

"Do you have a football inside there instead of a brain?" I point to his head. "Your favourite food. What is it?"

He sighs, tapping his fingers against the dog leash he has wrapped around his large hand while he thinks. I'm unsure if it's a nervous twitch. "I'm not sure. Nobody's ever asked me that before."

The media and fans ask him questions all the time, and I assume at least *someone* would be interested enough to know what his favourite food is.

But then I'm reminded that the news reporters want to sell a story, and unfortunately, an article about Nathan Slater's favourite food wouldn't be a hit.

"Probably peanut butter and jelly sandwiches. I don't really care for fancy food," he says after a few minutes—I thought he wasn't going to answer.

I'm surprised. He has enough money to eat at the most expensive and prestigious restaurants, and I was expecting the words 'caviar' or 'lobster' to be his response.

But it seems you can't go wrong with a peanut butter and jelly sandwich no matter who you are—unless you're me.

"I'm allergic to nuts, which sucks. I've only tried a peanut and jelly sandwich once, and it was when I was three. My face was so swollen I looked like a floating balloon on a stick." I wish my parents had taken a photo so I could laugh at it today, but I understand they were far more concerned with the fact that their child was struggling to breathe than getting the camera out.

"Really?" Nathan releases a husky laugh, his eyes darting to Mr No Name, who is still rustling around near the trees, pawing at rocks and barking at mice who race away from him. "I'll remember not to eat them around you, then."

I offer him a smile. "Thanks. Do you think you're prepared for the next game?"

His shoulders drop at the mention of football, that twinkle from his eyes now completely gone.

I realise I've never seen a football player so deflated at the mention of a game. I'd expect him to be excited, full of energy, but instead, he seems weighed down by it, like it's a burden he can't shake off.

I scan the field before Nathan can respond, my eyebrows collapsing. "Wait, where's Mr No Name?"

His eyes dart from side to side. "I don't know."

I do a full three-sixty and still can't see him. There's no sound or movement, either. We pick up the pace, weaving around trees and scanning the shrubs as we call out for him, searching through the tall grass. We find nothing but large boulders and rabbit holes, though, and I start to panic.

"We lost the shelter's dog. My mom is going to fucking love this. What if he's found his way onto a road and has been hit? Oh, shit." I pick at my lip, and Nathan takes my hand away from my mouth and sets it back down by my side, fingers skating against mine.

The contact has my entire body tingling, eyes round.

He crouches down so we're at the same level. "Mae, don't panic. We'll find him, okay? He's probably just off exploring."

I allow my lungs to expand as I breathe. "Okay."

"Take a deep breath for me. We can't look for him when you're not calm."

I do as I'm told, giving him a sharp nod, and I inhale, placing my hands on my lower belly.

"Good. Okay, so we're going to—"

"Whose dog is this? What the fuck! Get off!"

The shrill makes Nathan and me push through the thick cluster of trees to see Mr No Name prancing through a small fenced field. His snout is coated in thick dirt as he dips into a greenhouse, exiting a few seconds later with a purple vegetable hanging from his mouth.

A farmer is stomping his feet, and once he spots us, he storms over to the wooden fence and wiggles his finger. "Your dog's dug up my radishes inside of my greenhouse!" His sagging skin has mud splattered into the creases, his greying hair dishevelled from—what I imagine was— chasing Mr No Name.

"We're so sorry," I tell him with a frown, waving to try and gain the dog's attention, but I see him rip another radish from a pot through the open doors of the greenhouse, throwing it up into the air as if it's a rope toy.

"Sorry doesn't grow me back my radishes." The farmer gestures to the mess of dirt and deceased veggies.

"I know." Nathan pulls a spare receipt from his wallet and scribbles on it using a pen from behind his ear. He hands it to the irritated farmer. "Here's my number. Call me later, and I'll sort out some form of payment for the inconvenience."

Mr No Name spots us, and although he appears to be having a blast digging up the farmer's livelihood, he trots over without a care in the world, allowing me to grab him through the fence and fasten the leash back onto his harness.

The elderly farmer doesn't seem convinced, but he grunts in agreement as he pockets Nathan's number.

"We'll get someone down here to clean up the mess, too." Nathan speaks so calmly, and I honestly don't think you could put him in a situation that would cause him to freak out. "Don't do it yourself. Again, we're so sorry, but I promise you we'll pay you more than double what you would have received for the radishes."

The farmer's face twists at the dog panting by my booted feet, his dirt-covered tongue lolling out as he releases a loud bark of pride. "Keep your dog on a leash," he says as he shakes his head and waves us away.

I try to keep a straight face as we trudge back through the trees, but before I know it, Nathan and I have locked eyes, and a laugh is bursting from my mouth—with a huskier, calmer one coming from Nathan's.

It's not funny. It's really not. But the sight of Mr No Name with a limp radish swinging side to side from his slobbery lips while he bounced around the field like a lamb is burned into my memory

He was having a blast.

I don't have it in me to burst his bubble.

I've never seen Nathan laugh like this before. It goes beyond a chuckle—more like a throaty laugh that's husky and deep. It's filled with pure, intense amusement.

Mr No name barks, and I stop to crouch down to his level, scratching at his head. "Well, I think I have the perfect name for you."

"You do?"

I shoot Nathan a smile. "Yep, Radish."

15: Mae

"Mae! You're out of formation!" my mother yells above the booming music, shaking her head and tutting.

"I'm not," I complain back, and she shoots me a look that says *you better be quiet before I embarrass you in front of everybody.*

It's enough to make me click my teeth shut and nod. Daisy was the one out of line, but I'm not about to throw her under the bus when she's busting her ass. She has sweat dripping from every part of her body, and I know she almost didn't make the team because she can—apparently—be sloppy at times.

This is *her* dream.

Not mine.

So, who am I to stand in her way? She's trying, and I'll gladly take my mother's criticism if it means her mistake doesn't get noticed.

I'm stressing the fuck out. If I mess this up on game day, my mother will never let me live it down. In fact, I'm pretty sure she'll kick me out of the house and disown me altogether.

"Let's go again! Some of you looked like ten-year-olds at a school dance!" my mother calls, pressing pause on the music and starting it over, waving her manicured finger, lingering on me for a second.

The team feels different without Sophia. She's a natural-born leader, and everyone just seems to fall into place whenever she's around. And now I'm expected to take her place for the night—front and centre—something my mother isn't best pleased with. But that makes two of us.

The beat sinks into my bones as I dance, each step precise and calculated. My muscles relax as I give myself over to the music, forgetting about all the shit going on in my life, just living in the now.

But then someone's body collides with mine, and I land on the ground with a thud. "Shit," I grunt. A sharp pain shoots up my ankle.

For a fleeting moment, the world around me blurs, and dizziness takes over before I shake my head and blink.

"Are you okay?" Poppy holds her hand out, and I inhale deeply, pushing the aching aside, taking her hand and dipping my chin.

"I'm so sorry, Mae. I was out of line," Daisy says, biting her lip as Madison gazes down with worry. "Are you sure you're okay?"

My mom raises her eyebrows to her hairline and glares at me.

I glare right back. "I'm fine. Let's go again."

Putting weight on my ankle during the rest of practice causes me to grind my molars and clench my fists in pain. But I resist throwing in the towel. I summon every last bit of determination I have, forcing a fake smile as we repeat the routine over and over again until my mother finally stops the music and tells us to get going.

Once all the girls have filed their way into the locker rooms—with Poppy giving me a lingering worried glance—she juts her hip out as she stares at me.

I like to play nice with my mother. I honestly think it annoys her more that I don't lash out. She wants me to react, but instead, I give her nothing.

"Want me to make dinner for the both of us tonight?" I offer. I already know the answer, but kill 'em with kindness, am I right?

"I meal prep," she responds, raising her eyebrows questionably.

"Doesn't hurt to offer."

She takes a moment to gather her thoughts. "Mae, this is very important to me." Her voice—she almost sounds defeated.

"I know. I'm trying."

Her eyes analyse me for a good few seconds, softening slightly before they calcify again. "Don't let me down." She flips her hair behind her shoulder and stalks down the tunnel, away from the field.

I make my way over to a bench on the sidelines and plop myself down, holding my head in my hands.

My mother showed a sliver of vulnerability just then, and I haven't seen that since Dad left. It was a rare moment. For a heartbeat, I almost saw the woman who'd raised me, not the one constantly wearing that mask of animosity.

But as quickly as that side of her had appeared, it'd vanished. Her walls are built high, and it's evident my mother is far more comfortable in her fortress of emotional distance she's spent years constructing.

I get why she cares so deeply about the Missarali Storks Cheerleading Squad—it's the only thing she has left.

It doesn't excuse her behaviour, but I *do* pity her.

"Mae?"

The voice gives me goosebumps. I lift my head to see Nathan standing before me. His black T-shirt is tight over his muscular body, and the grey sweatpants he's wearing cause my eyes to dip briefly before I blink and hope he didn't notice.

"Why are you sitting here?" He sounds concerned—with a deep crease formed between his eyebrows, his mouth flipping downwards.

"Just relaxing," I say, jumping up but immediately regretting it. I feel my face falter, and my ankle complains under my weight. I can tell the injury isn't anything serious, but it's in need of rest.

"What was that?"

"Nothing." I smile, moving past him. I can already feel my ankle beginning to swell. However, I attempt to walk as normally as possible, knowing I probably look like a zombie dragging their twisted foot behind them. All I need now is rotting skin and an intense desire to eat brains.

"Why are you limping?"

"I'm not."

Nathan speeds up beside me, cocking his head and dragging his bottom lip into his mouth. "Mae, stop." He holds his hand up to cease my movement, hovering a few centimetres in front of my breasts, and the action causes sweat to form on my upper lip. He looks fed up with my antics. "Don't lie to me. You're hurt. Why are you hurt?"

I guess the jig is up.

My tongue moves to press behind my teeth, but before I can reply, Nathan tells me to sit down. His face tells me there's no room for defiance.

After he gestures to the bench I was previously sat on—tucked away in the corner—I huff and move back over to it. The icy metal bites into my skin, causing my body to shiver, but I'm not entirely sure it's *just* because of the bench.

Nathan grabs a first aid box from a cupboard and taps my knee, signalling that he wants me to lift my leg as he crouches.

I roll my eyes. "Nathan, I—"

"If you walk on it without wrapping it, you'll make it worse. Are you going to let me help or not?"

Why does he have to look at me like that?

I want to say no. To tell him I can do this myself. But his gaze is making my mouth feel numb. Like I can't move it.

"Actually, don't answer that. I don't want to hear whatever snarky remark you have up your sleeve."

My eyes slim. "I want to be a vet. I know how to wrap an injured ankle."

"There it is." He shakes his head and scoffs in humorous disbelief. Looking down at my foot, his fingers curl upwards in unison as he moves them in a *"give it to me"* motion.

I sigh softly, pulling off my tennis shoe and sock, watching as he pulls some wrap from the box and grips my ankle tentatively.

"And I didn't ask you if you knew how to do it, princess. I'm aware you're smart. I asked you if you were going to let me *help* you."

My mouth goes dry.

He examines my foot before beginning to wrap it. I focus on the warmth of his fingers against my skin, which makes my skin twist. I'm fighting to keep my breathing steady, trying to push through the pain while concentrating on the fact that Nathan Slater is tending to my ankle, gazing up at me with a hint of emotion other than annoyance.

"How did you do this?"

"Fell over." He eyes me up with a small chuckle, and I retort back, "We can't all harness the grace of a gazelle, you know?"

"Hmm, I've seen you in practice. I beg to differ."

My heart skips a beat, and Nathan's tongue darts out and wets his bottom lip as he concentrates, manoeuvring my foot carefully so he can wrap the cotton all the way around my ankle.

He finishes and double-checks that it's not too tight. "Keep off it for a few days. You'll need to sit out of cheering for the next game."

"I can't. Sophia's not here, and I'm filling in for her."

"Well, you can't cheer with your ankle like that, princess."

My *down-there* region flutters. It literally *flutters.*

Am I starting to like the nickname?

What the fuck?

"I have to. There isn't another option." I glance down at my foot, slightly self-conscious. Feet are weird. "But thank you. I appreciate it."

Nathan lowers his gaze. He's not used to praise. He's always facing criticism—whether from his father, the media, or even his own fans—and I can tell he feels slightly uncomfortable with the approval.

He doesn't do good things for the applause.

I've seen it first-hand.

When he paid for my wine.

When he babysat Evan's son.

When he butted in to make sure I wasn't falling for Riley's fake charm.

Those are the little things the world doesn't get to see, and I know they wouldn't treat him the way they do if they saw who he really was.

A grumpy, guarded jock, yes. But he's a grumpy, guarded jock with a heart. Even if he doesn't want to admit it.

He's been conditioned to brace himself for the storm, so when someone finally appreciates his efforts, his body wants to reject the commendation.

"No other option?" He crosses his arms over his chest, biceps bulging.

"I'd be fine never cheering again, but my mom wants this." I pause. "She needs this."

Nathan exhales deeply, settling on the bench beside me and resting his elbows on his knees with his fingers laced together. His gaze is fixated on the ground below. "For someone who treats you like crap, you seem to care about her a lot."

I shrug. "I don't want to be the one who takes this away from her. It'll just give her another reason to hate me. And as much as we don't get on, I don't want to see her fail."

My father and I were extremely close, but I have to remind myself that Cam and I aren't the only ones who lost someone. My mother also lost her husband.

She's always been a sharp and rigid person, but ever since he left, her skin has thickened. She's afraid of emotion.

Of letting people in. It's a coping mechanism that I can't entirely blame her for.

Two wrongs don't make a right, though, and watching her world crumble wouldn't make me feel any better about mine.

Nathan shakes his head, chuckling slightly. "I can't relate to that. I wish I could, but you're just a better person than I am."

"They're different situations, Nathan."

His expression shifts as I use his name, but then his gaze glides across my face and down my neck. "Mae, you're pale."

"I think I'm just nervous. I've never performed in front of such a big crowd before, and frankly, I'm fucking scared. I don't want to mess it up. I don't know how you handle all this pressure all the time."

His eyes soften as I catch his gaze briefly glide to the white scar beside my eyebrow before he looks away. It's something I've caught him doing a few times.

"You won't mess it up. I've seen you dance. You don't stand out at all."

I cock my head at him, laughing. "Thanks, I think?"

"I mean, you blend in with the team. You look like you're meant to be there."

His words bring a smile to my face. My mother's never said anything like that to me before.

"Do you ever get anxious about playing?" I'm curious. Nathan always appears so confident. So sure of himself.

I'm unsure if it's all an act or if he is just that lucky to be so self-assured.

"Sometimes. But I don't let it get to me. You can't. Worrying about what could happen won't change the outcome."

Anxiety can twist your imagination, painting futures that haven't even happened yet. Small, insignificant little worries can quickly pile into a mountain of what-ifs, the peak impossible to reach. Yet, it controls so many of us.

"Worrying about tomorrow won't make it any brighter. Coach Darrell likes to use that line," Nathan says, and I blink, suddenly feeling oddly calm about the situation.

"Yeah, I guess you're right."

He turns to me, his eyes intense. It isn't until now that I realise how close we are, our arms brushing as we breathe. His eyes flicker down for a split second, hovering on my lips before he knits his eyebrows together.

My palms begin to sweat as he looks down at my chest. He doesn't shy away. He doesn't pretend not to be looking. He relishes in it for a few greedy seconds before gulping and standing up.

If this is how he looks at me when I'm clothed, how would he look at me if I were naked underneath him? Fingers gripping his forearm. Tits pressed into his chest as I arch my back. Legs spread.

"Bennett needs me to run through some media training with him." Nathan stands, stretching his shoulders, face sullen.

I don't want to get up. I'm afraid I've soaked through my spandex shorts. Why do I feel like some horny teenager around him?

"Thanks for patching me up." I slip my sock and shoe back on, the fabric a little snug due to the slight swelling.

Nathan's lingering and muscular arms hang limply beside him as he grinds his teeth together.

Would it really be so bad if he were to fuck me right here on this bench? Would anyone know? Do they have cameras in here?

"What are you looking for?"

I snap my head back to his, not realising I'd been searching the roof for surveillance without even realising.

"Nothing. I thought I saw a... bird."

A chuckle falls from his lips as he nods slowly. "Right." The word is long and drawn out.

"I'm gonna hang here for a bit. Take a breather, you know?"

He doesn't look convinced, and it appears he's battling with himself on whether to object, but after a few seconds of deliberation, he nods. "Alright, I'll see you tomorrow."

I glance down at my ankle, placidity coursing through my veins.

Why is it that someone so anxiety-inducing can also chase it away with just one conversation?

Because now I'm looking at game day in a whole new light. I'm not scared shitless anymore. In fact, I'm looking forward to it, and the fact that Nathan managed to do that to me in a matter of minutes is redirecting my worry to a whole new place.

How the fuck am I supposed to survive being around him for the rest of the season without fantasising about doing things we can't?

16: Nathan

It's our final day volunteering at the Missarali City Animal Shelter.

I didn't think I'd care about leaving when I first arrived, but after four visits, I'm actually going to miss Mr No Name—or Radish, as Mae's now called him.

The workers loved it, and they even changed his name on file and created a little makeshift sign to tape to his kennel.

"She's impressive," Poppy remarks, nodding towards Mae, who is completing a five-point check-up on one of the dogs. The shelter is supposed to conduct these every few weeks, but they've fallen behind since the vets are busy on some training course.

"What do you mean?" I quietly question as I watch Mae peer into the dog's ear, using the torch on her phone to light the dark abyss.

"With animals."

I dip my chin in a nod.

I understand why Mae has a deep affection for animals. They embody a sense of innocence, untouched by the complexities of the world. They don't judge based on wealth, height, weight or skill—they simply love.

She's going to be a great veterinarian nurse. Any practice will be lucky to have someone with such passion join their team.

My smile drops from my face.

"Are you going to miss your little friend?" Bennett laughs as Radish bounces up to me.

"You know what?" I scratch the top of his head. "I will."

I know Radish will go to a good home, though. He's a loving and energetic dog that will make a great family pet. I'm sure when he gets his chance to shine, he'll flourish.

"I'll miss you, buddy." Mae cups Radish's face for the final time and presses a kiss to his wet nose, a bark escaping his mouth as he watches her grab her coat and bag.

I think I see her eyes coat with tears, but she keeps her head low as we exit the animal shelter for the final time.

It's spitting with rain, and the clouds above are grey and gloomy, the air frigid.

"Looks like a storm is on its way," Bennett groans.

"Scared of a little thunder, Quinn?" my sister teases, and Bennett glares at her.

"Who are you? Lightning McQueen?"

They head to their separate cars, leaving Mae and I alone.

I should say something.

"You okay?"

"Yeah, of course," she responds. "I can't allow myself to get attached to every animal I care for. Otherwise, I'll end up wanting to bring them all home."

I can tell she's playing her feelings for Radish down, but if there's something I've learned about Mae, it's that she doesn't enjoy being vulnerable. It's not the norm for her. Discussing her anxiety about performing yesterday must have been hard, and yet she did. With me.

"Are you having a stroke? What are you looking at?" she volleys at me, her voice is light and airy.

I clear my throat, realising I've been staring. She's wearing those damn jeans she was in when I first saw her in Emmanuel's store, and fuck... it's testing me. "I'll see you tomorrow for the meeting," I say before I embarrass myself.

She drops her brows and turns to her car, and I watch her—because it's an excuse to stare at her ass—before starting my Audi and turning my heated seat on.

As I exit the parking lot, rain cascades heavily, splattering against my windscreen. Given the slick roads, I keep my speed well below the limit.

The wind is fierce, forcing me to grip the wheel tightly, worried I might be blown off the road, but when I glance in the rear-view mirror and see Mae stepping out of the parking lot in the heavy rain, I hit the brakes, almost skidding to a halt.

"What the hell is she doing?" I mutter to myself as I head back toward the shelter. I pull up alongside her and undo my window. She's already drenched, her hair clinging to her forehead like dark ribbons, her knitted sweater hanging heavily with droplets dripping from the hem. Her arms are wrapped around her midsection as she walks, feet gliding through puddles with swift steps.

"Mae! What the fuck are you doing?" I call over the pounding rain, and she cocks her head.

She can barely hear me.

I immediately fling open my passenger door and hike my thumb towards it. "Get in."

"I'll get your seat all wet. It's fine, I can walk," is her response, and I curse under my breath.

If she thinks I'm going to let her walk home in this, then she's dead wrong.

I unbuckle my seatbelt and step out of my car, the icy rain hitting my skin, the sensation feeling like pinpricks. It's a sudden shock compared to the warmth of my car.

"Mae Bexley, get in the fucking car now, or I'll make you get in."

She gives me a look that could freeze the precipitation into ice.

Her ankle is still tender, and walking home will take her forever. I'll drive alongside her the entire way just to make sure she gets home safely if she's that adamant about not getting in the car with me.

I raise my eyebrows, my jaw set, and eventually, Mae releases her stubbornness and mutters, "Okay, fine," before rushing around the front of my vehicle to clamber in.

"Why the hell are you walking in a storm? People can get hit by lightning, you know? It's rare, but it happens," I say as I buckle myself up, eyes trained on her.

Mae looks at me like I'm crazy. "My rental car is like a million years old. It won't start."

The precipitation drums against the car's roof, and it only worsens. I give Mae one last concerned look before I begin to drive.

She's shivering, and I turn on her heated seat.

The car sways with each gust of wind. Thunder rumbles above us as a warning, and after a few seconds, a flash of lightning lights up the darkening sky. My windshield wipers are working on overdrive, and it surprises me they don't snap off.

The road's a blur in front of us and visibility is nearly zero as we creep along it—the street having turned into a treacherous river.

"It's too dangerous with all this rain. I'm going to have to pull over." I turn down a barely-used side road, putting the car into park.

"We'll have to wait for the worst of it to pass." I scrub a hand over my stubble.

This isn't where I should be right now. Sitting just inches away from Coach Renee's daughter, feeling like all I want to do is make her mine for the evening. Nobody would see. Nobody would know.

How is this woman torturing me without even knowing it?

The lightning outside illuminates her face, accentuating her white scar, and I can't help but focus on it for a few seconds too long before I realise what I'm doing and stop.

Mae notices it clearly, swallowing before her finger subconsciously glides over the scar's surface. She appears ready to speak, evident by her softly parted lips and shallow breath.

But she doesn't.

"What's on your mind?" I ask as rain beats down on the hood of my car, creating a rhythm that feels almost like a heartbeat, syncing with the pounding in my chest.

She shifts in her damp seat. "I just need to know... why did you pay for the wine for me that day in the store?"

My teeth snap together. I don't want to explain this to her, mostly because I don't fully understand why I did it myself—other than the fact that seeing her pretty face so troubled when the bottle broke made my insides strain.

I *wanted* to help her. And I don't feel that way often.

Which is what fucking irks me.

"I don't know."

Mae scowls. "That's not an answer, Nathan."

My eyebrows collapse. "Why do you need an answer?"

"Well, because *that* guy didn't know me, and not only did he pay for my mistake, but he falsely admitted to being the one to make it, too." She raises her head high. "When I joined the squad, you could barely even look at me. You were considerably different to that guy. You're only just starting to tolerate me now."

The storm outside mirrors the whirlwind of emotions brewing inside me, and my chest expands as I breathe. "What do you want me to say, Mae?"

She shakes her head. "You put on this big boy act, but that person in the wine store that day—that was the *real* you. Helping someone struggling with no expectation for something in return. Paying and walking out without so much as an explanation because you *wanted* to help. It made you feel good. I saw it. You're not as cold as you try to perceive yourself to be, Nathan."

My eyes are hard as they refuse to break from her determined face.

She's so incredibly bold and outgoing, and, at the same time, compassionate and sensitive. They're the very qualities I admire in a person—traits I was never exposed to while growing up.

I clench my fists by my side as lightning strikes again, a streak of light flashing over her face. She's so fucking beautiful it hurts. Too beautiful for her own good. For *my* own good. Because all I want to do is say *fuck the contract* and kiss her.

She sees me for who I am—or who I want to be—and even when I showed her nothing but disregard, she still gave me the benefit of the doubt.

But my contract with the Storks is all I have. The only thing that gives me purpose.

"Emmanuel, the owner, is a friend of mine," I state.

"That doesn't explain taking the fall. You could have paid and left it at that, but instead, you claimed that *you'd* dropped the wine."

"I invited you into my car to get you out of the rain, not to quiz me on my past decisions, princess." I'm deflecting, but I don't know what to say.

Does she want me to admit that seeing her all flustered and frustrated in Emmanuel's store that day bothered me?

That just her laugh had made me feel things that had been dormant for years?

That I all I want to do is bend her over in this car and fuck the questions right out of her?

"Fine." Mae drags her bottom lip into her mouth, her finger picking at the skin as she remains quiet for a moment too long. "My father did it."

"What?"

"My scar," she says. "You look at it a lot."

My heart skips a beat, heavy like lead in my chest. I'd thought I'd at least been subtle with it. But perhaps I'm not as slick as I think I am. "Your father?"

"He didn't mean to." Her face falters. "I mean, he did, but he also didn't. He was in the military but was discharged after being diagnosed with PTSD. He would have blackouts where he'd freak out, and even though we'd try to calm him down, it never really worked. He threw a vase at my head, and it cut me. I had to get stitches."

I blink a few times. "Where is he now?"

Mae shrugs. "Hurting me was the final straw for him. He left because he thought it wasn't safe for us, but he promised to come back when he was better. Haven't heard from him in years."

Her voice doesn't crack as she talks. It's almost like she's prepared herself for this moment. Prepared herself to be strong and stoic. But her eyes tell me something very different. The sadness in them... it's not just in the past. It's something that's still haunting her, still living inside. My heart hurts for her.

"And you have no idea if he's still in the country?"

"I have no idea if he's even *alive* anymore." Mae rubs at her nose, but she doesn't cry.

Cam had mentioned she'd had a tough childhood, but at the time, I'd assumed it was linked to how her mother treated her. Then, when Poppy asked about her father that day in her apartment, and I saw the way Mae began to spiral mentally, I knew there was more to the story.

Mae's expression suggests she's not used to saying this aloud, so I ask, "Have you talked to your family about it?"

"No, not really. My mom blames him for joining the military in the first place, and Cam and I don't discuss it often. I think he believes he's dead, but I can't give up like that."

"Military men are tough. They don't give up easily, especially when a family is waiting for them. I think it's admirable you aren't assuming the worst."

Evan's father was in the military. He died in action, but he always has incredible stories to tell about his father. There was nothing that he loved more than his family.

"It used to really bother me." Mae points to the scar. "I know it's not overly noticeable now, but I spent so much money on creams and ointments to try and fade it because of how ashamed I was when it first happened. I thought it was ugly."

That's like a slap in the face. "The word ugly and you don't even belong in the same sentence, Mae."

She rolls her eyes.

"No, don't do that *roll-your-eyes-thing* you do whenever someone tries to compliment you," I tell her, waiting until she's looking at me. "I never want to hear you thinking of yourself that way. Because it's not true."

She twists her lip to the side before smiling, hazel eyes glistening as they dart all over my face, ending on my lips. But only for a second.

I clear my throat to cut the silence, breaking eye contact. "I'm sorry you went through all that. It's not fair."

"Life isn't sometimes, but if it was fair all the time, I think it would be pretty damn boring."

She's trying to break the heaviness with humour, and I can't blame her for it.

A small smile graces her lips, and I follow her action. "I appreciate you telling me that."

I long to have the confidence she possesses as my mind flashes with memories from my own childhood.

The sheer amount of empty bottles filling the trash.

The slurred words.

The tape.

The police sirens.

The realisation that my efforts had failed.

I frown while looking through the car's windshield. The rain has eased up slightly, improving visibility, and after starting the car, I manoeuvre back onto the road.

"I don't just tolerate you, by the way."

Mae releases a small laugh, pressing her lips together to stifle her growing smile as she stares out the window.

I'm not just saying it to make her feel better, though.

Because I really am way past tolerating her.

17: Mae

I lean my head on the bus window, tucking my knees into my chest on the seat. We've travelled to Oregon for a game, and Peter's got some charity gigs lined up for us while we're here.

He donated some money to a climate change charity, which is now inviting all players and cheerleaders to meet with them. Again, it means excellent press, and Peter snapped up the opportunity without questions.

My eyes linger on the back of Nathan's head a few seats in front, and my fingers skate over my scar.

Opening up to him wasn't something I'd been expecting to do, but it had felt right in the moment. I wanted to remind him that paying for my wine and falsely admitting to my mistake was a selfless gesture I don't take lightly. It shouldn't be brushed under the carpet because he needs to realise he has so much more to offer than just his football skills.

I was a stranger to him, and he wanted to help me and his friend, Emmanuel, out of the goodness of his heart.

He's not as heartless and insensitive as he tries to portray.

I also hoped it might give him the courage to open up to me at some point, but I get that's wishful thinking.

My father fills my mind. Laughing and yelling reverberate through the empty space he's left behind, happiness and sadness mixed together in an odd combination that simultaneously brings me joy and despair.

Cam always tried to calm him down during his episodes, and he'd order me to take a walk, being the protective brother he was. But the night my father threw the vase at me was the first time I'd refused to leave. He'd been getting progressively worse, and I was worried for the safety of Cam and my mother.

The day he left is still etched into my brain.

The way he looked at me with dead eyes, silently saying *I'll see you again. One day.*

"Hey, Mae," Samuel says from the seat in front of me. "Are you coming tonight?"

"To what?"

"The press conference," Poppy responds, smirking. "They're kind of fun. They mainly consist of the guys getting berated."

"I know. I've been watching them."

After hearing me, Nathan turns around and asks, "I thought you said you didn't like football?" A knowing smile toys his lips.

I pinch my eyebrows together. Truthfully, I haven't *just* been watching the conferences because I want to learn more about the team I'm supposed to support.

It's because I want to embrace my potential inner horny football fiend and drool over Nathan Slater as he sits at the conference table wearing that cap he looks far too good in.

"Research," I snap back, and he hits me with a look that has my toes curling.

It isn't long before we reach the hotel, and I shield my eyes from the flashes of the few paparazzi cameras who wait out front. One particular stocky man stands in my way, refusing to move, and I faintly hear Nathan tell him to "have some respect for women" before he ushers him out of the way.

We're shown to our rooms. I'm sharing with Madison—courtesy of my mother's booking—and although she's a nice girl, I don't know her too well. She's pretty quiet. Constantly practising, spending every minute running through our routines. I think she's secretly terrified of my mom.

I wear jeans and a knitted cardigan for the press conference, finding a seat next to Poppy towards the back of the room. The reporters hum with anticipation as they ready themselves, growing silent when the selected members of the Missarali Storks chosen to represent the team enter the room and take their places on stage behind the long desk.

Nathan scans the room, and it looks like he sighs in relief, causing my eyebrows to furrow.

"He's looking for our Dad," Poppy says, following my gaze. She cranes her neck to look at the wave of people before us. "It looks like he's not here, which is good. Means Nathan can actually relax."

Darrell is in charge of the questions, which surprises me. I expected Peter to at least make an appearance, but it seems he has better things to do than show up for the team he's supposed to manage.

"Evan, do you think—"

"If you ask me anything about my son or who his mother is, I'll get you kicked out of this conference," is his response as he leans into the microphone, his eyes challenging. He's an intimidating guy who I don't think I've ever seen smile. If I were the reporter, I would shut my trap.

He doesn't finish his question.

"Bennett, Riley Donovan has come out with a statement about an argument between the Missarali Storks and the Pittsburgh Pilots. Anything you have to say about it? What happened, and why has Riley turned against a team he, up until now, had a mostly friendly relationship with?"

Bennett gulps, and I can visibly see him choking on his words.

Nathan immediately jumps in. "Riley Donovan has blown a minor disagreement out of proportion. It'll just be in preparation for our next game against one another. To rile the fans up and get people to watch. We're all good."

He's not spilling any secrets. The perfect way to stay out of the media's limelight is to refuse to give them what they want.

"That scumbag," Poppy grumbles as she pulls up a news article on her phone, in which Riley's criticising The Storks for their poor sportsmanship. He's butt-hurt about how Nathan treated him at the bar, and like a child, he's acting out. It's borderline hilarious.

"God, he's such a jerk."

The reporter's shoulders sag with disappointment, but he doesn't release the microphone. "Do you not think this will hinder your team, Nathan? You're the captain, and surely you need to take some kind of responsibility? Do you not even want to defend yourself?"

Nathan narrows his eyes, his jaw ticking. "And why would I benefit from getting involved with Riley Donovan's drama?"

Poppy audibly growls, and a few reports seated in front of us turn to give us concerned looks.

"It seems to me you're not concerned with how your team is perceived," the reporter continues, stepping away from the employee trying to take the microphone away. "What kind of captain does that make you? There's been an allegation against you, and you have nothing to say."

Anger bubbles up inside me. These guys don't deserve this. They play because they love football, and these press conferences do nothing for them. Peter needs a stern talking to.

"I believe I've already responded." Nathan is calm, although I can tell he's becoming agitated as he nods towards another employee to take the microphone away from the reporter. "I have nothing more to say on the matter."

"Well, don't you think—"

"Why are you making such a big deal out of something so insignificant?" I say loudly as I sit with my arms crossed, and Poppy turns to me with wide eyes, her mouth popping open.

She's a bold character, but it seems even she wouldn't dare speak out of turn during a press conference.

"Excuse me?" the reporter bites.

"This is a football conference, correct?" I raise my eyebrows. "Why don't you actually ask him something to do with it instead of focusing on petty drama? If that's what you're looking for, go and find some trashy celebrity to harass."

The corner of Nathan's lips curve upwards under the brim of his cap, and he chuckles to himself. "You heard the lady. Now, hand the microphone back before you *really* embarrass yourself."

Protectiveness swarms me. Nathan doesn't deserve to be subjected to this.

It must be exhausting.

All eyes are on me, and I even see Darrell smirking, shaking his head in disbelief at the prospect that someone would stand up for his boys at a time like this. I stifle a laugh and shuffle further down into my seat, gesturing for the questions to continue.

They do. And they're a whole lot more respectful. Some reporters push the boat out a bit, but the guys refuse to answer anything unrelated to their upcoming game against the Medford Heroes.

Poppy spends the rest of the conference giggling to herself at my brazenness, and once it's over, the reporters file out, leaving just us and the team.

"That reporter looked like he was about to burst at the seams," Bennett bellows as he sends me a wink. "Nice work, Mae."

"Brave of you," Evan adds.

They leave the room with the others, and Poppy follows Bennett, gazing up at him with bold eyes. If I didn't know she was adamant about sticking to the no-fraternisation rule, I'd think she had the hots for him.

I turn to leave, but Nathan calls my name. He's hopping off stage, his triceps flexing, and his large hands are splayed out on the set.

"You didn't have to do that. That could have majorly backfired if that guy had a temper."

I shrug. I'm not afraid of a sleazy, grease-covered asshole. "Someone had to stand up to them. And I also learned judo in high school, so I would have been able to beat his ass if he came anywhere near me."

"Judo?"

I bow my head. "Granted, it was only for one week, but I can land a mean punch."

"I'm pretty sure punching isn't allowed in Judo."

I make a quiet *pfft* noise. "Like *you* did Judo."

"I didn't, but maybe you could teach me? With your one week's worth of experience." A mischievous smile tugs his lips upwards.

I fold my arms over my chest, shooting him a stern look. "You may be able to tackle six-foot-five ogre-like men to the ground, Nathan Slater, but I'll have you know, I'm tougher than I look."

"Say my full name again."

"What?" I blink.

"You heard me." He raises his eyebrows, still smiling.

I pause for a second before saying a firm, "No." My eyes narrow before I head for the door.

"That's fine," Nathan calls after me. "You'll be saying it sooner or later, princess."

I stick my middle finger up at him as I leave.

I thought I didn't like cocky men, but Nathan Slater has just proved me fucking very wrong.

I lie underneath the crisp sheets in the hotel room, staring up at the ceiling, and I can hear Madison's laboured breaths as she sleeps. The cold air wraps around me like a shroud, making it hard to find comfort. I can feel the weight of the upcoming performance pressing down on me.

I'm not nearly as nervous as I was, thanks to Nathan's reassurance, but my ankle is still a little sore, and I'm panicking that it's going to give out mid-jump and I'll land on my ass in front of millions of people.

Although it would make for a great viral video.

I toss and turn, finally pulling the sheets off as my mouth feels parched. I need water, but the irritating sign in the bathroom warns that the faucet water isn't safe to drink.

Slipping out of the room in my pale blue pyjama shorts and tank top, I pad down the steps to the hotel reception. I purchase a bottle of cold water from the vending machine and climb the stairs back up to the floor where my room is as I sip at it.

But my face drops when I realise I've forgotten my key card, and the time is currently one in the morning. Nobody was manning the desk, and I curse under my breath as I gently rattle against the door, trying not to wake anybody nearby.

But Madison doesn't hear me, and I don't have my phone.

"Give me a break," I complain.

Sliding down the wall and resting my head against it, I thump to the floor. It's freezing out here, and goosebumps cover my skin.

I'm hoping Madison will miraculously wake up after hearing me telepathically begging. There's nothing I can do besides pounding on the door and pissing everyone else around me off, and I don't want to do that. The boys have a game, and I don't want to disturb their sleep and be the reason they lose concentration tomorrow because of lethargy.

My fingers pick at my lip as I sit on the floor, contemplating what to do.

"You're doing this to me," I grunt as I point to the sky.

But, just as I thought the situation couldn't get any worse, a door a few rooms down from me opens, and a shirtless Nathan stalks out. He's dressed in only tartan pyjama pants, hanging low on his waist and showing off his impressive V-line.

"What are you doing on the floor?"

I'm about to faint. His muscles ripple under his skin, each one defined, like he's been sculpted from marble. The way his shoulders taper down into his chest—a chest that I want to be pressed up against—has me infatuated. By looking at him, you'd think Nathan spends every spare second he has in the gym, but I know he rarely goes. His striking physique is from years of hard work on the football field.

"You need glasses?" I almost splutter the words.

They're not the round Harry Potter type. No, the glasses he has on are sharp and sleek. The frames are thin, and the angular shape somehow makes his face look even more defined.

Who would have thought that Nathan having bad eyesight would be a turn-on?

"No, I'm just wearing them for fun," Nathan says sarcastically, shaking his head.

I stand. "Did I wake you up?"

"No. Why are you out here?"

"I forgot my key card."

"So you're locked out?"

I nod.

"Have you tried knocking?"

I can't help but glare. "You know that? That didn't cross my mind. Thanks for the advice."

He chuckles, swallowing. And then, on a sigh, he says, "Alright, come on." His head beckons me.

"What?"

"You're not sleeping out here."

I watch with my mouth agape as he waltzes into his room. My feet feel frozen to the ground, as if someone spread super-glue on the carpet while I wasn't looking.

I hear Nathan loudly shuffling around in his room, and worried it's going to wake other people up with his door open, I follow him in.

A quiet whistle of appreciation leaves my lips. "I see someone's receiving star treatment," I say, nodding down to his king-sized bed, the room significantly bigger than mine and Madison's.

"Your mom booked me one of the best rooms. What can I say? I think she secretly loves me."

"Yeah, I dare you to say that to her face."

I stand awkwardly at the foot of the bed, my fingers finding my lip as they pick at it.

"You always do that when you're nervous."

"I'm not nervous."

"Mmm-hmm, sure." He shoots me a dazzling smile. "Worried to share a bed with me, princess? Concerned you won't be able to keep your hands off me?"

I cross my arms over my chest. "More like concerned for your career if anyone finds out I'm in here. Trust me, I'm perfectly capable of keeping my hands to myself."

Nathan takes a small step closer before removing his glasses and setting them aside. "Good to know." He pauses, eyes skating down my bare legs before he clears his throat. "I'll take the armchair."

I pinch my brows together, and he whips a blanket off the end of the bed and settles down on the armchair—that's far too small for him—in the corner of the room.

"Are you kidding?" I snatch the blanket from his body. "Nathan, you have a game tomorrow. You're not sleeping on the chair. Move."

I attempt to shove him aside by pushing his shoulder, but his gaze remains fixed on my hand, gripping his muscle. A jolt of electricity surges through my arm, and the tingling sensation quickly becomes addictive.

We're silent for a few seconds.

He then gestures back to the bed as I release him. "Mae, seriously, take the bed."

"I know you're trying to be a gentleman right now, but it's not the time. If you lose your game tomorrow because you wake up with a crick in your neck, I'll be the one to blame, so get your ass over there and get into bed."

"Someone's bossy in the bedroom."

His innuendo makes me freeze, and I narrow my eyes. "Not the time. I'm sleeping on the chair, so get off."

He stands up, and just as I'm about to take his place, he snatches the bottle of water from my hand and pours the contents onto the fabric armchair, leaving a huge wet patch. "Now no one's sleeping on it."

"What the hell are you doing?"

"Get in the bed, Mae."

I wait as I watch him slip into bed, raising his eyebrows at me as he waits.

"Nathan, this is—"

"I have a game tomorrow, and you have a performance. Neither of us will benefit from sleeping in that chair, and since you won't let me and I won't let you, I guess the bed is our only option." He cocks his head. "Now, will you get in, or will I have to pound Madison's door down so she lets you into your room?"

My eyes round, and I shake my head as I slip into the bed beside him. It's big enough that we don't have to touch, but I can feel the heat radiating off him, breaking my body out in a light sweat.

It really isn't helping that he's fucking shirtless.

"Do you need any more of the comforter?" he asks me after he sees me shivering, and as he grips the top of it and shifts it over to my side, I rest myself back on one of my elbows to take it from him.

But in doing so, his hand grazes my hard nipple, and an involuntary hushed moan escapes my mouth.

Nathan's jaw clenches. He's already snapped his hand away, but I swear I see his eyes shift from an olive-green colour to a dark emerald as he looks down at my breasts, accentuated by my position.

My stomach is twisting from the contact, and it's longing for it again.

My lashes flutter, lips parting slightly as I take in one short breath. I don't know what kind of look I'm giving Nathan right now, but I'm pretty sure the desire is written all over my face.

Swallowing, his Adam's apple shifting up and down in the sexiest way, Nathan slowly moves his hand over to me again, the back of it skating over my nipple again. His tongue darts across his bottom lip before he asks, "Is this okay?"

"Yes," I immediately say, and I arch my back so my tits are higher.

His hand moves again, the sensation causing my entire body to flame. I'm soaking through my shorts, and I attempt to keep my breathing steady as I re-focus my eyes to see Nathan staring at me with furrowed brows.

"Fuck, Mae," he says huskily. "What are you doing to me?"

I release a whimper in response, eyes turning half-lidded. He curses, and when I drop my eyes, I can see the outline of his hard dick against his pyjama pants. His very *big*, hard dick.

We should stop. I know we should. But I have tunnel vision right now. All I see is Nathan. And all I want is his hands on my body. Everywhere.

Nothing has ever felt this good, and all he's doing is teasing my tits.

I tip my head back, my tongue feeling heavy inside my mouth.

All that can be heard in the room is my short breaths, and after a couple more strokes, Nathan pulls away. "I'm not taking this any further with you in a hotel room like you're some fling. I respect you more than that, Mae."

I gulp but eventually nod in understanding, taking a deep breath before I pull the comforter up over my flaming body as I compose myself. However, a small giggle slips from my lips. "Now who can't keep their hands to themselves?"

18: Nathan

My helmet feels too tight on my head, squeezing my skull and compressing my thoughts. All I see is the ball—honing in on its position and where it's heading. The Medford Heroes are losing by eight points, which relieves me, but I know how quickly things can change. We need to stay focused.

Except I can't.

Because my head continues to snap to last night when Mae was in my bed, whimpering for me. She'd begged me to touch her with her eyes, and I knew that if we were to go any further, we wouldn't be able to stop.

I'd still been so hard this morning thinking about it that when she left, I had to jerk off in the shower with her name lingering on my lips.

She'd managed to slip out of my room and back into hers, and when Madison opened the door for her, Mae lied about *when* exactly she'd gone down to reception and realised she'd forgotten her key. As far as Madison knew, she'd only been gone a few minutes.

Adrenaline soars through me as I watch one of the opposition's quarterbacks fling the ball, sending it spiralling perfectly into his teammate's grasp. Their players move like a well-oiled machine, but Evan is fast, and he tackles the guy to the ground.

We've been playing well lately, but as the games go on, our opponents keep getting better. It's making me nervous.

The referee's whistle sounds, indicating the second fifteen-minute quarter has ended. There's a twelve-minute halftime break, and our cheerleaders are due to perform. Most of the team heads down the tunnel towards the locker rooms, but Bennett and I stick around.

I want to watch Mae's performance. I know she's nervous.

I want her back in my bed. It's going to feel lonely tonight without her. The soft rise and fall of her chest when asleep was both comforting and torturous. Every instinct in me begged to reach out and touch her again. I couldn't stop staring at her. Her tits in that slinky tank top. Her midriff slightly on show, tanned and toned. The curve of her ass underneath her frilly shorts.

But the weight of reality is burdensome.

This girl has the ability to fucking ruin me.

And my life.

I had wanted to savour the moment. I haven't had a woman in my bed for a long time—not that I'd missed it—but having Mae so close to me was different. It felt *right*. And yet, our contracts tell us it's wrong.

She'd opened up to me about her father, and I know how hard that was for her. She showed me the reason behind that fake confidence. The jutted-out chin and puffed chest. The sassy comments. The narrowed eyes.

It wasn't just because of Renee.

It makes sense now, and I realise that Mae Bexley is nothing like her mother. She's not the princess I initially believed her to be—although the nickname has stuck.

She's not condescending or insulting. Instead, she's a woman who's endured a shit ton of stuff she doesn't deserve but who still plasters on a smile to make everyone around her happy.

I dislike people judging me. I don't like when they make assumptions, yet I'd done the exact same thing with Mae. And boy, had I been wrong about her.

The stories of my own childhood are on the tip of my tongue around her, but I reel them back every time. The thought of being vulnerable sends a shiver down my spine.

I don't want to feel as helpless as I did as a child. I know things are different now. Circumstances have changed. But reliving the life I once had takes me away from who I now am. A confident man. An unbothered man. I don't want to take backwards steps.

The crowd roars as the cheerleaders step out, holding their red and white pom-poms to their hips. There isn't a person out of place as they skip across the grass, all smiles and flowy hair.

"Wow, they look great," Bennett mutters, and I clip him over the back of the head.

"That's my sister you're talking about."

"You know I didn't mean it like that." My best friend snickers.

I watch Mae. She takes a deep breath, and her eyes meet mine, rounding in the realisation that I'm here.

The girls move in perfect unison as the music starts, their bright uniforms shimmering under the shining stadium lights. The blend of athleticism and artistry is impressive. I've never paid much attention to their cheerleading routines, but wherever Mae goes, it seems to spark my interest.

She could sit and watch paint dry, and I'd find the action fascinating.

Renee stands on the sidelines. She's scrutinising the girls, her eyes narrowed into slits as she stands with her hands on her hips. She isn't clapping along like everyone else.

Then, her eyes catch mine, and she cocks her head, eyes bouncing between Bennett and me. It appears she wants to ask what we're still doing out here, but she wouldn't waste her breath on us.

I laugh inside. If only she knew I was rock fucking hard for her daughter last night.

The music fades out as the girls finish their routine, and I cheer with the rest of the stadium, a small smile gracing my lips as Mae's head twizzles to take one last dazzling look at me before she follows the rest of the girls back down the tunnel.

Pride swarms me. I know it shouldn't. I shouldn't care. But I do.

Mae doesn't want to be here. She doesn't want to be a cheerleader, but I admire her for putting her desires aside just to make someone else happy.

Not many people would do that, and it just emphasises how much of an honourable person she is.

I fiddle with the neckline of my navy shirt outside the fancy restaurant. It's too tight, and I'm not used to wearing them. I practically live in jerseys.

The team, including the cheerleaders, are here for a meal with the founders of the charity ClimateAid—organised by Renee at Peter's request. Not that she's coming, though. She doesn't want to spend more time with us than necessary.

I feel guilty being here, though.

Peter was behind the donation, which the team and I didn't even know about until last week.

And now we have to sit with the founders and pretend their charity is something we're passionate about when, in reality, we don't know much about it.

I'd tried to brush up on some facts last night, but then I'd heard someone's footsteps outside my room and the soft cursing of a particular honey-haired, hazel-eyed beauty, and my mind decided it was going to morph itself into a dry sponge—unable to soak up a thing.

Poppy's waiting beside me, her lip pulled into her mouth. Everyone else is inside at the bar, mingling with the founders. But Mae's not here yet, and it's starting to worry me.

"Why aren't you inside?"

She shoots me a knowing smile. "Same reason you're not. I'm waiting for Mae."

"Who says I'm waiting for Mae?"

A laugh escapes her. "Then tell me who you *are* waiting for, brother."

I pause. "I want to make sure everyone's here. It'll reflect badly on the team if people are late." I'm lying through my teeth, and all it takes is one look to know my sister isn't buying it.

"Riiiight." She pats my back. "She's interesting, isn't she? Did you know she has a tortoise? I went round the other day and met him. He's actually really cute."

I roll my eyes. "Yes, I did know that."

"Oh, so she's sharing personal things with you?"

"Why are you saying it like that? We're partners and have to spend a lot of time together, so naturally, I'm going to notice things."

She smiles and nods toward Mae, who is rushing toward the restaurant entrance wearing a baby pink sundress that bounces as she strides over to us. I can tell by the sheen on her legs that she's got natural-looking tights underneath. "That's not what you said when you were first paired with her," Poppy mutters quietly before widening her arms. "Hey, Mae!"

"Sorry I'm late." She's clearly flustered. "I was being held captive in my mother's hotel room."

"What?" Protectiveness swarms me as I take her words literally, causing Mae to shake her head and chuckle.

"No, like, she wouldn't stop talking about our next performance."

"Ugh! Enough about working!" Poppy says loudly, slinging her arm over Mae's shoulder. "Even if you were incredible." She shoots her a wink. "I, for one, can't wait to eat. Scallops. Truffle calamari. Lobster stuffed potato skins. The menu for tonight looks unbelievable!"

I pull the gleaming glass door of the restaurant open, but my feet freeze when Mae says, "I can't actually have anything. I called them as soon as I knew about the dinner, and apparently, because I notified them too late, they can't accommodate a nut allergy."

"You *are* kidding?" I grunt, heels digging into the ground. I understand the meal was planned last minute, but restaurants need to be prepared for this kind of thing. Allergies are common. "Did you at least eat beforehand?"

She shakes her head. "I was going to order something at the hotel, but my conversation with my mom went on longer than expected, so I didn't have time. I'll just have something later. It's fine."

I can practically hear her stomach growling, and I swear she looks paler than usual.

"So they expect you to sit at the table with nothing?" I gesture to the silver italic writing that reads *Velvet Fine Dining*.

It's an upscale chain with only a handful of locations in the country, where the price of one single dish could cover an entire family's weekly grocery bill. It's not my scene—packed with pretentious snobs who convince themselves they're content with the tiny portions just to look wealthy.

"Poppy, tell the founders I apologise, but I wasn't feeling well and had to head home." I hike my thumb over my shoulder towards the rental car I got for the few days I'm here. My eyes find Mae. "Let's get you something to eat."

Her lips part. "Nathan, it's fine. What about the dinner?"

I shrug. "Evan can speak for me. He's prepared. You can't wait until later to eat."

"I'll tell them," Poppy says, placing her arm on her friend's. "And they won't even know you're missing. In all honesty, they care about the guys more than the cheerleaders. Daisy and Madison aren't coming, either, so I'll tell the others you caught the same stomach flu as them."

My sister waves us away quickly, trying to contain her grin, and I lead Mae to my car.

"Why are you wearing that?" I ask, sighing. She looks fucking incredible, but it's not the weather for a sundress. She's only got a thin cardigan layered with it, and I can tell by the goosebumps across her skin that she's cold.

Mae's face drops as she looks down at herself inside the vehicle. "What? I thought it was—"

My eyes round. "No, no. It's beautiful, princess. You look beautiful." The words fall from my lips a little too naturally. "I'm just worried about you freezing to death. It's cold today."

Relief seems to spread across her face. "Well, it's the only thing I had that was semi-nice."

Oh, that will have to change.

"Okay, wear this," I instruct her as I reach behind my seat to grab a spare jacket. She takes it and slips it on without hesitation. "What do you want to eat?"

She hums. "I know we were just about to enter a snooty booty restaurant, but because they were so rude to me over the phone, is it bad if I want to go and eat at some gross burger joint just to say a massive *fuck you* to them?"

I laugh, winding down the road to the grossest fast-food place I know. "Say no more."

The burger joint ticks all the boxes. It smells of overused grease, sweat and stale buns. The biggest smile stretches Mae's glossy lips, and I have a sudden urge to kiss them.

Her perfume is sweet and fruity, and I breathe it in greedily as I admire her in my jacket. She looks good in my clothes. We order our food, and I pull the brim of my cap down—I always have one with me on hand—to hide my face so no one recognises me.

I wasn't looking forward to eating the *snooty booty* food anyway.

Mae dips her fries into her pot of honey mustard, a sigh of contentment slipping past her lips. "This really hits the spot. How do places like this get their fries to taste so good?"

"Maybe they wipe their armpits with them."

A laugh bubbles up her throat. "What's with you and armpits? You got a fetish or something?"

I chuckle, shaking my head before taking a bite of my burger. "I can't believe your mom, of all people, didn't tell the restaurant you had an allergy when booking."

"My mom? She told me Peter booked it."

I cock my head. "Peter told us he left it up to Renee since she's into fine dining."

Betrayal flashes across Mae's face, but it doesn't last long. "Why am I not surprised? It's just another way to spite me."

"Even after your performance last night?" Dislike blooms in my chest. "She doesn't appreciate you. It's fucking wrong."

Mae lifts her shoulders in a shrug. "It's just her. There's no changing it." She looks at me. "Sorry you had to eat this instead of—"

"Mae, I don't care. The food portions in that place wouldn't feed a mouse. I would have ended up getting a burger afterwards, anyway."

"Okay, good." Her response is breathy, and it takes me right back to last night. We haven't spoken about it, and I don't know if we're going to. But all I know is that I want to do it again.

I crave her underneath me. Desperate for me. Pussy throbbing as I swipe my finger over her clit. Her lips parting so I can slip my cock—

"Those women are checking you out." Mae nods to the group of women a few booths away from us. They're whispering to one another, giggling as they pretend to focus on their food. I doubt they've recognised me when they can only see a sliver of my face, but it's apparent that they've had a bit to drink, eyes hazy and movements sloppy.

I turn my head away from them. "I don't care."

"One of them could be your future lover. You could miss your opportunity." Mae's teasing, but there's a glint in her eyes that gets me—like she's jealous. Envious. I love it.

"I haven't had a girlfriend for seven years. I think I'll survive."

Her eyebrows fly up. "Seven years?"

I snatch up one of her fries, finished with mine. "Is that a surprise?"

"I mean... yeah. That's a long time without a woman. Unusual for someone who has the good looks and career."

"So you think I'm good-looking?" I smirk, but she just rolls her eyes at me. "And I didn't say it's been seven years since I've been with a woman," I clarify. "Just since I've had a girlfriend."

If you could call her a girlfriend. It fizzled out pretty quickly. Partly because my father got in the way but mainly because she wasn't fun. Snarky. Vivacious. Not like the woman sitting in front of me.

"Right." Mae drops her gaze, and I realise how poorly my comment came across.

If I don't want her thinking I'm some kind of manslut who used her last night, I need to be honest.

"It's been three years."

She peeks between long lashes.

"Three years since I've slept with anyone. Seven years since I've been in a relationship. Or something you could maybe call a relationship." I'm not embarrassed about not having slept with anyone for so long. No shame comes with the admittance. It's not like I haven't had the chance. Meaningless sex just doesn't do anything for me anymore.

But the thought of doing it with Mae doesn't seem so meaningless.

I grind my teeth together, attempting to pull my mind out of the gutter.

"That's... I wasn't expecting that."

I send her a wink. "Like I told you in the beginning, princess, I don't mess around with women."

"Unless it's me," she laughs, but my face is set.

"You're not *just* a woman."

Mae releases an exhale, eyebrows flicking up at my comment. "Most men I meet are pigs. They can't commit, and the ones that can have no ambition. No drive. There's nothing more attractive to me than a hard worker."

I like to think I'm one of the hardest workers in the NFL. I'm known as the guy who lives and breathes football, and even though it doesn't always work out for my team, I never give up. Never throw in the towel.

Hearing that Mae likes hard workers makes my stomach flip.

I want to be something she wants, even though we can't have each other.

"You've got a little—" I say as I reach forward and wipe the smear of mustard from the corner of her mouth.

The action comes naturally, and I don't realise I've done it until my thumb is pressing against the soft skin of her pouty bottom lip.

She tenses but then immediately relaxes at my touch, smiling at me, her teeth slowly scraping across her bottom lip.

I pull away.

And then something occurs to me that I never thought would.

I'm really fucking jealous of a set of teeth.

19: Mae

"Here's your Moscow Mule," I say from behind the bar of the Salty Dog—we're back in Missarali—as I place the fruity drink before the customer, who I'm pretty sure is just scraping twenty-one. Amber checked her ID, though, since I'm not trusted to sniff out a fake one yet.

I got a part-time job to save up before I—hopefully—secure a position at a veterinary practice. I've already applied to a few across the country. Sure, I'm getting paid to cheer, but having something to occupy my free time is healthy.

I liked how quaint the little bar was, and when I came in with my resume, expecting them to tell me that the *Help Wanted* sign taped to the window was old and they'd forgotten to take it down years ago, Amber hired me on the spot.

It's busy tonight since it's Saturday, and Poppy came to support me.

"You're sweating," she says as she sips her diet soda, stifling a snigger.

"It's called *working*, Poppy," I tell her as I pile as many used glasses as possible into the tiny dishwasher. "You could help if you want."

"Sorry, I'm too busy not listening." She peeks back at her laptop. I appreciate her coming, especially because she has some assignments due, so she's double-tasking, supporting me, and working on her essay simultaneously.

"Hey, Maya!" calls Jack from his stool, waving his empty beer glass. "Can I get a refill?"

I groan, taking the glass from him. "It's Mae, Jack, and don't you think you've had enough?"

Jack's a regular. He's here every time I work and spends hours drinking himself silly, but I've never seen him as drunk as he is now.

His eyes are glazed and unfocused, demonstrating the effect of countless hours spent nursing drinks in a stuffy bar. A scruffy beard frames his jaw, and his under eyes are deep and dark.

"Enough? It's barely eight o'clock! Come on, I'd really appreciate another."

I glance over at Amber, but she's too busy handling the small crowd waiting to be served, looking frustrated as she tries her best to get through everyone in record time.

I study Jack, who's swaying on his barstool, and his state is enough to make me shake my head. "Sorry, Jack, but you've had enough for tonight. Feel free to stay and have some water or coffee."

Turning my back on him, I take the next person's order, only to spot two large forms entering the rustic bar, looking very out of place in a venue with such low ceilings.

Poppy waves Nathan and Evan over.

My stomach tenses, and I quickly dab my forehead with a napkin, worried about Poppy's earlier sweating comment. This is the last environment I want Nathan to see me in. I'm flustered. Stressed. And fed up. At this point, it's making me question whether this job is worth the money.

"Poppy, did you invite them?" I ask in a whisper as the guys move through the crowd towards us.

She dips her chin in a nod. "Evan's trying out a new nanny for a few hours, so Nathan wanted to get him out of the house."

Judging by Evan's face, he wants to throw hands, appearing to be the last place he wants to be. I don't blame him, though.

"You said it wasn't going to be busy, Poppy," Nathan complains, but his eyes land on me, eyebrows hiking up in surprise. "Mae?"

I flatten down my apron. "What can I get you?"

"Why are you working here?"

I notice Amber's lingering glance. She's a nice girl—pretty quiet. But she takes her job seriously, and I know she's seconds away from asking me why I'm talking instead of working when the bar is so rammed.

"I need the money," I say matter-of-factly, ignoring Nathan's concern. I know bar work is stressful, but during the week, it's pretty much dead—it's only because there was a hockey game down the road that it's now packed.

Nathan presses his lips together in what seems to be worry, but he keeps quiet for the most part, his eyes travelling down my entire length before he snaps them back up.

"Hi, Evan," I say in an attempt to distract myself.

He nods, his jaw stiff. "Can I get a coffee, please, Mae?"

"Of course."

There are so many people here that nobody notices Nathan and Evan, especially since their caps shield their faces.

Had I known that caps could act as masks that prevent people from noticing you, I would have bought one and begun wearing it around my mother long ago.

As I serve people, I can feel Nathan's eyes on me. He's watching my every move, studying anyone that talks to me. Looks at me. Breathes near me.

He doesn't touch the water Amber's placed in front of him, and by the time Jack snaps his fingers at me and says, "Can I get another drink over here?" the bar has quieted down.

Nathan raises his eyebrows and takes a look at Jack. He opens his mouth to speak, but Evan taps at his bicep, stopping him. I imagine he doesn't want a scene.

"Jack," I sigh, "I've already told you you've had enough for tonight. You won't be getting any more drinks."

He doesn't like my reply, and he stares angrily at me, his fingers wrapped around his coffee mug—I gave him one about forty minutes ago to shut him up—so tightly it looks like he's trying to strangle it. But with his strength, Jack couldn't strangle a marshmallow. "I'm at this bar every damn day, and you think you can just show up out of the blue and cut me off? I'm the reason this bar is even staying in business, you little bitch!"

"Woah," Evan calls, scowling.

Nathan immediately stands, the sound of his barstool scraping back rumbling over the soft country music playing from the speakers. He towers above Jack, head tilted and his eyes daring. "What the fuck did you just say?"

Jack's face flickers with concern, but he doesn't let up. "You heard me. I'm a paying customer, and it's within my right to be served a beer when I ask for it. Since when did a woman belong in a bar anyway?" His words slur.

A chuckle slips past Nathan's lips, but it's not out of amusement at Jack. The laugh carries an intimidating tone. He places a firm hand on Jack's shoulder, jostling it slightly. "Alright, here's what you're not gonna do, buddy." His eyes are piercing. "You're not gonna sit here like some entitled dick, demanding alcohol you clearly don't need. You're not gonna make sexist comments about the women who work here, and you're most definitely not gonna call her a bitch in front of me again."

Jack's tongue darts out to wet his dry bottom lip, eyes shifting to Nathan's large hand that's still gripping his skinny body.

"Nathan, it's fine," I say, placing my hand on his that's splayed out on top of the sticky bar counter, but as soon as I do, I snap it away, realising we're surrounded by people who would view the action as unprofessional.

Luckily, it doesn't look like anybody noticed.

I turn to Jack. "I'm not putting up with this crap today, Jack. I may be new to this bar, but I'm not a pushover, and after speaking to me like that, you need to get the hell out."

He seems shocked at my remark, but after a few seconds and another glare from Nathan, he stumbles towards the door, grumbling under his breath.

"Come back and apologise when you're ready," I tell him before he leaves, my eyes narrowed into slits.

"Wow," Amber snickers, applauding me as the door slams shut. "I loved that."

"I'm not putting up with being called a bitch, especially not by a drunk old man who thinks I work to serve him beer all day," I huff, wiping my clammy hands on my apron. I'm riled up, and Nathan can clearly tell.

Are you okay? he mouths at me, and I roll my eyes and bob my head up and down.

The way he'd stood up for me—he'd seen red, and watching him that protective of me did weird things to my stomach. The warmth in my cheeks is betraying me.

He still looks incredibly ticked off, his jaw popping as he intertwines his fingers. Leaning his elbows against the bar counter, he takes a deep breath, and though Evan and Poppy act oblivious to his reaction, I know they can see how the altercation has affected him.

"Mae, do you mind changing the Sprite keg in the basement? The syrup's run out," Amber asks me. "Be careful. It's heavy."

"Sure. I got it." I need the escape, and I take a breather once down in the dimly lit basement, the cold air making my nipples harden against the cropped dark green T-shirt I'm wearing. My upper lip is no longer sweating, and I lean against the frosty wall. "Fuck my life."

"You sure do have a potty mouth for someone who looks so sweet on the outside." The voice makes me turn, and a small gasp escapes when I see Nathan standing at the entrance to the basement. He turns his cap backwards so I can see his face. "Only me, princess. No need to scream." The corner of his lip quirks up. "Unless you want to."

I scowl at him. He's getting braver. "What are you doing down here?"

"I wanted to make sure you were okay. And Amber said you might need help changing the keg."

I've been shown how to do it once before, but I can't lie and say I remember how to do it step by step.

"Yeah, I'm fine. Thanks for sticking up for me. You didn't have to."

He's wearing a hoodie today, almost as green as his eyes. I like it, and I have a sudden urge to steal it. As women, I'm pretty sure stealing men's hoodies and claiming they're ours has become instinct at this point.

Nathan cocks his head. "You handled Jack well."

"I know how to stick up for myself. I'm an independent woman." I wince. I know it doesn't look like it when it comes to my mother, but she's the only person I let get away with treating me like crap. I'd love to call her out on her shitty treatment, but we need something from each other right now, and I refuse to stoop down to her level and join in with the toxicity she brings to the table.

I move over to the stack of kegs, grab the Sprite from its pile, and roll it towards the pipe the old keg is hooked up to. My biceps complain, and my eyebrows scrunch up.

Nathan's eyes twinkle as he chuckles. "I can see that."

"Did you come down here just to laugh at me?" My tone is semi-playful, but I side-eye him.

"No," is his response as he lifts the keg off the ground and carries it over to its tap, dropping it down as if it weighs nothing. His arms ripple, and I give my eyes permission to check him out.

I find lengths of muscle. There's such raw power in his frame. That night in his bed...fuck. It's all I've been thinking about. *He's* all I've been thinking about. I so wish I'd had the confidence at the time to reach for him. Touch him. Pleasure him.

"Thank you," I say, gesturing to the keg.

There's a brief pause, but then Nathan steps around the keg, boots thundering against the concrete. His forehead creases as he looks at me, eyes so scorching I feel like I'm burning alive. "Do you know how easy it would be for me to kiss you right now?"

My heart stops, shock coursing through me like an electrical current. The comment ignites a hurricane of emotions inside me, and I attempt to swallow the lump in my throat but fail miserably.

"Nobody would know. Nobody would see," he continues, his finger finding my chin.

My entire body is tingling. My skin is on fire, and Nathan is the only element that can put it out. I need his lips on mine. His hands on me. I'm just as bad as the horny football fans that want him. But I want the *real* him. The *real* Nathan Slater. Not the cocky heartthrob they see on TV.

I force my face to deadpan him, though. "Who says I want that?"

"Don't pretend you look at everyone the same way you look at me, princess." The corner of Nathan's lips curl.

"Look at you, how?"

"Like you want me to fuck you."

Oh shit. My body is working on autopilot.

My breath hitches, and as I take a challenging step towards Nathan, our chests almost touch. Warmth emanates from him.

My heart is rattling against my ribs. I feel like they're about to break, but the pulse is addictive.

The air between us crackles with an unspoken challenge, Nathan's eyes flickering with desire. As the seconds stretch out, every one of them feels like an eternity, the both of us daring each other to bridge that gap. To make the move. To cross that boundary.

"Fuck it."

Arms snake around my waist, pulling me to a hard chest. I immediately respond as Nathan's lips find my own.

God, am I going delirious? This doesn't feel fucking real.

Our bodies fit so perfectly together. All I can do is moan into his mouth as he swipes his tongue across my bottom lip, demanding entrance.

I'm self-conscious that I smell like old wood and sweat, but it doesn't seem to bother Nathan if I do.

Electricity rockets through my body. My fingertips. My Legs. Right up my spine. It's making it almost impossible to feel okay with telling myself that in a few months, I won't have this anymore. Mine and Nathan's ships will sail away from each other.

Because we're very much on different paths.

My breath is hard to catch, and the more I chase it, the more desperate I feel for this not to be the one and only time I'll kiss Nathan Slater.

His large hands cup the back of my neck as our lips explore one another's, fingers tugging at my hair, forcing a subconscious moan from me. The kiss is full of desperation, my hands clawing up his chest and gripping his hoodie between white fingers.

I can feel his boner against my stomach—hard and thick—making my head spin. I know I'm soaking through my underwear and jeans, and I want nothing more than for him to unbutton them and feel it for himself so that he knows what he does to me.

Nathan pulls back and looks at me like I've hung the moon. "Do you have any idea how long I've waited to do that?"

"I thought you hated me."

"I hated the way you made me want you, princess. But I never hated *you*."

I scrunch my nose up. "Well, that's a shame, Nate. Because I hated you." I attempt to suppress my brewing giggle.

"You're going to regret saying that one day," he tells me, lips melting against mine again before Amber's voice yelling for us above the basement causes us to pull away.

Then, I spend the next two hours of my shift having to pretend that Nathan Slater—the man sitting and waiting for me to finish my shift with his sister, pretending to be interested in her assignment just so he can stay at the bar—isn't altering my brain chemistry beyond recognition.

20: Nathan

"How was she?" I ask Evan hopefully, and he deadpans me.

"She gave him a chocolate chip cookie ten minutes before bed and didn't even make him brush his teeth," he responds, nodding down to Leo, who's fiddling with his building blocks on the floor of Evan's kitchen. "That's not the kind of example I want set for my child."

Evan's search for a nanny for Leo isn't going well—not that I had high expectations.

I roll my eyes. "Ever heard of second chances?"

He shoots me a look, and I know I need to shut this conversation down. Evan and his finding a nanny fiasco isn't my business as long as it doesn't affect the way he plays, and in the past few games, he's been on top form. That might have something to do with the endless amount of coffee he drinks, though.

If he's happy with dropping nannies after one shift, so be it. As long as Leo is cared for.

The kid turns to me with a big, goofy smile, waving his toy elephant, trying to shove it into my hand,

"Sorry, buddy," I tell him, ruffling up his hair. "I wish I could stay and play, but I've got to go. Duty calls." I turn to Evan before I leave, pointing my finger in his direction. "Find a new nanny."

He wiggles his phone in hand. "Yeah, yeah, whatever. I've got a list of about ten applicants who responded to the ad you and Darrell set up."

"Good. Call them. Today." I exit Evan's house before he has time to argue, heading for Emmanuel's store.

Again, I'm worried I've been neglecting our relationship, but he understands how busy I am when the NFL games come around. He understands how important it is to me. Or rather, my father.

As I step inside, a warm comfort envelops me. This place, filled with memories of the day I marched in with a point to prove, is engrained in me. It might seem like it would trigger some old feelings, but surprisingly, it doesn't. Emmanuel has a soothing quality—his bright smile always makes me feel safe.

"Nathan, if I'd known you were coming, I would have cleaned the place!" he hollers.

The ground is covered in cardboard boxes, and wine is stacked in every corner.

"Let me help you."

Emmanuel's children lend a hand with the store, but for the most part, he runs it alone. He's not getting any younger, though, and I'm worried that one day, he'll blow his back out lifting the heavy boxes.

"No, no." He rushes over and snatches the box from my grip. "NFL stars do not work for free."

I chuckle. "They do when they consider the store owner to be family."

My remark is enough to shut Emmanuel up, and he mutters to himself humorously and shakes his head, working alongside me in silence.

I need this, though. I need to feel like I'm giving back to the man who offered me an escape from my childhood. Who cared enough to listen to a flustered and troubled kid. Who actually *wanted* to help me, although he didn't know me.

He's an inspiration to me. I want to be more like him.

Help people.

People I don't know.

Like the day Mae strolled in here, bright-eyed and bushy-tailed.

Paying for an expensive bottle of wine and owning up to someone's mistake was never in the cards, but it's very clear that where Mae is concerned, all logic flies out the window.

"We miss you!" Poppy says to the screen of her phone as she waves, and a beaming Mae sits beside her. My sister begged me to let her and Mae use my large flat-screen TV to watch a new gag-worthy rom-com film.

But am I going to watch it with them just as an excuse to spend more time with Mae? Probably.

According to Poppy, screen size and quality matter, and watching the film on her pea-sized television wouldn't do it justice.

But if my sister wants something, I usually give it to her. What sort of big brother would say no to the puppy dog eyes?

I never let anyone come to my house except Poppy, Bennett, and Evan. It's mine—my space, my refuge. There's something about it that feels sacred. Like it's my space to breathe. A no-judgement zone.

But when Poppy asked if Mae could come over, mentally, I didn't hesitate. However, I had to make it look like I wasn't sure just to keep up the narrative that Mae and I are professional.

Except we're not. Because there was nothing professional about the way my cock swelled for her as we locked lips, our hands exploring each other down in that basement.

But I'd do it again in a heartbeat.

"I miss you girls too!" I instantly recognise the voice on the phone as Sophia.

"How's the Maldives?" Mae asks, voice giddy with excitement, and I can't help but watch her from the kitchen before I tear my eyes away and begin to prep my whole chicken for cooking.

"So amazing!" Sophia responds, and I hear both girls make a collective *Oooh* noise as I assume Sophia shows them her surroundings through the video call. "Oh, I saw your performance the other day! Watched it online. Great work. Super proud of you."

I can see the pride on Mae's face. She didn't just do the team justice, she danced her ass off on that field. To say I'd been mesmerised would be an understatement.

"Everyone was so impressed," Poppy says before bombarding Sophia with questions about what the weather is like over in the Maldives.

No one was as impressed with Mae that day as me, though. She looked so sure of herself out there. So confident. So happy.

She looked like she belonged.

Belonged on the team.

Belonged in Missarali.

Belonged with... *me*.

"You like butt play or something?"

I freeze, staring at Mae standing on the other side of the kitchen island. "What?"

She laughs, nodding toward the chicken my hand is stuffed in, the lemon still in my palm. "You've had your hand up that chicken's ass for the past few minutes."

I remove it, not realising how I'd let my mind wander. "Watching me or something, princess?"

She hums, keeping her voice hushed. "Oh, always."

And as I let my eyes flit down to her curved lips, having to resist the urge to pull her to me and tell her how fucking perfect she looks standing in my house, I realise that I'm in over my head when it comes to this girl.

21: Mae

"Thanks again, Mae!" Sheila from the Missarali City Animal Shelter says as she takes Radish's leash from my hand. He's worn out from our hour-long walk across the fields, ensuring we stayed away from the farmer and his crops this time.

I missed him too much to never come back, so I've offered to volunteer twice a week for as long as I'm in the city.

Radish has had a few potential adopters turn their noses up at him. Even though he's a boisterous character, he doesn't show much interest in anyone who comes to meet him.

I told the centre that it's his way of letting them know they weren't suitable adopters for him.

I give Radish a gentle boop on his damp nose as a farewell before leaving the shelter—the rental place repaired my car free of charge. The crackly radio plays a song from one of our cheerleading routines, and I mentally run through the moves, feeling a mix of relief and disappointment that Sophia's now back from her honeymoon, which means I don't need to take her place any longer.

She bought me a big box of chocolates to show her gratitude for stepping up while she was gone, and I invited Flo over to my place to indulge in them over a hefty glass of wine.

My mother adores Sophia. I think she sees her as the daughter she never had, which stings when I'm right here in front of her. But comparing myself to others doesn't help me when my mom does it enough for both of us.

Sophia is Sophia.

And I'm me.

I'm perfectly fine with that.

As I step into the house, my mom's floral perfume hits me. She stands in the kitchen with her hands on her hips, the setting sun rays streaming through the window behind her.

"I've been watching back the last two performances without Sophia," she says as she prepares herself a green tea—the kind I think tastes like swamp water. But she enjoys its health benefits.

"Okay."

"You were out of time for the final eight counts."

I roll my eyes. Trust Renee Bexley to flip something I've done that I'm proud of and turn it into something negative. But she's not the glass-is-half-full kind of woman.

"I don't think I was half bad for a rookie who only agreed to do this last minute because she lost her job."

My mother stirs her tea. "That's what Sophia said."

"Wait, what?"

She cocks her head, but her eyes linger on me with faux surprise. "Sophia. She agreed that you—"

"No, no." I hold my hands up to stop her. "I heard what you said. Did you just tell me that you told Sophia I lost my job?"

My mother feigns innocence. "Yes? Is that a problem?"

Betrayal rockets through me. I hadn't asked much from my mother, but the one thing I'd requested was to keep the fact that I'd been let go from my job to herself, and she'd agreed. I thought we had come to a mutual understanding that we wouldn't reveal that information to anyone.

"Why?"

I rarely feel embarrassed, but knowing the cheerleading squad know that, at the age of twenty-five, I had to depend on Mommy to rescue me from a tough spot makes me want the ground to swallow me whole.

No doubt the word has spread.

If Poppy knows, then it won't be long until Nathan finds out, too.

He's going to think I'm a mess.

"What's your problem?" I bite, snatching my bag from the table and pulling my coat on. "I'm here, helping your squad. Why do you continue to try and make things difficult for me?"

My mother sets her mug down a little too harshly, the green liquid sloshing over the side onto the granite countertop. "Mae, please, not everything is about you. Don't be so self-centred."

"Don't do that. Don't pretend you haven't been trying to hurt me. You continuously treat me like crap, and I've been nothing but nice to you." I take a deep breath. "I'm sorry you lost Dad, okay? I'm fucking sorry, but I did too. And it's neither one of our faults. But I don't know why you're trying to torment me as if this is some kind of punishment. I'm your fucking daughter."

My mother releases a small scoff. She's shocked at my outburst, and I swear I see the tiniest glimmer of guilt flash in her eyes before she covers it up. "Sometimes I really don't understand how you think, Mae. What do you want me to say, hmm? That I'm sorry? That I want us to build bridges and work this out?" She pauses, a blank look masking her face. "Well, I'm not going to."

My chest is tight, and I feel physically sick. My bottom lip is wobbling, and I drop my eyes in disbelief.

My mother is a master gaslighter, and I don't understand how my father tolerated her for so long. They're nothing alike.

"Nothing?" I ask her, shaking my head in disbelief. "You feel nothing?" My hands shake, and a chill wracks my spine. I don't want to be here. I feel like I can't breathe.

My mother stares at me, blinking and turning her back to me.

Like she always does.

Before I cry in front of her, I leave the house. I don't know where I'm going, but I need to get far away from her.

Does she really hold that much resentment towards me just because I couldn't give her the carbon copy of herself as a daughter? Just because I had a better relationship with my father than with her? Just because I couldn't be *her* version of successful?

I know she still loves Dad deep down. I know she's hurt, but we all are.

And she has the nerve to call me self-centred.

Tears leak from my eyes as I drive, and I wipe at my nose, cursing myself for allowing myself to crumble. But I've been bottling it up for so long it's taking over. Consuming me. Bleeding into every cell in my body. It feels impossible to think about anything else.

I stare at my white knuckles as my hands clutch the steering wheel tighter, the metal groaning under the weight. What's this car made of? Tissue paper?

Poppy's with her mother tonight, Flo's seeing a movie with her work colleagues and Cam's on a date, so I either drive around aimlessly all night or see if Nathan's busy.

My mind is whirling a mile a minute, and I drive to his house before I can talk myself out of it.

Sitting with my thoughts momentarily, I gaze out into the darkness towards his gated residence. I grab my things and buzz, swallowing my shame.

There's no response, though, and I rest my forehead against the white brick for a few seconds before I shake my head.

Coming to Nathan's house was a stupid idea.

But then I hear the click of the speaker, and Nathan says, "If you're another cold caller, I swear to God—"

"Um, sorry, I just..." My voice trails off.

"Mae?"

The black iron gate immediately begins to swing open. My shoes click against the rocky path as I walk towards his front door, eyes wide as Nathan opens it with a down-turned mouth and a worrisome crease between his eyebrows.

"I'm sorry," I tell him as I stand on his porch, my voice wavering. "I—I didn't have anywhere else to go." I don't know what I look like, but I have no doubt my cheeks are flushed, and my eyes are glassy.

"Come here." He opens his arms for me, and I hurry into them, burying my face into his chest.

I shouldn't be here—crying into Nathan Slater's chest. But I can't find a cell in my body that cares about the contract right now. My world is disintegrating around me, and the only thing stopping it is having Nathan's arms around me.

"Tell me what happened. Seeing you cry is killing me." His finger tilts my chin up, his frown emphasising when he gets a better look at my tear-streaked face. I fucking hate crying in front of people, and I feel like an idiot right now.

He leads me away from the chill of the open door.

"I'm sorry, this is so embarrassing," I sniffle.

"Never apologise for having feelings, Mae." Nathan crouches in front of me as I sit on his couch. "Now, there's got to be a good reason you came to me, of all people." He chuckles.

Him of all people? Does he not realise what he does to me?

"My mom—she hates me." I attempt to calm my racing heart. I'm unsure if Nathan already knows, but I don't want him to hear this through the grapevine. I want it to come from me. "The reason I came to Missarali was because I lost my job."

His face is blank, and he just nods, not an ounce of judgment staining his features.

"The company couldn't afford to keep me any longer, which meant *I* couldn't afford to stay in Colorado, so I had to move back here. But my mom only agreed to have me if I joined the cheerleading squad for the season. We agreed to keep it between us, but she told Sophia, and now I'm really fucking embarrassed."

Nathan is silent for a few seconds before he says, "Well, it's no surprise that your mom wanted something in return for having you stay with her."

"I don't get it. I understand I'm not the daughter she wants, but why would that make her hate me? I thought love for a child was unconditional."

"Some people just aren't supposed to be parents."

It's true. My mother's never been overly maternal. But she got worse when my father left. I often think that he was the one who pushed to have children.

"It's not a reflection of you, though. You need to remember that, okay?" Nathan cocks his head at me, waiting for an answer, and I nod doubtfully. "Just because you love the ocean doesn't mean you have to drown in it, Mae."

My heart throbs at the comment, realising how true it is. I love my mother. She's my flesh and blood, but she makes it hard to breathe, and I deserve to respire painlessly.

I know when it's time to let someone go, but it still kills me inside.

"I'm a big believer in choosing your family," he continues. "Just because she was born your mom doesn't mean she has to stay."

It's logic I haven't had the strength to try to process yet.

"Everyone on the cheerleading squad probably knows now."

Nathan shrugs. "And who cares? So, your previous company failed to see your potential? That's their loss. I've seen the way you are around animals, Mae. You love them. Unconditionally. You want to help them because it makes you feel good. That's the kind of person you are. You're selfless." He pushes a strand of hair away from my face. "Never lose that. It's your gift."

More tears fall from my eyes as I smile, realising how close we are. My eyes flick down to his lips, and I stare at them. I'm feeling vulnerable right now, and I don't give a fuck if Nathan knows I want him.

"I can't, princess," he says, sighing, his eyes trained on me. Intense and strained. "Not when you're like this. I want you to have a clear head if it happens again."

If. I don't like that word.

I swallow and nod. I fully understand why he doesn't want to kiss me right now. Emotions are high.

He huffs, grinding his teeth together in frustration as he cups my cheeks. A torn groan slips past his lips as he drops his forehead down onto my thigh. "Trust me, I want to kiss you, Mae. But I want you to focus on processing your emotions right now. Not distracting yourself from them."

"No, I get that. Thank you."

"If you still want to kiss me after that, though, I'd happily oblige."

I smile, hand running through his hair, gently tugging at the strands. Nathan sighs in contentment. "Just as I thought," I say.

He lifts his head. "What?"

"Your hair. It's soft. Just as I thought."

A nervous, perplexed laugh rumbles from his chest as he shakes his head. "You're a little weirdo."

Nathan and I spend the next hour watching TV in silence, his arm wrapped around me and my head on his chest. My previously tense muscles relax, much like my mind.

I've never felt so comfortable in someone's presence before—as if they just fully get me. Want the best for me. No matter what.

The silence isn't awkward. It's just what I need. It gives me time to sift through my emotions and gather my thoughts without being clouded with my need for Nathan. Having him beside me is enough right now.

But guilt floods me when I realise the time. I straighten myself. "Oh, shit. I didn't know it was so late. You're probably tired. I should go."

"You're going back to her?" Nathan scows. "No. Not when you're in this state of mind. Absolutely not. I don't want you around that."

Without another word, he grips my hand and leads me to his simplistic, blue bedroom, the scent of musk and lemon whirling around me. It looks precisely how I imagined it would—because I've imagined it many times—and he pulls a jersey from his chest of drawers.

I take it from him, my fingers skating over the soft red and white fabric, arching my eyebrow when I read the name *Slater* embroidered on the back.

"Would you prefer something else?"

I chuckle. But I know the humour doesn't reach my eyes because of the look Nathan gives me. It's full of compassion and worry.

Entering the bathroom, I change, using his spare toothbrush.

Logic is long gone from my mind. But there's something satisfying about staying here with Nathan. It's almost a little fuck you to my mother because I know she'd probably sprout a second head if she knew I was here with her most-hated football player right now. Wearing his jersey. About to sleep in his bed. Fantasising about him making me feel good.

Would he push me away if I were to roll closer to him right now? Touch him?

There are so many people who are hot in this world. But Nathan Slater is on another level, and not just because of his looks. The way he cares for me makes my stomach twist. The area between my legs throb. I've never felt this out of control around someone before.

All I can hear is my heartbeat as we lay next to each other, our legs inches apart. My throat is dry, and even though I attempt to swallow, I can't. Our breathing syncs up, and I can tell Nathan wants to say something by how his eyebrows pinch together and his lips part, fingers tapping against his shirtless chest.

"My mother died. Suicide." I look at him with surprise as he shuts his eyes tightly, then opens them a few moments later, his chest rising as he takes a breath. "She struggled with an alcohol addiction."

I can tell he's extremely uncomfortable. His jaw is so tight it looks like the bone is going to burst through the flesh.

"Nathan, what are you doing?" I ask him as I sit up, my head shaking slightly. The last thing I want him to do is open up to me if it's excruciating for him.

"Helping you not to feel so alone," is his response before he hushes me. "It's why I don't drink. I can't stand the stuff. I also know that children who grew up with a parent who had an addiction are more likely to develop one themselves, and I don't want to take that risk. I was thirteen when I stormed into Emmanuel's store to demand he stop selling my mother alcohol. We'd just moved here. He agreed immediately, even though it would hurt his business, and we've been close ever since."

Nathan has never mentioned his mother, but I always wondered if she was in the picture. It hits me hard—the pain he's carried since childhood. The grief he must feel every day.

He hides it all so well.

"I should have done more. But I was always training, leaving my mother to turn to alcohol because she was lonely. My father claimed she wanted this for me, though. She wanted to see her son succeed. It's why I can't quit—not until the team wins. My mother's death can't be for nothing." He clears his throat but doesn't take his eyes off me, and I place my hand on his chest.

"It's not your fault, Nathan."

He does nothing but hum, unconvinced. "It got to a point that all she'd talk about was alcohol. Her favourite wines. Her not-so-favourite. The cheap stuff. The expensive stuff. I know more about wine than anyone who doesn't drink would ever need to."

My heart stutters inside my chest.

"I still remember the day I came home from training to see police everywhere. The house was taped off. I was seventeen. It should have discouraged me. It should have made me realise I'd wasted so much time playing football instead of spending time with her, but it lit a fire under my ass instead. I'd been considering talking to her and asking what she'd think of me if I gave up football competitively, but I never got the chance."

I've never seen Nathan look so broken. So lost. He's usually a composed man who knows what he wants and isn't afraid to speak his mind. But the man before me is a far cry from him.

"Listen to me, Nathan. It's not your fault. Your mom was sick, and you were a child. She decided to take her life, and that wasn't because of you. You can't blame yourself. I know no one else does." I whisper the final part, and Nathan dips his head in a nod. He studies every inch of my face, tongue skating across the front of his teeth. His nostrils flare, and he leans forward to kiss my forehead softly, making my stomach backflip.

"I've never told anyone other than Poppy, Bennett and Evan that before." He runs a finger along my collarbone and down my shoulder, his eyes following the movement. "Thank you for not judging me."

I smile at him. "I would never judge you."

"How are you feeling?"

I contemplate for a few seconds before saying, "Better. I just needed... a cry. Thank you for letting me stay over."

We glance at each other once more before letting our heads hit the pillows, and I feel his hand grip mine and squeeze it before he pulls the comforter up to tuck me in.

"Anytime, princess."

22: Nathan

I've never opened up to anyone like that. Never told them the whole story. Never told them how it affects me on the daily.

But seeing Mae cry broke my fucking heart right in half. Especially because it was over her witch of a mother.

I wanted to divert her attention somewhere else for a minute. To let her know she wasn't alone.

I'd offered her to stay and have breakfast, but we both decided it wouldn't look good if we showed up at this morning's practice together. We're partners, yes, but some things would just look suspicious.

We have a game tomorrow. The team is prepared, as far as I'm concerned. We've been playing well, but my stomach sinks knowing my father will be attending. Now that the Super Bowl is approaching, he's becoming more demanding, and his pressuring texts haven't gone unnoticed.

I can't wait to retire so I never have to see his face again. It'll be like Christmas. I'm counting down the days.

"How's your hamstring, Nathan?" Cam asks me as I walk into the locker room, and I stare at him. His sister was in my bed last night, and he has no idea. Granted, nothing happened between us, but somehow, consoling one another felt far more intimate than if we were to lock lips. There's something about confiding in someone else when, for the most part, you've been silent, which makes you realise how far you've fallen.

How deep you are.

How deep *I* am.

Because Mae Bexley does something to me—something no other woman has ever done. She makes me forget about my problems. She makes me feel alive again. Like *me* again, and fuck, he's been lost for a long time.

"It should be good for the game tomorrow. Thanks, man," I tell Cam. It could use a massage, but I want to avoid him. The last thing I want is his reminder that Mae doesn't need this. Doesn't need *me*.

Irritation begins to grow.

Because I want her.

But she still feels so out of reach, knowing she's leaving at the end of the season.

I can't help but imagine how good she'd feel wrapped around me, arms laced around my neck, with her lips chanting my name into my neck as I slip my cock into her.

Fuck.

Getting a boner in front of Cam wasn't on the cards today, so I nod at him and quickly head out of the locker room towards the field.

My eyes immediately land on Mae, and they widen when I see she's wearing my jersey from last night—the one that clearly says *Slater* in bold on the back. She's got her honey-coloured hair down, so the embroidery is slightly covered, and luckily, only Sophia, Madison, Bennett and Sam are here.

Renee and Darrell have yet to arrive for the pre-practice meeting.

Mae turns to me, and I beckon her over to the tunnel with my head, where no one can see us.

She gazes up at me with her hazel eyes that capture me every time, and I shake my head, pinching the jersey's material as I back her up against the wall. "Are you trying to get me in trouble, princess?"

Confusion masks her face briefly before she fists the jersey, her lips popping open. "Oh, fuck."

I release a small sound of exasperation as she pulls me into the women's locker room, locking the door behind us. She slides the jersey off, only wearing her tight, black sports bra underneath. The swell of her round breasts stares right back at me.

"Here, take it."

I fist the jersey she's thrust into my hand, and my eyes skate down her body. "Is it bad that I want you to put it back on?" I take a step towards her, chests close together.

"And risk everyone seeing it?" Mae tilts her head to the side and smiles. "That's very risky of you, Nate."

"Don't call me that, princess."

"Don't call me princess, then."

"Yeah, not going to happen."

I drop the jersey and bite down on my lip. I'm well-aware Mae can see how hard I am for her, her eyes dropping down before she gulps, face flushing.

"Nathan," Mae says, her voice breathy, and it's enough to send me into a spiral.

"Is this what you wanted last night, Mae?" I close the gap between us so our faces are inches apart, her minty breath fanning across my face. I tilt my head down until my lips latch onto the spot under her ear, and she immediately moans. "Is this what you were so desperate for?"

Another soft groan.

"Use your words for me. Tell me." I smile against her skin. I'm so fucking hard right now. My cock is aching.

"Yes," she responds. "Fuck yes."

Her raspy voice powers through me, and her eyes collide with mine as I pull away. Within seconds, our lips are locked.

It's instinct—her hands fisting my hair and my fingers digging into the skin of her hips.

Knowing that we shouldn't be doing this... where we are right now... it adds an element of excitement to the kiss.

Time stands still.

Her lips are desperate, her teeth bumping against my own, causing me to groan into her mouth.

But kissing Mae no longer feels enough. I want to pin her to the wall and fuck her senseless until she's screaming so loud everyone knows what we're doing.

She's been punishing me for too long with her smart mouth.

I want to return the favour.

I give her my best cocky smirk after I pull away, enjoying how her chest quickly rises and falls as she breathes. "Is this pussy wet, Mae?" Dropping down in front of her, I grin, eye level with the front of her spandex shorts. If she's not soaking, I haven't done my job properly.

My fingers grip her ass, and I pull her forwards so her pussy is just inches away from me. It would be so easy to lap at her right now. Dip my fingers into these shorts and fuck her with my fingers.

Mae's tongue darts out, wetting her bottom lip. "Nathan, I need it."

"What do you need?" I palm her ass cheeks, squeezing the muscle. It fits perfectly in my hands.

"You. Your tongue on me. Shit." Her head lolls back against the locker room wall. "Why do you have to make a woman so fucking horny?"

I narrow my eyes. "*You*, Mae. I make *you* feel horny. I'm not making anyone else feel this way," I tell her as I press a tentative kiss to her shorts, just over her pelvic bone.

Mae's hands are in my hair, fingers pulling at the strands with force, but it feels good.

My hands slide up her toned stomach, and they hover above her breasts, wrapped tightly in her tiny sports bra. I cock a brow at her, silently asking for permission.

She wastes no time in nodding, and within a second, her sports bra is on the floor beside her, and my tongue is swirling around her nipple.

"This is what I wanted to do that night in the hotel." My voice is husky.

"I would have let you," is her response.

I growl, lips making their way down her body, back towards her—what I know is soaking—pussy. "I was trying to be a gentleman."

Mae's eyes are intense. "Well, don't."

Suddenly, multiple loud voices sound outside the locker room, and Mae pulls away from me, lips puffy and eyes hazy.

I groan and rest my forehead against her stomach.

"You should get out there quickly before the girls try and come in here," she tells me, fingers running across her lips. "Can't risk ruining your career, now can we, Mr Slater?"

"Are you happy with yourself?" I smirk.

She drops her head to her chest in a nod. "Very. Good luck with that." She nods to my raging boner.

I pick up my jersey, which I dropped during our make-out session, and hand it back to her. I want her to keep it. I like it when she wears my name, even if the only place she can do so is in private. "Just so you know, next time that happens, you'll be wearing my name on your back."

I don't think it's possible for Mae to flush anymore, but she somehow turns an even pinker shade.

I exit the locker room, checking that nobody is around, and as I turn the corner towards the men's locker room, Renee strolls past me. Her face creases, and she shakes her head in disgust as she passes.

But all I can do is chuckle.

Because she has no idea I've just left her daughter in the women's locker room soaking wet and fucking needy for me.

"You brought your tortoise with you on a camping trip?" my sister asks Mae as we drop our bags down in the open space we're camping on tonight. We're helping another charity and are participating in a *clean-up-the-forest* event.

Spending tomorrow picking up trash isn't anyone's idea of fun, but it gives me an excuse to ignore my father. Darrell and Renee have taken away our phones.

"Nobody could look after him," Mae responds, peeking at Chump, who's content in his little hutch, snacking on a large chunk of kale.

"We're only here one night," Sophia laughs.

"One night too many," is Evan's response, yanking his one-person tent from his rucksack.

Darrell claps his hands to gain our attention. "Alright, everyone! Let's get set up before the sun sets. We can spend the evening roasting marshmallows around a campfire or whatever you kids like doing. The hard work begins tomorrow."

"I'm a thirty-two-year-old man," Evan scoffs. "I hate marshmallows."

"Well, then you can cry yourself to sleep in your tent while everyone else has fun, West. We're here to show Montana that we care about the community. That we're at one with nature. So let's put our brave faces on."

Evan's not usually one for talking, but he's out of his depth here—far away from Leo—and I can tell it's getting to him. "If I piss in a bush, does that count as being at one with nature and means I can go home?"

Darrell narrows his eyes playfully. "My wife's given up her evening to care for Leo for you. Don't push it." He turns to the rest of us. "Get in your groups and start setting up your tents. I need to get some good shots."

I immediately begin helping Mae. I try not to make it look so instinctual for me, keeping my face sullen and my shoulders dropped, but I can't get last week out of my head.

All I want to do is have it happen again. And again. And again.

Bennett begins unpacking his tent alongside Poppy, their eyes lingering on each other for a second too long. It appears as if they're talking telepathically. I can't put my finger on the way Bennett looks at my sister. It's protective, for sure. I know he cares for her a lot, but he looks at her like she's the only person he sees.

"Your mom looks like she's ready to have a blast," I whisper to Mae as I nod behind her, stifling my laugh.

Renee is standing with her arms wrapped around her stomach as she glares at everyone, her perfectly done-up hair and pristine makeup looking entirely out of place in the middle of the forest.

"She's scared of bears. She doesn't know it's a fenced-off area, but I won't tell her that." Mae giggles, and the sound goes through me like always.

I feel like a gooey pile of, well, goo. Why the hell am I here about to fall to my knees just because she laughed?

This woman could ask me to jump, and I'd probably say *how high?*

"That's an impressive tent, Nathan." Mae's words force me from my train of thought, and I look at my pants with confusion. She bursts into laughter as she nods to the tent we're currently stabilising, knowing precisely what she was doing with her wording.

"Well, someone wants to wake up with a Sharpie moustache tomorrow morning." I keep my smirking to a minimum. Little does she know, I indeed did pack Sharpies. You can never be too prepared when camping out in the forest with a bunch of football players.

The tents are pop-up, so all we have to do is secure them down to the ground to ensure they don't blow away, and after the sun has set, Samuel uses his Boy Scout training—or lack of—to try and make us a fire. In the end, Evan has to shove him aside and take over.

"Smile, everyone!" Darrell says as his phone camera flashes.

"How come *you're* allowed technology?" Bennett complains as he sits on one of the logs we've moved to circle the flames.

"I need to take photos. Peter's orders. And Mr Father-Of-The-Year over there," he points at Evan with a smirk, "demanded I have it on hand in case something goes wrong with Leo."

Evan responds with a grumble about wanting to shove the phone up Darrell's asshole, but all it gains him is a friendly back slap from his coach.

The winter air is chilling, but luckily, we brought a few portable battery-powered heaters, which we set up around the small camp. I have no idea why Peter didn't plan this at the beginning of the season when it was warmer, but then again, I don't understand much that goes through that man's head.

Samuel begins telling some stupid ghost story, and I roll my eyes as I spot Mae and Poppy climbing out of a tent, clutching unopened bags of marshmallows to their chests. They're doing their best to be quiet, though, and I raise my eyebrows questionably.

Mae holds her finger to her lips to silence me.

I give her a subtle, knowing nod.

Bennett looks like a fish out of water, with his eyes wide and mouth ajar as he listens to Samuel's—definitely fictional—story of how he got pushed into a lake by the ghost of an old fisherman when he was younger. He claims he almost died, and Bennett seems to be eating up every little detail like some gullible child.

Mae and Poppy stealthily move towards Bennett's back, each step muted. They're avoiding the crunchy leaves, and luckily, the crackling of the fire covers any sound they make.

"Boo!"

Bennett yells loudly as the girls grab his shoulders and shake them. He crumbles to the ground in fear and throws his bag of potato chips into the air, the crispy snacks landing all over the floor.

I can't contain my laughter, and even Renee cracks a small smile before dropping it, which shocks me to my core. She may hate us, but she can't deny we're a boatload of fun to be around sometimes. When football's not the topic, we're just a group of genuine guys who want to laugh as much as the next person.

"I'm gonna smother the both of you with pillows in your sleep." Bennett grabs the marshmallows from them and stuffs three in his mouth, sulking like a little boy.

"What was that?" Renee demands as the bush beside her rustles, and she shoots up into a standing position, clutching her hot water bottle tightly. "Is it a bear?"

"Maybe," I say, chuckling. "I wouldn't worry, though. The bears in Montana only eat dolled-up cheerleading coaches wearing *pink*." I nod to her purple velvet tracksuit, "so you should be good."

She takes a deep breath, calming herself before trudging over to her tent. I can already tell she isn't going to get a wink of sleep tonight. People like her don't belong in environments like this. The fact that she doesn't have electricity and won't be able to curl her hair in the morning is going to send her over the edge.

"Peter wouldn't let her out of it," Darrell tells us with a laugh before standing. "I'm going to hit the hay, too. Gotta be up early for a fun-filled day."

Mae releases a yawn. "Me too. I promised Chump I'd read him a bedtime story."

I love this easygoing side of Mae. It turns me on.

After a few minutes, everyone disappears into their separate tents, and I'm left staring at the hissing fire. I'm not tired. All I can think about is Mae. She's mere meters away from me—probably braless underneath an oversized band

T-shirt and leggings that accentuate every curve of her body.

Great.

I've got a fucking hard-on in the middle of the forest.

Scraping my hands through my hair, I kill the fire by pouring a pot of cold water over it and enter my tent. We're all pretty spaced out, so I'm sure my rustling isn't going to wake anybody up.

I strip down into just my boxers, staring at the roof of my tent. The material is flimsy, and my sleeping bag offers little comfort. I just know this is going to be a long night—torturous having Mae so close yet out of reach.

Can bears climb fences?

It's supposed to be a bear-proof area, but that's never guaranteed.

Could I fight a bear off?

Maybe I could befriend it?

Suddenly, I hear footsteps outside my tent, and I quickly unzip it, half expecting to be greeted by a snarling grizzly, but my eyes land on Mae.

"Hi," she whispers.

"What are you doing out in the cold dressed like that?" I ask her, placing my hands on her waist, pulling her into the tent and zipping it back up. She's wearing a pair of pyjama shorts and an old T-shirt. And I was right... she's very much braless.

"I thought I heard a ghost. Samuel's story was pretty scary," she mutters, her lashes fluttering innocently.

"Mmm-hmm," I hum sarcastically. "And what do you think I'm going to be able to do to keep you safe from that?"

"I don't know. Scare it away with that grumpy scowl you always do."

I hike my eyebrows up. "I don't *do* a grumpy scowl."

"Do, too." She pokes her slender finger into the middle of my forehead. "This area's all crinkled. That means you scowl too much."

My fingers trace the space between my eyebrows. She's making shit up now. "Okay, well, my wrinkles—that I definitely don't have, by the way—aren't going to frighten off a ghost."

Mae flicks her hair behind her shoulder, face lifting to mine as she leans back to rest on her elbows. "Okay, maybe you could just distract me from it instead, then."

I dance my fingers down the column of her neck. "And how am I supposed to do that?"

"I'm sure you can think of something."

My fingers grip her waist, gently massaging the skin as her legs slide out to either side of me. I study her, completely in awe. Her plush lips are damp, and I shiver when her gaze drops to my crotch that's pulsating for her.

"Do you like looking at me?" I tilt my head to the side. I know what her answer is going to be. I always catch her staring.

"Yes."

I pinch the fabric of her T-shirt between my fingertips, rolling it, raising it so her toned stomach is on display.

"Well, that's good because I certainly *love* looking at you."

Pressing my mouth to the soft skin just underneath her belly button, I kiss it.

Nip it.

Bite it.

And it drives Mae crazy.

Her hands are in my hair. Gripping my neck. Nails scraping the skin of my back.

She relaxes as I press my lips to her exposed collarbone, a moan slipping past her lips. I cover her mouth with my hand for a second. "You're going to need to be quiet for me, princess, or I'm going to get in a shitload of trouble."

I drag her lips to mine, her back arching so her chest is flush against me. Warmth radiates from her—not just from her body, but from how she touches me, too. The way she scrapes her fingernails down the back of my neck. The way her legs hook over my own. The way her core gravitates towards me, pressing firmly against the bulge in my boxers.

"Are you wearing underwear, Mae?"

"No."

Fuck. She's completely bare under these shorts. The only thing between us is two fragile pieces of fabric.

I increase the pressure my hips are applying to her core, and she gazes up at me with such want. Such need. Such desire.

I know she's craving it, and all I want to do is give it to her.

However, she can sense my reluctance. "Nathan, I know what you said about not wanting to make me feel like I'm some fling by doing it in a hotel room, but does the same still apply to a tent?"

I hum. I've never been with a woman in a tent before. "I just don't want you to think—"

"The only thing I *think*, is that I'm fucking desperate for you right now."

With my finger twirling around the waistband of her shorts, I gauge her reaction as I slowly dip into them, stroking her skin. The tent suddenly feels a whole lot warmer.

"Is this okay?"

"Yes, you don't even need to ask." The words rush from her.

"I definitely do."

I refrain from touching her just yet, though, because if there's something she needs to know about me, it's that I'm a tease.

"Nathan," Mae mutters pleadingly, her hands reaching forwards to stroke my cock over the top of my boxers. I feel it twitch, and a shiver wracks me.

No woman has ever made me feel this way with just one touch. I immediately want more, but more than that, I want to give *her* more.

"Do you need me, Mae?" I ask, twirling a strand of her hair around my finger. "Does this pussy need me to fuck it with my fingers?"

I can feel her trying to grind herself against me, small whimpers filling the small tent, and her lips sweep against my chest, peppering kisses on the muscle.

She raises her hips once again, and I hook one finger under the waistband and slide them down. I know it would be easy to just slip under the shorts, but I want to see her.

Her bottom half is bare, and I look at her pussy, glistening with wetness for me.

All for me. *Only* for me.

The small light I have in the corner of my tent creates a sultry aura, and Mae lifts her top to bare her breasts, the curve of them casting shadows onto my chest. "Nathan, please, do it. Make me feel good, or I will."

The thought of watching her pleasure herself fills my mind, and my cock immediately pulses with excitement. I can't think of anything hotter, but I'll save that for another time.

My fingers start at the space just above her breasts, and I trail them down, refusing to neglect her hard nipples. A breath rushes from her lips, eyes fluttering shut.

"I'm not going to rush this, princess. I want to take my time with you."

Her eyebrows pull together at my statement, and she opens her mouth to say something, but I shush her.

"We've got all night. Be patient." I try to fight my smile but quickly let it take over.

Teasing the area where her thigh meets her pussy, I linger there for a little while, tracing delicate circles on her smooth skin. Then, I run my finger through her wetness, releasing a soft grunt. "You're fucking soaked, Mae. And it's all for me."

I'm tempted to shuck my boxers off and fuck her so I can listen to her scream my name while trying to be as quiet as possible, but I know this isn't the environment for that. Sex is meant to be loud. I'm not going to make her be quiet when it happens.

Her hands grip my neck, her legs widening to give me better access. The tip of my finger inches in, and Mae squeezes around me, mumbling a quiet, "Oh, God."

"More?" I question, sliding in further.

"Yes, more."

My finger slips in with ease, and I curl them with every stroke. I know my tempo is cruel, and when I add a second finger, Mae's slick heat clamps around them.

"Shit, Nathan."

I take it slow at first, allowing my thumb to graze over her clit with every other pump, but after Mae delivers another needy whimper, I can't tease her any longer. I need to see her come for me.

The sound of her wetness fills the tent, but I make sure to keep the noise to a minimum, just in case. Although, most people should be asleep by now.

"Nathan, oh, God." Mae's head rolls back. "Fuck, don't stop."

"I don't plan on stopping until you've come all over my hand."

Her eyes are bold, staring up at me. Her mouth forms an *'O'* shape as she grips my forearm, which is moving in perfect rhythm, and after a few more seconds, she begins rocking with me, lifting her hips with every pump.

"Is that how you like it? Just like that?"

"Yes, fuck, yes."

"Watch me. Watch me fuck you with my fingers."

Mae doesn't hesitate, and she raises her head to stare down at my fingers pumping in and out of her, eyebrows knitted together in fascination.

"That's it, my pretty girl."

Pressing my lips to hers, I bite at them, and the feeling of Mae moaning into my mouth makes me lose it. I move my fingers faster, wrapping my arm around her waist and hoisting her closer to me, sitting back so I can get a good view of the way my fingers glide in and out of her pussy.

The view is fucking mesmerising.

If I were to die right now, I'd die happy.

"I want to feel this pretty pussy come for me."

"It feels so fucking good." Her eyes roll back, and she grabs my hand and brings my palm to her mouth to stop herself from being too loud.

It looks like my little cheerleader's a screamer.

"That's it," I say, talking her through the approach of her orgasm as I tweak her nipple, my spare hand running down her toned stomach. "Show me how good it feels. Let me see it. Let me see what I do to you."

She comes. Hard. With my hand clamped over her mouth to muffle her pleasured moans. Her body's trembling, her breathing choppy.

My dick feels like it's on fire—desperate to release—but after seeing how exhausted she looks after such an intense orgasm, I dress her back in her shorts and pull down her T-shirt to cover her.

"Nathan, Holy shit," Mae mutters, her hazy eyes fluttering as her chest rises and falls with each effortful breath.

"Get your breath back for me." I kiss her forehead, checking her over. "Get some sleep."

She pinches her brows together, eyes dropping to my still rock-hard dick. "Don't you want—"

"I had enough of a good time watching you come for me." I can't stop the smile that threatens to split my lips. I don't want to rush this with Mae. I don't want her to think I expect anything back because feeling how soaking wet she was for me was all I needed tonight. "I'm an early riser. I'll wake you up before anyone else notices. Just sleep for me."

Mae hesitates for a few seconds before nodding, and she rests her head on my chest as we lie together.

I wrap my arms around her, but I'm unable to fall asleep because all I can think about is how this girl is driving me up the fucking wall.

And I absolutely love it.

23: Mae

"Who's my favourite boy?"

There's something so wholesome about cooing over a dog. Their soppy eyes, wagging tails and soggy noses. Radish licks me as I wish him farewell. I've been taking care of him all day and have put my trust in Flo to drop him off at the shelter for me since I've got a shift at The Salty Dog.

Amber will kill me if I'm late.

"Is it a good idea to get this attached to him, Mae?" Flo asks, frowning as she bends down to scratch Radish's head. He's staring at me with doe-like eyes.

I tell myself I don't get attached, but I'm really starting to. I'm not making it any easier for myself with Radish, but I can't bear the thought of him spending his days cooped up, alone in his kennel when he could be out exploring with me.

"When the time comes for him to be adopted, I'll be able to let him go. But for now, I want to make sure he's not wasting away at the shelter."

"As long as you don't end up hurt." Flo opens the back of her car so Radish can jump in. "Both of you. Dogs can get attached, too."

I laugh. "He'll forget all about me once the right person comes along."

My comment makes me scrunch up my nose in distaste, but I push the feeling aside and enter the bar, gaining a *What time do you call this?* look from Amber.

I sheepishly put on my apron and load the dishwasher.

It isn't busy tonight, and thank God, because I can't face another manic shift—not after having spent all day researching and applying to more veterinary programs.

The thought of leaving... I don't like it. I couldn't wait to get out of Montana when I was younger. Granted, we didn't live in Missarali, but I never thought I'd dread moving away.

Moving away from Flo—again. Away from Poppy and the girls on the team. Away from Radish. And away from... Nathan.

It hurts like a bitch.

"Cheerleading didn't work out, huh?"

I jump at the voice, turning to see Riley Donovan staring at me across the bar. He's wearing his usual cocky grin, eyebrows raised.

"It's a side job," I state moodily. "What are you doing here, Riley? Shouldn't you be with your team?"

"They all left for California this morning. I thought I'd make a quick pit stop on the way. I had some meetings with my new sponsor."

I feel like scoffing. He's so wealthy that he can hire his own private jet and divert it to a different state on the way to a game.

I'm not going to entertain it, though. I'm here to do my job. Right now, Riley is just another paying customer.

"Humble as always, Riley." I fake a smile. "What can I get for you?"

"A Sprite will be fine."

I fill a glass for him and accept his cash, staring at him when he doesn't immediately leave the bar and find a seat. "Can I help you?"

He shrugs. "Not really. How was your camping trip? I saw the photos. It looked cute."

It went well. We spent the entire day litter-picking the area, with Nathan and I secretly making out behind trees whenever we hung back from Poppy and Bennett. Bennett was too distracted, staring at the ground to notice. And Poppy was too busy rambling about her psychology assignment to him.

"You're not going to get any information out of me." I turn to the small crowd behind him "Who's next?"

"Just trying to make friendly conversation, that's all," Riley says as I serve a middle-aged couple.

I'm unsure if Riley knew I worked here and came to irritate me just because of his conflict with Nathan or if this is merely some incredible coincidence.

"Mmm-hmm. Well, I'm not interested. I'm trying to work."

"Feisty. Interesting. How's Nathan doing?"

"Why don't you ask him?" My tone is bitter, and I sneak a glance at Amber, who's studying Riley with suspicious eyes. She can tell he's frustrating me, but she understands I can handle myself.

"I can't tell if you're frustrated because I'm asking about Nathan or because I'm—"

"Here," I finish for him. "Well, it's both." I can't help but be rude to him. He's still egging the media on, making statements and giving interviews about the so-called argument between the Pittsburgh Pilots and the Missarali Storks.

Riley sighs, taking another sip of his drink. "Look, you and I got off on the wrong foot. My girlfriend and I, we're casual."

"I think you're missing the point of the term girlfriend."

"I can't lie, Mae, I do love a woman who—"

"Alright, you're gone," I order, taking his drink from him and pouring it down the drain. "Get out. I already warned you."

His eyes narrow into slits, and he scrunches his nose. "That was my drink. I paid for that."

"Oh, my bad. Here, let me pay you back in fucks I give." I pull out my purse from my back pocket and open it, faking a gasp. "Oops, all out, sorry."

A chuckle seeps from Riley, who's smiling and holding his palms up defensively. "You're funny. Alright, I'm going. Thanks, Mae. I'll see you around."

After a few minutes, Amber turns to me with a grin, laughter ringing out. "I fucking love the way you talk to assholes."

It causes me to chortle, too, tilting my head to the ceiling and cursing under my breath.

For the most part, I'm going to miss this stupid little bar.

Things are still frosty between my mother and I.

Well, frostier than usual. She hasn't apologised for spilling my secret, but luckily, none of the girls have asked me about it.

Poppy invited me over to Nathan's house for another movie and snacks night. She really does like to take advantage of having a brother with a huge television—a television he rarely uses.

I talked to Poppy about my mom's actions, feeling comfortable enough to share it with her, and she's been trying to fill my spare time.

It's a gesture I love her for.

I enter the house with an armful of food. "Did you even ask Nathan if it was okay for me to come over?" I whisper to Poppy as she flings the door open.

She has no idea that I was writhing underneath him in the middle of the forest just days ago, and a piece of me feels guilty that I'm fooling around with her brother without her knowledge.

But it's more than just fooling around. Nathan makes me feel... enough. Wanted. Confident.

"I didn't exactly give him a choice," she snickers.

Nathan has arranged the living room with pillows scattering the carpeted floor and blankets draped everywhere, creating the ideal atmosphere for watching a movie.

He rounds the corner, and my mouth goes dry. He's all grey sweatpants, wet hair and that fresh man smell.

"I'm surprised you don't have a home theatre," I chuckle, trying to distract myself from how attractive he looks.

"Got rid of it. Turned it into my very own sex dungeon instead."

Poppy gasps, slapping her brother's chest. "Nathan!"

"What? I was just kidding."

She rolls her eyes. "Fine, I'm just so happy you two are getting along now. It makes things so much easier. We can actually sit in the same room without you wanting to kill each other."

Nathan scoffs. "To clarify, I never wanted to *kill* you."

"Unfortunately, I can't say the same."

His eyes shift, a smirk forming.

"Oh, the ice cream!" Poppy declares, and Nathan orders his sister to sit back down, entering the kitchen to get it.

My eyes follow him, but I snap them away before Poppy notices.

"Okay, horror or comedy?"

"For what?"

She quirks a brow. "For the movie? What's clunking around in that head of yours, Mae Bexley?"

Your brother.

I force a snicker. "Oh, um, horror. I could use a good scream."

There's a scoff from the kitchen, and I rest my hand over my mouth to cover my smile, telling Poppy, "I'm just gonna get some water quickly."

She nods as she sifts through the movies on Nathan's TV.

The polished countertops gleam next to the stainless steel appliances in the kitchen, while the gentle illumination of the pendant lights overhead creates soft shadows on the clean, white walls.

Nathan's casually leaning against the granite countertop, effortlessly handsome as always, looking at me as if he could eat me.

He'd given me the best orgasm of my life in that forest, and he fucking knows it. I get wet just thinking about it, but all I'm desperate to do is return the favour. It had been pretty dark in the tent, and all I could see was the outline of his cock.

I imagine his size far more often than I'd like to admit.

He lifts his arms above his head and props his weight against the high beam running through the kitchen ceiling, his shoulder muscles ticking as he rests his weight on it.

He's doing the typical leaning, sexy guy move, but I can tell he's not even meaning to, and that makes it all the better.

"I'll get you some water. Get the ice cream out for me, okay?" He nods towards the bottom drawer of his fridge-freezer.

My eyes widen once I lift out the tub of my favourite snack. I've already eaten dinner, but my dessert stomach just opened wide. Cinnamon ice cream does that to a girl.

"How did you know this was my favourite?" I prop my hip out, keeping my voice low.

"Maybe because every other thing you eat contains cinnamon. I wasn't sure what brand you liked, so I got a few. All nut-free, see?" Nathan crouches down to take the other tubs out, gesturing to them, giving me the pick of the bunch.

"You're so stupid," I tell him with a laugh.

But really, my heart is faltering. I'm thankful. Nobody has ever done something like this for me. It warms my heart that he's actually taken notice of the things I like. The things that make me happy.

Even if most people think cinnamon is disgusting.

I like it... mainly because it was my Dad's favourite, and he fed me the stuff like there was no tomorrow when I was a kid. I believe he once stated he'd have to ask for a paternity test if I ever grew up to hate cinnamon. I still laugh about that to this day.

Nathan's eyes darken, and he takes a step toward me, trapping me in between the counter and his rock-hard chest. "What did you say?"

I narrow my eyes at him. I was just about to thank him, but when he gets all cocky like this, all I want to do is push him further. It excites me. "I said you're stupid." I'm smiling from ear to ear.

"I'd like to hear you say that the next time my fingers are making you come so hard you're seeing stars."

My eyebrow arches. "They'll be a next time?"

"Oh, it would be a tragedy if there wasn't a next time, princess."

24: Mae

The crowd roars inside the Missarali City Stadium, and the clock shows two minutes left until halftime. The Storks are winning, and I can see in their opponents' faces that they know there's a slim chance of beating them.

Sophia waves her pom-poms beside me, and the crowd go wild. She's an adored member of the team—a striking, tall brunette with olive skin who has a mesmerising smile that makes me wonder if her teeth are naturally that white or if she had something done to them.

I'm glad her reappearance has relieved me of the pressure to perform, but watching the girls shuffle into their starting positions as the halftime whistle sounds fills me with an ounce of longing. I felt somewhat safe when I'd been there, dancing my socks off with Nathan watching me with adoration.

The football players pat each other on the backs as they file into the locker rooms, and I take the time to slip through the tunnel and down the corridor to grab a drink from the water fountain.

But husky muttering takes me off guard, and I peek around the corner to see Nathan talking with an older man who looks just like him but around thirty years older.

"There were a few close calls there, son."

I narrow my eyes—Nathan's father.

It's the voice of the man I'd heard berating the team through the wall of the female locker room when I'd first joined the squad. He has some nerve.

"Has it ever occurred to you that I actually play better when you're not here, watching me like an obsessive hawk?"

"No," his father responds, "it's not that. It's not me. What's distracting you, huh? What's going on in that empty head of yours, Nathan?"

Empty? The insult infuriates me.

If he bothered to spend time with his son outside of football, he'd learn that he's actually a very intellectual man.

"I scored two touchdowns. Get off my back."

Kevin Slater leans against the wall, stare intimidating. "You could've scored three or four. If you want to be the greatest player in the NFL, then you're going to have to—"

"I don't want to be the greatest player in the NFL. *You* do."

"Your mother—"

Nathan raises his hand to halt him. "Enough. Get back to your seat."

Within a few seconds, Kevin Slater has chuckled, shaken his head in disbelief and walked away, leaving his son staring up at the ceiling with a frown.

Seeing him like this—my heart constricts.

"You can come out now, princess."

My heart leaps from my chest, and I step round the corner. "How did you know I was there?"

A small smile graces Nathan's lips as his eyes find mine. "You can't hide from me, princess."

A blush rises to my cheeks as I move closer. "Ignore him, Nathan. He doesn't know what he's talking about."

"Unfortunately, he does." He sighs, fingers scraping through his tousled hair.

"Well, even so, he's wrong to bring up your mom as some kind of pressure tactic."

"Protective of me?"

I give him a dead stare. "Would you prefer it if I wasn't?"

"That's the last thing I want."

I comfortingly place my hands on Nathan's chest before pulling them away, realising we're out in the open. Anyone could round the corner and see us.

"Are you afraid someone will see us?" he asks, tilting his head to the side, challenging me.

"Aren't you?"

Nathan hums, dragging his bottom lip into his mouth as he studies me. His eyes dart to the side, and he leads me into the men's locker room beside us, locking the door.

"We have roughly ten minutes before we have to be back out there."

The way he talks to me. So lustful. So tentative. Wetness pools between my legs.

"I can easily make you come in that time," I say, dropping to my knees before him, and his eyes darken.

"What the fuck did you just say?"

I stifle my smile as I run my hand over the bulge in his shorts. "I've been told I have the mouth of a goddess."

"I really don't want to hear about you and other men, Mae." Jealousy sparks in his irises, and I play with the waistband of his football pants, silently asking permission.

He lowers his chin in a nod, and I pull his cock free, all thoughts dissipating from my mind.

I expected Nathan to have a big dick, but fuck me…

I don't know how I'm going to handle it.

But I can sure as hell try.

The crowd is whooping, and I have no doubt it's because they love the cheerleaders' performance. No one will notice my absence, especially not my mother, who will be too busy studying their every move.

Nathan looks at me for several beats, his Adam's apple working.

We're like yin and yang. We live entirely different lives. But everyone in the stadium is utterly oblivious to the fact that I'm about to make one of their favourite football players moan my name in the locker room, and it fucking turns me on.

On a chuckle, Nathan asks, "You just gonna sit there and stare at it?"

I meet his eyes, sticking my tongue out and sliding it over his tip. There's a bead of pre-cum dripping from him, and the sweetness explodes on my tongue.

"Oh, fuck."

I'm already full and haven't even taken half of him.

Nathan groans, leaning forward to rest his arms against the lockers, caging me in. He watches me, eyebrows drawn together. "You're desperate for this cock, aren't you, princess?"

I lower my head in a quick nod.

"Tell me, how many times have you imagined yourself doing this? How many times have you imagined what my cock would taste like?"

"Too many," I tell him as I pull away, gripping the base, my eyes shining with anticipation. I lean closer to lap at him again, and he shivers.

He rests his forehead against the locker, the force shaking them. "You have no idea how many times I've thought about filling this smart mouth of yours."

I moan as I slide my mouth down him, tongue swirling.

My eyes flicker up to gaze at Nathan, who's powerless to me right now. I'm doing this to him. I'm making him feel good. I've always been a giver.

My throat opens just as he begins to thrust gently. My eyes fill with tears.

"Too much?" he asks, pulling out, but I shake my head and inhale deeply through my nose, relaxing my throat muscles.

It's not too much. It's not *enough*.

Nathan's hand reaches down to cup one of my cheeks as he watches me with fascinated eyes. He looks at me like I'm a rare piece of art he can't believe he's seeing in the flesh—like some sleazy robber might come and snatch me away.

I take him again, the feel of him in my mouth causing an involuntary whimper to come from me.

"That's it. Moan on my cock, Mae."

When I glance up again, his eyes are half-lidded, and the pad of his thumb trails down the side of my cheek.

He groans as I take him deeper, tilting his head to the ceiling.

I can feel his body tensing under the palms of my hands, and I know he's enjoying this just as much as I am.

"Five minutes, sweetheart," he reminds me with a smirk, but he finishes it with a light tremor.

Sweetheart.

We'll add that to the list of names he calls me, which I would have hated upon our first meeting but now love.

"Look at you, so desperate." Nathan brushes the stray bits of my curled hair away from my face, gazing down at me with adoration. If I can't make him finish before he has to go back out on that field, I'll swallow my pom-poms whole in front of everyone.

He *will* finish. And it will be the best orgasm of his fucking life.

"Oh shit." Nathan jolts. "Mae, fuck."

I love the way he says my name. It does things to me.

"You want me to fuck your mouth? I can tell by the look in your eyes."

That's exactly what I want.

"Mmm-hmm," I manage to say right before Nathan begins thrusting, hips advancing before he reels them back, plunging into my mouth again.

My hands trail over his ripped abdomen, wanting to touch every inch of his flesh.

"This mouth is driving me fucking crazy."

My hands move on autopilot, and I yank my top open and reveal my breasts, palming them. I point to them.

"Yeah? You want to go out there with your chest still wet with my come?" he questions with gritted teeth, his thrusts strengthening, but he's still gentle. He still looks down at me to make sure I'm okay.

I've never been better, though.

My instincts make me want to gag, but I push the impulse away, soft moans escaping from him as he tries to steady his short breathing.

His large, athletic thighs flex, and he shakes his head at me in disbelief, eyes cloudy.

"I love fucking this mouth of yours. Fucking love it."

If I didn't have a mouthful of cock right now, I'd be smiling from ear to ear.

I can tell Nathan's close by his shuddering muscles, and his hands fist my hair and tug gently.

"You take my cock so well," he grunts, tone low. "Fuck, you're unbelievable."

His encouragement spurs me on, and I remain still as Nathan fucks my mouth, opening my eyes wide and gazing up at him.

I want him to see me—mouth stuffed with his cock. *His*.

"Holy shit," his palm hits the locker above my head with enough force to shake it slightly as he leans forwards, but not enough to startle me, and he then brings it back to my face, soft and tentative. "Mae, I'm gonna—"

And after a few seconds, Nathan draws his hips back and pumps his dick a few times. With his free hand, he tilts my chin up, telling me what a good job I've done.

Strings of hot cum spray across my chest and drip onto my cheer uniform. His chest rises with each heavy breath he greedily takes.

We're silent, and a dazzling smile takes over Nathan's face before he crouches down and kisses me—hard and feverish. "Holy shit, Mae," he says, chuckling. "Your mouth is fucking incredible. *You're* fucking incredible."

I use a wet paper towel to wipe my chest, the red and white uniform covered in a few spatters that darken the fabric. I don't think anybody will notice. But even if they do, I doubt they'll assume it's anything other than sweat or water.

I inhale deeply through my nostrils, trying to calm my growing arousal.

"You need to get back out there." I link my fingers together behind his neck. "You've got two minutes." But then I frown. "Wait, you missed the whole tactics talk. Won't Darrell—"

"Not with my dad here. He'll assume I was being scolded." Nathan smiles. "This was well worth missing the talk, though."

"I'm glad I could help relax you," I say on a chortle, giving him a quick kiss on the lips.

I ensure my uniform is straight before ducking out of the spare men's locker room, releasing an exhale of relief when nobody's hanging around outside. A tiny part of me was worried we'd have an audience.

"Mae?"

I whirl around as I shut the door, my eyes meeting Sophia's confused ones as she hurries around the corner. "I came looking for you. We're back on." She's standing with her arms crossed, and her gaze darts to the locker room door. "Why were you in the *men's* locker room?"

I'm not a good liar, but now's the time I need to deliver an Oscar-worthy performance.

"*Men's?*" My eyes widen with false realisation as I look at the black stickman clear on the red steel door.

"Yes?" Sophia raises her thin eyebrows.

"Oh, shit. Thank fuck there wasn't anyone else in there," I laugh casually, stalking away from the door. "I didn't even realise. I just needed a breather."

I don't want Sophia to see my face. My expression will give me away.

"Oh… right." She bobs her head before following me down the corridor, taking one last look at the locker room door. She quickly replaces her mystified expression with a cheerful one and slings an arm around my shoulder. "Come on. Let's go wow that crowd."

25: Nathan

"You're burning the water," I say as I peer into the pan bubbling on Bennett's stove.

"You can't burn water, genius."

Evan arches an eyebrow. "I beg to differ. Look at that." He gestures to the water now pouring over the side of the metal, and I roll my eyes and nudge Bennett aside so I can take over.

This man lives off ready meals and takeouts. Granted, he chooses the healthy options, but it would help if he knew how to boil pasta without setting his apartment on fire.

Leo gnaws on his toy block while sitting on his dad's lap. "See? You've driven my kid to eat plastic."

Bennett grumbles while we chuckle, and a knock from the door catches our attention.

"Who's that?"

"I invited Cam over." Bennet rushes to let him in.

My eyes round as I stare down at the cubed chicken frying.

Cam's a nice guy. He's a great member of the team, but he doesn't know that his sister had her lips wrapped around my cock in the men's locker room almost a week ago. He specifically told me to stay away from her, and I'm doing the complete opposite.

I've never hung out with him besides in a professional setting, so I'm not sure what I'm supposed to talk to him about.

"Great win last week, boys," Cameron congratulates us as he strides in. He's a confident man who can command a room, but he's not cocky or smug, which is refreshing.

"Thanks, man."

Leo releases a small gasp of excitement once he spots Cam. He sometimes sits in on Evan's physio sessions, and Cam sneaks Leo candy and plays his favourite soul-crushing toddler music while he abuses his father's muscles. I know it chips away at Evan's mental stability a little more each time.

While the guys converse, I focus on fixing Bennett's food disaster. I add to the conversation now and then, but for the most part, I remain quiet.

I don't feel guilty about what happened with Mae—not one bit. But it feels strange standing face to face with her brother when he has no idea all I want to do is rip her clothes off until she's in nothing but her lacey underwear and sink so deep into her that she won't forget me when she leaves.

The thought of not having Mae here makes me feel physically sick.

But I know it's reality.

I'm staying here where I belong. And she'll be moving on with her life after the season. I don't know where she'll be going, but another state sounds likely, and with busy schedules, it'll be unlikely that we'll be able to see each other.

Not that we'd be able to anyway. If Peter were to find out about Mae and me and put the pieces together, I'd be thrown off the team.

I clench my fists.

Fuck, I hate this.

Evan's phone buzzes, and he squints at it before grunting. "Seriously? Does this guy ever give it a rest?"

"What?"

"Riley's spoken to Essence Sport and commented about us as a team again."

I pinch the skin between my eyebrows. "What's he said now?"

"The usual crap," Bennett says, reading off Evan's phone. "We're a group of unruly swine who only care about the title, and it doesn't matter how we get it. We'll throw anyone and everyone under the bus to win."

"Unruly swine," I chuckle. "Well, that's a new one."

Cam's face scrunches up. "Riley's a weirdo. I stopped off at the bar to see Mae during her shift earlier, and she told me that he's been showing up and trying to talk to her."

Everybody goes silent, and I feel my heart thud. "What?"

He seems taken aback by the gravel in my voice. "Yeah, he's been in a few times. He says he's here on business, but I swear next time I see him, I'm gonna warn him to leave Mae alone. She's working herself into the dirt and doesn't want to be bothered, even if he is just trying to be friendly. He can find another bar to hang out at."

Aggravation surges through me. All I want to do is storm down to The Salty Dog, grip Riley by the back of his neck, and throw him into a saltwater river. If he loves The Salty Dog so much, he can become one.

Lucky for him, there are no saltwater rivers in Montana.

I have no idea what his game is, but he clearly has nothing better to do than torment my team, and harassing Mae is something I will absolutely not tolerate.

As we eat, my brain can't focus on anything other than Riley being in proximity to Mae right now, chatting to her over the bar even after she's told him to leave her alone multiple times.

His stupid cheesy smile—all gleaming teeth and dimples.

I don't get angry often. I usually keep my emotions in check, but this is fucking killing me.

After swiftly texting Poppy to inform her that I have to get out of something and need her to call me, claiming there's an emergency, I wait for her call. Tapping my foot against the stool I'm sitting on is grating, but the noise serves as a distraction from my whirring thoughts.

My phone buzzes, and I snatch it up, listening intently to Poppy's lie about a pipe bursting in her apartment. The others can hear, and I immediately jump up and tell her I'm coming over.

It's one of the things I love most about my sister. She'll ask questions later, but when someone is in need of help, she'll do it. There and then.

I ruffle Leo's hair before rushing to the front door, Bennett close behind me. He eyes me up suspiciously, his deep brown eyes flickering. "Say hi to Mae for me."

"What are you talking about?"

He releases a scoff as if it's obvious. "Maybe you should work with an acting coach or something in your free time. Your facial expressions give a lot away, Slater."

I curse.

"Cam definitely didn't notice. It's fine." He smiles. "I only gathered because Poppy's not at home tonight. She's at Sophia's house with Madison."

"Look, Bennett, you need to keep it to—" I falter. "Wait, how do you know where Poppy is tonight?"

My best friend shrugs, his face blank. He gazes at me for a few beats, and I can practically see the cogs in his head turning. "I talk to her now and then. She's your sister, so we're practically family, right?"

A sceptical hum escapes my mouth.

"My lips are sealed, Nathan. No need to panic." He pretends to lock up his lips and throws the imaginary key behind his shoulder as I hike my eyebrows up to my hairline.

"Okay, thanks. I need to go."

My friend rests his hand across his heart, allowing his eyes to turn doe-like as he fake pouts. "You're such a knight in shining armour, Nathan. Go and save the girl and kick Riley Donovan's butt. I can't wait to hear all about it."

I roll my eyes as I slip out the door.

The bar stinks of cigarette smoke and liquor, and I crinkle up my nose in dislike, but I immediately forget about it when my eyes land on a hard-working Mae. Her hair is pulled back into a tight ponytail, the front layers hanging by the side of her flushed face.

She's wearing an apron that accentuates her waist, her perfect ass causing my dick to stiffen in my pants.

But I'm not here for that. I want to hear all about Riley's provoking.

"I'll get ten Mai Tai's."

"We don't sell—" Mae double-takes and laughs, wiping the top of the bar with a rag. "What are you doing here?"

"Didn't recognise my voice, princess?" I tut. "We'll have to work on that."

She scowls at me.

"When does your shift end?"

Amber rounds the corner with a tray full of empty glasses. It seems she heard my question as she sneaks a glance at her watch and says, "We aren't busy tonight, Mae. You can head home a few hours early if you want."

Mae's face drops, though. I understand she needs the money, so I reach into my pocket and take out some cash, pushing it into her palm. "There, that should cover more than your wage for the rest of your shift. Come on. We've got... an emergency team meeting." My voice is hushed, but I accentuate the final part as Amber throws a glance our way.

"Nathan, I'm not taking your money. I'm staying."

Amber disappears down into the basement, so I lean in close. "You can either walk out with me, or I'll throw you over my shoulder and carry you outside. I'm not above it, so which one would you prefer?"

"Try me."

"Alright." I click my tongue and move closer to the small wooden doors that separate the customers from the staff, causing Mae to hold up her hands to stop me.

"Okay, fine. Don't get your panties in a twist. I'm coming." Her eyes twinkle with slight amusement.

I know she's secretly enjoying this.

With a small—fake—sigh, Mae follows my lead, grabbing her bag and saying goodbye to Amber and a few regulars before exiting the bar. "Right, what was so important that you had to pull me away from work?" She's still holding my money, and even though she tries to hand it back to me, I stuff it into her bag and open my car door for her.

"You looked like you needed a break." I start the car and head towards the animal shelter, where Mae feels most comfortable. "That, and I wanted to make sure Riley wasn't in there bothering you."

Mae's teeth click shut. "You heard about that."

"I did."

"You can't be annoyed that I didn't tell you, Nathan."

I shake my head, glancing at her. "Why do you immediately assume I'm mad at you, princess? I'm not." I know why—her mother has always made her feel like she's to blame for everything.

Mae scrubs a hand down her face. "Sorry."

"You don't need to apologise. I just want to make sure you're safe. Riley has it out for the Missarali Storks right now, and I don't want him taking his anger out on you."

"I know, I know. It sounds like he's fishing for information, but I think he understands he's not getting anything out of me. He never stays for longer than one drink."

"As long as he's never said or done anything to make you uncomfortable." Agitation rockets through me at the thought of him flirting with her. Eyeing her up while she bends down to grab a glass from the bottom shelf, her top riding up slightly, showing off her smooth, tanned skin.

"Nothing I can't handle," Mae says, face is determined.

"I like a woman who treats shitty men just as shitty."

"It's one of my many talents."

"And what are your other talents?" I cock an eyebrow as we pull up outside the shelter.

Mae's teeth pierce her bottom lip. "Making football players come in under ten minutes."

I hum. "I better be the only one who made you realise you possess that gift."

"And if you weren't?" she asks as we head towards the doors.

I shake my head, glaring at her teasingly. "Then they'd leave the field with more than a few broken bones."

"Careful, Nate," she chirps. "If I didn't know any better, I'd say that you're jealous."

"Oh, I am. Very much so." I hold the door open for her, patting her ass. "Now come on, there's a dog named after a vegetable that's been missing you."

26: Mae

"I didn't know you could cook." I sit on Nathan's kitchen counter, legs swinging over the side as I suck on an apple-flavoured lollipop I found at the bottom of my purse. I'm not much of a candy lover, but I'm jittery and need something to do with myself while Nathan cooks.

We haven't spoken about what's going to happen between the two of us when the season ends, but we both know that this isn't something that looks like it can last.

I think we both *want* it to.

But it can't.

"My mom and I would cook together sometimes," Nathan says. "After football practice. Not often, but I find it calming. It reminds me of her."

I smile at him, tipping my head to the side.

A man that can cook? *Swoon.*

"What was she like?" I hope I'm not overstepping, and when Nathan doesn't even falter, I know I'm not.

"Amazing. Incredible." He smiles as he stirs the tomato sauce he's just made from scratch. "When my Dad was working, she'd take me to the store and would let me pick whatever I wanted to make cupcakes with. We did it all. Chocolate. Cookies and cream. Banana. Cinnamon." He shoots me a wink. "But then she started to drink. It was only on the weekends at first, but that quickly turned into weekdays as well. And soon, she couldn't function without the stuff."

I shuffle closer and cup his cheek. "I'm sure she was still an amazing mother. I know she loved you right until the very end."

"I hope so. I hope... I'm making her proud."

"You are."

Nathan and I settle into silence, but it's not awkward. Instead, we revel in it. We don't need words to fill the space. The quiet between us is warm and familiar.

"It smells amazing." I peer down at the half-cooked roasted vegetables he's flipping over on the tray, sprinkling some extra salt and pepper onto them.

Nathan catches my eye after shoving the tray back into the oven. He steps closer, takes the lollipop from my mouth and places it into his. His nose skates over mine.

Does he have any idea how hard I've fallen for him?

So hard that I'm contemplating my future.

Contemplating actually moving away.

Contemplating what I really want.

Becoming a vet is my dream, but do I really want to restart my whole life? Especially when Missarali is starting to feel like home. The girls on the cheerleading squad are my friends now, and I enjoy it.

I've worked so hard, though, and given up so much.

There aren't any opportunities for me here.

But I just know they'll never be another Nathan Slater. No one will ever make me feel the way he does. Mentally and physically.

Fuck.

Well, isn't this just a shitty turn of events?

Nathan's eyes dart to the scar on my temple, and he skates his finger over it. His expression silently asks if it's okay, and I dip my head in a nod.

"Does it ever hurt?"

I shake my head. "Not anymore." Physically, I'm healed, but mentally, I'm still very much torn up. However, Nathan provides the balm for my fractured mind, smoothing the jagged edges and giving me the peace I didn't know existed. He doesn't try to change me and erase the cracks. He lets me be me.

"You're so beautiful."

I smile, leaning into his touch. "I'm sure that's not what you thought when I first arrived."

"It's exactly what I thought, and I was pissed at you for distracting me."

"Oh, so I'm a distraction?"

He cups my cheeks and places the lollipop back into my mouth. "Oh, the biggest distraction." Nathan's smirk is driving me wild. "You look good on top of my counter."

I study him. "I think I'd look better on top of *you*." The comment slips out, and I blink.

"Is that so?"

"Yes."

He steps even closer. "Is that something you'd like, princess? Would you like to ride my cock?"

My body tenses.

I don't think *like* is the right word. I *need* to.

Nathan reaches behind his shoulder and pulls his T-shirt off with one hand, his eyes remaining on me. An undeniable urge soars through my body, and all I want is his on mine. It's as if I'm starved of oxygen, and I can't breathe without him. He's the only thing grounding me. Making me feel like I'm alive. Making me feel human.

"I'm waiting for an answer, Mae. Tell me what you want."

I place the lollipop on the counter. "You. I want you."

"You want me? All of me?" His lips find my neck, sucking on the sweet spot where my neck and shoulder meet. His teeth graze my skin, and my lips pop open and I tilt my head back to give him easier access. "Is this what you want, princess?"

"Yes. Fuck, yes."

Heat pools between my legs. I've never felt like my body wasn't mine before, but right now, Nathan's the puppeteer. He has complete control of me, and I have no shame in handing over the power.

"You want to be filled with my cock?"

I shiver. There's absolutely nothing else I want more. "More than anything, Nathan."

He pulls back, challenge blazing in his eyes. "Say my full name."

I flatten my lips. I'm a stubborn girl.

His fingers find the back of my neck, and he grips my hair and tugs on it, making a moan slip past my lips.

"More than anything, Nathan Slater," I say, arousal wetting my leggings.

Okay, maybe *not* that stubborn, but a woman can only take so much.

"That's my girl."

His girl.

"I need to get a cond—"

I rest my hands on his chest, rubbing smooth circles. "No, I want to feel you. I'm on the pill. If that's okay with you?"

A smile touches his lips. "I'm absolutely okay with that." His eyes roam my body. "Fuck, I haven't touched a woman in years, but this is well worth breaking that streak."

His soft chuckle vibrates against my skin. After a few seconds, he drops and hitches my legs over his shoulders, pushing me back on the counter and peeling off my leggings. A smirk finds its way to his face as he catches sight of my lacy thong, the fabric cutting into my skin and barely covering me.

"Is this for me?" he asks as he pushes my thong to the side, refusing to enter until I answer. "You have the prettiest pussy, baby."

Baby.

That's three on the list now.

I turn to putty in his arms.

"I'm going to need an answer."

"Yes, it's yours, Nathan," I moan, tilting my head to the ceiling as he sinks two fingers into me. The sound of my wetness fills the room and moves at a tortuous pace, teasing me.

I hate it but love it at the same time.

His other hand is on my chest, and I rip off my cardigan and tank top as he pulls my underwear from my legs and tosses it behind him. "Part these legs a little more for me." He taps at my inner thigh, and I do as I'm told.

I don't usually like being bossed around, but I'd do anything Nathan asks of me when it comes to this. He can be in charge as long as he likes in the bedroom because I crave his leadership. His attitude. I love the way he claims me.

It isn't long before his lips find my clit, and his tongue swirls around it until I'm a writhing mess on his cold kitchen counter. My back arches, and I grip his shoulders as I rock into his face, chanting his name repeatedly.

"Do you have any idea how long I've wanted to drown in your pussy? How many nights I've spent jerking myself off to the thoughts of you moaning my name?" He smiles.

"Well, this surpasses all expectations, princess. You were fucking made for me."

I lick my lips, staring down at him. My toes are already curling.

"Is this what you like, baby? Being eaten out on my kitchen counter?"

It's clear that Nathan's a fan of dirty talk, and I love it equally as much, so when he tells me how unbelievable I look with his fingers shoved inside of me, I feel the stinging sensation of my rising orgasm.

"Nathan! Oh, fuck!"

Nathan groans into my pussy as I come on his face, fingers pumping into me quicker. I study the liquid dripping down his chin as he pulls away. "You're perfect. So perfect."

"I thought about you, too," I admit, catching my breath. "In the beginning. I was so annoyed at you, but all I really wanted was to swallow your cock."

Nathan hosts me off the counter and up into his arms, dropping down onto the floor so I'm straddling his waist. "Is that why you were so sassy with me? Because you were really just pissed off that you couldn't have my cock?"

"Yes... and I may have thought you were an asshole."

He hums, fingers twirling around my nipples, tweaking them. "Still think I'm an asshole, Mae?" His thumb presses down on my clit, making me jolt.

"No," I tell him, all breathy. "No, not at all."

"Good. Now that you're nice and wet for me, show me what you were imagining doing to me while you were fucking your pussy alone at night." He arches his eyebrow at me—as if to challenge him on the fact I've touched myself over him.

He isn't wrong.

I lean down to kiss him, cupping his cheeks, my fingers grating over his stubble. My hips rise, and one of my hands moves down his body to grip the base of his cock, pushing it against my entrance.

But I tease him, even though I'm so desperate that I feel like I might burst.

"You're so fucking wet." Nathan watches me with so much intensity as I swirl his head against my wetness. "Fuck, you're killing me. You know that, right?"

"Uh-huh."

A gasp suddenly escapes me as he raises his hips, causing a few inches of him to sink into me. I kick my head back in pleasure.

"Nathan, fuck..." I mutter. "It's—it's too fucking big."

"You can take it, though, can't you?" He tilts his head to the side, waiting for an answer.

"Yes, I can take it."

"Good girl."

I place my hands against his chest and raise myself, sliding up and down his length. It feels incredible. I'm absolutely stuffed, and the delicious stretching sensation causes me to whine.

"Look at you. Fucking my cock. Taking it like a good fucking girl."

I had no idea Nathan would have such a dirty mouth on him. But it makes this all the better. I've always been a sucker for praise during sex, and fuck, is Nathan telling me what a good job I'm doing.

I bounce on top of him as both of our hands roam.

His on my ass.

Mine on his chest.

His on my tits.

Mine on his hips.

We can't get enough of each other, and our moans of pleasure sync up.

I want to give myself over to this man completely. I need it. *He* needs it. I can tell by how he's looking up at me—eyebrows furrowed and teeth gritted.

Nathan sits up, resting his back against the counter. He places two hands behind his head and watches me in awe.

"Fuck, you fucking know how to ride my cock, baby. You're doing such a good job."

My pussy is clamping onto him with each time I raise and lower my hips, tits bouncing.

But it's not long until Nathan can't take it anymore. He flips us over and begins pounding into me, his hips perfectly aligned with mine.

"Wider, baby," he tells me, gripping my hipbones as he thrusts. "Let me get deep in that pretty pussy of yours."

His words cause me to ache, and I stretch myself wider for him. I'm pretty flexible, and my knees are almost to the floor on either side of me.

"Right there," I instruct him as he hits my sweet spot. "Fuck, Nathan, right there." My fingers find my clit after spreading my wetness over it, and Nathan watches with dark eyes as he focuses on pumping in and out of me at a pace that has me writhing beneath him.

My head falls back. "Shit, I think I'm—"

"You're not coming again just yet, baby. Not until I say so, " he says with a chuckle as he pulls out of me, and I whine in frustration.

I was so fucking close.

"Asshole," I grunt.

He picks me up and wraps my legs around his waist, pushing me up against the wall of his kitchen. The cold sensation makes me arch my back into him. He slips his cock back in, and we both release a breath of contentment.

"Your cock is so big," I grunt, leaning my head back against the wall as I'm fucked into oblivion.

The sound of wet slapping fills the room, and my entire body throbs.

"Have I mentioned to you how perfect you look like this?" Nathan asks, slowing down, eyes level with me. "Pussy full of *my* cock. Mouth moaning *my* name. Against *my* kitchen wall."

He's sliding in and out of me at a tormenting pace as he drags his lips over my collarbone, his stubble grating against my flushed skin.

"Please, Nathan." I attempt to swallow. "Please. Fuck me faster. I need to come. Please."

"A princess gets whatever she wants." He returns to his previous pace, wild and unhinged.

Cries of pleasure fall from my lips as he slams into me. I swear the wall is shaking, but I can't bring myself to care.

Everything is Nathan right now. Nothing else matters. We don't know how long we'll have with each other, so right now, it's just us. Reality can come later.

"Come for me."

I'm reduced to a puddle of hormones, with his tough hands gripping me like I might disappear into thin air. He works into me like it's our last day on Earth, and to be honest, now that we've *really* broken our contracts, it might be.

"Shit. I'm—I'm gonna..." I whimper.

"Let me hear it." One of Nathan's hands reach around and press against my clit, the pressure sending me over the edge. "Come around this cock, Mae. Let me fucking hear it."

And I do. I come so hard that I can't see anything other than a flash of white light. My body is shaking, and pleasure wracks through every cell in my body as I clench around Nathan's cock, calling his name. My fingernails dig into the back of his neck tightly as if my life depends on it.

He continues to rock into me, cock hitting just the right spot every time, and after a few seconds, he grunts. "Mae, fuck…"

Hot liquid fills me, a sheen of sweat coating both of our bodies.

My heart is working overdrive, pumping so erratically that for a second, I'm concerned I'm having a heart attack. But I feel no pain—only pleasure.

It isn't until minutes later that my body has calmed down. I still have my arms wrapped around Nathan's neck, but he's placed me on the couch and has a wet cloth in his hands.

"You're going to need to let me go eventually so I can clean you up." A chuckle rises from his throat, and I release him and rest my head back as he wipes me, his eyes glinting as he watches himself seep from my pussy.

"We have a problem," I say.

Nathan's eyes round, and he looks concerned. "What?"

"Now that I've had this, I'm going to want it again and again." A laugh bubbles from my chest.

"Well, it's a good thing I'm prepared to *give* it to you again and again, then, isn't it?"

"You have the face of a woman who's no longer sexually frustrated." Flo grins at me from her side of the couch.

I bite into my slice of pizza, nodding towards the TV. "Good show."

"Oh, fuck." She flails her arms and crawls towards me. "Something happened between you and Nathan. Fucking tell me now."

My face remains neutral. "How do you know something's happened?"

"The fact you haven't actively denied it means I'm right." She releases a squealing noise similar to a pig. "My best friend is getting the pickle."

"Flo, I hate it when you call it that."

She cups my cheeks, forcing me to drop my pizza back down in the box. "Does *the* Nathan Slater have any hot friends? I want a football player."

I wiggle my eyebrows. "Evan's single. You want to be a mommy?"

"I'll be *his* mommy," she jokes, and I smack her away with a laugh. "I hope you're ready. I can see it now. You'll be on the front page, clinging onto Nathan's arm as you walk into a fancy restaurant in Paris, ready to dine with the other millionaires of the world. My best friend is gonna be famous."

"I can't think of anything worse than being followed around my whole life."

My best friend snorts. "It wouldn't be your *whole* life. Just until Nathan dwindles to irrelevancy. And judging by his age, that shouldn't be too far away."

"Do you possess a filter, or were you just born without one?"

Flo groans, flopping back on the couch. "God, you sound like my mother. Speaking of, how's yours?"

I snort. "Is that even a question?"

My best friend sighs. "You're right. Sorry."

It isn't until now that I realise how tired Flo looks. Even the layer of concealer she's wearing isn't disguising her under-eye bags. "How's work?" I pry.

"Killing me." Flo works for a talent agency. They work with a bunch of celebrities, and she's always getting invited to fancy dinners and lavish parties—events she tries not to attend. "My clients are driving me crazy. Ella Baxter is a bitch. There I said it!"

On a chuckle, I say, "Really? Her music's pretty good, though."

"I know, and that's what makes it worse! I wanna kill her, but at the same, I don't because then she'd stop singing. My ears need that woman's voice."

"Why don't you just quit?"

"Mae, I am so close to a promotion, I can practically taste it. I don't want to give up now."

I beam at her. "That's the spirit."

My phone pings, and I snatch it up, staring at the screen. The world seems to freeze around me. I only pick up on a few words in the email because my heart is rattling against my ribs so hard they feel like they might break.

Congratulations.

Veterinary nurse.

Acceptance.

Florida.

I release a yelp.

"What?" Flo demands, eyes wide like saucers.

I'm still staring.

"Mae, tell me!"

"I got accepted..." My voice trails off. "Fuck, a practice accepted me, Flo."

My best friend wraps her arms around me. "Oh, shit! I knew you would. I'm so happy for you. Where is it?"

My body feels cold. "Florida."

Florida.

As in states away... Florida.

Flo tries to hide her sadness, but she forces a smile. "I'm so proud of you. You're gonna love Florida. You'll get so tanned!"

A laugh trickles out my throat, but even though I should be jumping for joy, I'm not. In fact, my body is filled with disappointment.

Dread.

Regret.

While this was my main goal when I first moved here, I'm beginning to feel my stomach churn at the thought of leaving Missarali.

And it's fucking scaring me.

27: Nathan

Mae and I fuck anywhere and everywhere. At halftime during games. After practice. Evenings off. I've never felt this way for anyone, and it fucking sucks that I have to pretend she's nothing more than a friend when we're around other people.

As Bennett said, I'm not great at acting.

Whenever the Missarali Storks win a game, she's the first face I want to see. The first person I want to hug, and it takes all my strength not to turn to her and wink whenever I score a touchdown.

The media would undoubtedly eat that shit up.

I'm tired. So fucking tired. Football drains me, and I know everything would be so much easier if I were to retire. But we *have* to win. My mother wanted this for me. I need to do this for *her*.

"You look like shit," my sister says, and her gaze shifts to my phone on the counter, which has pinged for the seventh time in the last fifteen minutes since she arrived at my house.

It's our father. The Missarali Storks had another press conference, and he specifically told me that I looked like I wanted to drop dead.

Apparently, there's no passion behind my eyes anymore, which concerns him. I think he's worried I'll fly off the handle, but I'm not sure why he's only just bringing it up now. My passion for football died long ago.

My phone pings again.

"Is that him?" Poppy narrows her eyes and snatches my phone from my kitchen counter before I can stop her. She reads the messages aloud, cursing. "Jesus, Nathan. Does he always use language like this with you?" She grimaces in revulsion. "You know, it would be so easy for me just to call him up and—"

I shake my head. "What would that accomplish? I don't want you on his radar, Pops."

"Nathan, you're my brother." She gives me a *I don't give a fuck about him* look.

"It won't change anything. He'll be snapping at my heels until we win. And I can't quit until we do."

"Because of your mom."

It feels like someone's just punched me in the gut. Poppy and I don't speak about my mother often, but she knows everything she needs to about the situation.

"Look, Poppy, my relationship with my parents is and was complicated. I don't—"

I'm cut off by someone knocking on my front door.

Either Bennett and Evan are here to pester me, a fan has discovered where I live, or Mae's here.

I inhale deeply.

"Who's that?"

I pinch the bridge of my nose as my sister gestures for me to open the door, raising her eyebrows at me questionably.

"Are you gonna answer that or sit there like a frozen woolly mammoth?"

I scoff at the analogy before staring at the door. I don't have any other choice.

I pull it open.

Mae stands on my porch with a bunch of ingredients in her arms, and she strolls in. "I bought some stuff to make some carbonara, and then I was thinking we could stop by the shelter and take Radish for a—oh."

She gazes at Poppy wide-eyed, and my sister's mouth hangs open. She shuffles off her stool and laughs out loud. "So, she knows the code to your gate, huh?" A loud hum fills the room. "I see."

"Poppy, it's—"

"Don't try and tell me it's not what it looks like." She's grinning ear to ear. "Renee would have a meltdown if she knew about this." My sister doubles over as she laughs, bracing her hands on her knees. "I had my suspicions, but I love this."

Mae rolls her eyes and dumps the ingredients on the counter. "Poppy, okay, I'm not even going to try and deny it, but you seriously can't tell anyone."

My sister fake scoffs. "What do you take me for? My mother didn't raise no snitch."

"Right," I say, bracing myself against the kitchen island. "I know you love gossip, but please keep this to yourself. I'll buy you a new laptop for school if you promise not to say anything."

"I can't believe you'd even try and bribe me into silence, and just because you did, I'll take that laptop as payment."

I cock an eyebrow. I'll buy her the most expensive one there is. "Done."

I want nothing more than to announce to the world that Mae is mine, but then I'll have to kiss the Missarali Storks goodbye. Those boys are my life. They keep me—mostly—sane. And if I've come this far just to fall at the last hurdle, I don't know how I'll feel.

I also know Mae doesn't deserve to be thrown into the limelight. She doesn't deserve to be part of some scandal. Not when she's working so hard to find a vet practice that'll take her.

Poppy shrugs on her coat. "Well, I should get going." She shoots Mae a wink. "Please wait until I'm off the premises before you start fucking. As much as I love you both, it's the last thing I want to hear."

I release a strained chuckle and walk my sister out, making sure she is indeed off the premises before I throw Mae over my shoulder and onto my bed, sinking into her and making her come over and over again for me.

The way she smiles at me with adoration when I clean her up reminds me how much I love this. How much I want this.

But it's always the things I want the most that I can't have.

The girls have just finished practice, and we cross over as ours is about to begin. My father's been calling me non-stop today, but I haven't picked up. I'm usually good at putting up with him, but with my head feeling as frazzled as it is, I don't have the patience to deal with him today.

I should be excited about getting closer to the Super Bowl. But I know that one step towards it means another away from Mae.

She appears dead behind the eyes as I cross her in the tunnel. She tries to force a smile, but it doesn't fool me. It's the way she looks whenever she leaves practice with her mother.

Defeated.

She may get over it quickly, but I can't help but feel infuriated with Renee Bexley. Her words hurt her daughter, and even though I know Mae's learned to enjoy cheerleading now, her mother doesn't make it easy for her.

I attempt to catch Mae's gaze again, but Sophia's already slung her arm over her shoulder and is asking if she's okay.

Poppy catches my wrist as the others head to the locker room. "Renee was extra hard on her today. Said some things that were just plain nasty. Just so you know."

My eyes shift to Renee straightening her tracksuit—because even the tiniest crease disgusts her—and I release a sigh of frustration.

"Thanks, Poppy."

My protectiveness flourishes. No one is going to make Mae feel less than perfect, especially not her control freak of a mother.

"Wanna tell me what your problem is today, then?" I ask Renee as I waltz over to her in the middle of the field. No one else is around.

She scoffs. Even the fact that I'm talking to her doesn't sit well with her. "Do I look like I have a problem?"

"Sounds like you do."

A small smile of realisation appears on her face, and she nods, rolling her eyes. "How I speak to my cheerleaders is none of your business. I give all my girls constructive criticism. Why do you care?"

I sigh. I don't know how to get my point across without giving away that I see Mae as more than a professional partner. I'm really trying to bite my tongue here.

"Sounds like it's a little more than a constructive criticism. In fact, I've heard out of everyone on the team, you treat Mae the worst. Want to tell me why that is?"

Renee's face contorts. "And you're speaking to me like I'm a child because...?"

I arch an eyebrow at her. "You got something against your own daughter?"

She's silent.

"Cat got your tongue now?" I shake my head, reminding myself I need to be nice. "Listen, Renee, I've got to know Mae a little since we've been partners. She's become good friends with my sister, and I don't understand how you have it in you to treat her the way you do."

"You don't know anything about me, Nathan Slater."

"And I don't want to," I respond. "But the way you treat my sister's friend," it pains me to refer to Mae as that, "is not fair. Do you know how lucky you are to have a daughter who tries with you after all you've done?"

"You don't know the half of it."

But I do. I know about Mae's father. I know the effect his PTSD had on the family. I know Renee feels alone. I know she projects her inner turmoil onto other people.

"I don't need to. You're pushing her away, which will only hurt you more in the long run. She's your flesh and blood. You probably don't care, but I don't have a mother. I wish I did, but I don't. You don't realise how lucky you are to have a child, or two for that matter, that stick by you. I'd do anything to be in their position, so stop taking family for granted because they're all you've got."

She's stunned.

"That's coming from someone who wishes their mother was still around. Things can change in the blink of an eye. Don't waste the time you have with them by being... well, *you*." I turn and walk away without another word.

I want to tell her I know it all. I know everything there is to about Mae, and I see the good things in her that her mother refuses to.

If she won't support her daughter, then I will, and I'll do it without complaint because caring for Mae Bexley is no skin off my back.

"There's the star of the NFL!" Emmanuel hollers as I walk into the store. He rushes over to me, gripping my shoulders. "Your last game was incredible. I'm so proud."

"Thanks, Emmanuel." I nod a greeting to his son, who's unloading boxes. "How are sales going?"

The man's face drops as he sighs. I can tell he's trying to be nonchalant about the situation in front of his son, but Emmanuel's store isn't doing well. "Not as good as I would like. We've sold one bottle today. One. Profit is barely over ten dollars."

I've offered Emmanuel financial assistance countless times, yet his pride stops him from accepting. I get why. He created this business from the ground up and doesn't want me rescuing him. Even when I've tried to boost his sales by buying wine, he refuses to sell it to me, knowing I don't drink and won't have any use for it.

The store was a booming business when it first opened.

One: because my mother was one of his top customers when we moved.

And two: because people were excited about something new.

But now that the store's old and outdated, it blends in.

It's no longer shiny and new.

People would prefer to purchase from a billion-dollar company rather than a man trying to make a better life for his family. If Emmanuel's store doesn't get the footfall soon, though, he'll be forced to close it. And I can't bear the thought of him losing everything he's worked so hard for.

It's why I come and help him. I know he can't afford to hire staff to restock the shelves and clean the floors, so I will. For free. Because it's the least I can do for him.

I don't care how many times he protests.

Grabbing the mop from the utility closet, I fill the bucket with soapy water in the break room. I ignore Emmanuel's glowers, working on the floor coated with muddy footprints.

His son snickers behind the tower of boxes, and I throw Emmanuel a humoured smile before ducking my head down.

The bell rings, and I whip around as that sweet, fruity scent I adore so much smacks me in the face.

I blink in shock. Mae beams at me before turning to Emmanuel. "Hi, I'm looking for a few bottles of wine."

I told her about Emmanuel's store a little while ago. About how I'm concerned he'll be forced to shut because of lack of customers, so here she is, purchasing from him even though I know for a fact she needs all the money she can get.

I don't interrupt. Instead, I get lost in my thoughts, smiling to myself.

How does someone so effortlessly good exist in a world that doesn't deserve it?

Mae's not doing this for my approval. My praise. She's doing this because she knows what Emmanuel means to me. What his store means to me.

I marvel at how perfect she is. How perfect she is for *me*. But she doesn't wear perfection like most people do. She's perfectly *imperfect*. Authentically herself. Her humility is quiet. But clear as day to me.

"These are perfect," Mae says as Emmanuel suggests a few options. She clutches three bottles in her hands and waltzes up to the counter.

She works hard to make her money. She doesn't have it sprouting out of her ears like some, and I know this wine will put a dent in her bank account.

But she's an independent woman who can make her own decisions. If this is what she wants to do, who am I to second-guess her?

Emmanuel doesn't seem to recognise Mae from months ago, or if he does, he decides not to say anything. I see joy spiralling in those grateful eyes of his, and after Mae pays and leaves—shooting me a wink—he turns to me and says, "Well, things are looking up."

I watch as Mae drives away in her rental car, which looks like it's going to fall apart any day now. My lips tilt into a smile. "Yeah, they are."

Who would have thought that the cocky and impenetrable Nathan Slater would melt like butter for a girl?

Not me.

And yet, here I am.

28: Mae

I really thought the second I got accepted, I'd be booking my flights and packing my bags, but I haven't even responded to the vet practice.

I'm sitting on it.

Thinking.

Or, more like stalling.

I need to get my ducks in a row before making a decision I could regret later.

But I only have a certain amount of time before they move on to the next candidate and offer them the place instead.

"So, how long exactly have you been fucking my brother?" Poppy stares at her fingernails as she paints them in the bedroom of her apartment.

I flop down on her bed, covering my face with her pillow.

"The only reason I'm not pulling that off you so I can see if your face is blushing is because I've got wet nails, so consider yourself lucky," Poppy says, followed by a giggle.

I owe her an explanation. I know she's happy for us, but guilt still stabs me in the chest, knowing I was hanging out with her and sleeping with her brother without telling her.

"Not long."

"Is that all I get? Mae, I want details."

I grimace in disgust. "You want details on me fucking your brother?"

Poppy shivers. "No, not like that. Just—you know what I mean? I wanted—Ew. I'm thinking about it now."

I burst into laughter. "I'm sorry I didn't tell you."

She makes a loud *pfft* sound as she waves my concern away. "Please, don't apologise. I just feel bad you have to put up with Mr Grumpy pants for... how long are you actually staying for?"

My mouth goes dry, and I swear I swallow my tongue. I don't even know the answer. I seriously need to talk to Nathan about this because we're in this waist-deep now.

"Um, I don't know."

Poppy sighs. "I thought you might say that. Still heard nothing from a practice?"

Looking into her ocean-blue eyes, there's no way I can lie. She'll see right through me anyway. "Well, actually, I heard from one place. In Florida. But I don't even know if I'm going to accept it yet. It's so far away."

A smile breaks out on Poppy's face as she blows on her metallic white nails. "You're not sure about going because you'd miss me too much, right?"

I roll my eyes, but she's right. "Yeah. And your brother."

"And my brother." She sits herself down on the bed beside me.

"It's just hard to know the right thing to do."

"Tell him, Mae. Talk to him about it. I know he'll appreciate it."

I nod. "You're right. I will" I nudge her shoulder with mine. "Wow, Poppy. It's like you're studying for a psychology degree or something."

She shoots me a wink. "Just doing what I do best. But seriously, Mae, if you do leave, I'll miss you like crazy." Her face drops, teeth scraping against her bottom lip as she sighs.

"I'll miss you too, Pops."

My mother hasn't spoken to me since three days ago when she was in a bad mood during practice. Granted, we never really converse much, but she didn't say anything even when I used my left foot to move forward instead of my right during practice today. And I *know* she noticed.

I'm watching the girls during their halftime performance on the Missarali Storks Stadium field. Poppy winks at me as she twirls, and I let out a loud "Whoop."

The crowd is going wild, and I shuffle back until I'm hiding in the tunnel, wanting to find Nathan. The Detroit Eagles and Missarali Storks are neck and neck, and I know he's panicking.

I'm also preparing to tell him about my placement in Florida later.

I'm worried he'll tell me to go. To go and not look back. I don't know how to explain to him that being with him in Missarali is tiers above moving states away and restarting my life, even if I once thought it was all I wanted.

But as I walk through the corridor, someone clears their throat behind me, and I jump, slamming into a hard chest. I blink a few times, craning my neck to look up at the giant of a man before me.

Kevin Slater.

"Oh, excuse me," I say as I take a step backwards.

"No worries... Mae."

My throat constricts. I have no idea how Nathan's father knows my name. But he does. "You know who I am?"

Kevin beckons me over to the corner with a nod of the head. I'm under the impression that he wants to talk to me about Nathan and his performance, and I prepare myself to tell him that he doesn't need the added pressure. Nathan's fighting for his life out on that field, and no amount of criticism is going to make him play better.

However, it seems I'm wrong about the topic Kevin Slater wants to discuss with me. So very wrong.

Because in his hands are photographs.

Of Nathan and I.

On dates.

In his car.

In the stadium locker room—me, smiling up at him with my hands laced around his neck.

He flicks at them.

"Where the fuck did you get these?" My blood runs cold, and I try to snatch the photographs from his hand as sweat trickles down my spine. My words hang heavy in the air, suffocating me.

My thoughts are spiralling. I can't think straight.

"It doesn't matter how I got them," Kevin begins. "What matters is what you do next. My son is a very talented player. He *will* take his team to the Super Bowl, but he won't be able to do that with you stuck to him like a leech."

I recoil.

I'm the leech? Ha, Kevin should see what he's saved as on his son's phone.

"Nathan doesn't need any distractions, and you, my dear, are a big one that could cost him his title as team captain. I can't have my son sneaking around with a *cheerleader*, of all people."

I'm so fucking ready to launch my fist into this man's nose.

He uses the word 'cheerleader' as an insult.

I know Nathan and I shouldn't be sneaking around, but this isn't just a fling. It's not just sex. "We happen to care about each other."

Kevin chuckles. "He cares about football, Mae. That's all he cares about."

He's wrong. Because Nathan Slater doesn't *just* care about football.

He cares about his peanut butter and jelly sandwiches being made with the jelly first because he claims it makes them taste better.

He cares about always having the same lemon-scented laundry detergent stocked in his laundry room because he hates the scent of the flowery ones.

He cares about making sure Radish is fed a high-protein kibble you can only buy from select stores, and he donates money to the shelter so they can provide it for him.

He cares about *me*. I see it in the way he looks at me. The way he traces my scar with the pad of his thumb, asking me about what my father was like. The way he smiles at me, those adorable crinkles appearing beside his eyes. The way he scans the stadium for me, face subtly lighting up when his gaze lands on me.

"And what if I tell you to go fuck yourself?"

He shrugs. "I thought you might say that. Tell me, Mae." Kevin pauses for dramatic effect. "Do you want paparazzi following you around everywhere? Do you want your name plastered on the cover of every sleazy tabloid, with these pictures printed for everyone to see? I could make that happen. And in the process, I'm sure all hope of reconciling things with your mother would be lost."

The metallic taste of panic sits on my tongue.

"I assume these veterinary practices research their applicants, correct? Do you really think they'd accept someone connected to such a scandal? With this dragging behind you, I imagine it'll be incredibly hard to find a job in that field." The words roll off his tongue with deliberate slowness, the condensation accentuated.

Kevin is right. If these photographs are leaked, I'll never get accepted by a practice.

Animals. It's all I'm good at.

"Why would you want to get your own son kicked off the team?"

"Nathan would receive offers to sign with other teams. He'd be snatched up in seconds. You, however, would be named and shamed. Your life will never be the same, Mae. Everything you've worked so hard for. Gone." His fingers snap. "Just like that."

My body feels numb, and I lean back against the wall and inhale. This isn't happening right now. There's no way in hell I'm actually being blackmailed by Kevin Slater.

"Do you seriously have no shame?"

Kevin's wrinkled face is blank. "I'll do anything to ensure my son achieves this. I won't allow him to throw it away for..." He looks me up and down. "Some whore."

"Excuse me." I poke him in the chest. "You don't know a damn thing about me. Or your own son, for that matter.

You're living through him. You want him to achieve what you never could just to feel some sense of accomplishment."

Kevin taps his foot impatiently, glancing at his watch. "Think about it, Mae. I can get these photos out by the end of the game. I don't care about Nathan's image. I don't care about how he looks to the media. All I care about is him lifting that trophy, so don't underestimate what I'll do to ensure that happens. Make the right choice."

I can hear the crowd settling down. Halftime is coming to an end, which means I'm expected back out there.

"Well?" Kevin hikes his eyebrow up.

My nostrils flare, chest burning. If these photos get out, Nathan's image will be ruined. He lives and breathes the Missarali Storks. Not only are they his team, but they're his family, and getting kicked off would crush him.

He wouldn't want to sign a contract with anyone else.

He's worked so hard to mop up the team's image, and these photos will take them right back to square one. People would see Nathan as a player. Someone who cares about getting his dick wet over football. They wouldn't understand. He'll be eaten alive.

"Cut it off with him, Mae. You have ten seconds before I send these to fifty different tabloids."

I clamp my eyes shut, balling up my fists. As the seconds stretch, my heart begins to ache painfully. I'm tangled up—unable to escape.

Nathan needs to win this for his mom.

And that can't happen if he's not on a team.

"I need an answer, Mae." Kevin waves his phone, showing me the mass email he's already drafted. His finger hovers over the *Send* button, and my stomach flips.

My mouth begins to move without my permission. "I'm leaving anyway. At the end of the season."

He shakes his head. "That's not good enough, Mae. I need you—"

"To Florida." The words feel like ice on my tongue. "I'm moving to Florida. To join a veterinary program. I'll be states away, so I'll never see Nathan again."

He narrows his eyes at me. "You'll never contact him again?"

I'm doing this for Nathan. He won't survive losing his position on this team. It will crush him.

And I won't be able to handle that. The way he speaks about his mom—he *loved* that woman.

I dip my chin, glaring at the narcissistic man before me with gritted teeth. Would I get arrested for stomping on his head? I'd only give him *minor* brain damage.

The impatient tapping of his foot drags me back to reality.

"I won't contact him again." My voice is strained.

Could Nathan and I have been anything anyway?

He needs to focus on his career.

I need to focus on following my dream.

Or what I *thought* was my dream.

Because my priorities are changing.

I thought I knew exactly what I wanted. Who I wanted to be. I spent so long convincing myself that it would make me whole again.

But now I'm here questioning everything—like waking up from a dream where your world has been flipped on its head.

But it's too late now.

Because I know Nathan needs this more than he needs me.

29: Nathan

Mae barely looks at me during the game. I'm so used to her grinning from ear to ear whenever we score a touchdown or field goal, but she keeps her gaze on the crowd, and even when I try to catch her eye, she positions herself away.

We win the game, but it's close, and as I file down the corridor, my father snaps his fingers to gain my attention. I roll my eyes.

"We won, so save the criticism. I don't need it today."

"You're no longer allowed to see Mae."

My Adam's apple bobs up and down as I stare at the man I despise. I take a threatening step forward, towering over him. I'm a few inches taller. "What the fuck did you just say?"

He pulls a stack of printed photographs out of his pocket, and I stare at them with gritted teeth, my pulse skyrocketing. "What the fuck are these?" I snatch them away, but my father isn't fazed, which means these aren't the only copies he has.

The thought of anyone seeing these makes me livid. These moments were supposed to be private between me and Mae. My body shakes. "What are you going to do? Release these? You can't threaten me."

He nods. "I know. That's why I threatened your whore instead."

I snap, grabbing him by the front of his shirt and shoving him against the wall. "Call her a whore again, and I'll break your fucking legs."

My father only shakes his head, stepping away after I loosen my grip. "Is it really worth it, Nathan? Getting kicked off the team? Having your image disassembled?"

"I don't give a shit about myself."

Kevin hums. "But think about her. If you care about her, which, unfortunately, I can tell you do, do you think she'll enjoy being followed around everywhere? Being stopped in the streets to get asked about her scandalous relationship with the famous Nathan Slater? Do you think she'll enjoy seeing her name tarnished—known as a slut and a whore? It'll be awfully hard for her to get a job with a reputation like that."

I curse under my breath. Those are the last things I want for Mae.

"Why continue this when you knew she was leaving anyway? And to Florida of all places." My father cackles.

My face contorts with confusion, and the buzzing of the fluorescent lights above us suddenly sounds ten thousand times louder, the brightness dizzying.

"What?"

A smile forms on my father's face as the realisation hits him. "Oh, you don't know? She's moving to Florida to join a veterinary program. Soon, too, and she agreed never to contact you again. Seems she doesn't like you as much as you think she does."

My stomach twists in the most harrowing way, causing me to almost double over in pain. The last time I'd spoken to Mae about her veterinary program search—which had been around two weeks ago—she'd claimed she hadn't been accepted by anyone yet. I was holding out hope that when she was, it would be by a program close. Somewhere near me so I could still see her.

But Florida is a six-and-a-half-hour flight away.

I hear the voices of the cheerleaders behind me, and I drop my head with a tense jaw, my eyes flickering to a doe-eyed Mae who's gazing at me with parted lips. She hangs back as everyone else files into the locker room.

"You're leaving," I mutter to her, and my father backs up and chuckles as he strolls away, leaving the volcano he's just set off to erupt.

"Nathan, I—"

"How long have you known?"

Mae is silent.

"Mae... how long?"

"A week."

Her reply cuts me like a knife, and I rest my head back against the wall, hands scraping through my hair.

"I didn't know how to tell you," she starts. "I didn't even know how to feel when I got accepted. I wasn't set on going, Nathan. I hadn't made up my mind."

"I wish you'd told me." My voice reveals my disappointment.

"We both knew I was leaving anyway."

"I know, but I didn't know when." My jaw pops.

I'm imagining living my life without Mae. I can literally feel the colour draining from the world around me, leaving it grey and lifeless. Everything will feel wrong. Everything in my life will shift, and knowing I can't stop it... there's a dead weight in my chest.

I don't want to go back to the way things were before. She's shown me I *can* be happy.

"We signed contracts, Nathan. We never should have started this in the first place—not when we both knew I'd be leaving and there was a chance we'd get caught."

I crouch down to her level, eyes lasering into hers. "But we did, Mae, okay? We fucking did, and we can't take it back."

She shakes her head, dropping her pom-poms to the ground. "I won't allow you to lose the Storks."

"But in turn, I lose you." It's a punch in the gut. Everything is blowing up in my face, and I don't know how to handle it. My chest feels hollow, and I raise my eyebrows at Mae, waiting for her to say something.

I'm going to fucking kill my father.

I roll my lips together painfully.

She's worked so hard to get where she wants to be. She's been through so much. The last thing she needs is to have her name blemished. Once the tabloids know you, that's it. There's no escaping.

Her fingers pick at her lips, and I reach forwards and stop her. Even if I am angry right now, I don't want her hurting herself.

I don't hold onto her hand, though. Instead, I place it back by her side, fingers skimming her wrist.

"I can't let this ruin your career. It's not worth it. You've spent years trying to win this for your mom, Nathan. So, after the season ends, I'll leave, and we won't contact each other again."

My heart practically turns to ash in my chest. "You want that?"

Mae's fingers press into her temples, and she rubs, sighing. "No, of course not, but it's no longer about what *we* want. It's more complicated than that."

"It's very complicated," I say. "Complicated because I've allowed myself to develop feelings for you. Feelings I can't stop or take back."

Mae's eyes fill with tears, but she blinks them away. "Me too." She shakes her head, allowing her palm to cup my cheek one last time before she drops it as if she's been burned, stepping past me.

She turns and walks away, and I swear I can hear my heart cracking inside my chest. I watch with dark eyes as she turns down the corridor, taking my love with her.

Because it's not until now that I realise I love her. I *need* her.

And yet, it's not enough.

"Are you sad?" Leo asks me as he squashes my face together, gaining a groan from me.

"No, Leo," I respond, gently prying his hands from my cheeks. "I'm not sad."

I'm fucking heartbroken.

The media likes to paint the Storks as heartbreakers.

And I guess it's true.

I'm a heartbreaker, alright. But it's not anyone else's heart I've broken. It's my own.

"Ease up, Leo," Evan orders his son, taking him into his arms and planting a quick kiss on the side of his head.

"Uncle Nathan isn't sad." Evan's stormy grey eyes flicker to mine. "He's..."

"Miserable? Mournful? Troubled?" Bennet chimes in from the couch, tilting his head to me while he lays there as if he owns it.

"Get your feet off my couch." Evan kicks Bennett, so he tumbles off.

My friends are aware of Mae. They understand me and can easily see when I'm off—every day over the past week. Yet, we haven't discussed it openly, aside from a few check-ins to see if I'm okay. They recognise it's a line not to cross right now.

According to Poppy, Renee has eased up on her daughter. She hasn't made any efforts to reach out and bridge the cavern-sized gap between them, but she's less offensive to her.

Perhaps I got through to her.

Good.

Because I won't be able to sleep again knowing that Renee still treats her daughter like crap.

Even if we don't see each other again.

I've purposely avoided sticking around before or after training because Mae needs time to think about everything right now. I'm the last person she needs to see, and truthfully, I'm still hurt she didn't tell me about Florida. I understand her mind wasn't made up. She was still weighing up her options.

I wouldn't have tried to convince her to stay or go. That's not my place. It's her life, and she needs to live it. But it's a conversation I would have loved to be a part of.

My father's been calling me, trying to talk to me as if nothing happened despite my demands he tell me where he acquired the photos. He's always working in South Dakota, so I know he couldn't have taken them.

I haven't slept. I've spent most of my nights putting the pieces together. Trying to work out who would be pathetic enough to work for my father. The paparazzi came to mind, but there's no way they would have been able to get into the restricted area of the stadium to get near the locker rooms.

There's someone I've been meaning to speak to, though, and knowing he's in the city after returning from a game in Texas, I snatch my phone from the coffee table. He answers after the first ring, and I can hear the smirk in his tone as he says, "Slater, I've been expecting your call. Ready for a chat?"

Riley's voice is as off-putting as always.

My jaw ticks, and Evan and Bennett arch their eyebrows.

"Is that who I think it is?" Bennet wonders, pursing his lips. "Wait until I get my hands on whoever took those photos." He cracks his knuckles, and Leo watches him with adoration, attempting to do the same but bending his little fingers too far back and hurting himself.

Evan shoots a glare at Bennett as I grumble into the phone, grabbing my car keys and nodding goodbye to my friends. "Fine. I'll meet you there."

"I hope you're going to beat someone up!" Bennett yells after me.

I dip my chin in a nod. "Maybe."

I meet Riley in a local gym, heading to the weights section where he's pumping iron. Sweat is trickling down his forehead, and he grins at me. "Nice of you to reach out."

I hum. There's a reason Riley's been hanging around Missarali, and in my head, I'm sure it's because he's been secretly spying on Mae and me. Now that he's back, I can speak to him in person because this isn't a conversation I wanted to have over the phone.

"Let me guess, you're tired of the slander, and you've come to apologise?"

A scoff forms in my throat, but I keep it down. "No, actually."

Riley seems genuinely surprised, and he pushes his damp, light brunette hair away from his face. "Alright, enlighten me, then."

"Kevin Slater... the name ring a bell?"

He laughs—loud and obnoxious. "Well, obviously, he's your daddy."

"Please never use that word again." I grimace. "Have you spoken to him before? Hung out with him?" My nostrils flare. "I think you know what I'm getting at."

He pulls his eyebrows together and shakes his head. "Nathan, this is a first for me, but I genuinely have no idea what you're talking about. No offence, but your father seems like a dick. Why would I want to hang out with him?"

It's frustrating that Riley isn't just admitting he collected the photos for my father. But he has too much pride to deny it. If he really went to all the effort, he sure as hell would want me to know he had one-upped me.

There's no reason why he wouldn't confess to it... unless he actually didn't do it.

"So you've been in Missarali doing what exactly?"

"Working with my new sponsor. Their headquarters are here. We lost our last game, so we're out of the playoffs, and my cousin just moved into the city, so I've been helping him settle in." He shrugs as if it's public knowledge. As if I keep up to date on what he's doing with his life.

Besides the fact that his team lost. I know all about that. And I smiled when I found out.

"The Salty Dog... why?"

Riley rolls his eyes. "It's a quiet bar. It's mostly filled with older people whose eyesight is so bad they can't see who I am. Just because I love the limelight doesn't mean I want to shine all the time, Slater. A man can only take so much."

"You have no idea what I'm talking about? You're sure?"

Riley chuckles, slapping my back. "You get tackled too hard during your last game, Slater? I thought you were here to talk about the comments I've been making to the press."

"I'm not. I don't care about that."

He pauses. "Yeah, you know what? I'm tired of our little feud. The fact that you came here to see me speaks volumes. I'm willing to forgive you." He flashes his whitened teeth at me, and I huff in disbelief.

But in all seriousness, I don't want Riley Donovan against me. I don't need the trouble. He may be a dick, but I have bigger issues than him.

I hold out my hand.

Riley shakes it. "Friends?"

I cock an eyebrow at him. "I wouldn't go that far, Donovan."

30: Mae

"Hi, boy." I grin as I ruffle up the tuft of hair on Radish's head. He has a potential adopter coming today, and the shelter asked if I could be present to see if it helps. He comes out of his shell when around me. "Listen to me, buddy." I crouch down in front of him. "Show them how amazing you are, okay? Give them a few kisses, sit on their lap, all the good stuff. Got it?"

Radish responds with a lick to my cheek, and I hop to my feet as the shelter doors are pushed open.

A short, middle-aged man walks in. He has a friendly face, and his eyes brighten as soon as they land on the dog by my feet.

"Hi, I'm Mae, a volunteer here. And this is Radish." I gesture down. I know the smile I'm faking isn't reaching my eyes. I haven't been getting any sleep, and I must look haggard.

Every inch of my mind is filled with Nathan. I can't even escape him in my dreams.

"Radish?" the man asks, cocking his head as he pets the dog. "Am I stuck with the name?"

My stomach drops. I've always known there's a chance that an adopter wouldn't keep the name, but I can't think of Radish as anything else. He always comes running when I say it, but I need to disassociate myself from our connection.

"Not if you don't want to be," I tell the man as I lead him into the adoption meeting room. It smells like dog shampoo and kibble, and the walls are lined with posters representing the responsibility of pet ownership and insurance costs.

Radish has been in a few times but tends to plop himself down in the corner and nap. I'm praying he picks up one of the toys and shows some personality today.

"Does he know any tricks?"

"Does ripping up root vegetables count?"

"What?"

"Nothing." I shake my head. "He doesn't, but he's a very smart boy. He'll quickly pick up anything you teach him."

The man nods and moves closer to Radish, who is sniffing at my feet. He gazes up at me with adoration, tongue loose and floppy. The man tries to gain his attention, but Radish doesn't drag his eyes from me—not even when the man offers him a treat.

Minutes go by, and Radish doesn't leave my side. Even when I move to the other side of the room and sit in the chipped plastic chair, I'm followed.

"It seems he has a favourite."

I sigh, scratching under Radish's chin. "I swear, he's a great dog when you get to know him. And when he gets to know you."

"I don't doubt that." The man's smiling at me, but then he nods towards the door. "I think I'm done here. Is that okay?"

Disappointment and relief swarm me simultaneously. "Are you sure? I swear you won't regret getting to know him."

The man chuckles, face warm and bright. "It seems he's already made his choice. I can't compete with that. I'll see myself out, thanks, Mae."

I blink as he exits the room, running my hands through my hair before I kneel on the floor and wrap my arms around the proud dog before me.

"Happy with yourself?"

His response is a nuzzle, making me laugh.

I sigh. "You're just like me, buddy." A sad smile stretches my lips. "We haven't quite worked out where we belong."

"So let me get this straight. My father threatened you with photos of you and Nathan? What a piece of shit!" Poppy gags. "And now you and Nathan are...?"

"Nothing," I say, my breathing slightly shaky. "We're nothing."

"Because you're leaving?"

My shoulders rise in a shrug. "And because he'll get kicked off the team."

"So? He hates football." Poppy focuses on her hair she's braiding in her living room mirror. "I mean, he likes it but hates it at the same time. Likes to play it but hates the competitiveness."

"I know, but he's put up with his father's abuse for years so that he can win for his mom. I can't let that all be for nothing."

"It's not for nothing if he has you."

The ground has been pulled from beneath me, and my heart has been wretched from my body. How can something that seemed so right suddenly vanish into nothing?

Memories of our time together flood my mind. Walks with Radish. Home-cooked meals. Sex in his bed where, after, I spent the night curled into his chest, watching chick flicks I know he secretly enjoyed even though he claimed he didn't. I even managed to convince him to try my favourite brand of cinnamon-flavoured ice cream, and despite his belief that he'd absolutely hate it, he actually enjoyed it. I even caught him throwing an extra tub into the shopping cart for himself when he thought I wasn't looking.

"Mae?" Poppy whispers, and it isn't until she sighs that I realise my eyes have welled with tears.

"I love him, Pops." Fuck. I hate crying in front of people. This year, I told myself my New Year's resolution was to let emotions get in the way less… so far, it's going fucking great.

"I know." Tears drip down her own cheeks. "It fucking kills me to see the both of you like this. My brother has never opened up to anyone like he has with you. I can see it in his eyes. He loves you too, Mae. So much. He deserves happiness. You both do. I'm so pissed off it's being stolen from you both."

I dab at my face, worried the tears have smudged my makeup.

"I know you don't want me to get involved, but—"

"No, Poppy. Please, don't. Confronting your dad won't change his mind. It'll make things worse for everyone."

She clicks her teeth shut, looking frustrated. "Okay, fine, but I swear, if I see him in person, I'm gonna crack his spine."

I wipe my face. "We've got to get to practise."

"Can we just skip it?"

"My mom would have your head if she knew you'd said that."

My friend shrugs. "She can have it. With everything going on, I don't want it anyway."

I drive us to the stadium. It's Tuesday, and the guys don't have practice today, so I won't have to see Nathan training from a distance.

Because I can't lie and say I don't watch him when I leave or arrive.

Every time I do, I get flashbacks of his lips on my own, his chest flush with mine and cock stroking into me so incredibly it brings me to multiple orgasms. Just the thought arouses me, and knowing no one will ever compare to him sets me up for a life full of crappy, meaningless sex.

How am I going to settle for anyone else when I want him?

Welcome to a life of celibacy.

There was something about us—we bounced off one another. We were able to understand what the other needed without the use of words. When we needed comfort. Inspiration. Excitement. We were tethered to each other, and now that rope has snapped, I feel like I'm missing half of me.

I'm incomplete.

Madison and Sophia are stretching early on the field, and I plaster a smile on.

"You feeling okay, Mae? You don't look so good," Madison asks, and Sophia shoots me a concerned look. As team captain, she always ensures her team are coping well, and if she sees someone struggling, she'll do her best to help. It's one of the things I like about her.

"I'm coming down with a cold," I lie, hoping they'll stop the questioning. Thankfully, they do.

"Can you guys believe we're four weeks away from the end of the season? We're so close to the Super Bowl!"

Sophia's comment has me jittery. Four weeks until I leave for Florida. Until I say goodbye to Nathan forever. Until I start a whole new life for myself and forget about everything. Until I become the new Mae Bexley—the woman who doesn't have a missing father and controlling mother. Who doesn't have a man she loves but can't have.

"Even less if the guys don't win the game on Sunday," Madison adds.

Oh God, I'm about to throw up my lunch.

"These lights are giving me a headache," I say as I pinch the bridge of my nose, and Sophia hikes her thumb towards the tunnel.

"I have some Tylenol if you need it. It's in my bag in the locker room. Front pocket."

"You're a lifesaver, Sophia." Rushing into the women's locker room, I unzip her bag and rummage through, but I frown when I come up empty-handed.

My headache intensifies, and thinking that Sophia may have accidentally misplaced her Tylenol in her coat instead, I quickly feel around in her pockets. I'm met with her phone, so I pull it out to find the small bottle of Tylenol underneath.

I swallow the pills dry, sitting down on the bench and taking a deep breath.

Can you die from sadness? I swear people have before.

What would happen if my heart were to give out right here in the locker room? What would be written on my death certificate? I'm a victim of a heartbreak-induced fatality?

Heartbreak is weird because it's all in your mind.

Nothing is physically wrong with me. But it feels like someone's taken my heart out, run it over with a truck, and then given it back to me with a smug smile. There are no bruises. No wounds. And I'm expected to go on because I'm only falling apart internally.

Suddenly, Sophia's phone buzzes beside me. I don't pay it any mind, though, resting my elbows on my knees and placing my head in my palms.

Cheering should perk me up a little bit. I enjoy it, and I feel alive dancing on that field. But I'm swapping my pom-poms for a stethoscope pretty soon. And I need to come to terms with the fact that all of this will be gone pretty soon. It was always supposed to be temporary.

Sophia's phone vibrates again. And again. And again.

I try not to read the texts that come through. I really do. But my eyes skate over the screen for a brief second.

Money has been transferred into your account.
Glad we could both get what we wanted.
Now, delete all our messages.
And don't speak about this to anyone.

My spine goes rigid. The texts don't make much sense to me until I see the initials they were sent from.

K.S.

My heart falters, and I feel like I can't breathe. With clammy hands, I pick up the phone, peering at the screen, convinced I've got it wrong.

But I haven't.

K.S

You have to be fucking kidding me.

There's no doubt in my mind who the contact stands for.

Kevin Slater.

I hold up another knitted sweatshirt, and Cam shakes his head at me.

"Mae, Florida has highs of about eighty-eight degrees. I doubt you're going to need a case full of sweaters."

I'm not leaving yet, but like the good big brother Cam is, he's helping me sort through my clothes while our mom is out with some friends.

I wasn't even aware she had friends, to be honest.

"Ew," he squeals like a little girl, throwing an item of clothing onto my lap. "What the hell are *they*?"

"They're hot pants, Cam." I ping them onto his face, and he leaps up as if I've thrown a snake at him.

"I never ever want to imagine you wearing them. That's disgusting."

Cam and I don't get to spend too much time together, and I'm definitely going to miss him when I move. He's promised to come and visit, but I know how busy he is.

He did specify he's never been with a woman from Florida, though, and that the idea tempts him. He was kidding, but there was a kernel of truth to his words.

We laugh, but again, I'm holding back. It's a facade because, deep down, I don't feel like laughing at all. I don't feel like packing my suitcase. And I certainly don't feel like pretending everything is okay right now. Because it's far from it.

Sophia... it was her. I trusted her. I thought we were friends. I don't trust easily, and this is a massive reminder of why. People will often chew you up and spit you out, keeping you around until it no longer benefits them.

I keep thinking this isn't real. That it's some big misunderstanding.

But I'm not stupid. I saw the texts. This was premeditated. Planned. Sophia's a fake, and I wasted so much time with her.

My phoney smile fades when Cam reaches into my drawer and pulls out an item of clothing. His face immediately drops. He holds it up, his white fingers gripping the red and white fabric.

My throat constricts.

The jersey.

The jersey with Nathan's name on the back.

My heart sinks, and I know I've gone as white as a ghost.

"Mae," Cam says slowly, teeth gritted. "What is this?"

I don't know what to say. My mouth is opening and closing like a fish gasping for breath. I'd completely forgotten the jersey was even in there.

My brother looks at me with betrayal, eyebrows tugging together. He drops the jersey, pushing it away from him as if it's poisonous. His fingers are running through his hair, gripping at the brunette strands. "No, no, no. Tell me you're not fucking Nathan Slater, Mae. Please."

I stay silent, my face blank.

"You can't, can you?" Cam growls, standing. "Oh my God, you're fucking him. What the hell, Mae? What the fuck is wrong with you?"

"Nothing is wrong with me." I also clamber to my feet. "It's over between him and I anyway."

"Is that supposed to make it okay? Mae, you have so much going for you. You're better than that. You don't need to have sex with people to get to where you want—"

I hold my hand up to stop him. "Don't give me a speech on how I don't need to fuck my way to the top. I'm well aware of that. I didn't want anything like that from Nathan. I'm not some gold digger, Cam."

"No, I know you're not, but—"

"It's the complete opposite of what I was doing. I didn't do it to gain anything. I actually care about Nathan."

My brother's face is red. "Well, does he care about you? Because I would bet my left leg he just sees you two as—"

Anger courses through me. "You don't know anything about Nathan, do you? Sure, you're his physiotherapist, but that doesn't mean you know him on a personal level, Cam."

He's taken aback. "What? And you do?"

I remain silent.

"Fuck, Mae. Nobody can know about this, okay?"

"I already know that."

"I swear to God, if he hurt you—"

"He didn't hurt me, Cameron Bexley." He jumps at the way I use his full name. Our father used to do it. "In fact, I'm probably the one who hurt him."

Guilt hits me point blank in the chest. I feel like a stone sinking in water—gradual at first, but as time goes on, it gets deeper and deeper. There's no swimming my way back up to the top now.

"It wasn't just some fling, Cam," I say, my voice cracking.

My brother doesn't know what to do. He stares at me, jaw set and mouth curving downwards. He rubs a hand down his face. "I have no idea what Mom was thinking getting you involved in all of this."

I scoff. "You don't need to try and make me feel worse than I already do, Cam." I try to keep everything in, but my throat betrays me, and a small sob lurches up. I cover my mouth with my hand in an attempt to quieten it.

My brother's eyes soften, and he immediately stalks towards me and pulls me to his chest. He rubs my back soothingly as he curses. "You made a mistake, Mae. It's okay. You're gonna be okay. Florida will be good to you. I'll make sure of it. You can put this all behind you. It was just a mistake; it's fine."

My heart rattles against my ribs as tears leak from my eyes.

Cam's right. I did make a mistake. But it wasn't getting involved with Nathan. It wasn't opening up to him. Or letting him see parts of me that no one else ever has. Nor was it falling in love with him.

No.

My mistake was letting go of one of the best things I'd ever had in my life.

Even if the world is against us.

31: Nathan

"Stop pouting. You don't have the lips for it," Poppy says as she waltzes up to me inside The Salty Dog. She texted me and demanded I meet her here, and I didn't dare refuse—after making sure Mae wasn't working. If there's one thing I know about my sister, she doesn't take no for an answer.

I sip on my water. I'm well aware I'm dead behind the eyes.

"You played like shit yesterday," my sister tells me. "Something on your mind?"

"I don't need someone else on my back," I say, pulling the brim of my red cap down.

Poppy's lips curl in disgust. "Don't even think about comparing me to our pig of a father. Unlike him, I don't give a fuck how you play, Nathan. As long as you're happy." She sighs. "And you're not happy."

"That psychology degree is serving you well."

"For once in my life, I'm not in the mood for jokes." Poppy's tone is serious, and she stares at me in desperation. "Please. Talk to me."

"You want me to talk to you about Mae?" My hands curl around my frosted glass of water. The sharp, stinging sensation feels good.

"She thinks she's saving you from swirling down the drain."

I cock my head.

"God, am I talking to a caveman? Mae wants to be with you. She doesn't want it to be the end for you two, but you let football get in the way." Poppy shakes her head. "Nathan, I know you want to win the Super Bowl for your mom, but I'm here telling you that your mother would prefer you to be happy than lift some stupid silver trophy in her name."

At the mention of my mother, my lungs tighten. "Her death can't be for—"

"Nothing... I know." Poppy releases a long breath. "I understand your logic. I do. But you're throwing your life away for someone who's no longer around. I know you think you're nothing if you don't have football, but that's not true. You're more than a football player, Nathan." Her eyes fill with tears. "You're my brother."

Fuck. Seeing my sister cry breaks my fucking heart.

I step forward off my stool and wrap my arms around her. "But the photos. Mae's career."

Poppy pulls away from my chest. "If you two love each other as much as I think you do, it's something you'll be able to work through. Look me in the eyes and tell me you love her. Forget about being cringy and mushy for a second. I'm a girl. I love that shit. Just do it."

I stare at her, eyes so starkly different to mine. "I've never met anyone like her, Poppy. Of course I love Mae. More than anything."

"Anything?" She quirks a brow.

"Anything," I clarify.

"Okay, good. Think about that last part for me, okay? Because that's all I wanted to hear." She takes a casual, loud sip of my water, blinking back her tears from seconds ago. "Be selfish for once. Please. No offence, but you're in your thirties, Nathan." A small smile marks her face. "Are you going to look back at this moment and be thankful you let Mae go? Be proud that you chose football over your happiness?"

I gulp. "No." It's a simple answer. I don't even need to think about it.

"I've been in contact with a certain someone who works for a talent agency, too. I have a feeling she can help soften the blow if you two decide to let the photos go public."

I shake my head at my sister. "Pops, what have you been up to?"

She grins. "Saving your ass. What are annoying little sisters for?"

I inhale deeply as I pull her back to my chest.

I love and hate how fucking right she is.

I've spent so long stuck on the fact that I need to do this for my mother. I kept pushing forward, hoping that if I won, everything would make sense. Everything would be worth it.

But now, even though I always knew it deep down, I see it for what it is—a dead weight pulling me down and stopping me from being who I want to be. Who I need to be.

My mom wouldn't want this for me. She wouldn't want me wasting my life trying to be something I'm not. I'm sure she would have loved to have watched me lift that trophy. Who wouldn't want that for their son? But she's not here anymore, and I can't let my life wither away trying to do something I know won't make me feel better in the long run.

Because winning the Super Bowl won't bring my mom back.

A strange sense of relief spreads through me. It feels like I can finally breathe.

I don't know if Mae will be on the same page as me, but if I allow her to leave for Florida without telling her how I feel, I'll regret it for the rest of my life.

There was a time when I thought cone drills were the death of me. Little did I know, they weren't. Not even close.

Mae Bexley is.

And there's nothing about it that upsets me.

I'm staring out at the wave of reporters before me in the Missarali stadium conference room as they flash their cameras and bombard us with questions. The playoffs are starting, and the only reason I'm here is because my team need me.

As of this second, football is all I have.

Only... football can't love me back. It can't make me laugh. It can't comfort me when I need it. It doesn't talk back to me and test my patience in the most enjoyable way.

Mae's the only thing that can do that for me.

"Nathan! Word on the street is that you're dating supermodel Emily Miller. Is that true? Rumours suggest you were spotted together last week."

Fuck, I'm too old for this shit.

I know my annoyance is evident on my face. I don't believe I've ever met Emily Miller, and even if I had, I have no interest in her because she's not Mae.

I glare at the reporter.

I can't wait any longer.

The question makes me push my chair backwards, and I turn to Darrell with gritted teeth. "There's something I have to do."

My coach asks no questions as he nods and waves me away, and I leave the reporters gasping and calling after me as I leave.

I waste no time getting into my car and driving straight to Mae's house. Renee isn't in. She meditates at the stadium early.

If I'm lucky, I'll catch Mae before she leaves for the stadium.

I kill the engine of my Audi. A light on in Mae's house indicates someone's home, and I knock impatiently.

She flings the door open, dressed in sweats and clutching her cheerleading duffel bag. Her body visibly stiffens. "Nathan?"

Fuck, she looks just as beautiful as she did the first time I laid eyes on her.

She looks like... mine.

"Hey, princess." The nickname sounds so right on my tongue.

"What are you doing here?"

"Making sure I don't lose the best thing that has ever happened to me."

Mae's eyebrows furrow as she steps aside, and I enter the house. "Shouldn't you be at your conference right now?"

I shake my head. "Not important."

"Then what is important?"

I shut the door behind me. "I'm looking at it."

Mae drops her bag and hums, sighing. She looks at me with soft eyes, dragging her lip into her mouth, her teeth scraping against the plush flesh. She takes a deep breath. "Sophia."

"What?"

A laugh of disbelief bubbles up her throat. "Sophia. It was her who was following us around, taking those photos. I saw a text from your dad on her phone. He paid her to do it."

Resentment surges through me.

And here I thought Sophia was one of the decent ones. But it doesn't matter right now. I can deal with that later. "They're not winning. They don't get to make this decision for us."

"Nathan," Mae sighs, "the Storks. They need you. You need them. I'm not letting you get kicked off the team for—"

"You're not *letting* me do anything, Mae. I'm making this decision. It's on me, and I don't give a flying fuck if they kick me off the team for it. If it means calling you mine, I'll give up football without blinking."

Mae's eyes are wide, her mouth popped open. She raises her eyebrows, a small gasp of exasperation leaving her.

"I know fame might not be something you want, and I'll do anything to make sure you don't have that. Fuck, we can leave Montana and live on some shitty remote island somewhere if it'll make you happy. I'm not losing you. You belong with me."

"But... you love football. I know you claim not to, but deep down, you do."

I cock my head. "Maybe, but not nearly as much as I love you." I cup her cheeks. "You want to go to Florida? Fine, go. But I'll be right there by your side to support you." I pause. "If you'll have me there." A hint of insecurity seeps into my voice.

She's stunned for a few seconds, but she quickly recovers. I watch her expression shift from shocked to something softer. Something warmer. Something... only for me.

Looking at her like this. I know I'm doing the right thing. This is fucking right. *We're* right.

"Does it make things harder that I love you too?"

I chuckle.

"Do I want fame? No, not really, but it wasn't the fame aspect that made me cut things off with you, Nathan. It was the idea of you losing everything you've worked so hard for."

I shake my head. "The Missarali Storks are a successful team. None of it was for nothing. But playing for them... it's not for me anymore. You are."

Mae releases a small laugh, but it looks uncertain. "You'd actually move to Florida?"

"Princess, I'd move to Mars if you were there."

She leans against the kitchen counter, and I hook my finger under her chin. She allows her hand to trickle down the side of my face, fingers grating against my stubble.

But her eyebrows are still pinched together as her gaze drifts over my shoulder, jaw working as she thinks.

"It seems I haven't made myself clear, so I'll reiterate it for you. There's no guilt on your part. You didn't make me do this. I did this. I lost the passion for football a long time ago, at least the competitive side of it, and even though I always told myself I needed to win the Super Bowl to make me feel better about my mother's death, in reality, I know I'd feel just as empty as I did when we weren't champions. All my mother ever wanted for me was happiness. She'd want me to do this. She'd want me to make this decision for myself."

I'm sure my mom has been screaming at me from the sky to quit football for years, but I never listened to her. I allowed my father to get inside my head and control me. I'm not letting that happen anymore, though. I'm not a puppet.

"You're so much more than Nathan Slater, the famous football player, by the way," Mae tells me. "I want you to know that. You're sensitive. Sweet. You're a good cook. You love your team, and you'd protect Poppy with your life. Radish loves you. And so do I. You have so many more layers to you than just football. I want you to know I see them."

"I need you by my side, Mae Bexley."

She dips her chin in a nod, arms wrapping around my neck. "I will be." Then, a smile appears. "I told Flo I'd never want a photo of you on my bedroom wall."

Confusion makes my eyes narrow.

"And that's still true," she continues, "because I want the real thing. A photo won't cut it."

"Is that so?"

"Mmm-hmm."

"You want to wake up to my face every morning?" I press my lips to her neck, circling my hands around her waist and pressing her against me.

"Maybe *on* your face."

An involuntary groan escapes me as I drop my forehead to hers. "Trust you to say something like that."

This woman knows just how to rile me up. I love it.

She smiles at me, cheeks pinched and lips stretched, but her eyes shift when she feels my boner sticking into her stomach. "Nathan," she sighs, eyes clouding with need, dropping her hand, running it over my length.

"Fuck, Mae."

Her fingers then find the zipper to my jeans, and when I hear the zipping noise of her undoing them, I hoist her up in my arms so she's straddling my waist.

"Bedroom. Now."

She points me in the right direction, and I drop her down on the sheets and shuck my jeans down to my hips so my cock springs free. My shirt is next, and I waste no time pulling her sweats off, leaving her bare for me.

"No underwear?" I ask. "My dirty girl."

Her skin is creamy, and I pepper kisses down it until I'm at her core. She arches into my face, and I chuckle.

"Someone's impatient."

I swear I hear her growl. "I need it, Nathan, please."

"What's my name, sweetheart?"

Mae groans, flopping her head back onto the pillow with a thump, but I can see the corner of her lip curling.

"You know you want to say it."

"Nathan... Slater," she mutters, hands in my hair. "Please eat my pussy."

I lap at her clit. "Good girl."

I tease her, on my knees as I pump two fingers into her already wet pussy. She moans, loud and entrancing, and it causes me to curse and tilt my head back to the sky.

She just knows how to make me tick.

I pull out of her, leaving her huffing in frustration before flipping us over so she straddles my waist. "Sit on my face, Mae."

"What?"

I raise an eyebrow, leaving no room for arguments. "You think you can make that *sit-on-your-face* comment and have me overlook it? Sit on my face. Now."

She shuffles forward until she hovers above my neck, and I arch an eyebrow at her.

"Are you sure?"

"Does my cock look as if I'm not sure, princess?"

She angles her head back to see me slowly stroking my hard dick, and a soft moan leaves her as she moves onto my face. Her legs shake, and I grip her ass.

I arch my head and lap at her, and her head kicks back.

I fuck her with my tongue, allowing it to swirl up over her clit every few pumps, and within seconds, Mae's shuddering for me, rolling her hips forward to add more friction.

"Fuck... it feels so fucking good."

"Hold onto the headboard, baby," I tell her, and she immediately leans forward and clutches onto the wood, making it easier for her to grind against my face.

The sight is hypnotic. The way she whimpers for me, muscles flexing and un-flexing.

"Fuck, Nathan, I'm so fucking close. Oh, shit."

"Is my girl going to come all over my face for me?"

Mae bobs her head up and down in a nod before one of her hands clutches my shoulder in a stiff grip. She comes for me, a symphony of moans falling from her lips—so unbelievable that I could come just from the sight.

With eyes hazy, she looks down at me. Her chest rises with heavy breaths. "That was amazing."

I smile because I'm not finished with her—not even close.

I scoot out from under her and grip her round ass, palming it before dipping my fingers into her pussy again. I then press my cock against her entrance. She's on all fours for me, and the view is captivating.

"Fuck, Nathan, I need your cock."

I pause at her entrance. "Tell me again."

"I need your cock. I need you to fuck me. Please." Her voice is desperate, and she attempts to push back onto me, making me chuckle.

I give her what she wants, pounding into her so hard that the sound of skin hitting skin fills the entire house. Her pussy wraps around me, squeezing tight. "Is this what you want every morning, Mae? Because this is what you're going to get. There's no way in hell that I'm letting you go. This pussy is mine. Only mine, got it?"

Mae's face is buried in the pillow as she attempts to muffle her loud screams of pleasure, but I hear her agree.

I thrust harder, making sure my jeans that sit right under my hips aren't grating against her skin. "Let me hear it louder. Tell me you want this, Mae. Tell me you want *me*."

I need to hear it. I need to know this is what she wants for life because I'm willing to give up absolutely everything for this girl. I won't look back with regret because she'll be worth it, but I need to hear the words from her lips.

I stop my movement. "I'm waiting, Mae. Tell me you want this. Tell me you want to be mine. All I need to hear is the word."

She reaches back and clutches onto my hand that's gripping her ass cheek. "I want it, Nathan. I want you. All of you. Forever."

"You sure?" I tilt my head, and her pussy squeezes my cock.

DANGEROUS

"Nathan, God, I've never been more sure of something in my life." She turns her head to look me in the eyes. "Please. I want you. I want *us*."

It's all I need to hear. I slam into her, sucking on my finger to make sure it's wet before I circle her clit.

She chants my name over and over as her legs quiver and her pussy tightens around my cock. It makes it almost impossible to pull out, but I roll us over and grip both of her wrists with my palm, pressing them above her head into the mattress. "Keep them up there." I shuck my jeans down the tiniest bit to give me more flexibility.

Her tits bounce with every thrust, nipples so hard they could be mistaken for diamonds.

Because they're fucking priceless.

Absolutely incredible.

I withdraw and plunge into her again, the bed sheets wet beneath us from how much she's dripping for me. She hums in satisfaction, and I grip her wrists again as she attempts to move them, making her laugh.

"Are you laughing at me, Mae?" I ask.

She shakes her head, biting down on her plump bottom lip. "No, not at all."

"Better not be," I wink at her from above, releasing her wrists, allowing her hands to roam my body.

Her touch feels like fire. Pure, burning, pulsating fire. But the flames are addictive. I'll never get tired of calling this woman mine.

Grabbing the pillow from behind Mae's head, I slide it underneath her ass, which raises her hips. She glances at me with confusion at first, but as I slide back in and hit her sweet spot, all the perplexity disappears from her face.

"Does that feel good, princess? You like being fucked like this?"

"Yes, oh my God, yes."

I press my lips to hers in a steaming kiss, nipping at the skin as I drive my cock into her tight heat.

Her lips part, and her toes curl as I bring her to another orgasm. Watching her come undone for me is something I'll never tire of.

"Mae, I'm going to—" I don't finish my sentence, kissing her softly as I spill inside of her, her legs wrapped around my waist, pulling me impossibly closer.

I clean her up as she catches her breath, pulling my jeans that are around my quads back up.

I stare at her, completely in awe.

She's such a fucking angel. I can't wait to be able to tell everyone she's mine. My father. Her mother. The team. The media.

There's nothing they can do to keep us apart.

"I missed you, Nathan," she says, rolling over on the bed and taking my hand. Her frizzy hair makes me chuckle.

"I missed you too, Mae."

She pauses, lips pursing. "Would now be a bad time to tell you my brother knows about us?" A small laugh falls from her.

I shrug, joining her. "Would now be a bad time to tell you I already know that because he threatened to give me a black eye?"

32: Mae

"I can break her nose if you'd like?" Flo says as we wander down the restricted stadium corridor. Once she takes in my lour, she purses her lips. "How about I just give her a nosebleed then? Not enough to break it, but just cause some damage, you know?"

My best friend looks at me hopefully, and although the thought of her pouncing on Sophia like a lion and wrestling her to the ground makes satisfaction blossom deep in my chest, I know it isn't worth it.

The last thing I want to spend my evening doing is bailing Flo out of jail for assault.

"Although I'm tempted, I'm going to have to reject your offer. Maybe next time." I shoot her a wink.

"Fine," she says, crossing her arms over her chest. "I guess a bitchy glare will have to do. But I'll be wasting my MMA potential."

I laugh. I haven't spoken to Sophia about discovering she'd been the one to gather the photographs of Nathan and me. He's been desperate to confront her, but I don't want her threatening to spill our secret before he has a chance to get his ducks in a row.

God, that saying is haunting me.

If this is going to come out, it's going to come from us. Nathan and I aren't a dirty secret.

He's accepted the fact that he'll have to kiss the Missarali Storks goodbye for breaking the terms of his contract, and although I've checked more than a few times, he keeps insisting this is what he wants and needs.

"I got you tickets to this game to support me, not to beat up my team members." My smile betrays me.

"No, you got me tickets to this game because even though you think giving Sophia a taste of her own medicine is unethical, your subconscious would love to watch me rip those hair extensions from her head."

"Well, the joke's on you. Her hair is natural."

"Lucky bitch," Flo growls. "Do you know why she did it anyway? Did she really go to all that trouble just for a bit of cash?"

I shrug. I've racked my brain trying to come up with reasonable explanations for why Sophia did what she did. She doesn't need the money. She's just married rich and works a job on the side of cheering, too. Money just doesn't seem like a good enough motive to me. "I honestly don't know. She was always so nice to me. I'm still having a hard time believing she'd do something like that."

My best friend sighs. "I guess some people really do love to keep their enemies closer." Her eyes widen as if she's just remembered something. "Your friend, Poppy's been messaging me, by the way. Sweet girl."

I freeze at Flo's admittance. "What? Really?"

"You told her I work for Starbound Talent Agency, and she clearly did her research because she was aware that the company also own Elevate Publications. They have a few tabloids they're in control of, and since I'm due a promotion, I'll use Poppy's suggestion and propose we run a few positive stories on *the* Nathan Slater finding his happy ever after. We can make it cute and restore people's faith in true love again. The readers will eat it up... as long as you provide us with exclusive photos and statements, of course. Once one tabloid does it, others will follow. I believe Poppy called it 'softening the blow'."

I shake my head in disbelief, a smile stretching my lips. "You'd do that? Seriously? Flo, I don't want my drama getting in the way of your work."

"They don't know I know you, Mae, and shut up. You're my best friend." She pulls me to her side. "This is the least I can do. Remember when I threw up in front of Bobby Macknell, the hottest senior in the entire school, and you took the fall and said it was you so that I had a chance with him? That's the kind of shit I'm talking about. You scratch my back; I scratch yours."

The fuzzy memory fills my mind, the smell of Flo's mac and cheese vomit forever etched into my brain. I shiver.

"Well, the game's about to start." Flo arches an eyebrow at me. "Shouldn't you be with your man, giving him an unforgettable blowie right about now?" I slap my hand over her mouth, but she manages to mutter out, "For good luck," before I can shut her up.

"Is this a conversation I should interrupt, or should I grab some popcorn?" The gravelly voice rockets right through me—sharp and intense. I turn to see Nathan leaning against the wall behind us, dressed in a pair of sweatpants and a tight white T-shirt that shows his pectoral muscles a little too nicely.

Flo shoves me off and takes a few steps forward. "So you're the man who's dropping everything and moving to Florida for my best friend." Her eyes dart up and down his form—like she's sussing him out. "You're shorter than I imagined." A mischievous smile breaks out on her face.

The mention of Florida fuels the restless flame of anxiety within me again. I accepted the practice's offer the other night, but I'm not finding myself thrilled about leaving. It doesn't feel the same as when I first left Montana for Colorado. I couldn't wait to move. I counted down the days, optimistic, but thinking about leaving now...

A niggling feeling has been growing, and it's now hollowed out my entire chest.

Nathan shakes his head as he laughs. "Nice to meet you too, Flo."

"You know my name? Wait, *the* Nathan Slater knows *my* name?" She fans herself comically and pretends to stumble before gripping onto my arm for fake support. "It's an honour. Will you sign my whole back?"

"Alright, that's enough out of you." I nudge her with my elbow.

"I should find my seat. Leave you two to it. Bye."

I roll my eyes at Flo's wink as she saunters away, waving her ticket behind her shoulder.

I know she's made a good first impression on Nathan. He likes firecrackers—finds them humorous and annoying simultaneously.

It's why he likes Bennett.

"I like her," he says as he nods after her. "She compliments you well."

I smile as he wraps his arms around me and brings me to his chest. His fresh, citrus scent triggers a rush of dopamine. "Yeah, she does."

"Will it be easier to leave her this time around since you've done it once before?"

I stare at the empty space where my best friend stood mere seconds ago, my chest tight. "I don't think so... I'll miss her. I'll miss it all."

Silence descends between us.

"Is it strange that I'll even miss being on the squad? Even though my mother, who hates me, and the captain who helped blackmail me, is here?"

A breath-taking smile takes over Nathan's features. One side of his lip tips more than the other. He's all masculine energy and sex appeal, and the way his eyes study me is doing something to my *lower* muscles. "No, I don't think it's weird. The human mind desires routine. This has become that for you."

Nathan's full of excellent advice and explanations. It's not like he has the answers to all my questions, but how he navigates his responses sounds like he does. He has this uncanny ability to make things make sense and bring clarity when I'm in a storm of wild emotions I can't escape from.

Cheering. Taking care of Radish. Seeing Flo. Working at the bar. They've all become part of my routine. A routine I'm content with. A routine I enjoy. A routine I... think I actually love.

Back in Colorado, I struggled with routine. I'd put all my eggs in one basket and even though I was supposedly living my dream, I'd never felt more alone. I know moving to Florida will be different, but it still doesn't ease the harsh uncertainty that I'm making a mistake.

I thought I'd be skipping for joy at the prospect of leaving a few months ago, but now that I'm facing it, I'm wishing for the days to stretch out so I can hold on just a little longer.

33: Nathan

The team captain of the Atlanta Goblins grunts in disapproval as Bennett scores yet another touchdown. He's furious, arms flinging up in the air with a growl trembling the corner of his lip.

My team are pulling through today. I can physically see the fire blowing up their asses and spurring them on. We're so close now. So close to lifting that trophy and being named the champions of the Super Bowl.

The thought isn't nearly as tempting as it once was, though.

At one point, it was all I wanted, and I needed to achieve it. But my thoughts are elsewhere now.

Every practice. Every game. Those were the moments that defined me. I thought I knew exactly who I was because I had the jersey and the ball in my hands. Every touchdown and tackle felt like I was getting closer to achieving it. Like I was chasing some version of success that would finally make it all feel right.

But things change.

My eyes flicker over to Mae, who's mid-chat with my sister, both of their cheeks pinched up as they grin. I've never seen Poppy this smitten with someone before, and my teeth worry my bottom lip as I think about how lonely she'll be when we leave.

Sophia had been a good friend of hers, but now, she can't even look her in the eyes, especially because Mae told her not to confront her about working with our dad.

She has Madison, though.

And Bennett.

She'll be okay.

"Slater! Get your head back in the game!" The voice takes me off guard, and I turn to see Peter, the manager of The Missarali Storks, glaring at me from the sidelines.

I can't help but grunt.

Nice of the guy to finally show up.

My feet push off the turf. The defensive back is at my hip, but I pretend he's not there as I glance up at the ball that's just been thrown in my direction. My legs pump harder, and with one more step, I swipe the ball from the air, clutching it to my chest. My fingers curl around the leather—cool and textured against my clammy palms.

The end zone is just ahead, but I can feel the defender's shadow creeping up on me—so close he's just inches away from swiping at me and crushing me to the ground.

I swear I hear Mae's voice, loud and encouraging, and with her in my mind, I take one final pace, the end zone line disappearing under my cleats. Then, I'm across it, the crowd hooting and my teammates rushing over to smack my helmet in appreciation.

I should have brain damage with the amount they do it.

The final whistle is blown, indicating that the Missarali Storks have won, and Evan pats my back as he beams. "Nice work, Captain."

Gazing out at my team, a warm feeling swells in my heart. These guys have been my family when I had no one. They've worked so hard. And I know they'll do it. They can win this. They just don't need me for it—not when my heart isn't entirely in the game, not when the media will focus on me and my scandal if I wait until after we win to announce what Mae and I are, detracting from their hard work and dedication.

Because although most people would feel ecstatic scoring that touchdown, all I can think about is never having to do it again, and they deserve a captain whose passion is spilling from his ears.

My father catches my attention in the crowd. He's watching me, head cocked and lips flat as he follows my gaze to the beautiful woman who's stolen my heart. He shakes his head subtly, and I notice his fingers fiddling with the pocket of his fleece, pulling out a thick wad of photos.

Another silent warning.

Reminding me of what he has on me.

Reminding me that my role here as captain for the Storks can be over in a second with the flick of his wrist.

Reminding me that he has the control. The power.

He always has.

Rage seethes inside me. This man is nothing to me. He may be my flesh and blood, but I'm not allowing him to dictate my life anymore.

Not when Mae is on the line.

Yanking my helmet off, I begin moving over to her, raising my eyebrows at my father. My face is blank as I stare at him.

His eyes are toxic, latching onto me, trying to suck all the courage from my flesh.

But he's nothing but an ineffective leech. Burdensome and irritating. Useless to me.

The crowd quiets, and I'm well aware my form is enlarged on the jumbotron above, the cameras following my movement. I stop in front of Mae.

"What are you doing?" she mutters to me, eyes flashing with a hint of concern, but I pick up on the way her teeth clamp down on her lower lip to stifle her smile.

Challenging.

Daring.

This woman.

"Taking the power back," I say, right as I wrap my arms around her waist and kiss her.

Nothing else matters right now. This kiss is being live-streamed to millions of people across America, and still, I can't find a fuck to give. Because football is no longer my priority. I've come to realise it never really was. It just happened to be one of the only things I actually cared about.

Mae has shown me I'm way more than football, though. And I hope she knows she's more than just a daughter her mother dislikes. More than a veterinarian student. More than a member of the Missarali cheerleading squad.

She's her. And that's all she needs to be.

All we both need to be.

Mae melts into the kiss. Her hands find the back of my neck, nails digging into my skin and making me groan.

People are hushed around us, and I almost want to pull away early just to see the look on everyone's faces. We'll probably get a mixed reaction, but I'm showing everyone this is our choice.

This is what *we* want.

My father's photos won't mean shit to anyone now. No tabloids are going to want them when they can plaster a photograph of Mae and I macking on with each other in front of a crowd of sixty thousand people on the front cover of their magazines.

I eventually pull away, but I don't bother looking around yet. I allow my thumb to caress Mae's flushed cheek, and she grins and presses her face into my jersey.

"Can't take it back now, princess," I tell her.

But she just looks up at me with those doe-like hazel eyes and says, "Wouldn't want to even if I could, Nate."

My head jerks at the sound of a deep "Whoop." Bennett's clapping, smiling from ear to ear. Evan's chuckling, giving me a look that says *impressive*. But the rest of my teammates are staring with their mouths open—so wide they could catch flies.

Cam isn't here, but I have no doubt the news will travel fast and I'll receive some choice words from him when I next look at my phone.

He came to me the other week after finding out about Mae and me, and although I took his threat seriously, I know he's clever enough not to follow through with it. Cam's not a violent guy.

The crowd are cheering. Because I'm showing them that Mae isn't just some fling. I've made our relationship public.

And even though a lot of them look fucking confused, as if they've missed something, I love it. I love *this*. I gaze at Mae. I love *us*.

My eyes travel to my father's seat, but I find it empty, and Mae sighs when she meets her mother's shocked stare. Her throat bobs, but Renee quickly averts her eyes and sits back on the bench, eyes latched onto the grass below as she takes it in.

She doesn't look happy, but she isn't enraged like I assumed she'd be.

Darrell strolls up to me and claps me on the back, the force harsh but friendly. He shakes his head and chuckles before saying, "About fucking time, Slater. I was wondering when you would get the guts to do something for yourself."

LOTTIE MOORE

"Slater, what was that?" Peter's stocky form steps in front of me, the fluorescent lights above beaming down on his bald head in the stadium corridor.

I wonder if he polishes it or if it's just naturally that blinding.

I shrug. I'm trying not to give Peter attitude, but he hasn't bothered to show up for any of our games until now. So, I don't understand how he demands respect when he doesn't even care about the team he manages.

Darrell's the one who puts in all the hard work. Peter just takes the money.

He pinches the bridge of his nose as my coach rounds the corner. "Darrell, you reminded them of the no-fraternisation rule, yes?"

"Of course. It's in the contract." Darrell tries to hide his smile. Although he wants me on the team, I think he knows I'm done with football. I have been for a long time. We've not spoken about it, but he's not an idiot.

"I understand the terms of the contract I signed and the repercussions I'll face," I tell them both.

"You surely can't proceed with legal action, Peter?" Darrell tries to reason with him, gesturing to me. "He's been a loyal captain. Nathan has done a lot for this team. More than most." He eyes him up, his subtle dig not so subtle.

Peter shakes his head. "Legal action will cost the team money. Sponsorships. Their image."

Of course. It all comes back to money.

"Nathan," Peter sighs, "Fuck." His hand finds his bald head, and he rubs it as if it's a crystal ball that will give him the answer on how to handle this predicament. "Right, we'll claim it was a publicity stunt. To get people talking about the team."

I cock my head. "Excuse me?"

My father's now joined the conversation, arms crossed over his chest as his nostrils flare. "So you're saying you won't kick Nathan off the team? As long as he runs with the narrative that it was all for show?"

Peter dips his head as he clicks his fingers. He truly believes he's just come up with the world's most fantastic idea. "Yes, that's what we'll do. We'll say this was planned. We can tell the rest of the team we were in on this. We can win the Super Bowl if we—"

"I quit."

All three heads turn to me, eyes bugging.

"What the fuck did you just say?" Kevin Slater seethes, face so red it looks like he's morphing into a life-size tomato.

"Your hearing aid not working, old man?" I ask him, pointing to my own ear mockingly. "I said I quit."

Taking a few steps back, I shrug as they gawk at me. Have I grown a second head or something?

I quit.

I quit.

I quit.

Two small words that hold so much power.

They've replayed over and over again in my head for years. And yet, I never had the ability to say them aloud. There were too many reasons not to, but since meeting Mae, those reasons have quickly dissipated.

"Nathan, think about this logically," Peter attempts to reason with me, desperation slipping into his usual monotone voice. "We're so close. This could be our year!"

"*Your* year." I nod towards him. "The team will be just fine without me. I've failed to follow the terms of the contract, so if you won't fire me, then I quit."

Darrell dips his chin in understanding. There's a sliver of disappointment lingering in his eyes, but he doesn't try to talk me out of it. He wants the best for me, and he knows that football has been an ever-growing burden for years now.

When I first joined the team, I could hide it. Tell myself it wasn't that heavy. But as time has passed, it's started to cling to me like a baby monkey to its mother.

Cracks have been forming for as long as I can remember, and it's finally all come crumbling down.

And I'm not the least bit disappointed about it either.

"All this… for a girl?" my father spits in disbelief. "What about when it doesn't work out? This would have all been for nothing, Nathan."

I eye him up, my chest tight with loathing for the man who wrecked my childhood. "It *will* work out, but my relationship is not your concern."

"So that's what you're calling it? A relationship?" He scoffs, and I'm shocked when Darrell turns to my father blankly.

"Nathan's a smart man. He can make his own decision. I, for one, am happy for you." He smiles at me before addressing my father again. "I don't believe you have the correct pass to be in this restricted area, anyway. It's in your best interest to leave before I get security down here." Darrell edges closer to me, placing a comforting hand on my shoulder. "Do what you need to do."

"Thanks, Coach."

He grins. "That's ex-coach to you."

And with that, I spin on my heel and turn my back on them.

Turn my back on football.

And it feels fucking euphoric.

Because my future isn't this sport anymore.

It's the beautiful woman who I can now publicly call mine.

34: Nathan

"Okay, you've been staring off into space for the past ten minutes, and it's creeping me out," Mae says to me as she kneels on my couch beside me. "What are you thinking about?"

I hum. "Just about where I want to kiss you first now that I can tell people you're mine. How about a restaurant? Or a bar? Or I could just do it out in the middle of a busy street so cars have to stop and people have to watch us?"

A soft blush rises to Mae's cheeks, and she releases a laugh.

A laugh that sounds like a thousand angels singing in perfect tune.

A laugh that causes my chest to tighten with adoration.

A laugh that captured my attention from the very beginning.

I hated having her as a secret. It felt dirty, and that's the last thing Mae is. Her existence shouldn't be hidden. It should be celebrated.

I nod towards the laptop on the coffee table in front of me. "I've been looking at apartments to rent in Florida near the vet practice. Found some really nice ones for a decent price."

I never fail to notice how Mae's smile subtly fades whenever Florida is mentioned. Her adverse reactions are discreet, but I know my girl. Something isn't sitting right with her, and even though I've tried asking, she insists she's just nervous.

I've offered to pay for her college tuition at a school of her choice so she can study anywhere she wants in the country if she doesn't feel prepared for this program, but she always scowls at me and says, "I don't want a handout."

Her glower is enough to shut me up because Mae Bexley is scary when she's annoyed. But I like it. It gets me going.

"Bennett's invited us out," she says, changing the subject, and I cock my head at her. She knows I'll bring this up later, but for now, I'll allow her to put her avoidance technique into play. "He said he wanted to celebrate finally being free of you."

I take the phone from her and narrow my eyes at the texts on her screen. "That boy is going to get it when I see him."

We make it to The Salty Dog quickly, mainly because Poppy kept messaging Mae and demanding she hurry up, and when we walk in, hand in hand, the lights flicker on, and a crowd of people jump out from poor hiding places to yell, "Surprise!"

My eyes shoot to Mae, but judging by her wide mouth and eyes, she also wasn't aware of this.

Balloons float through the air, and there's a huge banner taped to the back of the bar wall that says *congratulations on breaking your contracts.*

Bennett points to it proudly, and Poppy stands beside him with a smile so bright I'm sure it can be seen from space. Evan is standing next to a table covered in party snacks, and he marches over to hand us a card, Leo balanced on his hip.

I take it from his hands and immediately chuckle, the card reading *Happy sixty-fifth birthday!*

"Leo picked it out," he tells me as his son giggles, his chubby cheeks rosy. "Now you're gone, I'm the oldest on the team, so thanks for setting me up as the new recipient of all the old man jokes."

"You're very welcome, West." I squeeze his shoulder and thank Leo for the card, chuckling at how he's attempted to write his name inside. And I use attempted loosely. It looks like a bunch of squiggles.

Music begins to play and Poppy and Bennett rush over to us as everyone else starts to converse amongst themselves.

"It looks great in here." Mae beams.

"Bennett spent forever on the sign," Poppy tells us, flashing a grin at my best friend, who sends her a playful roll of the eyes.

"I can see that." Mae nods to the red paint spatters all over the white of the sign, the writing sloppy, the paper wrinkled.

"I'm a football player, not an artist," is Bennett's defence.

Amber works hard over at the bar, serving people their drinks at lightning speed, and when Bennett leads Mae away to buy her one, Poppy grips my arm.

"Are you two gonna be okay with everything going on?"

Mae and I have been featured in the tabloids, and people have been talking about us online. However, Flo pulled through and got Elevate Publications to run a few positive stories about how love conquered all for a football player and cheerleader.

As she expected, other tabloids followed suit, and although there will always be someone with something negative to say, for the most part, people have been mostly respectful. Apparently, people love love. She even did me a massive favour and got them to feature Emmanuel's wine store in some of the articles, and ever since, business has picked up significantly.

Some fans aren't happy about me leaving the team, but they'll soon forget about that when the Storks lift that trophy at the end of the Super Bowl.

"I love her," Poppy says, and I follow her gaze, my eyes latching onto a laughing Mae who's got Leo in her arms, bouncing him up and down as Bennett and Evan smile beside her.

Or what Evan would call a smile.

It looks more like he's trying to hold in a fart.

"I do, too."

"I know." She releases a sad sigh. "I'm really going to miss you two. Florida... wow."

Poppy's looking up at me the same way Mae looks at me whenever Florida is mentioned.

Like she's frightened. Like she's concerned. Like she's on the fence.

This shouldn't be an on-the-fence kind of decision, though. Mae needs to be sure this is what she wants, and right now, I'm not so convinced.

I sling an arm around my sister's shoulder, our gazes still on Mae, whose ass looks fucking phenomenal in her jeans. The jeans she was wearing the first time I laid eyes on her in Emmanuel's wine store.

"We'll be fine, Pops. You will be, too."

She leans against me. "I know you will. You have her."

We settle into a comfortable silence, but we both turn when someone clears their throat behind us.

Cam stares at me, hazel eyes that match Mae's boring into mine. "Poppy, do you mind if I talk to Nathan for a minute?"

My sister retreats, joining the others. I raise my eyebrows at Cam, whose eyes flit over to his sister before he sighs and scratches at the back of his neck. To say he looks uncomfortable would be an understatement.

"I want to apologise. Threatening you—that wasn't right. I realise I misunderstood how serious you are about my sister. You giving up football for her... that's shown me everything I need to know." Guilt flashes on his face.

I won't hold this against him. I can't lie and say I wouldn't be the same if I found out someone I didn't trust was banging my baby sister. It was coming from a place of protectiveness.

"You don't need to worry about it," I tell him, shaking his hand. "Mae means a lot to you. I get that, but I want you to know that she also means a lot to me. It was never just casual with her. Ever."

The thought of not spending the rest of my life with this girl makes me feel physically unwell.

"I appreciate that. Just please look after her. Because if you hurt her..."

I take another peek at Mae, who's watching me and her brother over Poppy's shoulder, her eyebrows slightly downturned as she tries to gauge what kind of interaction we're having.

I shook her a wink. "You don't need to worry about that, Cam."

The party is in full swing a couple of hours later. Apparently, Evan also couldn't say no to Leo when he picked up a giant rainbow unicorn pinata inside the party store, so people are currently smashing it to smithereens with a few branches Samuel retrieved from outside.

I'm not even sure there's anything inside.

I take the time to grab Mae's hand and pull her outside, pressing her up against the cold brick wall of the bar.

"We're going to miss all the fun if we're out here," she playfully says to me, rolling her lips together.

I raise a brow. "I can think of another way for us to enjoy ourselves without brutally beating a paper mythical creature into the ground."

"Hmm, I don't know." She tilts her head back towards the bar, where waves of shouts and cheers can be heard. "Sounds like they're having a blast."

"Trust me, you'll be making a lot more noise than that in just a minute."

My lips land on hers, and her fingers tangle themselves in my hair. When she pulls, I release a loud moan, full of pleasure.

My cock tightens in my jeans, and I trail my hands down to grip her hips. "You've been fucking teasing me with these jeans since the first day I first met you. With that round ass of yours. You know exactly what you're doing wearing these around me."

"I don't know what you mean. They're just jeans." Her smirk gives her away, though. She knows her ass looks incredible in them.

Her tongue darts out to lick her bottom lip, and my self-control snaps. My fingers unfasten the three buttons, revealing the top of her lacey red underwear.

Oh, you have to be kidding me.

I bend down and nip at the space below her belly button, gaining me a moan. She arches her back and presses herself into me, and I grip her ass, pushing her closer.

"Nathan, someone could see," she says, her voice all breathy.

"You think I'd stop just because someone could see us? Oh, you've severely underestimated me, princess."

My words cause her to tilt her head back as I dip my fingers into the front of her jeans and trace her pussy over her panties.

I'm teasing her. I'm well aware. But she's been teasing me for months.

"Fuck, Nathan." Her voice is barely above a whisper. "More."

"You want more?"

"Yes, I do. I need more."

It's enough for me to hoist her up in my arms and walk her over to my car. I slip into the front seat with her on my lap, and within seconds, I've discarded both of our jeans.

The parking lot is dark and quiet, with cars surrounding us. I know people could leave the party and see us out here, but there isn't a sliver of me that cares. I want them to know Mae is mine. Always has been and always will be.

"Pull your panties to the side."

She does as I tell her, and she bares her glistening pussy for me. So wet and needy.

I don't rush it. I want this moment to last forever, so I use my index finger to spread her wetness onto her clit, keeping my touch soft as I twirl over it. She moans, and I hush her, telling her, "I'm going to take care of you, okay?"

I slip two fingers into her and curl them, ensuring I'm hitting her g-spot each time I drag them out and thrust back in. I twist them, eyes trained on a panting Mae who's clutching onto me for dear life—as if she can't contain her desperation for me.

"You're so fucking tight." My voice is husky, laced with lust and love for this girl.

She's absolutely ruining me, and *I'm* the one pleasuring *her*.

I clamp my teeth down on my bottom lip when Mae orders me to quicken the pace, but I ignore her request, teasing her. Keeping the same rhythm, I watch in satisfaction when she begins rocking against me, trying to chase the pleasure.

"Nathan," she growls, nails digging into my shoulder.

"Yes, princess? Something wrong?"

Her free hand moves to play with her clit, but she draws her eyebrows together. "It's not enough. More, Nathan. Please."

Fuck. I love the way she says my name. I love it even more when she moans it, though.

So I give her what she wants, pumping my fingers in and out of her pussy at a merciful pace, watching her throw her head back and whimper.

My cock is throbbing, but I'm not one to skip out on foreplay. Pleasuring my girl and showing her that I care about her coming is one of my favourite parts of sex. Too many men don't do it these days.

My other hand presses down on her clit, taking over from her, and I feel her walls tighten around my fingers, indicating she's close.

"Is my girl going to come for me?"

Mae nods. "Yes, yes, I'm going to come."

"Fuck, my dick is so hard watching you like this for me."

Within seconds, she's shaking, nipples hardening even more under her top—if that's possible—as she erupts above me. The string of moans that leave her will forever be tattooed into my mind. Locked away. Only for me.

She comes down and rests her forehead on my chest. I plant a kiss on the top of her head, my dick twitching below. Even though she's just orgasmed, she takes one look at rock-hard cock and drags her bottom lip into her mouth, eyes sliding to mine.

I can see the want in her eyes.

"My fingers weren't enough for you, baby? You want my cock too?"

She leans back onto the dashboard and wiggles her hips, the wetness dripping from her pussy coating my thick thighs. "Nathan, I'm fucking desperate. Please."

I know she she is. She doesn't need to tell me. I can see it for myself.

"Take what you want, then."

With her red panties still off to the side, Mae lowers herself down on me, inch by inch, until I'm bottomed out. We groan in unison. It feels so unbelievably good. Like nothing else I've ever experienced. No woman has ever done this for me.

I need to take a few seconds to take it all in.

"Fuck, you feel like fucking heaven. Show me how desperate you are, Mae. Ride my cock."

She begins moving, bracing her hands on my shoulders as she bounces up and down on my cock. The sound of skin hitting skin fills the otherly silent parking lot.

I watch the space where our bodies connect before lowering Mae's cami top, latching onto one of her breasts, and swirling my tongue around the beaded nipple. "You're perfect, Mae. These tits are perfect." I bite down, not hard enough to cause pain, but enough to make her yelp. "This ass is perfect." My hands grip it, kneading the muscle. "This cunt is perfect. Taking my cock so well." I adjust my hips so my dick hits her sweet spot as she rides me, her head falling back as she mutters my name. "So fucking perfect. All of you."

"Nathan, give me more. I need more."

"You want to be fucked?" I ask her, holding on to her waist to cease her movement.

She nods, eyes hazy, a bed of sweat trickling down the swell of her breasts.

I manoeuvre her so she's on all fours on the seat beside me, fingernails digging into the fabric and ass high. I kneel behind her over the console, swiping my cock through her wetness. My fingers skate against her clit, and she jolts.

"I'm going to need to hear you scream my name when you come, Mae," I say as I push myself into her. "I want everyone here in Missarali to hear you. I want them to know what we are. Who we are. It's you and me, okay?"

"Yes," she responds. "You and me."

"Good girl."

I pound into her, and she chants my name. She's so warm. So wet. Her pussy grips onto me like it never wants to let me go.

I would die happy right here. Buried inside Mae, with her body trembling for me as she pushes herself back with each of my rhythmic strokes.

I can see her face in the reflection of the car window. Her mouth is open in an '*O*' shape, and her eyebrows are pinched together as she blushes.

"Nathan! Your cock feels so good."

"You're so fucking incredible," I bite out. "This was what you wanted from the very beginning, wasn't it?"

"Do you need any more of an ego boost?" Mae responds between groans.

I stop moving, balls deep inside her. "You know what? I do. Tell me, princess. Tell me what you thought of me the first time you saw me."

She's silent, and I see in the window reflection she's running her tongue along the front of her teeth in frustration.

"I'm waiting, baby."

She grunts. "I thought you were the most attractive person I'd ever seen. I didn't recognise you, but I was desperate to know who you were. I regret not going after you."

I begin pumping into her again, but slowly. "Tell me more."

"I wondered how big your dick was. Seeing you at practice... I wanted you."

I hum. "Is that so?"

"Yes."

My thrusts quicken. "Well, let me tell you what I first thought of you. I couldn't believe there was someone who existed as beautiful as you. I thought it was almost criminal. Then, you opened up that mouth of yours. That smart fucking mouth that knows how to put me in my fucking place. It was then that I knew I had to have you. I knew you were supposed to be mine."

We're having an entire discussion during sex. It should feel strange—talking like this while we fuck—but it only makes me harder, and I can feel that it's making Mae wetter.

"Tell me more," she says, throwing my own words back at me as she reaches behind her to grip my veiny forearm.

"You in that cheer uniform of yours. It does something to me. The way you look at me. The way this pussy grips me. We were fucking made for each other, Mae."

"I know," she responds. "Fuck, I'm gonna come."

"That's it, baby," I tell her as I grit my teeth, my lower abdomen twanging. My dick twitches, and the thought of Mae walking back into that party with my come dribbling down her thighs underneath her skin-tight jeans makes me explode.

My ears ring, and my muscles flood with bliss. My jaw pops as I continue to work into her. Condensation drips from the car windows.

Mae's body rocks against me, screaming my name before her orgasm dies down, and I pull out of her pussy and pepper kisses down the length of her back—each one a silent promise that we're in this together.

No matter where we are.

It's us.

Her and me.

35: Mae

I can't spend another second sifting through sites looking for apartments to rent in Florida. There are so many nice ones. They all look amazing, but I keep finding something to fault them on, even when I know that the bathroom layout or the fact that it's close to a busy road wouldn't be a deciding factor for me.

It's because I don't want to settle on one. Because the thought of Florida terrifies me. But I have to do this.

I can't shake the feeling that I'll disappoint Nathan if I allow this opportunity to slip through my fingertips. One of the reasons he quit football was so he could come with me.

The sound of the front door opening and closing sends a chill down my spine. I can tell by the silence that my mom's back after spending the past five nights with a friend, because finding out about Nathan and me was a total shock for her. I haven't seen her since the evening he kissed me on that field in front of everybody.

Instead of ignoring me like she usually does when she gets home, she heads into the plain living room and sits on the armchair opposite me. Bracing her hands on her knees, she takes a deep breath. "Mae."

My lips flatten. "Mom." I've prepared a speech, but now that I'm in the situation, all memory of it is gone.

I did the exact thing my mom didn't want me to do.

"Sophia's out."

My head jerks at her statement, and I blink, wondering if I've entered an alternate universe where my mom is actually on my side. "What?"

Frustration flashes in her irises, but she sighs and covers it quickly. "I said Sophia is out. She's gone from the team. She helped threaten you, Mae. That's not something I take lightly."

My mom's waiting for me to respond, but it feels like there's no air left in the room. I'm greedily breathing it in, my lungs desperate for more.

"Mae... I'm trying to talk to you here. I'm trying to.... do something good."

I immediately nod. "Yes, um, okay. So, you cut Sophia from the team?"

"I did. She came to me. Admitted everything. Not that she had much choice. Kevin Slater was this close," she pinches her finger and thumb together until there are only a few centimetres between them, "to ratting her out since he didn't get what he wanted. He wanted someone to go down the drain, at least."

"Did she tell you why?"

My mother drops her gaze. Her usually glossy hair looks dull. And her face is pale and lifeless. "She watched the routines where you performed in her spot while she was on her honeymoon. She was worried you'd take her place. Because you were good, Mae. You were a good addition to the team."

My face is blank. My mind reels, trying to process the words that just left my mom's mouth. This is the woman who, more often than not, makes me feel like everything I do is wrong. The one that hurts me just for fun. Who points out my flaws whenever she gets a chance.

I half expect to see that usual judgemental look in her eyes, but there's—what looks to be—shame. It shocks me.

"Sophia's action hit a nerve, I suppose. Jealousy makes people do ugly things. Say ugly things." She inhales deeply. "I was always jealous of you and your... father's relationship. I was jealous I couldn't be as happy-go-lucky as him. As parental as him. As easy to talk to." Regret masks her famous grouchy expression.

I don't know what to say. I've thought about this day more times than I can count—the day my mother would explain things to me. And now that it's happening, here I am, lost for words.

"Nathan came to me one day and demanded I treat you better. I didn't know how much he actually cared for you at the time, but he told me about his own mother. How she's not around. I–I don't know what I thought, really. Just that everyone around could see what an awful mother

I was. How life isn't guaranteed. How I was so deep in, that I felt like I could never change what I had done to us. I felt like we were too far gone. After what Sophia did, I was mad at her, and then I realised I had no right to be mad because I've treated you just the same over the years." Her bony fingers twitch. "I'm sorry, Mae. Jealousy made me ugly."

I sigh. "We could have been there for each other through Dad's disappearance. We *should* have."

"I know..." She gulps. "When you called me saying you couldn't pay your rent back in Colorado anymore, I wanted to help you. But I suppose I wouldn't allow myself to do a good deed just for the sake of it. I needed something from you, so it's why I offered you a spot on the team. I had plenty of girls I could have called, but making you join the team made me feel less... weird, I guess, about doing something for you."

My mother's explanation goes right through me. After years of being the recipient of words and actions that felt like daggers to my heart, she's finally sitting here in front of me, trying. She's putting her pride aside to tell me the truth. To tell me where it all went wrong.

I want to open up to her about the pain she put me through, but looking in her eyes now, all glassy and dead, I'm adamant she already knows. She feels it.

The knife she's hurt me with is still in my back, but I think it's cut her, too.

"Thank you for sticking up for me," I tell her, my lips tilting into a smile.

"I don't expect ever to be as close to you as your father was, but I think enough is enough… you don't deserve to be treated like this. I'm sorry."

"Thank you."

I don't know if I should get up and hug her, but that feels a little far for us right now. We aren't there yet, but we've just taken our first baby step.

And baby steps feel a whole lot more appropriate than breaking out into a full-blown sprint.

I bounce into the Missarali City Animal Shelter with a spring in my step. I haven't seen my scruffy little boy for a week now, and I've missed him like crazy.

"Hey, Sheila!" I call as I head past reception, straight down the corridor towards the kennels.

"Oh, Mae! There's something I need to speak to you about. Well, two things, actually." She rushes after me, but I'm already frozen in place, my hands shaking as I glance at the kennel before me.

The empty kennel.

The empty kennel that has an *adopted* sign taped to the front.

"He… he's gone?" Tears prick my eyes, but I blink them away.

This is what I wanted for him. He deserved to go to a good home with people who will love him so hard it hurts. He deserves a family.

For a little while, he was starting to feel like mine, though. Like *my* little Radish.

Sheila dips her chin to her chest as she catches up to me. "Um, yes, that's what I wanted to talk to you about. Well, that, and the fact that we have a job opportunity that you might be interested in. Or you might not be, but I wanted to give you the option to take a look anyway." She gestures to a bulletin board where a few posters are pinned up.

I step towards it and unpin the one she's pointing to.

Veterinary nurse opportunity available.
Speak to a member of staff for more details.

I sigh. "Thank you, Sheila, but I'm not qualified."

She nods, grinning. "We've recently joined the Veterinary Training Academy. Mallory and Tonya, our vets, have completed their courses, which means they're qualified to teach on the job. I can't guarantee the pay will be great, but it'll be enough. You wouldn't need any qualifications to start. Just a really good resume." Sheila winks at me before she releases a small sigh. "I just wanted to let you know. You're so good with the animals, and it really would be a shame to lose you, Mae."

I clutch the poster tighter in my flexed fingers, my entire body going cold as I resist the urge to smother Sheila in an inappropriate bear hug.

"And when it comes to Radish—" She's interrupted by the sound of someone walking into the shelter reception, the dogs releasing loud, bellowing barks. "I'm so sorry. It's been manic here today."

I take one last longing look at Radish's empty kennel, my stomach sinking, and follow Sheila to reception. A man is waiting, and I push aside my need to ask him if he's the man who adopted Radish.

I feel protective over that dog.

Sheila sees to him, but then the telephone rings and her computer pings, causing her to grunt.

My teeth worry my bottom lip. "I'll come back later, Sheila. You seem really busy."

Her mouth turns downward. "Are you sure? I can—"

Another person walks in, and I shake my head at her, mouthing *don't worry* before exiting.

Rain is trickling down from the sky, and I gaze up at the ominous grey clouds and sigh. I call Nathan to let him know I'm done early—since he agreed to pick me up—and I let my thoughts wander.

Radish is out there somewhere. It feels similar to the situation with my father, where I'm left wondering if our paths will cross again. I'm not sure I can handle missing someone else.

Is he looking up at someone else with those big, doe-like brown eyes? Tail swishing as he receives a little head scratch? What kind of food are they giving him? Are they taking him for long enough walks? Is he happy? A lot of people don't know that dogs can suffer from depression, too. What if they have a swimming pool, and he falls in when they're not looking and drowns?

A horn blaring pulls me from my worries. Nathan's looking at me through the rain-spattered windshield of his car, eyes asking me what's wrong.

My heart skips a beat, suddenly realising how bittersweet this situation is.

I have an opportunity to work here in Missarali—a place I now see as home. But Radish won't be around, which feels like a kick in the teeth. That, and I don't know how I'm going to admit to Nathan that I don't want to go to Florida. Because now that I have the choice, I know what I'd rather do. I know what feels right. I know that moving states isn't what my heart wants. It's not what it needs.

But it's not all about me.

"What happened?" Nathan asks when I slip into the car.

"How do you know something has happened?"

He gives me an *I know you* look, and his gaze flits down to the poster in my hand, trying to read the black printed words that are now streaky from the precipitation.

"Radish," I say, swallowing my tears. "I'm supposed to be professional, but that dog. He stole my heart. I loved him like my own. He was… adopted.." I take a deep breath.

"I'm happy for him, and I'm happy for his new owners because they've got such an incredible dog, but just the thought of never seeing him again. The thought of him not being called Radish anymore. That hurts. What if they pick some boring, generic name that doesn't suit him at all?"

Nathan nods as I talk, his stubble a little longer due to a lack of shaving. He looks damn good with it, but it only almost distracts me. "Who says he won't be called Radish anymore?"

I shake my head in confusion. "The new adopters aren't required to keep the name."

"I see." He reaches into a bag by his feet and pulls out something jangly, placing it in my hands. "I had this made. What do you think?"

My eyes are round as I gaze down at the turquoise collar on my thighs. The fabric is delicately woven and intricate. Flipping the metal pendant hanging from it, I see the name *Radish* engraved on it.

"It's nice, right?"

Tears well in my eyes. "What... what is—"

"You can come out now, boy."

At Nathan's command, Radish leaps out from behind his seat in the back, attacking me with kisses so slobbery I feel like I've just showered. My heart rattles inside my chest, and a laugh bursts from my throat as I cradle the dog in my lap and cry with relief.

"You? You adopted him?" I ask, tears dripping down my cheeks.

"Yep."

"What about Florida? I mean, I know you can transport dogs, but—"

"We're not going to Florida, princess." Nathan's tone is challenging, and he cocks his head as he cups my cheeks. "I know you. And you're not happy about going. If moving doesn't feel right, don't force yourself. We can work this out together, but I see the doubt in your eyes whenever I talk about going. You love Missarali."

Relief spills out of my eyes. It's like a giant weight has been lifted from my chest, and I can finally breathe again. The constant tension in my shoulders, the ache in my jaw—*poof*—gone. My skin is no longer crawling with anxiety.

"I don't want to go to Florida, Nathan."

He shakes his head. "I know you don't, baby. We'll create a life wherever works for both of us. Wherever you can accomplish your dreams while feeling at home. And if Florida isn't that, then we can find somewhere else."

I wipe at my eyes and lean forward to kiss him, gaining a grunt from Radish, who is frustrated that the attention isn't entirely on him. "I felt too guilty to bring it up. You quit football."

"Because I wanted to. Because it didn't feel like home anymore. But you, Mae Bexley, do. I belong wherever you are." He kisses the top of my head. "You can find another program. One that feels right."

My eyes flicker down to the soggy poster in my lap, now peppered with holes from Radish's claws. I laugh, my mind oddly still. Calm.

"I have one in mind."

Epilogue: Nathan

"Let's go, boys!" I boom, cupping my hands around my mouth so the sound travels directly toward the guys clipping each other on the backs of their helmets after the referee has blown the halftime whistle. It's the Super Bowl against the Nashville Wranglers—hosted in the Missarali City Stadium.

I'm standing in the stands, wearing a pair of worn jeans and a white T-shirt with a tartan overshirt hanging over my shoulder. It feels good to be here, *not* in uniform. Watching the guys play. It's so different seeing it from this perspective.

I feel fucking free.

Leo sits beside me on Darrell's wife, Hazel's, lap. He points down at Evan and yells, "Dada!" which causes the people around us to release loud *awwws* in unison. Evan glances up at his son with adoration and offers him a wave. I know he can't wait for the game to be over so he can have Leo back in his arms.

"How are your child coaching sessions going, Nathan? Has Leo joined yet?" Hazel asks me, bouncing the giggling child on her lap, making sure the protective earwear he's wearing doesn't slide off as she does so. Evan takes his son's ear health very seriously.

I ruffle up the small boy's hair as he reaches for me—it's our thing at this point. "They're going well, thanks, Hazel. And no," my eyes narrow at a staring Evan, who cocks his head, knowing we're talking about him, "Evan refuses to let Leo join my classes. Says he doesn't want his son getting into football."

I teach for fun. I let the kids enjoy the sport, and I put no pressure on them. We don't play competitively. It's simply a good time, which I wanted from football at a young age, so I'm happy I can give that to other children, even if I didn't get it myself.

Hazel cackles. "Well, that's going to be hard with how he looks at his dad when he plays."

It's true. Leo watches his father as if he's hung the moon down there on that field. Normal kids would get restless and want to play with toys or crawl around, but Leo finds entertainment in watching Evan tackle other men to the ground.

He claps his hands every time.

As the guys file down the tunnel to have their halftime pep talk with Darrell—who shoots me a smile before he disappears—I turn all my attention towards the cheerleaders who skip out onto the grass. They're all blown-out hair and cheesy smiles.

Mae looks fucking unbelievable, and my eyes flicker over to Renee for a split second to see her nodding along with the music, her lips curling into somewhat of a smile.

It's a huge improvement from what used to be a glower as she scrutinised each and every one of her girls during the performance—her daughter, especially.

Mae's eyes shoot to me, and she winks before spinning and dropping down into the splits with the rest of the girls.

Oh, she's definitely going to be doing that for me later.

I make my way down to the stadium stairs as she dances, eyes glued on her. There's no way I can wait until the game ends to have my arms around her waist and my lips on hers.

I climb the barrier, nodding toward the security guards who let me over with no questions. Renee spots me and offers me a simple nod before I join her.

"She's great, right?"

She's tense, but she clears her throat. "She gets it from me."

My head kicks back as I laugh. Was that a joke? It's hard to tell with Renee.

"You made the right choice... making her captain."

"Yeah... is she managing okay?" Renee asks me, sounding like a curious mother. But she doesn't look at me. Instead, her gaze is fixated on the field. "With her job at the animal shelter and this? It isn't too much for her?"

I can tell she's uncomfortable asking me these sorts of questions, but I don't bat an eyelid. At least she's doing it.

"She helps Amber out at the bar one day a week now, so don't worry, she's fine."

Renee studies me for a brief second before humming. "I hope you wait up for her."

I chuckle. Mae and I moved into a bungalow on the outskirts of Missarali. It's a quaint little home, but we didn't need anything lavish or regal. I did insist on getting the perimeter fenced off and cameras installed though. Radish has his own playroom bursting with toys Flo insists on making us. It turns out the girl can sew. We don't mention how he tears them apart the very day he gets them, but judging by the sheer amount of stuffing dotted all over the house, I'm sure Flo can tell.

He just loves ripping things up.

Shoes.

Toys.

Root vegetables.

"Don't worry about your daughter, Renee. I drive her to and from that bar every shift." I've offered to stay, but she always shoves me out the door while complaining she doesn't need a babysitter.

Renee dips her pointed chin. "Good."

I know that's her weird little way of saying *thank you*, and I roll my eyes and laugh as the girls finish their routine. Arms fly up into the air as they skip around each other in a large circle, one hand splayed over their stomach while the other is up high, shaking the pom-pom.

It's impossible for me to look at anyone other than my girl. Wherever she goes, my eyes follow.

The crowd cheers as they bow, and I clap and holler—louder than anyone in that stadium.

Mae rushes up to me and wraps her arms around my neck, and the sensation had me releasing a sigh of contentment.

"Perfect performance, Mae," Renee tells her daughter before she steps away from us, shoulders still high, indicating her discomfort. But she's trying, and I appreciate that. It's all we can ask of her right now.

"I still think she kind of hates me," I laugh as I kiss the tip of Mae's button nose.

She shakes her head, grinning. "She doesn't. She even told me how handsome you are the other day, but don't let her know I told you that. She'd probably kick me off the team."

"As tempted as I am to tease her about that, your secret is safe with me."

We lock lips, and the people nearest us hoot. But I pay them no mind as I snake my hands around Mae's waist and pull her to me, our bodies tangled.

There's no better feeling than kissing her.

Showing her how wanted she is.

How desired she is.

How *mine* she is.

"I love you," I say after I've pulled back.

"I love you too." She leans closer to whisper into my ear, a mischievous glint in her eyes. "And by the way, the only regret I have about you quitting the team is that you never got the chance to fuck me while wearing your helmet."

I feel my jeans tighten. Is this girl seriously trying to give me a rock-on in front of everyone? I smirk at her. "I still have the helmet, princess."

Mae presses her lips together to stop her smile from growing even more, and that's when I gaze into her glistening hazel eyes and know I'm not just in love with her. I'm *lost* in her. She's in the air I breathe. In every thump of my heart. She's the centre of my universe—a universe I didn't even know existed until I laid eyes on her that day in Emmanuel's wine store.

I used to dwell on the past. The time before I joined the Missarali Storks. Before my mom ended her life. Before my father took control and used me. Before I was thrown into a world of sleazy tabloid drama.

But that's all behind me now.

I don't think about my life like that anymore.

Everything before... that's just *before Mae Bexley*. And it will stay that way forever, because she's my future.

I thought allowing myself to love her was dangerous, but as the Missarali Storks finally raise that Super Bowl trophy in the centre of the field, gathering in a tight huddle, shouting and celebrating, I smile down at my girl.

DANGEROUS

Because with Mae by my side, I now know that the only dangerous thing about us was the warped belief that we weren't meant to be.

What's To Come

**Like a single dad x nanny romance?
Well, get ready for Evan and Flo.**

About The Author

Lottie Moore is an author from the UK who enjoys nothing more than heading out on long walks with her cocker spaniel and attending pub quizzes with her friends when she's not writing sizzling romance novels.

Unlike Mae, she, however, only enjoys cinnamon in the form of an iced cinnamon roll.

To keep up to date with all the latest information regarding upcoming books and sneak peeks, follow her Instagram: @lottiemooreaauthor

Printed in Great Britain
by Amazon